Tesla's Lost

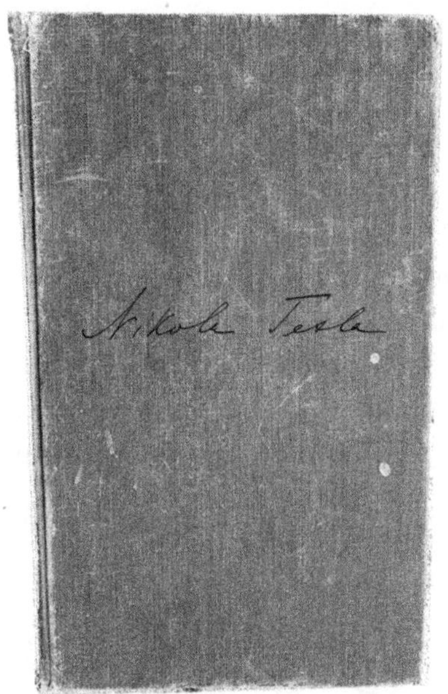

Notebook

by

Kenneth J. M. MacLean

A Big Picture Press publication

Disclaimer:

This is a work of fiction. Any resemblance of persons in this book (other than Nikola Tesla, President Eisenhower, and President Kennedy) to actual persons, living or dead, is purely coincidental.

ISBN: 978-0-9882125-4-1

Contact the author at www.kjmaclean.com. Email: kmaclean@kjmaclean.com

Contents

Part I

Tesla's Notebook

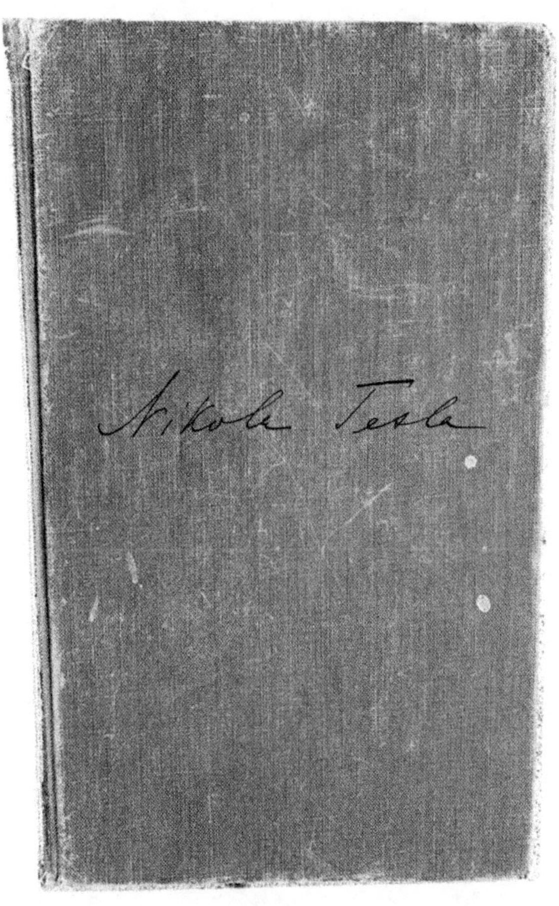

— 1 —

The Black Box

My name is Max Berglin, businessman and scientist. This is my memoir about an Independence Day attack on an American city.

It all started one day when I came across the long lost personal notebook of Nikola Tesla, the great inventor. History tells us that Tesla died a crazy old man but that's a load of crap.

I have to tell you about Midland, Illinois (where this all happened) and the people who lived through it, and how events slowly unfolded. This is a story about a typical American city and its people, and how they were forced to deal with a world that has a lot of dark secrets. These secrets have to be exposed before we destroy ourselves and this planet.

My part in the story begins one summer day when I was seven years old. My grandfather, Horace Berglin, told me a story about Dr. Tesla, whose inventions altered the course of history. This story was the genesis of my interest in physics and has motivated me in everything I have done in my life. I think Grandpa Horace told me this at such a young age because he knew he was dying.

We were sitting on the front porch of the family cottage on Portage Lake, in upper New York State. Grandpa had a bottle of whiskey and a small shot glass, from which he sipped from time to time.

"Now listen here Max. I'm an old man now and my memory isn't what it was, but I remember this as if it happened yesterday. You remember I told you I met Nikola Tesla?"

I nodded. Grandpa Horace was obsessed with Tesla, said he was the greatest scientific genius in history.

"Well, one day Tesla's nephew, a man named Slava Terbo, called me unexpectedly. He was very excited. He wanted me to come along with him to see the great inventor. I served in the Great War (referring to World War I) as an aviator and at that time I was an engineer. I knew this Terbo fellow from our days together in the War. He had no technical training and wanted someone more knowledgeable to observe. Anyway Max, we met Tesla at the Grand Central terminal in New York and rode to Buffalo on a train. Tesla didn't look like a happy man; he was in financial trouble. He didn't want me there. When Terbo asked him questions about where we were going and why, he just grunted out responses. Occasionally Tesla would bring out a leather notebook and write or sketch in it. I couldn't see what he was doing because I was sitting across from them. All he would say was that we were going to conduct an 'aetheric experiment.'"

I sat there, enthralled by the old man's passion and enthusiasm. My father was a self-employed engineering consultant with a bad temper and griped a lot about his life. He never showed interest in anything but a fast buck. Grandpa Harold called him a schemer. My mother was a mild-mannered, good looking *hausfrau* who, despite all reasons not to, loved my father. Both of them never showed much fervor for me. But I loved Grandpa Harold just as much as he loved me.

"You listening Max?"

"Yeah, sorry grandpa. I was just thinking that it would be better if you were my dad."

My grandpa's eyes teared up and he gulped another shot. I could tell he felt the same way. As young as I was, I could read his unspoken emotion: life deals us a hand and we have to make the best of it.

"Are you still with me kid?"

I nodded. "You were talking about some kind of experiment."

"That's right." Grandpa poured out another shot. I could see him becoming animated again. The old man still had a passion for life and I vowed, at that moment, to emulate him. "This sounded like a lot of hooey to me, Max, but I had already studied Tesla's AC motors and dynamos. They were brilliant, so I didn't say anything. Anyway, when we got to Buffalo Tesla took us to a small garage where there was a Pierce-Arrow automobile."

I frowned and Grandpa laughed. "Oh, they aren't around anymore, son. But they were well-engineered automobiles in their day. Dr. Tesla opened the hood of this vehicle and instead of an engine I saw one of Tesla's electric motors. Tesla remarked that he had built this motor himself. It was about three feet long and two feet wide. There were two thick cables from the motor that went into the dashboard. If I recall, there was also an ordinary 12-volt storage battery to get the system initialized. Dr. Tesla said that the motor could do 80 horsepower. I also noticed a 6-foot antenna rod fitted into the rear section of the car. In the dashboard was what looked like a short-wave radio. Back then, in 1931, we didn't have transistors or circuit boards. These radios were used to communicate with other amateur radio operators across the country."

I nodded, even though I didn't understand. Grandpa was building up to something and I could feel he was about to explode.

"It turned out that it wasn't a short-wave at all, but what Dr. Tesla called a 'receiver.' Dr. Tesla took out a box that had twelve specialized transmission tubes. He placed them into the 'receiver' in the dashboard, which also contained several meters that he was reading as he was setting this up. I got curious so I asked him about the tubes and the receiver. But Dr. Tesla refused to say anything about them or how they worked, which I bitterly regret to this day. He pushed two contact rods and announced that power was available to drive the car."

Grandpa must have thought I was getting bored. "Do you understand how unusual this is Max? Tesla was proposing to power the automobile not with gasoline and an internal combustion engine, but with a 'black box' with a bunch of tubes in it. I thought the whole thing was ridiculous."

I nodded. It didn't seem such a big deal to me, but Grandpa was excited.

"I asked him, 'Where does the power come from?' Dr. Tesla replied, 'This new power will drive the world's machinery and is derived from the energy which operates the universe, the cosmic energy, whose central source for the earth is the sun and which is everywhere present in unlimited quantities.'[1]

"I must have snorted or something because it sounded like metaphysics, not science or engineering. The great man turned to me, disgusted. 'Yes, that's what they all think.'"

Grandpa raised his shot glass. I could smell the sharp, pungent aroma of whiskey.

"The upshot of it was that Terbo was told to start the car. He put the key into the ignition and turned it. This engaged the battery to get the motor turning. We didn't hear anything but when Terbo put his foot on the accelerator, the car began to move."

I remember Grandpa's eyes getting misty at this point. "Max, we drove that car through the city of Buffalo and out to the countryside for several hours without fuel. We found a well-paved road and Terbo got that car up to 90 miles per hour. I couldn't get used to the fact that the car was totally silent. Just before we left the city we stopped at a streetlight. A motorist next to us in a Packard said, 'Your car has no exhaust fumes.' Terbo said, 'That's because we have no engine.' The guy stomped on his gas pedal and challenged us to a race. Fortunately the road up ahead was deserted."

I must have looked excited because Grandpa said, "That's right Max. A race! This guy must have been well-to-do because he was driving a 1930 Packard Deluxe Eight roadster, a beautiful luxury automobile comparable to a Cadillac of today. I think he was angry because he thought we were making fun of him. Well, when the light turned green Terbo stepped hard on the accelerator. Max, you should have seen it! We took off so fast we left that guy in our dust. It was totally silent. We heard the other motorist's car chugging along, trying to catch up, and Terbo let up on the accelerator. By this time Dr. Tesla was getting irritated. He must have been in a bad mood because he said, 'Drive on!' Well, that's when we went 90 for about thirty seconds and left that guy in our rear view mirror. Just before we got out of there I turned around and saw the man's face, which had an expression of total and complete astonishment."

I remember Grandpa smiling broadly here, and then he began to laugh. Tears were streaming down his face. "Max, I wish you could have been there. As we silently accelerated, the man in the Packard looked like a kid who just got a beautiful new bike for Christmas and then found out his older brother got a motorcycle. It was so funny!"

Then Grandpa sobered. "I asked Tesla several times on that journey about his 'receiving device,' and the special tubes he had built. But he was sullen and didn't say anything except that the device could be used to power the world's boats, planes, trains, and other automobiles. He said that the motive or power source was a 'mysterious radiation' that 'came out of the aether.' He told me that his device was able to gather some of it to power the motor."

He began coughing at that point and Grandma came in. "That's enough dear." She led him upstairs to bed. That was the last I ever saw Grandpa Horace. Two weeks later he was dead from pneumonia.

Ten years later my parents died in a car crash. This happened two months before my 18th birthday and a month after my acceptance to MIT, where I studied physics. Grandpa Harold had transmitted his enthusiasm for Tesla to me. I was determined to discover if Harold's anecdote was real, or just an old man's daydream.

The short answer is that it wasn't.

I studied Tesla's work and was able to determine that his "cosmic energy" was somehow utilizing "dark energy," the invisible energy that makes up over 68% of all the energy in the universe. This is what Tesla called the "aether."

When I investigated the September 11, 2001 incident I remember seeing photographs of workers clearing away debris just after the Towers were destroyed. I remember seeing an odd bluish-looking fire, which the workers were walking right through. It looked like fire, but the workers were walking through it, unconcerned and unharmed. Could it have been what Tesla described as radiant energy? I built and tested Tesla's radiant energy device (for which he received a patent) but I never got anywhere with it. I buckled down and concentrated on the physics.

Two years after my graduation from MIT I got my PhD (I have a natural aptitude for math and science, and I learn very quickly). Shortly after that I met a woman at a party. She told me that she lived in a building next to the Towers and the night after 9/11, she saw this same "cold fire" and started freaking out. She called the authorities; they said it was just welders at work. This satisfied her, but it didn't satisfy me. That's when I decided to start my own company, make some money, and try to investigate this so-called radiant energy. I also wanted to research Tesla's "receiver," the one the powered the Pierce-Arrow. But I needed money to do this. So I went to work for Lockheed for five years in Bethesda, Maryland and Palmdale, California. After that I moved to Midland, Illinois, a college town with lots of tech companies. I started my own company, Berglin Enterprises.

I never got anywhere with my investigations. I'm smart, but I'm a practical man without Tesla's genius, and I shelved it. I wanted to make some money and I gradually forgot about Tesla. I was too busy getting my business off the ground. One day, five years after I started my company, I heard about a mysterious notebook of the great inventor that had disappeared from his collection of papers shortly after his death in 1943.

— 2 —

1943

On January 9th, 1943, during World War II, a janitor was sweeping a long, dirty hallway at the Manhattan Warehouse & Storage Company building in New York City. The previous day, January 8th, the Office of Alien Property had barged into his area. Four men deposited almost two truckloads of material, including furniture, 30 barrels, and boxes of papers, into one of the storage areas. The storage area looked like a jail cell. It had an iron door with bars, and was shut and locked with a padlock. Two armed guards were posted. This material was the entire property of the genius Nikola Tesla, who had died two days before on January 7th. All of Tesla's technical papers were in there.

The janitor was sweeping the hallway when he noticed an old broken clock that must have fallen out during the storage process. As he picked it up he saw a notebook with a leather cover underneath. Both of the guards were playing cards, smoking, and drinking a bottle of gin. The two men were engrossed in their game. The janitor picked up the clock and placed it in front of the door, notifying the guards. "They missed something."

"Sure, just leave it," one of the players said. "We'll take a look at it later." The janitor noticed their guns lying on the cold cement floor and shivered nervously. He was about to put the notebook by the clock but decided to look inside first. A dabbler in electrical motors, he became fascinated by the designs. He put it in his pocket and forgot about it, finishing his chores for the day, and went home. Neither of the guards noticed.

Tesla was an American citizen. But two days after his death the FBI ordered the Alien Property Custodian to seize his belongings. The War Department called in John G. Trump (uncle to Donald Trump) to analyze the Tesla items in the custody of the Office of Alien Property. Trump was a professor at

M.I.T. and a well-known electrical engineer serving as a technical aide to the National Defense Research Committee. After a three-day investigation, Trump's report concluded that there was nothing in the documents that would constitute a hazard in unfriendly hands. "[Tesla's] thoughts and efforts during at least the past 15 years were primarily of a speculative, philosophical, and somewhat promotional character often concerned with the production and wireless transmission of power; but did not include new, sound, workable principles or methods for realizing such results."[2]

The War Department thought differently.

Two days later a full bird colonel and three men in fancy suits took all of Tesla's boxes and papers. When the colonel's team got back to Washington they quickly cataloged the great inventor's papers.

"Where is that damned notebook?" the colonel asked.

"It isn't here sir," replied the leader of the science team sent to check the veracity and value of Tesla's work. "We've checked everything three times."

"Trump did his part to deflect attention. We know that notebook contained material about his death ray, and other exotic devices that may have military application. Where is it?"

The junior scientist of the trio scoffed. "There's no such thing as a death ray. It's ridiculous."

The colonel turned on the little scientist. "Shut the fuck up kid."

The lead scientist tried to diffuse the tension. "The War Department thinks there is; that's why we're here, Alfred. In 1934 Tesla himself announced the creation of a death ray that he said would be capable of destroying 10,000 enemy airplanes at a distance of 250 miles. He said it could drop an army in its tracks. Hell, *Time* magazine even wrote an article about it that year, saying that Tesla already knew how to do it."

The second scientist said, "Listen to this." He brought out a folded newspaper article from his briefcase, from the *Philadelphia Public Ledger* dated November 2, 1933, and began reading.

"**Tesla Harnesses Cosmic Energy** is the headline. 'A principle by which power for driving machinery of the world may be developed from the cosmic energy which operates the universe, has been discovered by Nikola Tesla, noted physicist and inventor of scientific devices, he announced today. This principle, which taps a source of power described as "everywhere present in unlimited quantities" and which may be transmitted by wire or wireless from central plants to any part of the globe, will eliminate the need of coal, oil, gas or any other of the common fuels, he said. Dr. Tesla in a statement today at his hotel indicated the time was not far distant when the principle would be ready for practical commercial development.'" He paused. "That was ten years ago gentlemen. Lord knows what he's been up to since then."

"Ah bah," Alfred said. "He's been broke for years, no way he could've done anything like that. Just an old man scribbling fantasies and feeding pigeons, holed up in that room of his."

The colonel, exasperated, silently cursed all civilians.

"Tesla had an eidetic memory and could visualize devices entirely in his head and then build them without ever writing anything down," the lead scientist said. "And they would work. But we know he *did* write them down in his personal notebook."

The colonel snorted. "I don't give a shit about the wireless transmission of power. But the War Department is pretty sure that the designs for that death ray are in his notebook. We know he had it in that hotel room."

"What if the Nazis somehow got it?" Alfred asked.

"How the hell would they have been able to? We had two armed guards around that stuff from the moment it was taken."

The guards were questioned. The two men didn't want to admit they had been drinking and playing cards, and denied that anything unusual had happened. Both men never even thought of the janitor.

The janitor (whose name was Joshua Teague), found another job at an office supply company and did not return to work the next day. Although intrigued by the information in the notebook, he wasn't bright enough to understand it. Despite an exhaustive search the War Department never found the notebook. The colonel, in his report, noted that he thought it had been stolen.

2007

When Joshua Teague died in 2007 his son Kenneth went through his father's belongings and discovered it. Kenneth was an electrical engineer who worked for General Electric. The yellowed pages of the old notebook testified to its age. He realized its significance at once and turned it in to his superior. Before doing so he photocopied it for further study and then forgot about it in the press of his daily work.

After several years the notebook found its way to the Technology Acquisition Consortium (TAC), headed by Lt. Colonel James Stapleton (ret). Stapleton examined it but did not have the technical knowledge to assess its importance. He called in his aide, Lieutenant Spieth, a physicist fresh out of graduate school. When Spieth received the notebook he carefully flipped through its worn pages, careful not to tear anything. He was stunned. "You know what you have here sir."

"I'm sure you will tell me eventually," Stapleton remarked.

The lieutenant shuffled his feet nervously. He was tall and thin, and looked too much like a nerd for the colonel's taste. This kid was brilliant but too sensitive. "I believe that this is the personal notebook of Nikola Tesla, the one the War Department could never find back in 1943."

"You mean the one with the Death Ray?"

"The very same. Where did this come from?" Spieth asked.

"You don't have a need to know, son. Let's just say it came from a patriotic American somewhere in the bowels of industry."

Spieth shrugged. He still had not gained the colonel's trust, and he wanted to very badly. "Sir, shouldn't we report this to the Pentagon, or the DNI?"

"Son, we're running an unacknowledged special access program. No one, and I mean no one, who hasn't been read in has any knowledge of our existence. That includes – thank God! – Congressional oversight committees, the CIA, the ODNI, and other meddlers."

"But sir, what if the President —"

"The President! Lieutenant, the President does not have a need to know, nor should he. Let him kiss babies and dedicate buildings. We'll handle the security of this country."[3]

The young man's Adam's apple went nervously up and down. "I see, sir," he replied, even though he didn't.

Stapleton pointed at the aging notebook. "I want you to analyze everything in there and have a report on my desk by the end of the week. I want to know if the technology in that notebook is strictly legacy, and whether anything in there is a threat to the national security of the United States."

Spieth snapped to attention, ramrod stiff, and saluted. "Yes sir!"

Stapleton nodded his dismissal. He noted with approval the lieutenant's enthusiasm as he almost ran back to his desk. Spieth was as persistent as a junkyard dog. Once you gave him a job he would see it through, no matter what. The colonel was pleased. He would have something good to report to the odious Zbigniew Byrnes, his superior, at their weekly briefing on Friday.

Lieutenant Spieth, in his enthusiasm to complete his analysis, made a mistake. He was able to understand the importance of everything in the notebook except for seven of the drawings. He shared the notebook with a TAC scientist at Radical Systems, a classified research company outside of Chicago. "For your eyes only Brian," Spieth said. "I want your analysis of the diagrams under the 'death ray' section, and the wireless transmission of power section. I'll wait while you look them over."

Spieth walked around the lab, looking at Brian Palmerston's work. The scientist became curious as he studied the drawings and notes. He was able to photocopy some of the pages with his mobile after the lieutenant became absorbed while studying a bench experiment. "I'll have my report to you on Monday," he told Spieth.

"Make it Thursday. Stapleton has a burr up his ass on this one."

Palmerston nodded and returned the notebook.

After work, and at great personal risk, Palmerston decided to share the photocopied pages with a friend he knew in Belgrade. He encrypted an email using a program he had developed himself and shared it with his friend. Nervously pausing for a moment over the send button, he sent the information.

Present Day

After he retired from GE Kenneth Teague remembered the notebook he had copied. He dug it out from an old box where he kept memorabilia from his career at GE. As he began to study its contents he became more and more intrigued. His father had been convinced the notebook was Tesla's but Joshua only had a high school education. Kenneth had never believed him and so had dismissed its importance. Now he kicked himself for being a fool. His father had been right.

For the past month Kenneth had taken the photocopied notebook to Carleton University's Graduate Library as a reference for further study. The great old brownstone building with its old-fashioned plaster walls and long narrow windows was as silent as a church. He could concentrate better there than at home.

On the Thursday before Christmas he went back into the stacks to find an old engineering textbook, absentmindedly placing the notebook on top of a stack of books. As he rummaged through the book the notebook fell to the floor. Impatiently, Kenneth shoved it between the metal end of the stack and another book. He began to study the textbook.

After a while his feet began to hurt and he took the textbook back to his table, the notebook forgotten. He checked out the textbook and brought it home, remembering too late that he had left the photocopies in the stacks. Kenneth decided to wait until Friday to pick it up. He was tired and the odds of anyone finding it in that deserted stack were negligible.

— 3 —

That Friday morning before Christmas, Zach Ferrell went to the Graduate Library. He was a third-year engineering student majoring in electrical and power systems engineering at Carleton University in Midland, Illinois. The previous year, while studying turbines, he had been introduced to the work of Nikola Tesla. In Midland 90% of the residents had college degrees and everyone knew who Tesla was, even his not so brilliant friend Mike Parsons. Zach had become fascinated with Tesla's bladeless turbine, which had never been developed commercially. Zach had an idea to use the bladeless turbine as a waste pump in factories and mills where normal vane-type turbine pumps typically get blocked. He had scoured the Undergraduate Library's engineering section looking for more information. Now he was searching the database of the university's Graduate Library.

Zach walked to a deserted aisle in a dusty area of the library that held old books. He came across an old 1947 textbook called *Tesla's Turbines,* and decided to take it down from the shelf. At the end of the shelf he noticed a notebook with a thin black plastic cover, with photocopied pages inside. It had been stuffed (hastily, it looked like) next to some books on power systems generation. Curious, Zach picked up the notebook and began to scan its pages. They were filled with old-fashioned engineering diagrams with handwritten notes next to them. Amazingly, one of the diagrams was of a bladeless turbine. He stared at the handwriting, wondering whose it was.

After an hour of study Zach began to get excited. The designs were ingenious. Several of them were for devices unknown to him. One of them even showed a diagram marked "death ray." He knew he should put this thing back on the shelf, but when he looked at the cover it was unmarked. There was no copyright information, no date, and no ISBN. All of the other books on the shelf distinguished them as the property of the Carleton Graduate Library. Where had this thing come from? The notebook itself seemed to emanate a feeling of importance and intrigue, but he didn't want to steal anyone's property. It was clearly a photocopy and not an original. But it had obviously been copied from something very old.

Zach looked back and forth along the deserted aisle. There was no one. He knew he shouldn't take it; what if someone else was looking for it? But curiosity got the better of him. After all, he could just bring it home, copy the pages, and put it back. Zach placed the notebook carefully inside one of his textbooks and nervously walked out of the place. Nobody challenged him.

Zach went back to the rented campus house he shared with his four roommates. He shared the notebook with Max Berglin Jr., the son of the famous Max Berglin, of Berglin Enterprises. Max Jr. was majoring in physics and Zach was eager for his opinion. Max Jr. pronounced the drawings uninteresting. "I don't understand why you study that stuff. It's legacy technology that has already been developed and improved on."

Zach was appalled at Max Jr.'s lack of imagination, and showed him the other designs. "Do you recognize any of these? I don't know what they're for."

Max Jr. looked at the drawings and shrugged his shoulders. Zach could see he was bored. "Look Max! This drawing is for a radiant energy device. Do you know what that is?" Zach trusted Max Jr.'s opinion. Although cold and distant, he had a fantastic engineering mind.

"Radiant energy? C'mon Zach, that's just woo-woo science."

Zach didn't understand this attitude at all.

On an impulse he went to see Danielle Menard at her rundown home, showing her the notebook. "This looks like something my father would understand," she remarked. "He worked in a classified project before he fell apart."

"Why don't we go downstairs and ask the brilliant Pierce Menard about this?"

"Dad's moping again, and drinking beer. Ever since mom died he's been completely useless."

Disappointed, Zach went back to the rental house and packed. Rachel and Mark – he thought of his parents that way because they were getting more and more strange every day – wanted him to come home for the Christmas weekend. He put the notebook on a pile of textbooks and hauled them and his duffel bag out to the car. He promised himself that tomorrow he'd scan the diagrams and digitize them.

Max Jr. Comes Home for the Holidays

That evening my son Max Jr. came home for the Christmas holidays. We were drinking coffee together in the kitchen. "Dad, do you know of something called a radiant energy device?"

"Radiant energy? Are they teaching that now at Carleton?" In my investigation of Tesla's work I remembered seeing a patent for a device like that. I still kept up my reading in the physics journals, but radiant energy wasn't on any university physics curriculum I knew of.

"No dad. One of my friends, Zach Ferrell, showed me a photocopied notebook that had a strange looking device labeled 'cosmic energy generator.'"

My son was staring at me, judging my reaction. He was big and blond just like me, but unlike me there was something dark inside him I would never understand. "I told him it was just legacy technology, or some crackpot inventor."

I knew my son was testing me. He knew my interest in Tesla, and was implying that his roommate had discovered something of the great inventor's work. I replied as calmly as I could. "Do me a favor and see if you can get your hands on it."

Max Jr. smirked, knowing I was feigning disinterest. My son had always been able to read me like a book.

"OK, I'll see what I can do." There was a pause, and I knew what he was going to say before he said it. "You don't have a couple hundred on you do you?"

My son was brilliant but lazy and I was pretty sure he'd never amount to much. But that was mostly my fault. "Sure son."

I reached into my wallet and pulled out five $100 bills. "Here, that should tide you over for a while."

"Thanks dad."

My son was never more in charity with me than when I was giving him something.

Part II

Midland, Illinois

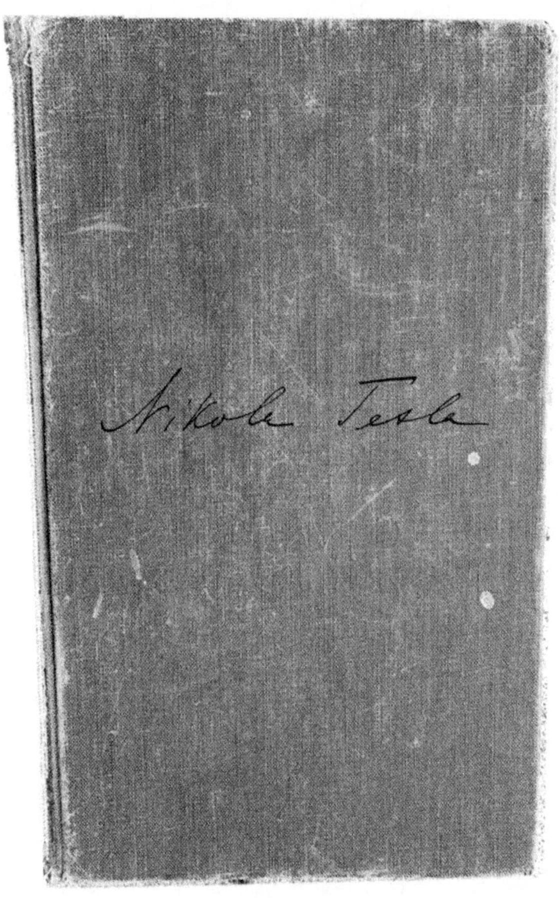

— 4 —

"Hi mom, hi dad!" Jessie DiPietro dropped her suitcase on the foyer floor and waited. The house seemed empty. It was odd, because mom had requested she come home for the holidays. Jessie walked from the foyer into dad's study, a small room with a picture window that looked out into the garden. The room was empty. She looked into the living room, then the kitchen. She walked upstairs, thinking that her parents might be in the bedroom fooling around. Sure enough, she heard noises and hurriedly walked back down the stairs.

About five minutes later Wayne DiPietro came down the stairs, smiling, and confirming her guess. Dad was a well set up man with thinning blond hair, about six feet tall.

"When's dinner?" she asked.

"Ask your mom when she comes down."

Jessie went into the bathroom to freshen up. Her face was always oily and she checked for acne, but there was nothing, thank god. She inspected herself in the long mirror hung on the door. A symmetrical face with large eyes and a button nose, black hair that hung straight to her should/ers, and nice legs. Not beautiful exactly, her chin was a bit too square, but pretty. She ran a comb through her hair and tucked her blouse into her jeans. She'd do.

Jessie walked downstairs into the kitchen, where mom was stirring a sauce. "Spaghetti?"

"Yes dear, my hand-made sauce."

Myra put the lid on the pot and turned down the heat. "We'll let it simmer for ten more minutes." Myra and Jessie sat down at the table. "So what's new?" Jessie asked.

"There's a big social event sponsored by the bank this weekend. Trevor Clarke is MC-ing."

"That guy?" Jessie was incredulous at her mother's implied approval. "When he smiles he looks like a used car salesman."

"He does not! I like him."

"You smile like him sometimes, mom."

"I do not!"

As Jessie was about to respond her father Wayne strolled lightly in to the kitchen. Jessie looked at her father as he sat down on one of the kitchen chairs and smiled at Myra, who smiled back at him smugly. Jessie thought that there was something...inconsequential...about both of them, which was probably why they had gotten together. Jessie hoped that the course of her life would take a grander turn than theirs.

"Are you guys talking about the fundraiser?" Wayne said. "Trevor will be there."

Jessie looked back and forth at her parents. "You guys don't seriously *like* that scumbag, do you?"

"How could you *not* like him?" Myra glanced meaningfully at her husband. "He's charming and successful."

Jessie noticed just the slightest emphasis on successful, and knew that mom was digging at dad again. She sighed.

Wayne ignored the slight and spoke in envious tones."Trevor Clarke knows all the bigwigs in town. I'm hoping to talk to him there. Maybe he can help me become head of Accounting."

Myra said nothing, but Jessie noticed her mother's air of dissatisfaction.

"Trevor told this great joke at the Finance meeting yesterday," Wayne said. "A computer programmer, a physicist, a biologist, and an accountant were sitting in a restaurant across the street from an abandoned building. A man and a woman go in and five minutes later three people come out. The biologist says, 'They must have reproduced while they were in there.' The computer programmer says, 'The third guy must have come in through a back door.' The physicist says, 'We must have made an error in our calculations.' The accountant says, 'if one more person enters the building then it will be empty.'"

Jessie saw her father laugh so hard he almost fell on the floor, and she smiled. Dad was a bit of a lightweight, but he had a good heart. Mom smiled but shook her head sardonically, as if her husband was one of her high school students acting up in class.

Jessie saw that Myra was about to make another sarcastic comment. She hated it when they dug into each other in front of her. She tried to relieve the tension. "So what were you guys doing upstairs?"

Myra and Wayne glanced at each other secretively.

Jessie sighed. Her parents had a strange relationship. Obviously they still liked each other enough to have sex, but she couldn't understand the underlying tension between them, which was mostly on Myra's side.

Myra jumped up out of her chair. "The spaghetti sauce is burning!"

"Don't worry honey. Just scoop the good stuff out and we'll eat it."

Jessie was so hungry she didn't care if the sauce had blackened to little bits of smoking ash. "Yeah mom, bring it on."

After she ate Jessie went up to her bedroom at the end of the hall. She lay down on the bad and wondered what Zach Ferrell was doing for the holidays. She hoped he wasn't with that degenerate Danielle Menard girl. Jessie sighed. Zach was so perfect but his taste in women was awful.

She told herself she should have stayed at the dorm with her friend Heather.

Jessie Calls Zach

Zach Ferrell drove to the Ferrell house, a two-story colonial that was too big for the Ferrell family. Dad had wanted a smaller house but Rachel had insisted on a larger one. As usual, Rachel had gotten her way.

He went up the stairs to his old bedroom. He threw his duffel on the bed and plopped his textbooks, and the notebook, on his old desk. It was only two o'clock in the afternoon and the day was a warm one for December. His parents were still at work, and there was still time to get his bag together and play some disk golf. As he changed into his sweats he heard his phone ring. Jessie! She knew he wanted her to text before she called. He ignored the phone as it went to voice mail and descended the stairs two at a time, still excited about finding the notebook and what could be in it. Jessie was smart and thought herself unconventional, but Zach knew he couldn't talk to her about it. He needed to show it to Danielle's father.

As he walked out the front door he saw Rachel's car come up the driveway. He groaned. Now she'd want him to sit and talk, she'd ask him about his classes, and it would be really boring. Zach waved, got quickly into his beat-up Mazda, and whipped past Rachel backwards down the driveway. He smiled when he saw her irritated face. He knew he'd have to face a grilling when he got home, but it would be worth it.

He called his buddy Mike, who worked in the local hardware store. They had been friends since junior high even though Mike hadn't joined their group from Midland East High in college. Their common bond was disk golf, which Mike had taught him only a year ago. "Hey, you got time to play today?"

"Yeah, I'm just getting off work."

"Meet you out at the Monster Course in ten minutes."

Zach drove out to the course and parked. He liked the old Mazda because he could easily put his 6' 5" frame into the driver's seat and stretch out his legs. His phone beeped. "What do you want Jessie?"

"What are you doing?"

"What do you think? I just got home and I'm playing a round with Mike."

"What are you going to do over the holidays?"

Zach walked up to the first tee and put his bag down on the table. "Try to stay away from home and play as much disk golf as I can." He looked down the fairway. There was only an inch of snow on the ground, pretty good conditions for winter golf.

"How did you do on your finals?" Jessie asked.

It was typical of women that they always wanted to talk when you were busy. He tried out a few putts at the practice basket next to the first tee, while holding on to his phone with his left hand. He liked disk golfing chicks but Jessie wasn't very athletic. Too bad. "Now that's a dumb question," he said.

"I get the idea you don't want to talk to me."

"Very good, girl. Mike just got here and we're about to tee off."

"Call me tonight, OK?"

"Uh, sure."

He'd call Jessie but he really wanted to get together with Danielle again. That girl was beautiful but totally jaded, like a war veteran who had seen too much action at the front. He'd score some herb from her and maybe he'd get lucky tonight. And maybe he'd be able to talk to her father about those schematics.

Trevor Clarke Schemes

Trevor Clarke sat in his corner office at PRC Bank, looking at his nameplate: "Trevor Clarke, President." Oh he was president all right, he muttered to himself. He had been hired almost one year ago after the former president, with the collusion of the head of the investment banking unit, had misused investor funds. The silly fools had a "can't miss" investment strategy they thought would propel them to the main office in New York, and banking fame. But the market had turned and the money was lost. To make things worse, a few of the locals had lost most of their savings and had created a big stink.

Just then Darren Bloom entered his office. Dammit, he had forgotten to shut the door again. "Hello Trevor," said the affable head of PRC's small Public Relations unit. "We have a problem."

Trevor sighed and put his arms on the desk, leaning in to look his auditor in the eye. "Sit down, Darren. You make me nervous, standing there like an addict waiting for his next fix."

Darren Bloom guffawed. "Well Trevor, it's like this. We're still seeing fall-out from that stock scam your predecessor pulled last year. Apparently the state legislature is ready to slap PRC with some hefty sanctions."

Trevor was calm and polite, as always. "Not to worry my boy, I've already checked on that. PRC is an investment bank privately incorporated in the state of Delaware. If Senator Blanchard wants to make some headlines, he's going to have to sue the parent company. Besides, he'd have to change state law. A local bank branch is immune from lawsuits unless, and I quote, 'an egregious and broad pattern of corruption or malfeasance is proven.' A small, local stock scandal doesn't qualify."

"That's all very well Trevor." Bloom spoke in a broad, flat, Midwestern accent. Trevor would never get used to how even casual acquaintances were on a first name basis here. "What I'm talking about is the public relations fallout."

Trevor found Bloom's bluntness rude. But almost all Americans are rude. "What is it this time?"

"Channel 7 is almost ready to air another set piece about 'corrupt bankers.' Even though there's nothing libelous in it, the piece will slam us just when the front office is getting back on its feet."

Trevor raised an eyebrow. "What do you want me to do about it?" He already knew the answer to that, having been hired for his sophisticated social skills and his British accent. He wanted to see Bloom squirm a little.

"Williams from Kent and Williams sent me over – with the approval of the Investment Banking division and the Board of course. To, uh, see if you could get the piece toned down a bit."

Trevor scowled.

Justin Williams was a blustering, vulgar man who was good in front of the camera but had no people skills. His firm had done more harm than good in the wake of the scandal.

Bloom spoke in conciliating tones. "Look, we know that this was before your time. We really need this one."

Despite his irritation, Trevor nodded his head and smiled. "Of course." He decided to use an Americanism. "I'll get right on it."

Trevor saw Bloom breathe a great sigh of relief. He quickly rose and left.

Trevor leaned back in his plush leather chair. Oh, Mr. Bloom, if you only knew. He was building up credibility here in Midland after what had happened in London. There was that little incident at Barclays where, in his earlier life as an investment banker, he had been a minor player in the Libor manipulation scandal. His parents were both in finance, and ambitious; their careers had given him a driving motivation for success. Unfortunately, his determination sometimes clouded his judgment. But in the City they knew how to handle these things. The bank was fined, Trevor submitted his resignation, and his involvement was forgotten. He had learned his lesson. The City of London was too disagreeable and so he had come to the United States to begin again. He had carefully chosen Midland, Illinois, as his destination. It was a town of about 120,000 people and dominated by Carleton University, an excellent private college with a worldwide reputation. Wealthy executives from Chicago lived here and the city had a thriving and diverse social scene. There was money in Midland. Before moving he had thoroughly scouted the city. The place was like a mini-London or mini-New York, with theaters, parks, concert halls, and cultural events. It was situated on the Midland River, fifty miles southwest of Chicago. When he drove into the place along River Dr. he liked it on sight. Green spaces had been placed at regular intervals even downtown, which reminded him of his native London. He got out of his car and strolled around downtown, seeing several high-end restaurants and shops. The people were friendly and the place had a comfortable feel. He could live here.

Although he had been educated at the London School of Economics, his strong suit was not banking but rather social relationships and networking. In London he had been a hit in society with his droll humor, his good looks, and his witty and urbane conversation. And so it had proved here in Midland, where he had wangled the bank job with relative ease. At first he had sincerely tried to fit in and begin a new life. He was thrilled when he had been voted president of PRC. It was an honest job. But soon his life became boring. He missed the hard-driving life of an investment banker and its excitement, where millions of dollars could ride on a single transaction. He couldn't risk applying for another brokerage job for fear that his earlier indiscretions would become known. As the weeks went by he realized that being president of a bank branch wasn't exciting enough, nor did it give him sufficient compensation. He needed more.

Trevor found himself drifting into the same pattern and seeking out risk-takers, just as he had in London. Then he hit upon an excellent scheme. It was something that satisfied his itch for adventure and promised some extra income. His first response had already come in the mail from Larry Potvin, a local accountant. He was ready.

Larry Potvin Gets an Email

"Karl, what are you doing?"

Larry had told his son to do something simple: take the doors off the new refrigerator and hang them on the other side. Jenny was left-handed and she liked the doors the other way. But the kid was fucking it up again. He already showed him how to take out the two screws on the left, and how to remove the plugs from the two holes on the right. All you had to do was loosen the screws, flip the doors over, and put in two screws on the other side. The damn doors were modular and the shelves inside could be arranged any way you wanted.

Larry watched as Karl fumbled around with the screws on the lower door. He could see that the stupid kid was going to undo the last screw without bracing his leg against the door. It was going to fall and crush his feet.

"I don't know dad, I'm no good at mechanical things."

"For godssake son it isn't rocket science. I showed you how to do it."

He saw the look of fear in Karl's eyes, and it made him angry. What was the kid afraid of? He was 18 years old now, almost ready to go off to college in January.

"Fuck it!" Karl said. Larry could see that the boy was about to cry. He dropped the screwdriver and stomped out of the kitchen, leaving the door hanging awkwardly. Jenny walked in. "Why can't you two ever get along?"

Larry bit his tongue. What he wanted to say was, "that kid will never amount to anything," but Jenny had taught him to be nicer around their son. It was too bad that Karl was so much like his mother, who had died of cancer when she was only 25. That was fifteen years ago. He had loved Lorraine but had never understood her. Just like his son.

Jenny read his expression. "You have to be more patient with him, dear," she said with a smile. Larry was just as frustrated as his son, but he held himself in check. He had vowed that after his stormy first marriage he would do better. After Lorraine died he started drinking heavily and knew he could never raise Karl alone. So he had married again. He was fond of Jenny but she was no substitute for Lorraine.

"I know, Jenny. But the kid has no common sense."

Jenny didn't deny it. "Maybe he'll find himself in college."

"Yeah, maybe." Larry quickly rotated the door, put the hinge on the right side, and re-arranged all the shelves. He did the same with the freezer door, and loaded everything up. Jenny helped.

"You really are good at that," she said. "Thanks."

Larry smiled. Jenny was a good woman. It was too bad he wasn't such a great husband. He'd had a few over the weekend and he felt the old devil inside him waking up.

The next day Larry went in early to work at the PANA auto parts store. A new hire was coming in and he had to train him. As he walked by the Assistant Manager's office, he saw that Bruce Nowicki was already at his desk. "What are you in so early for?" Larry asked.

"New computer system. That means everything doesn't work right."

Larry laughed. He was the branch's accountant, and that was a story in itself. After he got laid off as a mechanic he had gone two years at Midland Community College, receiving an Associates Degree in accounting. Everybody needed accountants, even when the economy was bad. He had a family to support.

"How's my Corvette coming along?" Bruce asked.

"I ordered OEM headers and they should be here tomorrow. After that all I have to do is put the engine back in and crank her up."

Bruce was excited. He'd given Larry his precious '77 Corvette and asked him to restore it. He knew it was work Larry loved. "Why don't you restore cars full time?"

"Some day I will."

"I've seen that little shop of yours in the garage. You need more space."

"I do. The family cars have to be parked outside. In winter that causes a lot of complaints from Jenny and Karl. I don't like it either."

"So do it."

"There's a little thing called money Bruce. I need about $100,000 to get some new equipment and rent a bigger building. The banks won't float me the loan I need to start up a real business."

"Don't I know it. I've been trying to get out of here for years."

Larry thought Bruce needed some cheering up. "Bruce, you are going to have an orgasm when you see this car. The new paint job is sweet. I had the body off and the entire chassis sanded, primed, and painted."

Bruce smiled. The 1977 Corvette was one of the best American muscle cars ever and he'd been bugging Larry for weeks now to get it done.

Suddenly Larry made up his mind. He was tired of this place; it was a dead-end job. Somehow he was going to set himself up to do the work he loved.

"I gotta get to work. I'll take you over to the shop next Monday and you can pick it up."

Bruce pantomimed a swoon.

Just then the new guy came in and Larry spent three boring hours going over the books and showing him the system. A fresh-faced kid right out of college who reminded him of his son. He gave him the two easiest accounts and told him to get busy. After that boring interlude he went back to his desk and brought up his email.

He needed a way out of here or he'd be off the wagon again. He could feel the tension and the frustration building up in him, just like his old Army days when he got sent to Iraq to fight that stupid war.

Hmmm, what was this? The header read: "You don't make enough money." Damn right. As he went through the email he couldn't believe what he was reading. ouched in accounting jargon, it was a fraudulent but brilliant scam. A short-term scam, six months max, and then you're out. It was crazy. He was about to delete it, but went back and read it again, looking for flaws. He couldn't find any. He'd just decided to leave PANA, he needed money, and now look at this!

After careful consideration, Larry decided that the email was a message from God. Screw PANA. As he thought of his new business he began to get really excited, but he took a mental step back. His military training had taught him to look at life realistically. Now he examined his own life as if it was an accounting ledger.

The truth was that he was living from paycheck to paycheck and would never be able to save enough to get his business going. He could see his life stretching out into the future, mundane and unsatisfying. He was bored out of his mind, and frustrated. He needed some action and this looked like a good thing. How could something wrong feel so great? In the Army they told you to go for it, so he'd go for it and damn the consequences. He had no loyalty to PANA and neither did any of the employees who worked there. The company was known for low wages and a demanding corporate structure.

Larry checked again for the sender but the email was anonymous. He'd have Karl check the email header, maybe he could figure out where it came from. Larry knew none of it mattered.

The email came with instructions. "If you are interested, reply to the email with a handwritten letter and send it to Midland East Post Office, P.O. Box 1773."

He sent the letter right after he got off work.

— 5 —

Danielle Menard took a break from organizing her stash. She sat on her unmade bed and looked at the tattoos on her right arm. Every one of these figures had meaning to her; they all represented parts of her life and her personality. Above her wrist was Aphrodite, the Greek goddess of love. She remembered the quote from Mother Teresa, which had inspired her to endure the pain of imprinting it. "In life we cannot do great things. We can only do small things with great love." She sighed. Above the half-naked figure, on her forearm, was a thunderbolt thrown by a powerful Zeus. She had made Zeus' face to look a little like Zach Ferrell's. She was attracted to big, powerful men. Medusa was next, with a face like her own with her hair flying out in all directions, caressing a figure half horse and half human. Medusa represented, for her, not the evil creature of the myth but the power of the feminine. A golden orb representing the sun was on her bicep, sending yellow rays up to her shoulder and illuminating a beautiful white unicorn. She smirked, remembering she had gotten that one in a rare fit of good humor. The unicorn was beauty and idealism, which had largely been superseded by cynicism. On her left forearm was a devil with glowing red eyes, symbolizing the evil that had infected her life.

Nobody got her, except maybe Zach and Jamelle the homeless guy. Certainly not her father.

Her phone rang. "Hey Danielle, what are you doing tonight?"

It was Zach. "I don't know, I'm bored."

"I know how you feel. You want to get some action tonight?"

"What did you have in mind? I want to get out of this pisshole. The holidays always depress me."

"You will face many defeats in life, but never let yourself be defeated."

Danielle sighed with pleasure.

"Maya Angelou. I love that quote." She remembered it from the literature class she'd had with Zach at Midland East.

There was perfect understanding between them. "I'll come over at 8 and pick you up," Zach said.

"I'll unlock the front door. Just come in." Danielle heard the click and her depression lifted. It would be a good night with Zach, whatever happened.

Before Zach left for Danielle's he remembered to take the notebook.

Zach arrived right at 8 and walked upstairs to her bedroom.

Danielle liked Zach as much as she could like anybody. It was a sign of respect, to get here on time. Zach was old-fashioned that way.

"Where's your old man?"

"He went out. Probably won't get home until 2 or 3. Why do you want to see him?"

"I have a notebook of old drawings. I think they're by Nikola Tesla. I want him to tell me if they are for real, or just doodles."

"If anyone would know, dad would."

"Oh well. What you got?"

Danielle went to her closet and the safe she kept inside. It was a fire-proof unit with a grade one digital security lock and steel locking bolts in all four directions. The safe was bolted to the floor on two wooden studs. Danielle placed a strip of soft plastic up to the keypad and quickly pressed the combination. Her fingers were so fast that Zach, concentrating intently, couldn't get the combination.

She waited to see if Zach would get why she did it.

Zach spoke admiringly. "You don't take chances. Nobody can tell which keys you press."

"God you're a hunk."

Zach ignored this. "Got any good weed?"

She liked that Zach didn't do meth or coke or any of the designer drugs. Weed would do for tonight. Just a nice high and a good time.

Without asking Zach handed her some money. She brought out a small packet and a couple of pipes. They lit up and sat together on the bed, silently smoking, feeling the mellow drug infuse their bodies.

"I don't want to go out tonight after all," Danielle said. "This is great."

Zach turned to look at her. She was beautiful, with blond hair over a heart-shaped but dissipated face that looked as if it had disappointment permanently etched into it. She wore her usual black man-shirt and jeans with rips in them over her slim legs. Black boots with pointy toes covered her small feet. Danielle was a mess, but he liked her anyway. He wanted her right now, but he could feel her putting up a wall as she felt his intention. He lay back on the bed against the wall. "Yeah, it is. Let's talk."

Sudden tears came to Danielle's eyes. This guy was so sensitive, and so smart. The only guy other than John Rosen, their high school mentor, as smart as her. And he totally got her.

"Marry me," she said.

Zach's eyes went bright in surprise. He looked her straight in the eyes. "You're the most interesting girl I've ever met. Maybe we should."

Danielle threw herself into his arms and cried, her heart almost breaking. She thought of Aphrodite on her arm. Was this love she was feeling? It was an emotion foreign to her. After a couple of minutes she felt better and looked up into his brown eyes. "Why, Zach?" she asked.

"I don't know Danielle," he replied, holding her quietly.

She sighed, knowing that this guy was the way out for her, but also knowing it was impossible. Was it karma? Something was holding her back. Maybe Zach would be able to figure it out eventually, if someone else didn't nab him. Like Jessie. She took another toke as Zach moved his hands gently over her breasts. She liked his touch and felt safe with him. He kissed her hair, liking how she smelled. Then he released her.

They talked until four in the morning, and fell into bed together with their clothes on. Danielle thought about their little gang that had graduated from Midland East. Her, John Rosen, Zach, Jessie DiPeitro, Heather McCloy, and Mike Parsons, Zach's disk golf playing partner.

John was two years older, the genius scientist who had gone off to MIT when they were juniors. The gregarious Zach was in engineering school at Carleton. Jessie and Heather had also gone to Carleton, while she had to sit home and take care of dad. All of them except her had a life. She fell asleep thinking about what it would be like to be married to Zach.

As Zach drifted off to sleep he realized he had forgotten to call Jessie, or his parents. Rachel would be steaming and he didn't like breaking his word to Jessie even though she was a pain in the ass. The last thing he saw was Danielle's face, smooth now with no worry lines. She looked like an angel.

Zach Goes Home

Zach woke up at dawn. Danielle was still sleeping and he wrote her a note on a piece of scrap paper. "Great time last night. You're awesome, keep the faith." He knew she'd know what he meant. He put the note on the little table on his side of the bed, grabbed the notebook off the end table, and tiptoed down the stairs. He saw Danielle's father sleeping it off on the couch in the untidy living room. He felt a sudden burst of anger and walked toward the sleeping man. He wanted to beat the crap out of this loser who had made Danielle's life miserable. As he got within a couple steps from the couch he felt the roiling emotions inside him deflate. He was Danielle's father and so part of her. Zach knew her father depended on her and that if he did anything it would only make Danielle feel bad. He looked at the pathetic figure sprawled on the couch and saw a face that resembled Danielle's, with fine even features, a pleasant face in repose. He knew from Danielle that Pierce Menard was a certifiable genius whose wife had died in a horrible accident, and who had gotten off track.

As he stepped backward to leave the house he tripped on the lamp and fell awkwardly against the wall. The man on the couch sat up, rubbing his eyes. "Who's there?"

Zach stepped forward. "Sorry Mr. Menard, I didn't mean to wake you up." The older man's eyes sharpened. "Oh yes, Zach Ferrell, I heard about you from Danielle."

Zach picked up the notebook, which had fallen to the floor. The rising sun was over the horizon now, and two shafts of light from the front windows illuminated the room. "I have something here I'd like to show you," Zach offered. He almost laughed, thinking how ridiculous it was to show a drunk technical diagrams at six in the morning.

Pierce Menard must have read his mind. "No, I'm not drunk. It's OK." He reached for the papers and began to examine them.

Before Zach could say anything the older man's head snapped up. "Where did you get this?"

"I found it in the Graduate Library."

"This is Nikola Tesla's handwriting." He thumbed through the rest of the drawings. "I'm sure of it." As quickly as he had awoken, the older man's eyes now began to close. He returned the notebook to Zach. "I think I'll go back to sleep."

"Thank you Mr. Menard." Zach let himself out softly, not wanting to disturb Danielle. He walked slowly to his car in the driveway, thinking. So that was Pierce Menard. A world class physicist and a deeply troubled man, Danielle had told him. Zach couldn't help but recall the sharp intelligence in his eyes.

Zach put his old Mazda in neutral and quietly backed down the driveway. When he got to the curb he started the car. Maybe if he drove home quietly he could sneak into bed without being noticed. He laughed. Why was he still worried about Rachel? He was a junior at Carleton now, and an adult.

On the way home Zach began to feel a buzz of anticipation. If only his old buddy John Rosen was still around! Danielle's father had confirmed that the notebook was Tesla's. But he needed someone more experienced to tell him whether the drawings were for real, or if they were just scribbling.

Zach switched off the lights on his Mazda and turned into the driveway as quietly as he could. Fortunately the car, although old, was in good shape. He parked it in the turn-around and walked slowly to the back door. It was almost 6:20 and everyone should still be asleep. He unlocked the door and tiptoed quietly up the stairs, avoiding the creaky one. He made it to his room and sighed thankfully, pulling off his clothes. Before he got into bed he got out his mobile and texted Jessie.

> Sorry I didn't call last night, I was over at Danielle's and we were talking until the early morning. I'll call you tomorrow sometime.

OK, he was clean of all obligations now. Today was Saturday and he'd sleep until noon, then call Mike and go golfing if it wasn't too cold.

"Hey sleepyhead, get up."

It was Rachel, pulling back the curtains, letting in the sunlight. He hated it when his mother trespassed into his space without knocking, even though he didn't live here anymore and this bedroom wasn't his space anymore. "Where were you last night?"

"Oh leave it please, I'm 21 now. I don't have to account to you for my actions anymore."

"As long as I'm helping with your tuition you do."

Zach was going to point out that where he went on his own time had nothing to do with his college tuition. But he realized the futility of arguing with his mother. She was damnably persistent and always had to have the last word.

"Couldn't we have this conversation over breakfast? I'm still sleepy."

In answer Rachel kicked the bed. "We'll have it now, sonny boy. It's already ten."

Zach groaned and rolled over on his back. "If you have to know, I went over to Danielle's."

"Danielle Menard? That tramp? Did you buy any drugs from her?"

"We smoked a little weed, that's all." Zach shot up in bed, angry now. "And NO, I didn't fuck her."

"You're as bad as your father. Both of you have foul mouths and a foul temper."

"Don't bring dad into it. This is between you and me." Zach paused. "I don't get my foul temper from him, I get it from you. I only get my foul mouth from him."

"I don't want you hanging out with that slut, son."

Zach realized again that the only way to deal with Rachel was to stay cheerful and ignore her bitter outbursts. "She's not a slut, mom, just a druggie."

Despite herself Rachel found herself smiling. Then she tried to be serious again, and gave it up. "You're both of you hopeless." She left the room, getting the last word.

Zach wondered how dad had put up with her all these years.

When Zach wandered downstairs he saw his parents in the living room, sitting by a fire. Dad was reading and mom was brooding.

"What's new, son?" Mark asked.

"Same old shit. School is boring, the only thing that really interests me is disk golf. Mike is going pro next month."

"And Danielle," Rachel added.

"Are you hanging out with her again Zach?" Mark asked.

"I just did it once!"

"Back off Zach. I'm not accusing you of anything. You're 21 now, you can screw up your life any way you want."

"You know, I'm really getting tired of this badmouthing of Danielle. She's beautiful, she's brilliant, and I like her." He remembered something. "Besides, she asked me to marry her last night."

Rachel exploded out of the wing chair. "What? Are you serious?"

"I'm very serious. I haven't decided yet."

Rachel stood in front of the fire with her mouth open. He had rendered her speechless for the first time in his life! Even his father couldn't believe it. "You mean you didn't say no?" he asked.

"I can't remember, it was three in the morning. I think we didn't decide one way or the other."

"You mean you'd consider it?"

Zach thought about last night, although it was hard when Rachel was standing there like an angry hippopotamus about to charge. "I would. She's the smartest and deepest person I've ever met. We connect on a very, very deep level. We understand each other without words being spoken."

"You'd marry a drug dealer?" Rachel asked.

It was what Zach had expected: a shallow response. "Do you know why Danielle deals?" Zach felt it was hopeless but he'd try to explain anyway.

"Yes son, because she's a slut and a scumbag."

"No mom. Danielle is the daughter of Pierce Menard. You know, the guy who was proclaimed one of the most brilliant physicists in the world. Won the Maxwell medal. Then his wife died, if you recall, and he fell apart. Went on the bottle and never recovered. Well, Danielle's father has totally annihilated her life. She's just as smart as he was, maybe even smarter. She's very sensitive—"

Rachel snorted.

"She's very sensitive," Zach repeated, "and she sees deep into people and situations—"

"Yeah, that's why she deals drugs. Because she so sensitive and deep," Rachel said derisively.

"If you'll let me finish I'll explain." Zach glanced over at Mark, who was looking at him strangely, as if he had never seen his son before. "As I said, Mr. Menard has totally messed up his life and Danielle's too. He was always on her, insulting her, telling her she was no good. She was just young enough when it started for her to believe him. She sells drugs because she and her father have blown through his savings and she needs the money. She told me once it's the only way she knows how to provide people with a little happiness."

Dad was still looking at him strangely. He was trying to understand, at least, but mom was unbelieving. "If she's that hard up it's all the more reason to avoid her. If you believe she sells drugs to make people happy, Zach, it's ridiculous. And sad, too, that you would believe such nonsense."

"Yes it is sad, mom." Zach said it with his mother's air of cynicism. He hoped she would understand that her distrust of people caused her to assume the worst about them. She didn't of course.

"If you marry that slut you are no longer welcome in this house," Rachel said.

"Rachel, no!" Mark said. "You'll always be welcome here with me, son."

Zach smiled wanly. "Thanks dad."

"You're both crazy." Rachel stomped out of the room.

Mark spoke hopefully."Don't worry Zach, she'll come around."

"Will she dad?"

Zach decided to ask his father a question, man to man. "How did you fall in love with her?"

Mark tensed up at first, but then relaxed. "Well, you're 21 now son, I suppose you have a right to ask. I had just come back from New York, worn to a frazzle. You remember, I worked for two years at that big firm out there, Calvert Middleton Edwards and Jankowski. Rachel was a young intern just out of college back then. She was the most beautiful woman I'd ever seen and I fell for her hard. To her I was the big advertising exec from New York, and she looked up to me. For a while anyway. Her personality changed when she was made a partner. She has ambitions to be president. The problem is that we both work for the same firm. She is bitter about what she calls my lack of ambition even though it conflicts with her own goals. She has became colder, brittler. I've never understood it myself."

"Do you still love her?"

"Yes, I do. I still see the woman I married in there. I'm still working to bring that back out but I don't know if I can anymore."

Wow, Zach thought. Ask a deep question and get an answer you might not want to hear. His father had never opened up to him like this. Zach's eyes suddenly filled with tears. "Give me a hug dad."

Mark stood up and hugged his son. Zach was three inches taller than his six feet two. "I'm glad you came home, Zach."

"I am too dad. I think we understand each other a lot better."

Mark patted his son on the back affectionately. He stepped back and nodded in agreement.

Zach was happy. No matter what happened now, he had established a bond with his father, adult to adult. It felt good.

Zach put on his sweats and drove out to play a round with Mike Parsons.

Mike at Home

Mike Parsons got home from his round with Zach at four. He was a little irritated because his buddy had talked about a notebook of Nikola Tesla all during the play. He felt as dumb as a circus clown at a Stephen Hawking lecture as Zach described some of the drawings. Everybody knew about Tesla, but Mike was serious about disk golf and found Zach's talk distracting. Even worse, Zach had beaten him by five strokes. Zach's easy competence at anything he did amazed Mike, because he had to work hard at *everything*. Even so, Mike knew he was good enough to go pro. That was exactly what he was going to do despite the old man's bitching about taking over the family business. To spend your life waiting on idiots in a hardware store! You got to be kidding. You could make some money on the pro circuit now, disk golf was getting bigger and bigger.

Mike walked into the kitchen from the back door with his bag over his shoulder and a beer in his hand. His father was sitting at the kitchen table, waiting for him.

"Where have you been?"

"What does it look like?" Mike said, taking the bag off his shoulder.

"Watch your mouth, son," his father said.

Mike knew he shouldn't have said that. Now it would be even harder.

"Have you thought about what we talked about yesterday?" his father asked.

Mike dropped the bag to the floor with a loud plop. His mother walked into the kitchen. There was silence for a few moments.

"Well?" his father demanded.

Mike took a deep breath and spoke without heat. "I've decided to go pro and play on the circuit. Workin' in a store isn't for me."

"Goddammit! I worked my ass off all these years for you! Now you want to waste your life throwing frisbees?"

"What you want isn't what I want." Mike spoke sharply, expressing his feelings perfectly.

Mike saw his father's beefy face getting redder and redder. It always happened when he thwarted his father's will. But Mike had had it.

The older man slammed his fist on the table. "It won't do, son. Who can I get to take over the business if you don't do it?"

Mike, desperate, glanced over at his mom, who was smiling suggestively. Suddenly he knew what to say. "That apprentice you got will do just fine. You want to give Abe the business anyway. He's smart and motivated. You're just angry because you think that the business should stay in the family."

Gerard looked over his shoulder at his wife and then back at his son. "It's a goddamn conspiracy. You were always more like your mother than me."

"That's right pops," Mike said. "And you love it." Mike could see a bunch of emotions flitting over his father's face.

"Damn right. You're too stupid to run a store. It's a complicated business."

Mike sighed with relief. "Neither of us is very bright, but we're smart enough to know that."

"All right, damn you! Get over here and let's have a beer."

Mike was amazed how easy it was after that. Dad discussed how he would retire, and how much responsibility he would give to Abe. "Don't know how you can make any money farting around with stupid games like that." After that he grudgingly wished his son good luck on the tour. Of course it was all mom's doing; she had been greasing the wheels for a while now. Mike knew she had been talking privately with Abe, guiding him on how to approach the Bulldog.

"You're the best, mom," he said.

"Damn right," Gerard said. He smiled affectionately at his wife of thirty years.

"Maybe you'll meet some nice girl out there," his father suggested.

"Lots of women play the circuit."

"You mean they got pro frisbee girls too?"

"Sure dad, just like ball golf. Separate pro tours for women and men."

"You know I want grandkids. Don't wait too long."

"Yes sir."

"Now I know you're bullshitting me when you're that polite."

Everybody laughed.

"You'll feel better when I'm out of the house," Mike proposed.

Gerard guffawed, and Mike knew he was right. His father's friends called him the Bulldog. Mike thought the comparison suited him. His wife was the only person Gerard could love, and he did a good job of it. Even if he wasn't a genius, Gerard Parsons was a straight shooter and people respected that.

It was going to be OK. Now he just had to figure out how to win enough on the tour to support himself. Even though his mom was great, he sure as hell wasn't going to live here anymore with his dad.

Jessie Calls Heather

Jessie woke up on Saturday feeling depressed. Zach hadn't called her, and he had a reputation for always keeping his word. She picked up her phone and saw his message. Danielle Menard! That druggie! Did he really like her? Jessie thought about it and admitted to herself that Danielle was really smart. Zach was too. But she was a drug dealer with a useless father. What did he see in her?

Jessie picked up the phone and called her friend Heather. "I'm depressed."

"Let me guess. It's Zach isn't it?"

"Am I that obvious?"

"Girl, you are definitely obvious. You need to back off."

"But I don't want to. How do I get him to like me?"

Heather said nothing and Jessie realized how stupid her question was. "I really like that guy and I know we'd be good for each other."

"You probably would be, but you have to let it play out," Heather advised. "It's never going to work out with him and Danielle."

"How do you know that?"

"Because they are fated not to work."

"I don't understand, Heather."

"Jessie, Zach has a sunny personality but that girl has bad karma. There's something dark about her that is eventually going to turn Zach off. You just have to wait and not be a pain. You know how guys don't like women who pester them."

"That's a good word, pester," Jessie admitted. "Do I pester Zach?"

"Yup. How many times did you call him yesterday?"

Jessie's face turned red. "I only called him once!"

"How many times did you text him?"

"Only three times!" She laughed. "I suppose I'm like the little girl at the petting zoo, always chasing the llama until he farts in my face."

Heather smiled. "Well, not quite that bad, but you have to go easy."

"It's hard, though. Zach texted me last night and said he was over at Danielle Menard's until four in the morning."

Heather was silent for a moment. "Yeah, that's bad."

"Do you think they hooked up?"

"Are you kidding? Who can resist that guy?"

"Heather! I thought you said they wouldn't make it?"

"I didn't say that, I said they wouldn't work out *permanently*."

"I'd like to smack that bitch." Jessie was angry, thinking about Zach and Danielle in bed together. "It just burns me up. She's no good."

"Watch that DiPietro temper. Don't do anything rash."

"I'd like to give *her* a rash." Jessie thought about an airborne virus that would turn Danielle into a bloated cow with pimples all over her face.

"Hang in there, Jessie. You have to be patient."

"I'm sorry Heather. I know I'm being unreasonable."

"Just don't say anything to him for a couple of days," Heather suggested.

"But then he'll ignore me."

"Just be alluringly silent and watch what happens."

Jessie liked the idea immediately. "Heather, you're a genius." She'd wear winter colors to set off her hair and creamy skin. She'd sort of find out where Zach was going to be and just be around for him to see her. If she had to go to the stupid disk golf course she'd do it.

"Thank you, I knew I could count on you."

As Jessie hung up Heather thought: I'd like to have a go at Zach myself. Why should Jessie have all the fun?

Jessie Goes to Meet Zach

Jessie knew that Zach and Mike played on Saturday mornings at 9 at Deerfield Park. At 8:40 she put on a pair of tight-fitting winter slacks, a winter shirt, and a ski jacket. She drove out to the hiking trail, which intersected the fifth hole on the pro course. She started walking, timing her arrival to get to number five at 9:20. Today she was going to find out a little more about Zach. She knew he loved disk golf and couldn't understand why. She would walk with them and keep quiet, letting him look at her and maybe see she wasn't like the other girls. She didn't like Mike very much but she'd put up with him.

As she approached the number five teepad she saw that Heather was walking beside both guys on the fourth fairway. The traitor! Angry now, she walked very quickly up to the threesome and almost blew it. She remembered Heather's advice just in time before she opened her mouth: lay back. She pretended to be surprised to see everybody.

"What are you doing here?" Zach asked.

Jessie's temper rose but she stifled it. "I'm going for a walk."

"Didn't know you were into exercising in the cold."

"It's nice out here."

Mike grinned. "Perfect day for golfing." Despite his nervousness around women he was glad the girls showed up. Zach had been babbling on about Tesla's notebook since the first hole. He had told him to either call their old buddy John Rosen or take it to the Carleton physics department. John was now a research scientist at Octagon Research and would know a lot more about Nikola Tesla than him.

Jessie avoided looking at Heather, for fear she'd say something rude. Heather was wearing a nice ski jacket and ski pants. Jessie could tell she had groomed herself carefully, with a long blond pony tail that bobbed when she walked. Zach grabbed a disk out of his bag and stepped onto the tee pad, which had a sign that read "538 feet." Jessie was behind him and saw him wind up and throw an incredible shot straight down a narrow wooded fairway. It went so far she couldn't even see the disk land. "Wow!"

Zach was prepared to be irritated because he knew Jessie didn't care for sports. He felt she was playing some game with him. But her genuine look of appreciation and amazement pleased him. "Great shot," Mike grunted. He was shorter and stockier than Zach and threw a shot almost as good as Zach's, but not quite as far.

The two players and the women walked down the fairway. Zach's shot was less than 100 feet from the basket; Mike's was about 40 feet behind Zach's. Despite her lack of enthusiasm for the game Jessie was impressed. "How do you not throw it in the trees?"

"Practice sweetheart, practice," Zach said in his best Humphrey Bogart voice. Heather was scowling as Jessie monopolized the attention from the guys.

"Do you mind if I walk with you?" Jessie asked. "I don't see how you can throw so far and so accurately."

Zach looked at Mike, who shrugged. "Sure. You can spot for us if you like."

"Spot?"

"Find the disks after they throw them," Heather said. Both women giggled, and Jessie's anger toward her friend evaporated.

At the next hole Mike and Zach sent both of their guests down the fairway.

"What's this all about?" Mike asked. "Those two chicks never wanted to come out here before."

"I don't know man, but they're both nice to look at. Kind of inspirational if you know what I mean."

To Zach's surprise, they all had a good time. Mike was in his element and didn't display his usual awkwardness around women. Both Jessie and Heather seemed into it.

After the round was over they walked to the parking lot, chatting amiably. Zach invited them all to his house for hot chocolate.

"Will your mom mind?" Heather asked. "It's Christmas eve."

"I don't care what she wants," Zach said, remembering what Rachel had said to him yesterday. "Dad does all the cooking anyway. She just sits around and complains."

"Uh, thanks but no thanks," Heather said. "I don't want to irritate anybody in your family." She could tell that Zach regarded her as just another female acquaintance. She didn't want to force the situation so she walked to her car and drove off.

Jessie was bolder. "I'd love to come over for a couple of minutes anyway."

"OK, follow me. Oh wait, your car is in the other parking lot for hikers. I'll drive you over there."

Jessie was pleased. She had spent some time with Zach and it was actually fun, even though her feet were soaking wet from the snow.

Zach motioned for her to take the front seat. "Get in." Mike gave him an evil look because he and Zach had driven to the course in Zach's Mazda. Mike had to squash his stocky body into the back seat. Jessie didn't say anything as they drove over to the other parking lot. She liked to talk but Zach and Mike were discussing their round as if it was as important as a summit meeting.

Jessie drove to Zach's and parked behind the Mazda, where Mike and Zach were just getting out of the car. At that moment Rachel came out of the house. "No guests today! The family is coming over for Christmas Eve dinner."

Zach looked apologetically at Jessie. "Sorry babe. Mom's in a bad mood."

Jessie was gracious. "I had fun today. I didn't think I would."

"It gets into your blood. If you want I'll give you a lesson sometime."

"I'd like that."

Zach liked her smile and her interest. This was a new Jessie from the pain-in-the-ass one. "Happy Christmas! Maybe you can come out again with us on Tuesday."

Jessie nodded and got in her car. It had been a great day. But she was going to have a little talk with Heather.

Jessie and Heather Talk

Jessie talked to Heather over the phone on Monday, the day after Christmas. "What were you doing out there on Saturday?" She'd been too mad to even text Heather on Sunday.

"Same thing you were doing: trying to get Zach interested."

"You were trying to steal him from me."

"Give me a break. Zach belongs to nobody. Half the women at Carleton are interested in him."

"Yeah that's true. I thought it was sneaky, Heather."

"It was not! Why shouldn't I have a go at the most gorgeous guy in town?"

"Sometimes I wonder why you're my friend."

"I'll tell you why. Because I'm the best judge of relationships you ever saw. And that's why you don't have to worry."

"What do you mean?"

"Zach has no interest in me. I could tell almost from the moment I got there."

Jessie's resentment evaporated.

"So what's your interest in Zach? Do you just want to get him in bed?"

"I've always liked Zach, I'm not sure why."

"Well girl, you'd better think about that some more."

Jessie felt uncomfortable and changed the subject. "Don't we have anything better to do than talk about guys?"

"Apparently not. But on a more serious note, I've decided I don't like pharmacology, Jessie. It's too boring."

"Really? You've slogged through two years of chemistry courses. You're changing your major?"

"I only took that career path because my father is a doctor and I admire him."

Jessie thought about Heather's father; a tall, imposing man who wanted a son and instead got two daughters. "Your father is a man difficult to say no to."

"That's true. But after two years of chemistry I discovered that I'm more interested in people than chemicals."

"My General Studies major is just an excuse to put off making a career choice."

"I've never told you that, but I've thought it."

Jessie sighed. Unlike her, Heather thought things through. Was she as shallow as her parents? It was a troubling thought. Maybe that's why she liked Zach so much. He was deep and smart and he knew where he was going. At least she thought he did.

"What do you want to be when you grow up?" Heather teased.

"I don't know Heather."

The two women left it at that for the time being.

On Monday night Jessie texted Zach.

I'll take you up on that lesson. How about tomorrow morning?

Zach texted back shortly after.

OK, come to Hudson Mills, the Original course, to the left of the parking lot, at eleven. Mike and I will be finishing our round.

Can Heather come if she wants?

Sure. Mike kind of likes her.

Jessie's lips curled at the mention of Mike. She called her friend. "Heather, Zach says we can get a lesson if we get out to the course tomorrow at eleven. Are you interested?"

"No thanks, honey. Especially not if that creep Mike Parsons will be there."

"He'll be there."

"Good luck then, he's all yours."

"Thanks Heather. I'll call you and let you know everything."

The next morning Jessie got to the course just as Zach and Mike were coming off. Zach waved. "Jessie! Over here!"

She ran over to them and smiled. "I'm ready."

Mike looked at Zach and they grinned. Jessie was bright and interested this morning. "All right, we'll practice on the first hole. The course is empty today, it's a bit cold."

As Zach showed her how to throw the disk Mike stood by and watched, occasionally commenting. After ten minutes it was clear to her that the men were all business. Zach really had no interest in her other than as another disk golf addict. They played the first hole and she actually made a good shot, but the game did nothing for her. They walked back to the parking lot. Zach said, "You have talent, Jessie. You could be good if you practiced. But I don't think you're really into it."

"No, I thought I might be," Jessie said. Well, she might be if Zach was more into *her*. "Oh well, it was fun coming out again."

"If you ever want to spot for us again, just call," Mike said.

She couldn't tell if he was being sarcastic or not, but she held in her temper. The stupid ass. No wonder none of the girls liked him. "OK, thanks guys."

When she got home Jessie called Heather and told her all about it.

"I thought so," Heather said. "He's not into either of us."

"You're right. I think I'm going to concentrate on my classes this year and avoid men altogether."

"Good idea. Let's make a pact: We'll stay away from men until next year."

Jessie agreed.

Danielle Goes Downtown

It was 11 p.m. and Danielle Menard had to meet Ricky, her supplier, downtown. She didn't like it because he was a creep and once had tried to force himself on her. She carried a knife for that. They had reached a detente after she'd put her knee to his groin and put the knife on his throat, drawing a little blood. He was a skinny little kid, and afraid. Like her, Ricky was probably out of options and just trying to survive.

She was small-time and didn't interfere with the other dealers on the streets. She dealt to a few of her high school friends who were still in town. She had only one big customer, a socialite who protected her for his own good. She only needed the one big sale each week to get the week's food money and pay the utilities for her and dad. With that money she could also buy the next week's stash. The money from the other small sales she kept for herself.

She never knew what her client would demand; often it was specialty designer drugs that she had to pay extra for. But she charged him plenty for it and he didn't complain. They had an understanding: the word on the street was not to mess with her. However, the client had made it abundantly clear that if she even hinted at his involvement with drugs, she'd be in "grave difficulty." Danielle believed him. She had only seen him once when he introduced himself as she was walking by the Radison downtown. At first she thought he thought she was a prostitute, but then she found out he wanted drugs. This guy wore carefully tailored designer clothes and he had a nice British accent. He was polite but there was a hard steely coldness behind his smile. He wasn't a man to fuck with, she was certain of that.

Danielle would show up in front of the Radison Hotel in the swanky part of downtown on Saturday afternoons, dressed as a courier. She had been given a badge to wear by the client: "Bloom Courier Service." She'd place the drugs in a packet the client gave her, which had the Bloom logo on it. She'd walk in to the hotel and simply hand the packet to the receptionist with whom she was on friendly terms. "Delivery for Mr. Haskins," she'd say. The receptionist would hand her a small manila envelope addressed to the courier service, which contained cash and a list of drugs for the following week. She didn't ask questions. As long as the money kept showing up, she'd keep supplying.

She carried a slim black suitcase in her right hand. It looked like something a businessman would carry. Whenever she met Ricky she wore her good clothes, even though she was going to a bad neighborhood. Danielle walked into the alley behind Ashley Street where a lot of homeless people hung out. Ricky was already there, leaning against the wall. He looked at her hungrily

"You got the stuff?" she asked.

"It's right here."

"Hand it over."

"You first."

Danielle grabbed her knife in her right hand and set the black satchel at her feet. She let him see the cash, which had magically appeared in her left hand, and waited. Ricky dropped a brown package at his feet, and she kicked the suitcase over to him. Ricky put the package in the suitcase and kicked it back over to her. At the same time she threw the envelope at his feet, picked up the suitcase, and walked the three blocks back home. It was the same every week.

When she got home she locked the suitcase in her safe. She'd deal with it later. She went to the kitchen and opened up the right-hand top cabinet, where there were some canned goods. She stuffed the cans into the paper bag and walked back downtown to Ashley Street. Everyone was huddling around the barrel fire. Nobody asked her any questions when they saw her approach; she was known and liked in the homeless community. When they saw the shopping bag people came over and greeted her.

"Danielle, how are you?" said a young woman about her own age, who called herself Rita. She was the saddest case. Whenever Danielle started feeling sorry for herself she talked to Rita, who had lost her parents in an automobile accident. Rita was now a prostitute and a heroin addict. Compared to her she was living like a queen.

Most of the homeless were men; she had to be careful. Some of them were mentally unstable but the others protected her because she brought food. She was especially welcome at this time of the year, when the winter cold seeped through worn and frayed jackets and coats, and hungry stomachs needed sustenance.

After she scoped out the situation and spotted potential troublemakers, she handed out cans to those who needed it most. Sometimes fights broke out and when that happened she just left. But almost always the people were polite and grateful. Talking to the homeless and hearing their stories was the highlight of Danielle's week. These unwanted cast-offs were living on the edge and some of them were desperate. Yet their lives were so much more meaningful than most people, who just went to work every day. They were living lives of such poignancy.

There was Ron, an old vet who had seen action in Afghanistan. His parents had died when he was a young child. He had been raised in the foster care system until he was able to fend for himself. He joined the army and although he didn't elaborate, he had been subjected to awful experiences in the war. He got involved with drugs and alcohol over there and "just sort of sank out of sight." When he returned to the United States he had a difficult time readjusting, and finally wound up living on the streets.

There was James, formerly a successful securities broker. As a child he had been raised in a nice home by loving parents. He and his wife had no children but eventually she filed for divorce. "I spent too much time at work," he told Danielle. While working as a broker he developed severe headaches but the doctors could find no obvious reason for their occurrence. He became depressed, lost his job at the brokerage firm, and "just fell of the face of the earth." James told her that since he had lost his wife, his job, and his "fair-weather friends," his depression and headaches had gotten much better.

Lois was about 60 and wore a very bulky and unbuttoned dark gray cloth overcoat over worn-out jeans. She was overweight and had some kind of nervous condition. "My husband left me," she told Danielle, and said she was going through a difficult divorce. Her children blamed her for the difficulties in her marriage. Her husband left her penniless and she lost her home. Her nervous condition made it difficult for her to hold a job. She had lost all of her "friends."

Danielle's favorite was Jamelle. He was only fourteen years old. His folks had passed away and he was being cared for by his older brother. He lived with his brother and several other boys in a house just south of Second Street. All of the boys living in the home worked long hours in order to pay for rent, food, and other living expenses. They often didn't have enough to eat. The boys were too busy to ever attend school. Jamelle and his friends had been hired by "the man" to be door-to-door salesmen. They sold an assortment of products which they carried in their duffel bags. Each boy was expected to wear a provided uniform. "The man wants us to look professional," Jamelle explained. Every boy was given a specific area to canvas. After a year the business, although well run, fell apart and he and his brother were on the streets. Tonight Jamelle was, as usual, bright and cheerful. She didn't know how he kept so positive.[4]

Danielle talked with a newcomer and told everybody the latest news in her life. After an hour or so she walked back home to her dingy, dirty home. She felt grateful. It was more than these people had.

She would rather spend time with the homeless than almost anyone she knew except Zach, whom she had met in high school and always had a crush on. The homeless were close to the edge, living day to day. She felt the same way. But despite their poverty and their problems there was something vital and real about them. She'd often stop by to hang out and always brought something to share.

Danielle went upstairs to her bed, throwing on her nightgown and flopping onto the bed. The house was always cold in winter to save money on the heating bill. When she thought about Zach she almost shuddered with desire, and imagined what it would be like to be with him. They had had a little fling in high school but nothing came of it. She fell asleep dreaming about Ricky, chasing her down a dark alleyway with a knife in his hand.

— 6 —

Elmo Tackett sat on the bank of the river that flowed by the orphanage. He was ten years old and small for his age, with a pinched face and ears that stuck out of his head. Nobody liked him, but he didn't care much about them either. It was a short walk from the front door of the Sisters of St. Mary to the river, which was swollen with snow melt on this warm, late March day. He saw a frog croaking in a little swamp filled with rushes by the water. Curious, he quietly walked over and snatched it. He put it down on the muddy grass and watched as it breathed in and out. How did the frog do that? Elmo could see the creature about ready to pounce so he tore one of its legs off. The creature hobbled about on three legs. Elmo thought it was funny so he tore off one of its front legs. Gloppy red stuff ran out from the stumps, and he leaned over to smell it. It smelled pleasantly sweet, and he licked some off. It tasted good. The frog was now completely immobilized, but it was still breathing. Elmo ripped off the other two legs and watched as the creature's energy began to slowly fade away. Now it was no longer breathing; did that mean it was dead? Would that happen to a person if he did that to them? Elmo walked back to the orphanage's front door. He was hungry now, it was time for dinner.

The orphans trooped into the cafeteria, a large room with a cold old-fashioned linoleum floor and metal tables and chairs. Shouting children shoved Elmo out of the way. "Watch where you're going, kid!" a bigger boy said.

Elmo hated this place. He hated the other children and especially the staff, who always gave him the dirtiest jobs in the kitchen, scrubbing floors and washing out huge greasy pots and pans. He particularly despised Sister Armitage, a tall, big-boned woman who called him "little devil" or "little bastard." Each of the orphans lived in small rooms with five bunkbeds, ten to a room. Each day they got up at 8 a.m., ate breakfast, went to religion class, and then worked like slaves until 5 p.m. The children were only allowed a half hour break for lunch. Sister Armitage said hard work built character, but it just made him very tired.

As the years went by Elmo thought there was something wrong with the place. Weren't there regulations to protect children? The orphanage was like something from the old days. Elmo learned to despise the adults who worked there, and the authorities who allowed it to happen.

Today Sister Armitage had cafeteria duty and she patrolled the room like a duty sergeant. When she came to his table she said, "Did you clean that big soup pot you little devil?" Elmo learned long ago never to answer her unless in class. She raised her hand to cuff him on the side of the head and let it drop. He could feel her contempt for him.

Elmo had no patience with religion, or God. All he knew was that his parents had dropped him off at the front door of the orphanage one day. In class he never spoke up and only did the minimum. The sisters referred to him as "incorrigible."

He knew would never last here until his eighteenth birthday.

When he was sixteen, after the big fundraiser on Friday, Elmo stole all the cash from the building fund. Sister Armitage managed the fund and for Elmo it was a small measure of revenge. She had stupidly (Elmo thought) locked the money in the safe until Monday's bank deposit. But Elmo knew the combination to the safe.

He found that life on the streets was much to his liking.

Danielle Meets Elmo

Three days after her night with Zach, Danielle met Elmo Tackett. She had just made a delivery on Ann Street, in the bad part of town, only two blocks from her run-down home. Even at 3 a.m. she felt at home with the cast-offs and the dregs of society. She was carrying three hundred dollars when a short, ugly man came up to her, staring at her. "Are you staring at my boobs?" she asked.

"Yes," he said. "I like how you move." Elmo liked her because she was all in black and looked like a blond raven.

"Get lost, fuckhead." Danielle started to move off but Elmo's hand shot out quickly and grabbed her right arm. He was incredibly strong, with a grip like iron.

"You have money," the little man said. "I saw you make that drug deal. I see a lot of things. You're down here a lot."

Danielle was feeling afraid. There was something creepy about this guy; he spoke like a robot.

"Give me your money and I'll let you go," Elmo said.

Danielle tried to wriggle her arm away, but his grip was like a vise. "Give me your money," he repeated, louder this time. Elmo didn't need the raven's money but he liked to make people afraid so he could study the life force. When people were angry or afraid it was easier to see.

Danielle knew she was going to lose a sale and she couldn't afford it. Dad was sick. She had to buy his prescriptions because he didn't qualify for Medicare or Medicaid. Her eyes darted about. She would have screamed and created a scene but the street was empty.

"I may be ugly but I'm not stupid," Elmo said. His grip tightened even harder on her forearm.

"Let me go and I'll give you the money." The ugly man didn't seem to care that he was inflicting pain. He was emotionless and that scared her even more. Was this guy some kind of serial killer? He looked like an escaped mental patient.

Elmo loosened his grip but didn't let go. He indicated the left back pocket of her jeans with a nod of his head. "You put the money there. No tricks."

Danielle decided to risk it. She was expert at sleight-of-hand. She moved her left hand slowly toward her pocket, which had a small wad of three $100 bills. That was to establish trust.

The little man was intently watching her hand, though, and she didn't know how acute his perception was. He didn't seem to be armed. Her knife, unfortunately, was down her jeans on the right side, inaccessible. As her left hand approached her back pocket she moved it upward, showing him that there was no weapon. He nodded slightly and she put her fingers in her pocket. Incredibly swiftly, she manipulated the wad and took out two of the bills, leaving the other one.

"Is that all of it?"

"You got my food money for the week. Now fuck off."

The corner's of Elmo's mouth rose up and then down again, in what Danielle thought was supposed to be a smile. The emotion seemed foreign to him.

"All right. I know you have more in there but $200 is OK." Elmo was disappointed. The raven didn't scream or become hysterical, as most women would do. Strong emotion, he had observed, activated the life force. He would have to try again.

Elmo released his grip and took a step back, signifying that she could go. Danielle walked slowly, aware that the little man's attention was on her all the way until she turned the corner.

God, she thought, now this creep knows me.

After the raven left Elmo stood there for several minutes. Her life force had displayed itself when she became agitated, and left when she relaxed. It was the same with the frog and the other animals he dissected. Why was this? He had never been able to understand it despite all his studies. Fortunately he had made contact with the Katelian family, and through them other clients. Now he had steady work. He no longer had to worry about finances and his needs were simple. The Katelians had set him up in a basement apartment at the Tavistock development by the Midland River. He liked the apartment because it allowed him to continue his experiments with the small animals who inhabited the marshes. His favorite experiments were with human beings, for the life force was strongest there.

Max Jr. Asks Zach about the Notebook

On Wednesday of Christmas week Max Jr. and Zach, both sick of their parents, returned to the rental house on campus. Max Jr. was unpacking in his upstairs room when he heard the front door slam. He had spent over $400 of his father's money at the 24 Club the past two nights, and was almost broke again. But he had promised his father he'd talk to Zach, so he waited until Zach had lugged his books and his duffel up the stairs into his room. He and Zach had the two bedrooms upstairs.

Max Jr. walked into Zach's room. "Hey Zach do you still have that notebook?"

Zach straightened after putting his underwear and socks into the old-fashioned dresser. "Yeah, but I haven't had a chance to look it over yet."

"Well, my old man wants to see it."

"The great Max Berglin wants to see my little old notebook? Why?"

"He thinks it might be Nikola Tesla's work, and he's a fanatic about Tesla. Personally, I couldn't care less."

Zach knew nothing about Max Jr.'s father. If he was as aloof as his son, he felt no great desire to do anything for him."I stole it from the Graduate Library. When I'm done with it I'll put it back where I found it."

Max Jr. was satisfied. He had earned his $500.

— 7 —

On a warm Thursday morning Zach Ferrell and Mike Parsons were standing on the first tee looking down a snowless fairway. Mike had some important news for Zach. Before he could begin Zach started talking about Nikola Tesla and his mysterious notebook again.

Mike was irritated. "Why don't you show it to someone in the physics department at the university?"

"I plan to. But it's Christmas week and the place is closed up."

"Let's just talk about golf today, okay? I don't know anything about physics or engineering."

"I'm getting a little annoying, aren't I?"

"Yeah."

Zach dug out a disk from his bag. Mike said, "I'm leaving town and going pro."

Zach was stunned for a moment. "But why? You have it good here."

"Are you kidding? Workin' in that hardware store with my old man yelling at me all the time? That's no life for anybody."

Zach didn't know what to say. He had always accepted Mike as someone who would always be there, his disk golf playing partner and occasional drinking buddy. "Uh, yeah, I guess you're right. I never thought about it before."

"You never think about anything, Zach. Everything comes so easy for you. You never have to study in school. You pick up a disk and throw like an expert. Girls slobber all over you. You're the smartest person I know. Do you ever think about the rest of us bozos?"

Zach was amazed at his friend's outburst. Normally sullen and taciturn, Mike had rounded on him this morning. Zach shifted his feet awkwardly. "I guess not."

"Yeah, well look at my life. It sucks. I'm in a dead-end job and girls think I'm putrid. That's what Bethany said to me the other day in the store. I'm not smart enough for college and I got no money and no way to make it other than disk golf. I'm desperate, Zach. This town's got nothing for me."

Zach's first response was to think: 'But who am I going to play with now?'

Mike caught that right away. "Yeah I thought so. Always thinking about yourself."

"I didn't say anything!"

Mike stared at him. "You really do think I'm a dumbass, don't you?"

Zach put his bag down and sat on the picnic table next to the tee. "Shit Mike, you're right. I'm an arrogant, selfish bastard."

"Goddam right," Mike said, echoing his father's favorite expression.

"So when do you leave?"

"I worked it out with the Bulldog. I'll stay in the store until the end of March, to get that apprentice of his up to speed and so they can hire a new guy. Then I'm gone."

For the first time Zach realized how important Mike was to him. "But what will I do without you?"

Zach's emotion was genuine and Mike grinned sarcastically. "For all your smarts you don't know a lot about people."

Zach thought about that. "No, I don't, I guess." He looked up into Mike's face. "Are people that important?"

"One thing I learned working in the store, Zach. If you want to be successful you gotta get along with people. All the bigwigs in town are good at it." Mike spoke resentfully. "Guys like me never get anywhere."

"You should have been a cowboy," Zach joked. "You're the strong silent type."

Mike kicked his friend in the shins. "That's not funny Zach."

"I did it again didn't I?"

"Yup. As Trevor Clarke said one time in the store, you treat people with casual contempt."

Zach's mouth dropped open. "Do I?"

Mike was satisfied. For the first time in his life he had really gotten through to somebody. It felt good. He knew Zach would be the better for it. "All right then, let's play. I'm going to crush you today."

After the round Zach went home and sat on the bed, sweat dripping down his face. Mike had been right today. He was coasting through life. He'd always had a little contempt for Rachel and her cold, calculating, and aggressive ways. Now he thought that maybe he was lacking in determination.. He needed to be more decisive, he had to plan for his future. He realized that he had taken the worst from both his parents. He was dismissive of people, like his mother, and too easygoing like his father. He decided to call Mike.

"Hey buddy, what are you doing?"

"Just sitting around."

"You mind if I come over?"

Mike was surprised. Zach almost never came to his house, he always had to go over there. "Yeah sure, if you want."

"Good, I need to talk to you. Break out some beers, I'll be over in fifteen minutes."

Mike could tell Zach wanted to work out something. It made him feel good to know that his opinion was valued. Mostly in the store all people wanted was advice about sinks and where to find toilet seats. He went downstairs and saw his mom sitting in the kitchen, reading a book. "Hey mom, Zach is coming over. I'm getting a few beers."

"What's the occasion?" she asked, smiling.

"He wants to talk. Don't know why he wants to talk to me but I'll oblige him."

His mother gave him a knowing smile, something she was doing a lot lately.

"Do you want to tell me something?"

Justine Parsons opened her mouth but then closed it. "No son. I think you are just about ready to figure it out for yourself."

"Figure out what?"

"Talk to Zach and then come down and see me."

Mike was confused. "OK mom, I'll do that."

He walked upstairs, thinking about Zach, the hardware store, and his life. Five minutes later Zach stomped up the stairs and burst into his room. Mike indicated a beer on his desk; Zach popped it open. He sat on the bed and Mike sat on his swivel chair by the desk. Just like Dr. Phil, he thought.

"I've been thinking about what you said today Mike," Zach began. "You're right. I have no idea what I'm going to do with my life."

Mike took a swig from his beer and pretended he was the famous TV personality. "Tell me about it."

Zach started right in. "You're right. I can do anything, but I don't know what I want." He paused. "I've been thinking about Danielle Menard a lot."

"Danielle Menard? Are you kidding?" As soon as Mike said it he saw Zach get angry. He had goofed. He realized that he had a responsibility now to help his friend, that somehow this wasn't a normal conversation. It was a new feeling. "I'm sorry buddy. Tell me about Danielle and your feelings for her."

Zach relaxed and looked up at him, grateful for the question. "I spent a night with her a couple of days ago. We didn't even fuck, we just talked until four in the morning. I think I love her."

"*Love* her?" Mike was startled that anyone could love that depressing girl.

Zach got really angry and rose from the bed, ready to walk out.

Mike knew he had blown it again. "Hey man, I'm sorry. I'm new at this." He got up and slowly walked over to Zach, putting his hand on his back and guiding him back to the bed.

He let Zach cool down a bit. "OK, continue. You were saying you might love Danielle." He could hardly get the words out without sounding disapproving, but he modulated his voice.

"Yeah, she's beautiful and deep and we connect." He looked up at Mike, almost pleading. "I can't explain it."

"You love who you love."

Zach jumped off the bed, startling Mike. "That's it! You love who you love. It's like my parents. Why does Mark stay with Rachel, who is getting more and more bitter every year? He said because he loved her. That's how it works."

"For better or for worse," Mike said.

Zach became even more animated and his eyes were bright. "That's right. You nailed it!" Zach was so excited now he began to pace the room, talking rapidly in staccato sentences. "The good and the bad, Mike. Nobody's perfect. Everybody has flaws. OK, I gotta figure out what I'm going to do with my life this semester. I'm going to call Danielle and ask her out."

Zach turned around and locked eyes with his friend. "She's a good person."

Mike didn't say anything, accepting the statement even though he didn't agree with it.

After that Zach sat down and they drank a beer together. They discussed the round and Mike decided to crow a little. "Beat you today."

"You putted out of your mind. You bounced one off a tree and it went in."

"Good players get the bounces."

They both laughed. After a few minutes Zach left, a determined look in his eyes. Mike went downstairs in a thoughtful mood and entered the kitchen.

"Zach looks a lot better," Justine said. "What did you guys do up there?"

"Just talked." He was silent for a minute. "Mom, I don't understand how words can be so powerful. I made two big mistakes with Zach and hit two winners. Every time I opened my mouth I got a powerful reaction."

"It's not just the words, son. It's the emotions and the intention behind the words that give them their power."

Something clicked in Mike's brain. "For fuck's sake, you're right! Uh, sorry mom." The Bulldog had a strict rule: no swearing around your mother, even though he did it all the time.

"That's OK son. I won't tell your father."

For the first time in a long time Justine saw her son smile brightly, and laugh unaffectedly.

"I don't know what it is, mom, but I don't feel like a dumbass today. Maybe I made some progress."

Justine smiled. "I think you did, Mike."

Zach Calls on Danielle

Zach was so pumped up after his conversation with Mike that he drove right over to Danielle's. She was probably still sleeping. The girl really was a mess; she dealt drugs and took them too, and stayed up all hours of the night. But he felt what he felt. When he walked up to the peeling front door he noticed that it was open a crack, so he walked in. The living room was in disarray, with rumpled bedsheets on the couch, but her father wasn't there. He walked up the stairs and knocked on Danielle's door, which had a poster of a white unicorn on it. "Who is it?"

"Zach. Can I come in?"

"I haven't got any clothes on."

Zach became hopeful. "That's OK."

He heard some noises and then she opened the door in her jeans and a hastily thrown on shirt. "It's early."

"Past eleven now."

She held the door open like a trainer would to a circus animal. "Come on in."

This wasn't starting like he wanted. "Danielle — "

"Zach. Have you ever seen a small, ugly guy with ears that stick out from his face?"

Zach was flustered by this spontaneous question. He had rehearsed what he wanted to say and was now completely thrown off. "Uh, no, can't say I have."

Danielle told him the story of her adventure last night. "Do you think I'm in any danger from this creep?"

Her shirt was unbuttoned at the top and she caught Zach looking. Danielle buttoned up the shirt. "I'm serious, Zach."

"I think you'd better be careful. Sounds like the guy is crazy and observant."

"Just what I thought. I'll have to arrange my business in the daytime." Which really sucked, because the police presence was much greater than at night.

"Danielle, I need to talk to you."

"We're talking."

Zach took a deep breath. "OK, just listen and don't say anything until I'm done, OK?"

Danielle shrugged.

"I've been thinking a lot about you lately. I like you a lot. I think I might even love you. I—"

"Zach, we really had a nice time, but—"

"Just listen, OK? I've been thinking about my own life and what I want to do. After I graduate I'm going to leave Midland for Chicago or New York, or maybe L.A., and join one of the big engineering companies. I want you to come with me. This town is no good for you; if you stay here you won't last long." As soon as he said it he knew he was right. Danielle glanced at him quickly. He knew she felt it too.

Danielle ran her fingers through her blond hair. "Do you mean it Zach?"

"I mean it."

Danielle was surprised and a little pleased. This was a new Zach, a decisive Zach, not the fun-loving, irresponsible joyrider. "I can't."

"Why not?"

"Because of dad."

"Screw your dad!"

"If you're going to talk like that, you can get the fuck out."

"I'm sorry babe. I've been thinking about all the girls I've met and all the girls I know. You're the one for me."

"You don't know anything about me."

In response Zach was silent, looking into her eyes, and remembering the night they had connected so deeply. 'You know it and I know it,' his look said.

She smiled sadly at him. "God, if it could only be." She got out of bed and stood at the window with her back to him. The way she moved excited him, and he wanted her right now.

"I'm a druggie and a dealer Zach, and I don't know how to do anything else. I'm a loser. If you and I get together I'd just bring you down." She turned to him and spoke, her voice full of bitterness. "I don't know how to be a good person."

"I don't care about that. I love you."

Her eyes widened. "Do you mean that Zach?"

In response he walked over to her and took her in his arms. He kissed her as gently and as lovingly as he could. "Yes."

She turned her head up and gazed into his eyes. She was almost six feet tall but she liked it that Zach was taller. "I believe you. Now let me go. And get out of here."

Zach was confused. "But why?"

"Because I'm bad news. I'm hopeless." She walked over to the door and held it open. Something was going on behind those eyes, though. He could tell she was just about to break down.

"But Danielle—"

"Please Zach. I'll think about it OK? Give me time."

Zach sighed. "OK Danielle, but I meant everything I said. I love you."

After Zach left Danielle threw herself on the bed and cried.

When Zach got home he sat on his bed for hours, thinking. He did some research on alcoholism and rehab facilities. Then he sent Danielle a long text.

> Danielle I want to marry you. I'm serious. I'm sorry about what I said about your dad. I don't know how much he's been drinking, but I thought we could get him into a rehab facility. He needs help or he might not make it, you know that. These facilities can be expensive but I have some money saved up. He won't be there forever. I'm not worried about money anyway. It would only be until he got back on his feet. Then, if you want, he could come with us. Think about it Danielle. I've never been more certain of anything in my life that this will work for both of us.

After Zach left and she had her cry, Danielle felt more depressed than she ever had in her life. Zach loved her! She knew he wasn't kidding. That night a week ago they had communicated on a level where lying was impossible. It had been almost telepathic. So why was she feeling so bad?

Just then she heard the door open and her father come in. She recognized the sounds. She didn't know where he'd been, but soon he would be screaming for his supper. Numbly, she walked down the stairs and began to prepare a ground beef concoction with onions and tomatoes. She tried to get him some protein every day.

"Danielle, when are we going to eat?" he yelled from the living room.

She supposed it was a good sign that he still desired food. She knew he tried to stay away from hard liquor and only drank beer. Fortunately, the former scientist was still lucid and hadn't lost his marbles. He was just stuck. When he did drink he got sad, not angry; but he still said harsh things to her sometimes.

Her phone sounded and she saw the text from Zach. Her eyes filled with tears and she almost ran out of the house, but she finished the cooking. She made sure an open beer was on the table. Her father drank half the beer in one swig as she dished up the food.

When dad wasn't moping they could talk rationally at the dinner table. "Dad, Zach Ferrell has asked me to marry him."

Nothing.

"He's asked me to leave Midland with him in a year's time. I'd either be going to New York, Chicago, or maybe L.A."

That got a response.

"But what about me?"

"We'll put you in rehab until you're better. Then you can come with us if you want."

She noticed her father's face lift in sudden hope, then it fell. "I like it here."

"No you don't dad. This is where mom died. This is where all your dreams fell apart. It's the same for me. If we don't get out of here we're both going to die, sooner rather than later."

Pierce Menard dropped his fork and it clattered off his plate and onto the floor. He looked at his daughter, slack-jawed. He was entirely present now. "Are you serious?"

"I'm serious." And she was. She had made her decision and her depression suddenly lifted.

"You mean, you'd have me?" There was a note of hope in his voice. She hadn't seen that since mom died.

"On one condition: you have to clean up your act and get back to work."

His face fell. "I don't know if I can do that Danielle. I've been avoiding life for the past five years."

"Do you like the taste of alcohol?"

"I hate it. I only drink sometimes when I can't stand the pain."

Danielle sighed with relief. It might be possible. She looked him over carefully. Despite his ragged and hopeless appearance, there was still some color in his cheeks. She saw him drink down the beer. He grimaced as he put the bottle down on the table.

"What was that?" she asked.

"As I said, I hate the stuff. I thought – never mind."

"You thought what?"

"I thought...you hated me."

Danielle was honest. "Sometimes I do hate you, you bastard. But why do you think I stick around this filthy pigsty? It's because of you."

Pierce Menard suddenly grabbed the empty beer bottle and flung it violently against the wall behind her. Glass shattered.

"What did you do that for?" she screamed. Her father had never gotten angry in all the years she'd known him. But when she looked in his eyes she saw that had come out of the daze he'd been in for so long.

"I'm sorry, that was uncalled for. I was expressing myself rather too demonstrably. Id est: my hatred of this vile substance, my pathetic life, and my sudden resolve to do better. If I can."

"Wow dad! I haven't heard you speak like that since mom died."

"I've been hiding. Like the coward I am."

He began to sob, big, heart-wrenching gasps, bent over. She thought he was having a heart attack. "Dad!"

"It's all right daughter. I can't hold back my grief any longer. Get me another beer, would you?"

Danielle didn't know what to do. Her first instinct was to call Zach, but she was more worldly than he was. She put her arms around her father and led him to the unkempt couch. She straightened up and set the pillows up for his head. Still sobbing, her father just fell on the couch and lay there.

Danielle's head was spinning as she went back and carefully swept and vacuumed the broken glass out of the kitchen. She must have said something to snap Pierce Menard out of it. But was he capable of change? She realized, appalled, that she knew almost nothing about her father. When she was a child he had been mostly absent, working. For the past five years he had been a burden; someone to take care of; almost a patient. A voice inside her head told her that her father would always be a loser and always be there to ruin her life. Danielle recognized how jaded she had become, how tenuous was her desire for life. Maybe with Zach she could find a new beginning.

And maybe it would all go to hell, just like always.

The next morning she checked on her father, who was sleeping peacefully. Then she thought for a long time and texted Zach.

> OK boy, you asked for me, you got me. Dad snapped out of it last night and agreed to go to rehab. He's a mess. You better realize what you're getting into. If I go with you I'm all in and you have to take care of me and dad. You have a year to get yourself together because your act now isn't going to cut it. Think about it Zach, think hard. If you want me I'll have your back, but you have to do your part and not complain. You have to be a man, not a little boy. I think I might love you too. Danielle.

When Zach woke up the next morning and saw Danielle's text his heart started to pound. She said yes! The responsibility of it hit him like a ton of bricks, but then he grew excited. To have Danielle as his companion to bounce ideas off of, to have that level of intimacy every day.... He thought deliciously about having her in his bed every night. She was so much different than any other woman he'd ever met.

He got out of bed filled with a sudden burst of energy. He quickly laced up his running shoes and hit the road. It was only 6 o'clock and so cold that the Canadian Boy Scouts called off their ice fishing trip. He took off at a dead sprint, and ran a mile until he fell over in the snow on somebody's lawn.

Zach got up and ran some more, he didn't even know where he was going. Then, as suddenly as the burst of energy claimed him, it let him go. He felt exhausted now, and couldn't figure out what he had been so excited about. One thing was for sure: he had committed himself. He was now responsible for three lives, not one. Was he up for it? Did he really want it? There was still time to back out.

— 8 —

Zach found himself two miles from the rental house, on the edge of downtown. On the way home he searched himself. The only emotion that came was a throbbing excitement at the thought of being with Danielle. Her old man, he could care less. He'd keep him happy because it would make Danielle happy. Maybe that was love, maybe not, but it was the best he had. Now he had to make some serious plans.

Larry Potvin was driving to work at 6 in the morning when he saw a figure running down the street like a crazy man. "Is that Zach Ferrell?"Sure enough, it was Zach. He was about to ask the kid if he wanted a ride, but saw he was in his sweats. Larry shrugged and drove on. He wondered what the kid was doing, getting involved with that Menard girl. He had heard that from Karl, who idolized Zach. Danielle Menard was a real loser. The kid shouldn't waste his time with riff-raff like that. Her father was worse than her; he was responsible for the way the daughter turned out. He hadn't played a man's part. Hell, I don't want to get up so early and go to this shitty job. But I do it because I have a family.

On the way to work Larry thought about having a talk with Zach. He needed some help with his new business. The kid was good with his hands and had a natural understanding of mechanics. Once when he stopped by to see Karl, he put him to work reassembling a carburetor. Larry chuckled at that memory. Karl had been really upset about it because he wanted to play chess with Zach, but Zach was more interested in the engine.

Maybe he could get Zach to work part-time for some extra money. It would be good help and he wouldn't have to pay a full-time mechanic. He could also clue him in about that waste of space Danielle Menard.

When Zach got back to his room his excitement was gone but he hadn't changed his mind. His best friend was leaving, his own life was going to change big time. Unlike Mike he had a whole year to get ready, because he wouldn't graduate until the following January.

A part of him wondered whether it would work out with Danielle but the rest of him wanted to go for it. It was Sunday morning, New Year's Day. Rachel and Mark would be home all day. He'd drive over to the house and announce his decision at breakfast.

When he got to the house his parents were sitting at the kitchen table eating eggs and bacon. "Happy New year, son!" Mark said. As usual, Rachel was in a bad mood in the morning, but it couldn't be helped. "You might not say that after I make my announcement," he said.

Rachel's head snapped up sharply and her mouth tightened. "What announcement?"

"I've asked Danielle to marry me and she has accepted. I'm going to finish school and then we're going to leave Midland next year."

Mark said nothing, searching his face for honest intent.

Rachel's eyes tightened. "So you've decided to throw your life away on that strumpet."

Any nervousness Zach felt abruptly vanished. "Don't ever refer to my fiancée as a strumpet again, mom." He said it politely but with firm intention, even though he didn't know what strumpet meant.

"That girl is no good. If you marry her it's the worst thing you could ever do."

"It's my decision to make and I've made it."

Rachel shook her head sadly. Zach could tell that she thought him a naive fool, and his feelings a mere infatuation. Mark held his hand out. "Congratulations, son. I hope you'll be happy."

"That figures," Rachel said. She slammed her coffee cup down on the table and left the room.

"I think you could do better Zach," Mark said. "Getting angry won't help. I sincerely do wish you happiness."

Zach was pleased that his dad had come around, but he didn't want friction between mom and Danielle. He walked into the living room. "From now on you pay your own way at school," Rachel said. "I won't support you as long as you are with that girl."

"Suit yourself, mom. But understand this. When Danielle comes over here – and I'm inviting her to dinner on Tuesday – I expect you to treat her with respect. You don't have to like her, but you do have to at least be polite."

"I won't be seen in the company of that woman. If your father chooses to accept her, that's his decision. I won't have her in this house."

Zach gave it up. "Very well Rachel." Rachel's head snapped up at the cold formality. "If you change your mind you can always text or call. You have my number." He said it as if addressing a client. Zach went back to the kitchen.

"I'll be leaving now dad. Mom has decided she won't accept Danielle, so I'll have a celebration dinner at Seva on Tuesday instead. You're welcome to come and I really hope you do."

"I'll be there son. What time?"

"Seven. I'm inviting all my friends."

Mark laughed. Zach had a lot of friends at Carleton. "Who's going to pay for all that?"

"Oh, they'll pay for their own dinners. We're all starving students."

"All right. I'd like to see Danielle in company, see what kind of person she is."

"So would I."

Zach turned to go up to his room. Mark said, "Don't worry about your tuition son. I'll take care of that."

Zach turned back to face his father, a feeling of love in his heart. "Thanks dad." He could see his father tear up so he left the kitchen and walked upstairs to his room. There were still a few odds and ends like his baseball glove, a couple of tennis rackets, and his store of disks. He packed them all into a couple of cloth shopping bags and hauled them out to the car. When he got back inside he could hear his parents arguing. He'd already said his goodbyes, so he left.

When Zach got back to the rental house he texted all his friends. He decided to keep it simple.

> Danielle Menard and I are engaged. We hope to be married next year, after I graduate. Come to Seva this Tuesday at 7 and I'll tell you all about it.

His finger hovered over the send button. He knew this text would get everybody talking, and he knew a lot of people. Once he sent it he would be fully committed. He hesitated for a moment and put Danielle on the send list as well. Then he pressed his finger to the screen.

When Jessie DiPietro woke up on Sunday morning, New Year's Day, she received the text from Zach. When she read it she couldn't believe it. "Danielle Menard? He's got to be kidding!" She called Zach immediately.

"Zach, what are you doing marrying that girl?"

"You're the fifth person this morning who's asked me that. Because I love her, that's why."

"OK Zach. I just wanted to make sure you were sure."

"I am sure. Nothing is going to change for another year except I can't go home because of Rachel. But Mark is cool with it."

"I always liked your dad," Jessie agreed.

"You're a good person, Jessie. Will you be coming to the party? I want you all to see Danielle and say hi."

"Sure, Heather and I will be there."

And so it went for the next 24 hours. He had to make reservations for 45 people. Danielle was getting worried. "What if your friends don't like me?"

"Who cares? It's not about them, it's about you. I want everybody to see you. I even invited the parents if they want to come. My father says he'll be there."

"But Zach, I don't have any good clothes!" That wasn't quite true, she realized. There was all of mom's stuff, and she was the same size. A little old, but there were some classic dresses in her closet. Mom had some nice shoes, slacks, blouses, a couple of business suits, even an Easter hat. Dad hadn't touched anything up there for five years, preferring to sleep downstairs.

"It will be OK Danielle. Just wear what you have. You look great in anything."

She was pleased by his confidence in her. She liked that he wanted to show her off to all his friends, even though it made her nervous. They had talked again in her room until two in the morning, she couldn't even remember about what. What was clear was that she really liked him and he really liked her. Moreover, he didn't care that she lived in a dump and dealt drugs and used them sometimes. He was already making plans. It was a good start.

Danielle Gets Introduced

When Zach and Danielle arrived at Seva the place was already packed. Danielle couldn't believe all the people who showed up! All of her friends were homeless people. She felt alone here, except for Zach.

There was an excited buzz of conversation as she and Zach entered the room. They were all looking at her; she felt their judgment. Their faces seemed to be saying, "Look, there's the loser who took Zach and is going to ruin him." Her old high school acquaintances had avoided her since she graduated (except the ones she sold to), but here they all were again. About half of them were at Carleton – the smart ones. The others had found various jobs in the city. She was the black sheep and felt like one.

She looked up at Zach, who was leading her to a table in the middle of the room. All the tables and chairs had been arranged around their table. Danielle felt like a guppy in a fish bowl about to be scooped up with a food strainer. Zach's face was wreathed in smiles. He was happy, she could feel it. That made her less nervous.

After they walked to their table Zach banged a water glass with a spoon. Everybody went quiet. Zach said, "Friends, I really, really want to thank you for coming this evening. I know most of you came to see Danielle and not me, but thank you anyway."

Most of Zach's guests were made uncomfortable by this artless statement. Danielle blushed fiery red.

"Zach! What are you doing?"

Zach said nothing. He kissed the top of her head and gave her a reassuring hug.

Jessie looked over at Heather. "Did you see that? I think he really loves her."

Heather nodded. "I don't understand it, but I think it's cute."

Jessie was a little jealous. Danielle was wearing a really nice dark blue dress with a classic square neckline, black heels, and a string of pearls around her neck. Her blond hair was straight with no frills. It hung around her shoulders as if it had been brushed out by a hair designer. Jessie had to admit the girl looked fabulous. She was very curious now and wanted to talk to Danielle. What was it about her that had enticed Zach? There must be something other than physical attractiveness. Zach wasn't that shallow.

Most of the guys were frankly astonished. Mike Parson's eyes bulged out. Zach's roommates were surprised. Barry Therion turned to Max Berglin Jr. "I thought you said she was some kind of poor sad chick with a bad attitude?"

"Just wait," Max replied. "She may yet live up to our expectations."

Zach made an announcement. "OK, here's how it's going to work. We're going to have a great meal, courtesy of Seva and your own wallets. Then Danielle and I will come around to every table and we'll talk. There's an open bar at the back, but you have to pay."

Zach drew a chair back for Danielle and seated her. Nobody had ever cared enough about her to do that, but Zach made it look like the most natural thing in the world. Conversation started, waiters came around to tables and took orders. Zach knew it would be a while before everyone was served but he wanted to talk to Danielle first. Just then Mike Parsons came around and was openly curious, staring at Danielle. She blushed and Zach could feel her acerbic wit assembling a nice set-down. He was relieved when she retracted her claws and smiled. "Hi Mike," she said.

Mike always felt clumsy around women. He fumbled a response. "Uh, Danielle, you look fantastic."

Zach laughed in a friendly way, breaking the tension. "You see, I told you she was great."

"I can see that." Mike blushed and walked away.

A waiter brought a drinks menu and took orders for dinner. Zach ordered a beer and a steak. Danielle, sick of the smell of alcohol, drank water and ordered chicken parm. Just then all five of Zach's housemates came over to the table. Zach saw they wanted to get a look at Danielle, who by now was feeling uncomfortable with all of the attention. Too late, he realized that he had put her on the spot in front of a crowd of people who were predisposed not to like her. He threw her an apologetic look that said, 'sorry babe, it won't happen again.' Danielle smiled.

Zach introduced them all. "Danielle, meet my housemates at Carleton." He pointed to an olive-skinned man with dark curly hair and a swarthy face. "This is Dharwat Jain. Engineering major at Carleton like me, comes from Delhi. The best cook in the world." Dharwat smiled and held out his hand. Danielle noticed there was a ring on it. "It's very nice to meet you Danielle."

"Are you married?" she asked.

"Yes, just recently, to that woman over there." Dharwat pointed to a small, dark woman with a sunny smile. She waved to Danielle and Danielle waved back.

"And this is Max Berglin." Max was almost as tall as Zach, with blond hair and a chiseled, handsome face. He looked like a young Robert Redford. Max inspected Danielle with just a touch of hauteur, which Zach didn't like. Danielle noticed it immediately. Max's eyebrows raised a little in approval. "Your fiancée is observant," he said.

Danielle noticed a current of sexual excitement coming from him, which made her nervous. Max laughed. "Sorry Danielle. Honestly, I came prepared to meet you in a negative frame of mind. But you have exceeded my expectations."

Danielle knew how to handle these science types. She nodded and quoted Max Born. It was something she had heard from her father. "Intellect distinguishes between the possible and the impossible; reason distinguishes between the sensible and the senseless. Even the impossible can be sensible."

Max's eyes widened in surprise. He took a step back. "Danielle, you have given me food for thought."

Zach grinned in appreciation for that home thrust. He pointed to a short, pear-shaped man who was already going bald on top. "This is Gary Cronin, aka Anjou, from Devon, England. He's majoring in psychology and will undoubtedly attempt to analyze your mental state and offer a diagnosis."

Danielle was amazed at Zach's language skills. She had never seen him in company and was impressed with his social acumen. Just then a waiter came with Zach's beer, and he opened it.

Gary extended a pudgy hand and smiled. Danielle took it, liking him right away. He had an open countenance and an unaffected, cheerful smile. "You'll go far," she said.

Gary stepped back in surprise and approval, executing a small bow. "Thank you Danielle. I sincerely believe that you will as well."

Zach was pleased to see how Danielle had said exactly the right thing to people she had never met before. He looked at her with admiration and was rewarded by a brilliant smile.

He introduced Barry Therion next. "Barry is majoring in French Lit." Zach's tone implied that studying French was a waste of time.

Danielle immediately understood that this was a joke of long standing between them. Barry was a barrel-chested man of medium height, with muscular arms and legs and a strong face. She was feeling much more comfortable now, and looked him over. "Very unusual, Zach. He looks like a weightlifter."

"I am. And while I work out I cite French poetry. My favorite is Baudelaire."

"My father reads Baudelaire. *The Flowers of Evil.*"

Barry was blown away. "You know it!"

"My father left a book out once, it was a collection of Baudelaire's poetry. I read The Flowers of Evil, I couldn't put it down. It's a masterpiece if you ask me, brilliant phrasing, rhythm, and expressiveness."

Barry was openly admiring now. "Who is this father of yours?"

"Pierce Menard." She said it with a little heat.

"Sorry Barry, it's not your fault," Zach said. "Danielle and her father have had...let's say, some problems."

Just then a very tall, thin guy who was hanging back snapped his fingers. "Of course. Pierce Menard, won the Maxwell in '05. One of the most brilliant minds in the world. Whatever happened to him?"

This uninhibited comment caused Danielle's eyes to moisten, and Zach stepped in. "Danielle, this is Kenny Wang. Known for being terminally obtuse in social situations, and a turn-off to every woman he has ever met."

Danielle recovered her composure and smiled. "Pleased to meet you, Kenny."

Barry smacked Kenny on the shoulder. "Dumbass, can't you see the lady is upset?"

Max agreed and tried a little humor. "Not terribly observant, Sheldon." No one got it except Danielle. She laughed, understanding it was a reference to a physicist in a comedy show.

"Well boys, I think we've done enough damage here for one night," Max said. "Our work here is done." He led them off, all talking together.

"You're a hit, Danielle." Zach was appreciative and also embarrassed. "I apologize for putting us at the center of the room. It was thoughtless of me."

"Apology accepted." She tilted her head to the side. "I've always had a crush on you. But there's more to you than I thought."

"Noted." He raised his glass to her in a salute and took a drink of his beer.

Danielle turned her head and saw the five guys who had come over, still talking among themselves. Occasionally one would turn his head to the right as they talked, toward their table. A couple of groups had formed and were approaching their table, but just then waiters started delivering food and everybody sat down.

Zach and Danielle talked comfortably during dinner. Afterward Zach got up and handed her out of his chair. "Now we've got work to do," he said. Danielle wasn't looking forward to more social confrontations, but she acquiesced with good grace. "We might as well get it over with."

They started at the back of the room and worked their way forward. Sometimes Zach had to introduce her, sometimes she recognized people from her high school days. Most of the women were frosty toward her but the guys were more friendly. "They like the look of you," Zach said.

There were a few curious parents, including Mark Ferrell and Max Berglin's father, who was a bulkier version of his son. Danielle noticed that Max Sr. was looking at her with an evaluating air, which made her nervous. He was also scrutinizing Zach but her fiancée didn't notice.

Zach was pleased his father showed up. "Great to see you here dad."

Mark was looking at Danielle. "You'll keep Zach happy, won't you Danielle?"

Danielle thought it was a stupid question but she replied diplomatically. "I'll do my best. Your son is very demanding."

Mark burst out laughing, and nodded approvingly at his son. Zach noticed Larry Potvin sitting with Mark. The two were old friends, apparently, from their high school days. Larry spoke up. "Zach, I have a proposal for you. I'm thinking of doing my car restoration work full time, and I'm going to need some help getting off the ground. Would you be interested in a part time job?"

Zach was intrigued. He had saved some money the last two summers doing landscaping, but he hated it. "I was remembering the time you put that carburetor together from the drawing," Larry suggested. Zach remembered that too. Automobiles weren't his focus, but it would be a way to learn some practical engineering. He could see Danielle studying him intently. "Yeah, sure, that might work out for me. When would I start?"

"If things go the way I've planned them, in six months. You'd have half a year to make some coin before you graduated."

"Sounds great Mr. Potvin."

"Call me Larry. You're a man now, and twice as big as me."

Zach and Mark both laughed. Maybe it might not be too bad, Zach thought. His last semester would be an easy one because he would have almost all the credits he needed to graduate. At least the old fart had a sense of humor.

Zach and Danielle were introduced to some more older people and then moved off.

When they stopped by Jessie and Heather's table, Jessie stood up and Heather leaned back in her chair. "Well done, Zach," Jessie said. "Both of you have handled this very well."

"Thanks Jessie. It had to be done or people would have talked."

"They'll still talk," Jessie observed. "But at least you satisfied the social imperatives. Everybody got a look at you both. Those disposed to dislike you won't change anyway."

"Yes, I guess that's true," Zach acknowledged.

When they were done with the social introductions, Zach and Danielle went back to their table. Almost everyone had already left except a few guys who were getting a little rowdy up at the bar. Max Berglin Sr. was still sitting at his table, talking on his phone. Danielle sighed. "Take me out of here. All of a sudden I'm really tired." Unspoken was her desire to avoid drunks. Zach picked up on that right away, smiling down at her.

Zach walked up to the bar and said goodbye to the other guys, who all congratulated him.

Part III

Tesla

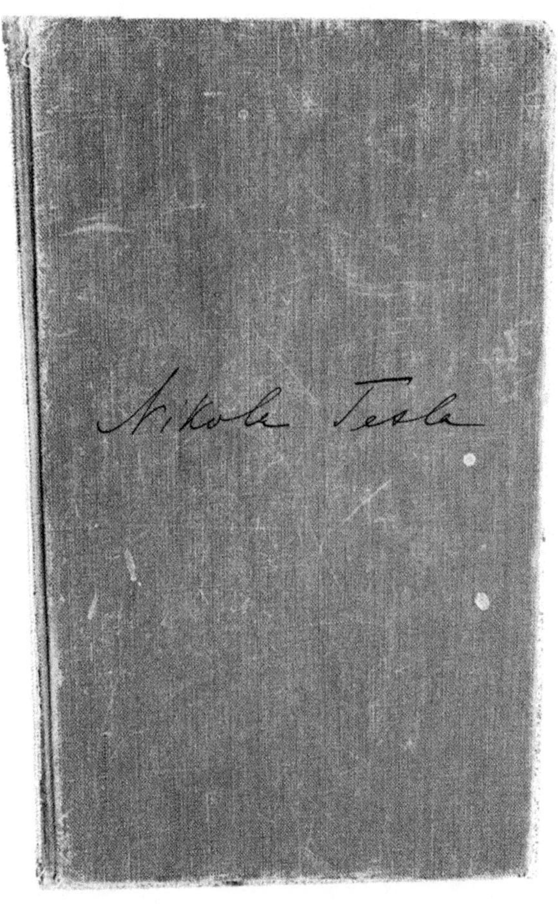

— 9 —

Slava Terbo III

On the Friday before the New Year I received a call from a man who called himself Slava Terbo the third. He claimed to be the grandson of the Slava Terbo my grandfather knew. I remembered the story Grandpa Harold told me when I was seven. Tesla, my grandfather, and a man named Slava Terbo had used Tesla's "receiving device" to motor a Pierce-Arrow car around Buffalo, New York, for over an hour without fuel. My heart began to pound in excitement.

The man said he had "some information that you should know," and that he wasn't trying to sell me anything. He asked me to come to his hotel room, which was about five miles outside of town. It wasn't very specific but my blood was up and I didn't waste any time. I left my downtown office at Berglin Enterprises and arrived at a nondescript Motel 6 in Bartonville, next door to a little cafe. When I knocked on the door I was met by a short, dark man with gray hair and a furtive look about him. He was about 25 years older than my 40.

"Were you followed?"

"How should I know? I came here at your invitation, I didn't know this was top secret."

"I'm sorry," Terbo said. "I'm on edge. I have some sensitive information concerning the personal notebook of Dr. Nikola Tesla. I was told that you might be interested."

I wasn't impressed so far. Terbo behaved like someone who wanted to pump me for money.

The older man held up his hands. "As I said on the phone, I'm not selling anything. I'm here on behalf of a friend who works in one of the classified programs."

"I'm interested, but you look more like an accountant or a schoolteacher than a scientist. What do you know about physics or Tesla?"

Terbo ignored my question. "I don't know how much Horace Berglin told you, if anything."

"How do you know my Grandpa Horace?"

The man looked at me blandly. "The aetheric experiment! I'm the grandson of the man he and Horace and Tesla were in the car with, back in 1931."

That confirmed my hunch about the man, but I was still suspicious. "All right. Break out some ID."

Terbo's face flushed in anger as he reached into his pocket and pulled out his wallet. "Look through that if you don't trust me."

"I've never seen you before in my life and I'm a cautious man," I said in explanation. I looked at his driver's license and skimmed through his credit cards. All looked in order.

I handed Terbo his wallet. "What's this all about?"

Without further ado Terbo brought out ten photocopied pages of drawings. We sat on opposite sides of the bed as I studied them. The drawings were difficult to read. They had been copied from pages that had severely darkened over time.

"Oh my God." There, in front of me, was Tesla's "receiving device," just as described by Grandpa Horace!

I held up the page to the light streaming in from the hotel window. "Do you know what you have here?" I asked. "If my grandfather can be believed, this is the device Tesla supposedly used to power that Pierce-Arrow back in 1931."

"What are the drawings next to it?" Terbo asked.

"Looks like an improved version of the receiver, but without vacuum tubes." These drawings were marked, "Pierce-Arrow, 1942." Tesla must have been working right up until his death in January 1943.

Terbo nodded vigorously in agreement and pleasure. "I'm so glad you have found something of value in there. I myself am technically illiterate, and didn't know who to turn to. My, uh, friend, suggested you. He is in the defense contracting industry and knows about you from your time at Lockheed. Needless to say, he is in great danger if it is ever discovered that he duplicated this material."

Terbo began to tell me the history of Tesla's personal notebook.

"I have this information from my grandfather, who knew Ms. Charlotte Muzar. In 1943 she was the secretary and assistant to Nikola Tesla's nephew, Ambassador Sava N. Kosanovic of Yugoslavia. In 1934, Tesla announced the creation of a 'death ray' that could be capable of destroying 10,000 enemy airplanes at a distance of 250 miles and that would drop an army in its tracks. On July 23, 1934, *Time* magazine wrote an article about Tesla's Death Ray. It said that Dr. Tesla had announced a combination of four inventions which would make war unthinkable, and described how he would do it. Needless to say, the military and the intelligence branches of the War Department were very, very interested."

I began to like this guy. He was obviously sincere and seemed to have a good heart. I am a fine judge of men and people – at least when it comes to business – which is one of the reasons I have been successful. I trust my instincts.

Slava continued. I already knew most of what he was saying, but I listened politely.

"Tesla died on January 7th, 1943 in the Hotel New Yorker, in Manhattan, in room 3327 on the 33rd floor of the hotel. The next day, January 8th, Ambassador Kosanovic went to his uncle's room. At that time Yugoslavia was a Communist country. Kosanovic was the minister of the State of Yugoslavia and a member of the Yugoslav Mission to the United States in New York. According to Ms. Muzar, that morning Ambassador Kosanovich, Ms. Muzar, a locksmith, and another person were present. Earlier that day representatives from the police, and government officials from the Custodian of Alien Property, boxed up all of Dr. Tesla's papers, books, records, and correspondence. Tesla's personal notebook was supposed to have been in there. Tesla's papers were eventually taken to the Manhattan Warehouse & Storage building on Seventh Street. According to Ms. Muzar, all of Tesla's things were eventually returned to Ambassador Kosanovic. Kosanovic used them to found the Tesla Museum in Belgrade, which still exists to this day. However, Ambassador Kosanovic never found Tesla's personal notebook. We know he had it in his hotel room. My father suspected that it had been stolen by the people who took Tesla's papers."

I looked at the photocopied pages again. Everything seemed genuine, including Tesla's handwriting, which I had become familiar with from old documents. "Where's the rest of it?"

"My friend only had time to copy a few of the most interesting drawings. He says that the complete notebook exists within one of the classified programs. He told me that the diagrams are complete schematics for working devices and not just doodlings or scribblings. I wouldn't know, which is why I came to you."

I thought of the notebook my son had teased me about. I didn't think it could possibly have any relation to the drawings I was looking at, having been so cavalierly treated. I made a note to ask Max Jr. for his roommate's phone number.

"One last thing," Slava said. "My contact thinks that the War Department back then was very concerned that these drawings not fall into the hands of the Germans, and after the war, the Russians. He says that whoever possesses the information it contains may, if they have the technical knowledge, be able to build weapons of tremendous destructive power. They would gain access to technology that is far ahead even of what we have today."

Slava made it clear that releasing any of the photocopied pages would surely endanger his contact. I nodded my agreement.

"May I keep these? I would like to hang on to the drawings and when the time is right, try to use the information."

I saw a sigh of satisfaction from Terbo. "My contact would like that very much. He is not in a position to do anything with the material."

I nodded, my mind racing. I knew a couple of guys from my time at Lockheed who worked for the Skunk Works. Those boys worked on some very advanced stuff, most of it classified. I would need someone more knowledgeable to decipher Tesla's information and put it to practical use.

I was intensely interested in Tesla's "receiving device," which had potential commercial application. I gazed out into space, thinking about powering millions of homes cleanly, without wires and electricity. I'd be filthy rich and help to solve the pollution problem and eliminate the scarcity and inefficiency of energy from fossil fuels. The industrial and scientific consequences were enormous.

Terbo and I chatted for over an hour in his cheap hotel room.

Amazingly, he refused payment for his documents but said he was looking for a job. That day I hired Slava to manage my household. I needed someone to take care of the house because my old housekeeper had left at the beginning of September. She said she was too lonely "rattling around in that mansion."

When I first came to Midland I bought a large house in Palmer Park, thinking to get married again and start a family. But I've been too busy with my business to have a long term relationship. Even so, I loved the house even though it was five sizes too big for a single man.

My other motivation for hiring Slava was simply that I didn't want him to tell anyone else.

If Slava worked for me his contact, whoever he was, would also be safe.

Max Jr. told me about the engagement party and that Zach Ferrell had a notebook that could be Nikola Tesla's, so I decided to go.

During the evening I became fascinated with Ferrell's fiancée, and almost forgot why I had come. I took an immediate liking to Danielle Menard. She was striking, and had an edge to her that I appreciated. Her adroitness in an obviously uncomfortable social situation was impressive. She was clearly nervous but had handled strangers with self-assurance, wit, and a charm the girl didn't even know she had. With training, she might make an excellent sales representative for my company. I hung around after the guests had left and approached her and Zach as they were about to leave.

The boy, who was three inches taller than me, bristled. I knew he felt I was encroaching on his territory. I approached Danielle and stood before her, looking her over just as some of my rather boorish clients might do. She stood there, trying to be calm and self-possessed, but I can be pretty intimidating when I want to. The girl held her ground and looked back at me as coolly as she could.

"Danielle Menard, are you looking for employment?"

Danielle's eyes narrowed. A job? She was a drug dealer and had no qualifications for anything. If it were anyone but the successful entrepreneur Max Berglin, she would have blown him off. "If this is a joke, it's in very poor taste."

"I'm sorry Danielle. I know about your personal history, but I am very impressed with your social skills. I also know you are the daughter of the brilliant Pierce Menard."

Danielle nodded and I continued. "My expanding company sells security software to intelligence and hi-tech firms, many of whom are run by hard-nosed ex-military types. I've been looking for another female sales representative for some time. If you are interested, I'd like you to apply." In my ultra-competitive business, many of my clients were pricks with lots of money, or ex-military security guys. It was a fact of life that some of these men responded to a personable, good-looking woman. But that woman had to be strong, intelligent, and not fold under pressure.

"You are talking to me, right?" the girl asked. "Not to Zach?"

I smiled at Zach. "My son already told me about you, Zach. I don't need engineers, but I'm desperate for a good presenter."

The boy relaxed and I could see that the girl was interested, but skeptical.

"What would I be doing?" she asked.

"Your job would be to pitch the product to potential customers. You would travel with a technical representative, who would answer all technical questions about the software. A monitor would also be present. This person's job is note errors in your presentation and to refine your approach until you became a polished presenter."

I could see Danielle's interest, but I had still not convinced her. "I understand that you're a high school graduate, Danielle, with no prior business experience. The job I'm offering you requires no academic knowledge. However, it does require specialized training, which I'm confident you'll be able to master." I wanted to be completely honest with her. "The job is less about substance and more about show. You have a certain look my company needs, but you would be protected at all times."

I wasn't used to begging, but this woman had potential.

I checked my digital calendar. "If you're interested, come to the Berglin Enterprises building at noon on the 30th of January for an interview. That's two weeks from today." Two weeks would give her some time to think about it and maybe decide she wasn't up for it.

Before the two could leave I spoke to Zach. "My son tells me you have a notebook that might have belonged to the great Nikola Tesla."

"I do, Mr. Berglin. I've been trying to show it to Danielle's father, but he has been, ah, indisposed."

"I understand." I told him about my background at MIT and Lockheed. "Would you be willing to entrust that notebook to me for a while? I have the resources to determine the validity of the information."

"Well sir, considering that I stole it from the Graduate Library, I can't really say it's my property."

I liked his open honesty. "Why don't I send someone over to the house to pick it up? If you want it back I'll see that it's returned to you."

"Very good sir."

I got Zach's number and walked out of the restaurant, excited on two fronts.

After Danielle and Zach got in the car Zach pulled out a small jewelry case.

"Zach!" she cried.

"It's just an engagement ring Danielle. Not a real diamond. I couldn't afford much, but it's a sign of my commitment."

Danielle smiled brilliantly and Zach had his reward. "I'll put it on now."

Zach drove Danielle to her house and there was a sort of happy tension between them that grew stronger and stronger. As they got out of the car Danielle wiggled her body at him. "We're engaged now. Don't you think it's time you made love to me?"

"I've wanted to rip your clothes off all night."

"Come on lover boy, now's your chance!"

On the drive back to Palmer Park I called Mildred, my secretary at the company, and told her to arrange with Zach Ferrell to pick up the notebook. I was eager to compare what I had gotten from Slava to Zach's documents. Zach Ferrell's notebook had to be fake. It seemed to me unlikely that something so important could have turned up twice in the same town after all this time.

I also wondered whether the Menard girl would show up for her interview, which I would conduct personally. I was more excited about her than as just a potential employee. Was I interested in a girl that was 18 years my junior? I had to admit I was. I would have to be very careful. I promised myself I would treat her as a fellow professional and avoid emotional entanglements.

When I got home from work at 7:15 p.m. Slava was there in the kitchen with my cappuccino. He was preparing dinner, which was always served at 7:30. I drink caffeinated coffee all day and into the evening but I have never had trouble sleeping. Slava and I always eat together. I tell him the latest company news, mainly to get things off my chest. In almost no time he had morphed from a housekeeper into my personal assistant. Slava told me Max Jr. had called earlier, asking for more pocket money.

"I don't know what to do with Max, Slava. Ever since he entered Carleton he's been demanding and churlish."

"All good parents blame themselves for the faults of their children," Slava replied. "Only the bad ones don't."

"I've indulged the boy, I'll admit, and that's my fault; but there's a dark side to him that I don't understand."

Slava looked up from his coffee. "That's because it's not in you. So you couldn't have put it there."

"I'm not so sure about that."

Slava began to tell me of his childhood and his life. He was born in Belgrade and lived only a mile from the Tesla Museum there. After graduating high school he got a job at the museum as a document clerk. He worked there until a staff reshuffle forced him out twenty years later. "Since then I've worked many jobs, but never found anything permanent. Did you know that the Museum has over 160,000 original documents? The cataloging and preservation of these papers is a full time job for a number of people." Slava sighed. "When the museum upgraded their staff they wanted professionals, so I had to leave."

Because Slava had opened up to me, I decided to return the favor. He was a good listener.

"My parents died in a plane crash. My grandfather Harold, who you know about, had a wife named Eleanor who died shortly after he did. I was raised by my grandparents on my mother's side of the family. But they were both dead by the time I entered university."

"Sounds like you didn't have much of a family."

"No, but fortunately I'm a loner and didn't really miss it. Harold was like a father to me before he died, and taught me the value of love." I began to tear up. "He was a great guy, Slava. I wish you could have met him."

"I have never been much of a family man. Other than Grandpa Harold I never had any strong family connections, and that sometimes makes me sad. But like Harold said one time, 'Max, wherever you land in life is the right place for you.' I have kept that in mind through good times and bad.

"I attended public schools and eventually found my way to MIT when I was 16." Slava's eyes widened and I smiled. "I'm bright, but not Tesla bright. I got my PhD in applied physics at the age of 23, hoping to use this knowledge to make sense of Tesla's work. I taught there for two years but grew weary of the academic life. During my time at MIT I got married but it didn't work out. I think it was mostly my fault. I've never been an intimate person, perhaps because everyone I loved most in my family died. At that time I was obsessed with Tesla and Barbara probably got sick of it.

"People I talked to in academia had no interest in the inventor. They regarded him as an eccentric genius whose time had long gone. I left MIT and went to work for Lockheed. I wanted to get some industry experience. At Lockheed I studiously developed a network of contacts in the intelligence and defense areas. I looked for people who might be receptive to my desire of building on Tesla's work. But, just like at MIT, I discovered that all of the scientists I met weren't interested. Everybody there was hard-headed and not open to new ideas. I thought that was strange. I knew I would have to postpone my dream until I had some money and my own business, and could hire my own people. So I concentrated on building my personal network at Lockheed."

"Eight years later I was ready and I founded Berglin Enterprises. I was determined to make some real money. Most of the people in my network were interested in computer security systems, so that's what my company is about. We sell sophisticated firewall and hacker-proof software to players in the high-tech, defense, and intelligence areas. These people are very concerned with cyber threats that attack their information networks. I already had a security clearance, so I had access. I started with three other executives who had had it with Lockheed. We hired five hotshot programmers.

"From the start it was a success. Now, after seven years, I am making money. But I still haven't found the guys who can help me with my Tesla project. I put the word out into my network that I was looking for frontier physics scientists. Even though I got several tenuous leads there were no takers. The sentiment in the scientific community is that the work I want to do is too far out of the mainstream, and won't lead to career enhancement."

I had talked myself out and my cappuccino was cold. Slava picked up the dishes and cleaned up. I went upstairs to my study and wondered when I could get my hands on Zach Ferrell's notebook.

Part IV

Midland

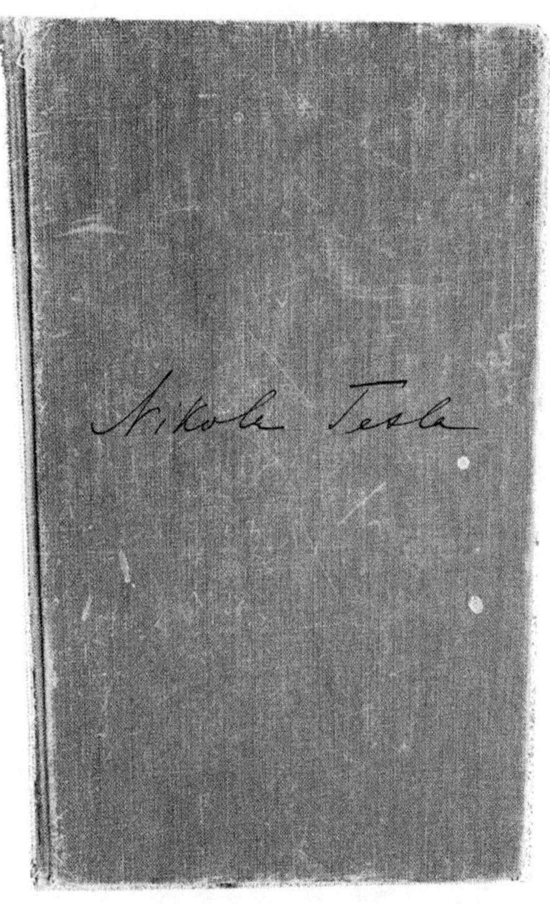

— 10 —

A week after the engagement party Danielle made her usual stop in the alley with her briefcase. Instead of seeing Ricky there was a scruffy-looking guy in a greatcoat. "Who are you? Where's Ricky?"

"I'm your new contact. I have your order, hand over the cash."

"Fuck off. Show me the drugs or get lost."

The man brought out a packet.

"Open it up, you fool. I don't know you or what's in that package. You could even be a cop." As soon as she said it she knew it was true. For some reason she couldn't stop. She had already been paid to bring her client an order, and felt it was her obligation. She laughed at her warped sense of duty.

"What's so funny?" the man said.

"I know you're a cop. If I hand over the money and take the drugs I'll be arrested."

The man drew back and hissed. The girl was on to him!

"Don't worry honey. I've already been paid to do the deal and my client won't take no for an answer. For my own protection I'd rather be in jail." Danielle handed over the cash and accepted the drugs. The man stepped forward and snapped the cuffs on her. "Danielle Menard, I arrest you for narcotics trafficking. Anything you say can and will be used against you."

After the cop read her her rights, she went quietly and the officer shoved her into the police car. When they got to the city jail her phone was taken away, and her knife. "You'll be arraigned tomorrow morning," the officer said.

Just before she was taken away the officer asked, "Why did you do it? You knew I was going to arrest you."

"I already told you. This was going to be my last deal but my client already paid me for the stuff and he isn't someone you can cross. If I didn't deliver he would have cut my hands off or something. Now he'll know I'm in jail and that I tried to honestly complete the transaction. I felt responsible."

"That's a very twisted mindset," the officer said.

This statement echoed her thoughts exactly.

"Who is your client?"

"I'm not sure. I address a package to a Mr. Haskins at the Radison Hotel and receive cash in an envelope. Our transactions are anonymous."

The officer nodded. Probably some white collar businessman looking for excitement, but it wasn't worth pursuing. "I've seen you downtown distributing food to the homeless. I checked and you have no priors. What's your story?"

Danielle told him briefly about her father and how she needed to make money to feed him and pay the bills every month.

"I know a little bit about you, Danielle Menard, and I know about your father and what happened. I'll put in a good word for you if you promise me to stay away from narcotics."

"I promise. I was going to stop anyway. I'm supposed to be getting married." Danielle was bitter. "When my fiancée finds out about my arrest he'll probably dump me."

After that another officer came and put her in a holding cell.

Danielle sat in jail that night and reflected sourly about how she had fucked up again. Whenever something good happened to her, she would find a way to mess it up. When Zach and his friends and their parents and Max Berglin found out about her arrest, she could kiss her marriage and her interview goodbye. It was just as well she didn't have her knife or she would have cut her throat.

Trevor Clarke Panics

When Trevor Clarke found out about Danielle's arrest he called Elmo Tackett.

He had met Elmo a year ago, walking downtown after a public relations event for a new car dealership. The bank had floated the loan; PRC sent him out every time they needed to boost their image. It was boring but he was being paid to do something he was good at. After the event he had been approached by a funny looking man in a suit. "Excuse me Mr. Clarke," the little man said. "May I speak with you a moment?"

Trevor was polite. A lot of people were still around, and a few reporters. "What can I do for you?"

"If you need a good man who knows how to keep his mouth shut, call me." He had then handed him a business card with the name "Elmo Tackett" on it and a phone number, and walked away.

The next day he had called the number. He had gotten a taste for cocaine and designer drugs when he was a broker in London. He was looking for a supplier that would operate discretely; someone he could trust to keep his mouth shut. Elmo had recommended the Menard girl as a dependable small-time dealer that might be suitable.

"How do I know I can trust you?" he had asked.

"You've seen me. Do I look like someone anyone would hire? I know I'm not normal."

Elmo was short and ugly, with ears that stuck out from his head. Thoroughly unlikable, with no charm at all. "All right. Why did you approach me?"

"Because I need money just like everyone else. Vahan Katelian will vouch for me."

Trevor knew Katelian as a client of the bank.

"I know a little bit about you, Trevor Clarke, and your involvement in the Barclays LIBOR affair," Tackett said. "I got your name from another well-connected client."

Oh dear, Trevor thought. He had finally been found out!

"Don't worry Mr. Clarke. I need you more than you need me. I only work for selected clients who are discreet and who have work to do that must remain below the radar of the police and the newspapers. I am extremely meticulous."

"How do I reach you?" Trevor had asked.

"Just call this number anytime, 24 hours a day, 7 days a week. I will return your call in six hours or less."

That was how it began. Elmo had been true to his word. The ugly little man didn't like people and didn't talk to them unless it was absolutely necessary. Shortly after their meeting Trevor called the number, wanting information about a bank client with shady connections. Elmo's information had proved out. He had used him several times since then. Now he called Elmo and asked him about the girl and her arrest. "Determine if the Menard girl mentioned my name to the police," he instructed.

"Yes, Danielle Menard. I like her. I like the way she moves," Elmo said.

Trevor ignored this irrelevancy. "She was busted an hour ago. I want you to find out if she said anything about me. Do you understand Elmo?"

"Yes Mr. Clarke. I will have the information for you in less than two hours."

Trevor waited anxiously for Elmo's call. The Menard girl had seen him once, briefly, at their first and only interview. It was the only mistake he had made since coming to Midland.

When Elmo called back he told him that the girl had said nothing.

"They're not interested in her, and the jails are crowded. She has no priors, she's just a small time operator. They know she does volunteer work in the community for the homeless. She'll be out on the streets tomorrow but you won't be able to use her again."

"Will she talk? If so, you'll have to find a way to get rid of her." After he said it he was shocked. He didn't see himself as a murderer. But the girl could ruin him.

"I don't think it will come to that, sir. I'll talk to her."

Trevor felt relieved. That was a good sign, was it not? A killer would not have cared. It meant he was still a good person. But he needed to find another supplier.

Danielle Gets Out of Jail

Danielle walked home from jail when she was released in the morning. The streets were crowded with commuters.

As she turned the corner from Maynard to First, two blocks from her house, she saw that little creep Elmo come out of the recessed doorway of a sandwich shop. He stood directly in front of her, blocking her path.

"Danielle Menard," he said.

"What do you want?"

"You cannot speak of Trevor Clarke's involvement in your drug dealing. Do you understand?"

So that's who it was! "Why shouldn't I? He's probably the one who got me arrested."

Elmo caught the slight look of surprise on the raven's face. He had erred volunteering his client's name. He should have been more subtle. "He didn't. Trevor was satisfied with your work."

"If Trevor Clarke didn't do it, who did?"

"I don't know yet, but I'm going to find out." Elmo studied her for a few moments. "It wouldn't go well for me if Trevor came to harm over this." His voice was stone cold, devoid of all emotion.

The creep was looking at the unicorn tattoo on her left arm. "I like that tattoo."

God this guy was creepy. She spoke carefully, not wanting to upset him. "Yeah, I like it too."

Elmo glanced up at her. "Keep what I said in mind, raven." He walked off.

When Danielle got home she saw her father on the phone. He had a beer beside him on the kitchen table, a laptop, and an open case on the floor. She looked into the living room and saw that the blankets on the couch had been neatly folded. The old bottles and the trash on the floor had been picked up.

She waited until he had finished his call. "What are you up to, dad?"

"Reestablishing old contacts," he said, drinking the rest of the beer. "I'm catching up on all the research I missed for the past five years."

It was a minor miracle. Dad had come out of his funk! When she was a child she had thought of her father as the smartest man in the world. After her mother died she thought of him as a pathetic loser. But now his eyes burned with a feverish intelligence and his presence almost filled the room, as if a great mind had suddenly stuttered back to life. "Dad, I was busted last night. I spent the night in jail and was released this morning."

"I know all about that Danielle." He reached for another beer. "I had a talk with the duty officer at the jail last night when you didn't come home."

"But how could you have known where I was?"

"I've been a miserable coward for five years, hiding in self pity, but not totally unaware of my surroundings. I knew about your drug dealing and had Brad on the alert in case you ever got arrested. He called me as soon as you arrived at the jail." Pierce swigged his beer, grimacing. "I'm trying to get off the alcohol as much as possible." He pointed to the open case. "I'm down to half a case per day, and I never touched hard liquor. It's been hard, but it's a start. Compare my efforts to a smoker who gradually weans himself from three packs a day and chewing tobacco, to two packs a day. That's where I am now."

"Do you want to go into rehab?"

"I think not. I'm gradually finding mental stability and getting my strength of mind back. Before Carol died...before your mother died, I had complete confidence, almost an arrogance, about myself and my mental acuity. Of course I was wrong but I'm feeling a little better now emotionally. I'm starting to get interested in life again."

"That's great dad. Before I got busted I was starting to feel the same way. Now I'm not so sure. I just messed up my life again." She explained about the party, and Zach, and the interview with Mr. Berglin that was supposed to take place on the following Wednesday.

She filled him in on her life for the past five years.

"I see. In my present condition I'm no good to you Danielle, but at least I will no longer be a liability. I agree that we should both get out of town. The only problem is what do we do for money until I get back on my feet."

"I was thinking the same thing on my way over here."

Her father reached for another beer.

"Let me cook you some protein. Maybe that will help stop the craving."

"It couldn't hurt."

As they ate Danielle felt like crying. She would have to tell Zach about her arrest, and wondered whether it made the papers or the internet. Should she go to the interview? If she did, should she tell Mr. Berglin about her arrest?

The problem of money was left unresolved. Unspoken was the hope that Danielle would get the job at Berglin Enterprises. Danielle left her father at the table, looking at his laptop.

She went outside in the cold for a walk.

Larry Goes to Work with a Different Attitude

After the holidays, Larry Potvin went in to work with a different attitude. He was throwing caution to the winds; he was going to go on a mission, just like when he was a grunt in the Army. He was going into action and it felt good. Fuck PANA, he thought, fuck life in general. This country was going to the criminals and the greedy bastards who wanted you to work for pennies so they could get rich. Every time he thought of his new shop he got excited, he felt a buzz. And if he kept doing it he wouldn't feel like drinking. Jenny would really appreciate that. Drinking was for losers. If he got caught, so be it. At least he'd go down with a bang. What was it his drill instructor used to say all the time? "I'd rather live one day as a lion than a lifetime as a sheep." Larry rubbed his hands together. It was time to get to work.

Bruce Tarpley noticed his new attitude right away, being in the office next to his. "What's got you so fired up?"

Larry had a perfect excuse. "I'm almost done with that Corvette. Friday you can come and pick it up."

"OK mate. Can't wait!"

Larry sat down with his accounts. The new trainee was part-time for now, only coming in on Wednesdays and Fridays. He had all day today and tomorrow to get set up. A response to his letter had come in Saturday's mail, a set of instructions printed on generic office paper. It was unsigned. The document outlined in minute detail the embezzling scheme and his role. His unknown benefactor would provide him with blank invoices with valid mailing addresses for fake vendors such as ABC Manufacturing. His job would be to decide how much to pay each of the vendors. He would fill out the invoices at home and mail them to his office at PANA. Then, when he got to the office he'd discover an invoice that needed to be paid. Then he would issue a check to that vendor at the mailing address, and his handler would deposit the money.

Larry looked for loopholes and couldn't find any.

He would have to make sure that the accounting profile on the expenses ledger didn't show too large an increase because there would be no corresponding increase in income. However, unless he got greedy, it would be easy. PANA had dozens of suppliers in the area and business was good. Larry would receive 50% of everything he deposited. A CPA might be able to figure out what he'd done with a little digging, but Larry could legitimately claim that he was just paying invoices sent by legitimate vendors.

If he did it right the accounting profile would never show a red flag and no one would be the wiser.

The letter hinted that there were similar operations ongoing in Midland, but he didn't care about that. It had also made clear that the writer (whomever he or she was) knew his identity. The good part of the scheme was that he was only involved for six months. He would always be blackmailable by the mastermind, but that was the breaks. The controller was also risking himself because he had to set up multiple imaginary vendors, but if he was smart he could set up P.O. boxes at the post office for each one. If somebody screwed up it could mean exposure for the mastermind, but that wasn't his problem.

That evening, Jenny asked him about it.

"I've never seen you bring work home before. What's up?"

"Oh, I've got an increased workload at the office for the next six months. I'll have to spend an hour or so a few days each week after supper."

"You seem to be a lot more motivated."

"I'm getting out of PANA. I want to work my car restoration business full-time. If I'm successful we can park the cars in the garage again."

"How will you get the startup money?"

Larry decided to be cheerful and light. "I'll tell you all about it in six months."

That first week he was able to invoice and pay almost $7,000.

On Monday morning Larry saw from his work computer that someone had deposited $3,427 to a special account for which he had a checkbook. That was his! If he could do about $3,500 per week, in less than thirty weeks he'd have a hundred grand.

After work he was so excited he decided to go to the bar and have a few beers. He promised himself he'd do it just this once, to celebrate.

The sharp, pleasant taste of the beer was making Larry feel mellow. He reminisced about his life, pleased that he could start over. He had one good friend, Mark Ferrell, and a few acquaintances he liked. He had met Mark and Rachel Ferrell and Wayne and Myra DiPietro ten years ago at a fundraiser for the local animal shelter. Larry remembered that fundraiser as if it were yesterday. Back then he was four years removed from his tour of duty but he still hadn't completely readjusted to civilian life. He wanted to be a professional and be respected and make a lot of money. He remembered seeing a tall guy by the pool with a drink in his hand, and a good-looking babe on his arm. He looked like a banker or a computer programmer. Larry introduced himself to Wayne and Myra DiPietro and told them he was an accountant.

Wayne remarked on the coincidence. "I work at PRC Accounting in the PRC Bank building."

Myra was polite. "I'm a teacher."

Larry could tell she didn't like the look of him, and was trying to steer Wayne away.

"Go ahead darlin', I'll stay and talk to Larry for a while." Myra moved off.

"Drink?" he asked Larry.

"Love to, but I don't want to get off the wagon again."

"Gotcha. You don't mind?"

"Nah."

As Wayne eagerly pointed out all the socialites in attendance, Larry got bored. This guy was just a wanna-be social climber; he wondered how long Myra would stay with him. Larry recognized that Myra's reaction to him was the right one. She saw through him, knew there was something skewed in there. At the earliest opportunity he excused himself and wandered over to another couple he liked the look of. The woman was beautiful but cold-looking. The guy looked like a success. They got to talking and he found out they were Mark and Rachel Ferrell. Rachel was ten years younger than Mark, who had just come back from a successful job in a New York advertising firm. Larry and Mark got to talking and they both hit it off. Mark liked hunting just as he did, and they agreed to go out in the fall. Mark was just the kind of professional he liked: not full of himself, quietly successful.

Larry twirled the beer in his glass and took a gulp. He laughed to himself about that fundraiser, because he'd been forced to attend. PANA prided itself on "involvement in the community," which meant that PANA employees had to attend insipid events like that one, usually on their own time. But Larry knew how to hump over a bad situation. He'd learned that in the Army, when he was sent to Iraq to fight those turban heads.

The Army thought they were teaching him discipline and love of country but he really learned how pointless fighting was. One time they'd busted into a home that was supposed to contain terrorists, but all they'd done was shoot up a man and his wife and his son eating dinner. Thank God he was driving that time and not shooting. It was explained later that they were sent to the wrong house. No apologies to the family, nothing. It was chalked up as "the fortunes of war," too bad for those guys. That, and all the political stuff he never understood, soured him on war for good.

Nothing ever changed, human nature never changed. People were destined to fight and kill each other until the end of time but he wouldn't do any more of it. When his tour was over he didn't re-up.

Somebody at the bar cursed loudly at the TV and Larry came back to the present. He could tell the liquor was making him sappy. He'd better stop and get home to Jenny and Karl. There was work to do that would lead him to a better life. He drank off the beer, put money on the counter, and left the bar.

Mark Confronts Rachel

When Mark Ferrell got home from work he was thinking about the impending marriage of his son. The Menard girl was beautiful in a weird kind of way with all those tattoos. There was a strength to her, he could feel it, but also a dark side. He hoped she was strong enough to overcome it.

Rachel had strength too, or used to. Now it was being warped somehow. His wife was getting more and more distant from him every week. Suddenly he thought that she might be having an affair. What if she were? At first he felt very angry, but he admitted it might be the best thing for both of them. They hadn't been working for a couple of years now.

Just then Rachel walked into the living room. She grimaced when she saw her husband.

"What's that look for?"

"I was thinking about Zach wasting his life with that Menard girl. Then I thought about you wasting your life at the firm."

"I see. But you haven't been wasting your time there, have you?"

She looked sharply at him. "What is that supposed to mean?"

"Please, Rachel. I know all about your tawdry little affair at the office."

She was shocked. "You do?"

"Of course I do!" he lied. "Who is it? Of course, Don Halloran, the charming and handsome VP. He's moving on to Platchon and Berger. You'd like him to recommend you for the presidency, which has been your goal all along."

"But I thought—"

"You thought I was a fool because I didn't know, and because I'm not ambitious. But your kind of ambition only causes misery."

Rachel laughed hysterically. "Misery! And what do you think this marriage has been for me the past several years? Living with a man who is happy to be a junior partner; who wants nothing else."

Mark didn't deny it. "I've been happy. That's more important."

"More important than what? Success? Money? Money buys you influence, Mark, and with money and influence you can change the world. But you just sit there at your desk all day, satisfied with your petty little life. Well, that's not for me."

"And what do you intend to do with this money and influence you're seeking, Rachel? How do you intend to change the world? Perhaps these are just justifications for a petty and shallow selfishness. It's just an excuse for greed."

"That's exactly what you would say. You equate money with greed, and influence with selfishness. That's the mindset of all underachievers."

"You didn't answer my question, Rachel."

"I intend to do some good in the world."

"I see. And you thought you'd start this program of benefaction by breaking your marriage vow, and going to bed with a married man."

Rachel laughed cynically. "Mark, you know our marriage has been on the rocks for a while now, and that Don is in the middle of a divorce. Your criticisms are just mewling platitudes from a man who has and never will amount to anything."

"Well, I'm glad we're having this out now, Rachel. It seems we have a fundamental clash of worldviews."

Rachel was dismissive. "You don't have a *worldview,* Mark, that's much too grandiose a name for your weak-kneed philosophy of life."

"I was at Zach's party," Mark offered. "Danielle Menard was very impressive. She's beautiful in a strange kind of way. She has an inner strength."

"Inner strength! You just placed your finger on why this marriage is no longer working, Mark." She stepped forward. "When I first met you I was impressed with the hotshot New York executive. But after I married you I slowly realized that you were just running away. The only reason I've stayed this long is because of Zach." Rachel was resentful. "His life is apparently settled now. You have helped him get together with a girl that is totally beneath him."

"I think not, Rachel. Sometimes strength comes in different forms. Danielle's strength is an inner wisdom that comes from a good heart and experience. Did you know that she does volunteer work with the homeless downtown? No, I'm not done yet. My strength is understanding who I am and being comfortable with it. You used to have that kind of strength, Rachel, but what you think is power and influence is just selfish ambition."

"Spoken like a true also-ran, Mark. What you see as strength is merely a justification of failure." She shook her head back and forth. "It's sad, really. You could have been a force in the world. Instead you choose to hide in a position where you know you can't rise."

With that she left the room. A few minutes later he heard noises coming from the bedroom upstairs. His wife reappeared carrying two suitcases. "I'm moving out. I'll come back for the rest of my things this weekend."

"Suit yourself."

Mark had finally given up on their marriage when she had refused to see Danielle and had boycotted the party at Seva. Was that his fault or hers? Probably a little of both.

Mark heard the garage door open, and through the living room window saw Rachel's BMW drive away. He probably should feel sad, but he didn't feel much of anything. He would have to call Zach and tell him the news.

Danielle Confronts Zach

That evening Danielle drove over to Zach's house in her father's old Camry. She usually walked the three or four blocks downtown to do her business, but Zach's rental house was the other side of downtown on the Carleton campus. She might as well get it over with; everyone would find out sooner or later. Perversely she hoped that Zach's roommates would all be there to hear it.

The Carleton campus was a joke for parking, with a lot of meters that charged you a dollar every fifteen minutes. She found an empty space almost a quarter mile away and put in four dollars. She had never liked the car because it always reminded her of the times when her mother was alive and they'd go out to dinner together. Dad hardly ever used it; if they towed it she wouldn't care.

When she got to the house she heard loud music. It was late January and it was cold. She heard raised voices inside. Sounded like the guys were having a good time.

She knocked on the door but no one heard, so she began pounding. A face appeared in the little window. When Gary recognized her his face creased in a wide smile. "Danielle, come on in!"

Danielle entered the house in her usual black jeans, black shirt, and pointy boots. "Zach is a lucky man, that's all I can say," Gary said.

"You might not think that after I tell you what happened to me last night. Is Zach here?"

"Yeah, he's upstairs. I'll get him."

Danielle stood in the cold foyer, not wanting to come into the living room and intrude on the space. She heard pounding on the stairs and Zach came rushing down two at a time. "Hey guys! Danielle's here!"

In two minutes the music and the talking stopped, and everyone had trooped downstairs. Gary, Max, and Barry sat on the frayed couch facing the front door. Dharwan sat on a beat-up wing chair to her left, and Zach sat on a small sofa in front of her. They were all looking at her with interest and a little sexual excitement. She stood in the middle of the room and felt like a woman who could send them all out onto a battlefield. Despite herself she smiled.

"Good news?" Max asked.

"Actually, no, but I'm glad you're all here." She turned to Zach. "I wanted to tell you, Zach, that I got busted last night."

She expected the guys to sneer and make deprecating comments to Zach about her. But nothing happened, except that Zach frowned. She looked over at

Max to see his reaction. Other than a little withdrawal, he said nothing.

"Tell me about it," Zach said.

Standing there in the middle of the small living room, Danielle told her story. She explained about Pierce and her drug dealing and why she had to do it. She almost told them about Trevor Clarke, but referred to him as "my bigwig client." She told them about her night in jail, her talk with the police officer, and how her dad was sobering up.

"That's it. So now you know I'm not really the witty girl in the nice dress that made such a good impression. I'm just what Zach's mom thinks I am: a loser." She hung her head.

The reaction she got was not at all what she was expecting. Zach came over and took her in his arms and kissed her. The other guys reassured her that it was OK.

"But it's not OK. Max! Wednesday is my interview with your father. What is he going to say when I tell him what happened?"

"He won't like it but he probably already knows about it, so what's done is done."

"He does?"

"Dad has a security classification and he has a wide network. There's very little in this town that escapes his notice, especially when it involves a potential employee. But if you explain your life he might be OK with it." He looked searchingly at her. "The authorities let you go, didn't they?"

"Yes. They weren't interested." She brightened a little. "They knew all about me though. They said I was way below the radar. The only reason they arrested me was a call from some VIP, but they didn't tell me who his name was." She looked earnestly at Zach. "Honest to God, Zach, I'll never get involved in that again."

"OK Danielle. But I have to admit it's kind of cool that my fiancée is such a bad-ass criminal."

"Zach!" The guys all laughed. She noticed that Max was a little reserved, but Zach said he was always reserved. She wondered what would happen on Wednesday. If she got the job, would she like having to be respectable?

Part V

Tesla

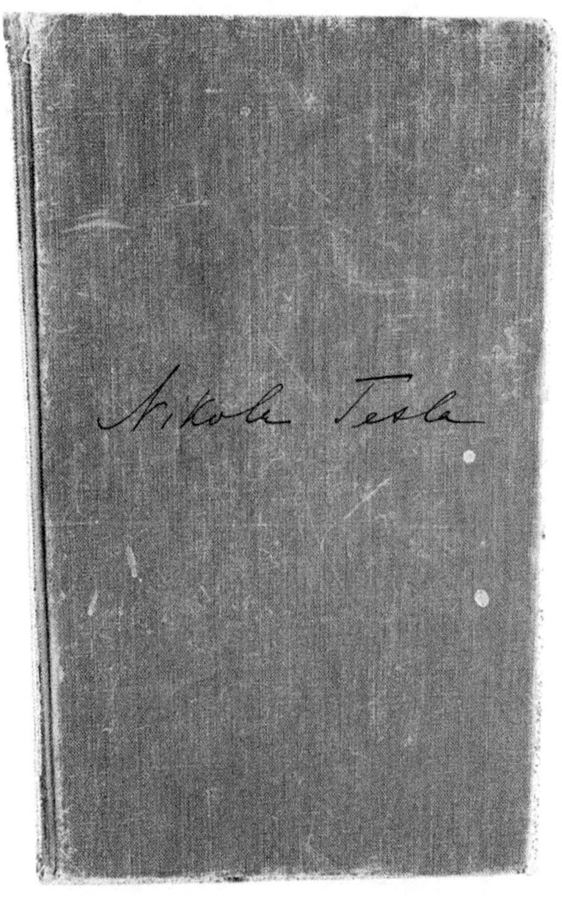

— 11 —

On a cold Tuesday afternoon at the end of January Mildred Harrison, my personal secretary at Berglin Enterprises, handed me a cheap spiral bound notebook with a black cover. "Here is what you wanted, sir. From Zach Ferrell."

"Thank you Mildred" I said, putting it into an inside pocket of my suitcoat. There was no pressing business so I left work early. When I got home I immediately went to my bedroom and got the photocopied pages Slava had given me. When I went down to the kitchen Slava handed me a mocha latte with whipped cream on top. I brought out Zach's notebook and opened it. Then I spread Slava's drawings out on the table top. "Max, sir!" Slava shouted. "The pages are a match."

I scrutinized the photocopied notebook pages, which were seven inches wide and eleven inches long. I compared them with Slava's drawings, looking for inconsistencies. I could find none."I believe you are right."

We both asked the question at the same time: "Where is the original?" There were approximately fifty pages in Zach's copy. I shuffled quickly through all of the pages, looking for the "receiving device" described by Grandpa Harold. If that drawing was in Zach's notebook, we probably had the real thing. "By God Slava, there it is." I flattened out Zach's notebook and put Slava's drawing next to it. The copy in Zach's notebook was more readable. Whoever copied it had taken the time to properly adjust the contrast and the brightness.

Our eyes met. "They look the same," Slava said.

"They are." I felt like dancing around the kitchen like Archimedes after he discovered how to measure the displacement of irregular objects. Supposedly the old boy ran around the town naked shouting "Eureka!" and I felt like doing the same. Then I sobered. How was I going to test the validity of these drawings without involving other people who might spill the beans? If the receiving device could be developed commercially I wanted to do it myself. I didn't want the military and the national security establishment to weaponize it or sequester it. Slava's contact must also be protected.

Slava saw me thinking and sat down across from me, ready to listen.

"I'm hamstrung by my business, Slava. I'm bored with it. Selling software brings the money in but it's a full-time job. Berglin Enterprises has over fifty employees now and we are expanding. My board of directors – the two men and the woman I had brought with me from Lockheed – are happy. All of them are conventional businesspeople and don't like to think outside the box. There is no reason to. Business is booming."

Like a good bartender Slava said nothing and remained receptive.

"I have traded one problem for another. I now have the funds (and hopefully the information) to begin my Tesla project but I 'm hemmed in by the very business that makes it possible. I have to devote so much time to Berglin Enterprises that I have little time for anything else. I promised the Board I would stay at Berglin Enterprises for ten years and I still have over three to go."

My latte was still warm and I drank the foamy cream from the top. I heard the doorbell ring. Slava left the kitchen and I heard voices in the foyer, which was down a short hallway to the left of the kitchen. Slava came in a couple of minutes later with an impeccably dressed man in his early thirties. He wore a perfectly tailored gray suit, Gucci black leather shoes, and a fedora hat with a gray ribbon around it. "This is Vahan Katelian. He has a business proposition I think you might be interested in."

"Hello Mr. Berglin," Katelian said, smiling.

I looked Katelian over and didn't much like what I saw. He looked like a con man with a flashy smile who obviously wanted something. But I was polite, for I had learned never to judge a person's character by his or her first appearance. "What can I do for you Mr. Katelian?"

"You don't know me Mr. Berglin, and my presence here could be regarded as an imposition. However, I know that you are interested in the work of Nikola Tesla, and that you are looking for research scientists for a, uh, frontier science project."

"How would you know that, Vahan Katelian?"

Katelian smiled a toothy smile. "My family, Mr. Berglin, has what you might call wide-ranging interests. It just so happens that my grandfather Apkar was an electrical engineer who developed a fascination for Tesla's work. He passed that interest along to me. Our family has a lab in the Octagon building in Research Park, where we employ a forward-thinking scientist. It's, uh, a project I insisted we fund, a big longshot with a huge payoff if anything ever comes of it. However, we are at present experiencing a financial shortage in our businesses. We are looking for an investor to help us continue the research."

"I don't know anything about you or your operation, Mr. Katelian."

Katelian smirked condescendingly, which irritated me. He reached into a slim black briefcase and pulled out a booklet, which was titled, "The Katelian Difference." It showed a picture of a construction site, the inside of a laboratory, complete with a scientist in a white lab coat, and various luxury and commercial properties. It was beautifully done, I had to admit, very professional.

"We are mainly involved in commercial and luxury property development. The image you see on the front cover is our lab at the Octagon building. The scientist in the picture is Dr. Austin Park, who said he knows you from your days at MIT."

I remembered Dr. Park, a brilliant researcher from South Korea who told me before I left the university that he was going home to take a job at Samsung. Apparently he hadn't.

"Dr. Park told me of your interest in Tesla and his work, which is why I am here. If our investment is successful it's going to mean a lot of money." He fiddled with the lock on his briefcase. "Our information is that you might have something very important that belonged to Tesla. Something that could make all the difference between failure and success."

"How do you know this?"

"The information came from your son Max Jr.," Katelian replied.

I was appalled. "How do you know my son?"

"Max Jr. gets around," Katelian said, with just the slightest hint of a sneer.

"I'm sorry Max Berglin, but you asked. He told me you were interested in a notebook of Tesla's that his roommate found in the university's Graduate Library." Katelian's eyes sparkled with excitement and greed. "If you do have such a document, it may be of interest to Dr. Park."

"Tell me a little about your interest in frontier physics," I said, leaning back in my chair. I wasn't sure about this guy at all, and I am usually a good judge of character. I wanted to draw him out. Just then Slava entered with a tray of little sandwiches and a bottle of dry Riesling from the wine cellar.

While Katelian talked, I ate and sipped wine.

It became clear to me that Vahan's interest was purely monetary. The man had no scientific training, nor did he exhibit any interest in the broader implications of Tesla's work for the good of the world.

Katelian drew out two documents from his briefcase. “I want to make it clear, Mr. Berglin, that the work of Dr. Park and his assistant John Rosen is actually the intellectual property of Octagon Research Co. and not Katelian Properties.” He placed the documents in front of me. “Here is the contract we had to sign. The second document is a proposed Research and Development agreement between our two companies.”

While I looked over the contract and the proposal, Katelian explained. “Octagon Research provides the lab and the equipment for rent. The Octagon building itself is owned by an outfit called the Technology Acquisition Consortium, who owns the Octagon Research Corporation, for which the building is named. Our understanding is that Octagon Research also does classified work.”

“My intention is to keep clear of the intelligence community and the national security establishment.”

Again that slight Katelian smirk. “Good luck with that. The arrangement we negotiated with Dr. Park and Octagon Research is the best we could do. We want to do real research with a reputable scientist, not a basement experimenter. We need the best equipment.” He paused for a moment. “We discovered very quickly that frontier science work is monitored closely by the government. Apparently it goes with the territory.”

I nodded. What Katelian said was true from my experience at Lockheed.

“Even though Octagon owns everything we develop, we get a share of anything that is commercially marketed.” Vahan pointed at the relevant phrases in the contract. “We are essentially an independent lab renting space at Octagon, but they have the final say. Nothing we develop can leave the building unless it is cleared first.”

Katelian must have sensed my skepticism. “I told you it was a long shot.” He paused for a moment and then spoke with suppressed excitement. “Mr. Berglin, successful commercial development along the lines of Dr. Park’s research could literally be worth *billions*.”

I couldn’t have agreed more. I considered Katelian as he sat there hopefully. The man was not an ideal business partner, but at least he had vision.

“I see one major drawback, Mr. Katelian, in this contract you signed: If your lab is involved in a classified program we’d never know it. Octagon Research could claim all of our research on the grounds of national security, or even shelve our development altogether.”

“Certainly. But great profit sometimes involves great risk. What do you say, Max Berglin?”

Katelian had shrewdly hit just the right note. He was a risk taker, just like me. "All right Mr. Katelian. I want to show these documents to my lawyers first. If they pass muster, and if you'll allow me to take a look at the lab in person and talk to Dr. Park, we might do business."

"I'll arrange that."

We talked numbers for half an hour. Katelian handed me the R & D agreement with the numbers filled in. All profits were to be split evenly. Everything seemed to be in order. We shook hands and Katelian handed me a laminated Octagon Research pass labeled *Authorized Guest*. "This will get you past the front gate and the guards in the lobby."

Katelian then put his hand on my arm. "The fewer who know about this, the better it will be for us."

I drew my arm away and Katelian smiled like the snake that tempted Eve in the Garden of Eden. "Nice doing business with you."

Slava escorted Vahan Katelian out of the house. I finished the little sandwiches and thought about the series of coincidences which had brought me Tesla's notebook, a research scientist, and a lab. My Tesla project was finally getting off the ground and fate seemed to be cooperating. If the Board objected to the expenditure I'd use my own money and make the agreement a personal one between myself and Katelian Properties. If Katelian proved not to be trustworthy I could start over.

On an impulse I drove over to the Centurion Building and went upstairs to the fourth floor, where I had turned a storage area into a lab. I looked at a couple of my old experiments, performed when I was just starting my business and had some free time. Nikola Tesla had been granted hundreds of patents, the most important of which (to me) was his Tesla coil, Patent No. 512,340, and the two patents he received for his radiant energy device: U.S. Patent No. 685,957 – Apparatus for the Utilization of Radiant Energy, and U.S. Patent No. 685,958 – Method of Utilizing Radiant Energy. Both were filed on March 21, 1901 and granted on November 5, 1901. In these patents was a diagram of his radiant energy device, and a statement by Nikola Tesla.

> "This new power for the driving of the world's machinery will be derived from the energy which operates the universe, the cosmic energy, whose central source for the earth is the sun and which is everywhere present in unlimited quantities."

I built and experimented with a radiant energy device, trying to understand his idea of "cosmic energy," but I had never been able to advance the concept. I just didn't have the great inventor's genius, but maybe Austin Park did. Perhaps the copied pages from Tesla's notebook would help.

The next day at work I got the OK on Katelian's proposal from a company lawyer, along with a word of advice: "Don't invest too much in this boondoggle."

After that I went to see Austin Park at the Octagon building.

Octagon Research Facility, Research Park

I gained entrance to the parking lot of the Octagon building after presenting Katelian's pass at the front gate and showing it again to the armed guards in the lobby. The imposing brick building was four stories high and eight-sided with thick walls, looking solid enough to withstand a siege. The building was surrounded by an octagonal cement courtyard with inlaid stone patterns and a fountain outside. Trees had been planted around the outside of the structure. Whoever had built this had the money to splurge a little.

When I walked in to Room 317 I saw Austin Park bending over a lab bench. Park was a fine-featured man of medium height, with intense black hair that ran into his face. He wasn't even aware of me until I stepped around him to the front of the table. "Austin Park! How are you?"

"Dr. Berglin! Wha – What are you doing here?"

"I was about to ask you that myself, Austin. I thought you were working for Samsung?"

"I used to. But it didn't work out."

"Too boring, wasn't it?"

"How did you know?"

"Because I've experienced the same thing with my company. I want to branch out, to change the world. And in the process, make a whole lot of money."

Park straightened and took off his glasses. "Vartan Nalbandian, the research director, told me I would receive a visitor today. What is this about?"

I explained my interest in Tesla and said I had some information that might help. "What are you working on?"

"My assistant and I have been investigating the work of Nikola Tesla and a researcher named Gabriel Kron. Essentially, both men claimed to be able to access energy from the quantum vacuum and use it to power loads. So far no luck, Dr. Berglin, but I'm as convinced as Kron and Tesla that it's possible. I feel I've made some progress."

"Didn't Kron work for the General Electric Company in the 1930s?"

"That's right Dr. Berglin. GE was formed by Thomas Edison in 1889 and was originally called the Edison General Electric Company. Kron claimed to have discovered what he called a 'negative' resistor that, instead of absorbing energy, would act like a battery and power the circuit."

"Isn't Kron's concept of a separate energy matrix outside the circuit similar to Tesla's idea of cosmic energy?"

"Yes, I'd say so."

"Why was the concept never advanced?"

"If the negative resistor had been developed commercially it would have made most of the electrical industry obsolete, including the products GE sold. So the company tabled Kron's discovery."

"If recall, Edison had a long-running feud with Tesla. Edison adamantly opposed Tesla's introduction of alternating current. Edison even electrocuted animals with it, claiming it was harmful."

"Yes. It's sad to think that even a forward-thinking person like Edison could be so closed-minded."

Just then a tall young man with curly hair that stuck out from his head strode into the lab. "Austin!" he shouted. "Where did you put that network analyzer?"

When he saw me he stopped and looked at Austin Park. "Who is this guy?"

I started laughing. Whoever he was, he looked like a clown at a child's birthday party.

"Dr. Berglin, meet my assistant, Dr. John Rosen. He's a theoretical physicist."

"Berglin...Berglin..." the young man muttered. "I've heard of you. Taught at MIT didn't you?"

"Is he always this impetuous?" I asked Austin.

"Almost always. But he's got a head full of new ideas and the brains to develop them."

"Not brains enough it seems," Rosen said. "And our funding runs out at the end of the month."

"That's why I'm here," I said. "I'm going in 50-50 with the venture capitalists who are funding you. You'll be able to continue your research."

"That's capital!" Rosen said. He grabbed my hand and pumped my arm up and down. The curly hair on his head shook like Dorothy's house in a strong Kansas wind.

After that we got down to business. They showed me their work and I began to feel energized. I didn't want to show them the drawings until Katelian and I had both signed the contract, but I couldn't help myself. I exhibited five of the photocopied pages from Tesla's notebook, the ones that described his "receiving device." When Park and Rosen saw these diagrams they began babbling physics to each other excitedly. I stayed for half an hour, talking to the two scientists, trying to enlist them on my side, feeling them out. I didn't relish Vahan Katelian as a business partner, but if anything went sour Park and Rosen would know I had money and resources. They were disposed toward me anyway because I was a fellow scientist. By the time I was ready to leave I felt I had done a good day's work.

As I walked out the door and past the guards I was feeling an inner excitement, an anticipation that something monumentally good was on its way. At the same time I felt an inner dread, as if that good thing was also accompanied by something alarming.

When I got back to the office I talked to the Board and showed them the contract. They were skeptical, but the monies involved were well within our R & D budget. Al Jordan, as CEO, signed off and joked, "I expect a fully operational flying carpet by the end of the next quarter!" Next I had Mildred Harrison, my secretary, phone Vahan Katelian and send over a signed contract. Within two hours it came back with Katelian's signature representing Katelian Properties. We were all set.

I went back to Room 317 at Octagon Research and handed Zach Ferrell's notebook to Austin Park. "See what you can make of that."

— 12 —

Danielle went to her interview in one of her mom's dark blue business suits, which would hide her tattoos. It felt weird to be interviewing for a real job. She had never had one. At 16 she'd been forced to fend for herself and her father as her dad went into an emotional shell and lost his job after the death of his wife. At 19, with her father's savings used up, she started dealing drugs to make ends meet. It was either that or become a prostitute. Now she was 21 and was interviewing for her first job at a prestigious company that expected, she was certain, the highest professional standards. Danielle admitted to herself that she was terrified. At the same time, she was determined to succeed.

When the driver saw the address he was disposed to be skeptical of the fare. When he arrived at the rundown house a tall, beautiful young woman walked out the front door looking the perfect businesswoman. "Where to?" he asked.

"115 Main Street."

As he took off the driver entered the address into the onboard computer, which showed the map on the display. "I know that place – the Centurion building."

"Yeah, I'm going for an interview at Berglin Enterprises."

"Right. The big IT company. Defense contractor."

Oh, so that's what it was. Danielle didn't even know. As she looked down at her suit she felt like a fraud. A business suit was way outside her comfort zone.

When Danielle arrived at the steel and glass building she felt intimidated. She paid the driver and strode as confidently as she could through the heavy revolving door into a large multi-story foyer / reception area. She looked around like a hick in the big city at all the glass, which sent sunlight streaming in to illuminate a big circular metal staircase. A solid black floor echoed the tap-tap her heels made upon it as she walked toward the reception area. There was *money* here.

The receptionist was dressed in a powder blue business suit. She looked cool and competent. The woman saw her approach and nodded with approval. Her name tag said Tara Bolshoi and her demeanor was crisp and professional. "Are you Ms. Danielle Menard?" she asked.

Danielle tried to keep her voice from cracking. "Yes."

"Mr. Berglin is expecting you. Suite 309." The woman handed her a badge with a ribbon. Danielle placed it around her neck.

"Thank you."

Danielle saw a bank of elevators but decided to walk up the beautiful spiral staircase, which had a lovely wood handrail. She found her way down a plushly carpeted hallway to Suite 309. Danielle knocked on the door, which was opened by an older woman wearing slacks and a lavender blouse. An ID tag hung around her neck, which read "Mildred Harrison."

"Danielle Menard? Please come with me."

She was escorted to a back office. Max Berglin was seated at an almost empty desk with a huge monitor and an optical keyboard in front of it. Suddenly the man moved his hands and a three-dimensional image appeared in the space above his desk. He moved his hands and the images shifted. He nodded his head, apparently satisfied, and the image disappeared. When he saw Danielle enter, she saw a look of pleased surprise on his face. He rose from behind the desk and approached her.

"Hello Danielle. You look very professional." This was said with cool reserve and a hint of relief, as if he hadn't been sure about a girl who came from her background. He was silent, waiting for her to say something. Danielle did not speak.

"Very good Danielle," Max said after a half-minute had gone by.

She wondered if this was some kind of test.

"Forgive me Danielle, won't you please sit down?"

Danielle obliged, sitting on a nice leather chair in front of a steel and glass desk.

Max seated himself behind the desk. "Did you know that Pierce Menard, your father, had a security classification?"

"I didn't sir." This seemed to be going nowhere, and she began to feel irritated. Was this a job interview or an interrogation?

"Let me come to the point," Max said, reading her mind. "Did your father ever mention his work to you during the time after your mother died?"

Danielle was getting angry now. "Excuse me sir, but the personal life of me and my father is none of your business. I was led to believe that this was a job interview."

"You're right Danielle," Max said. "I have the unfortunate habit, I'm told, of being obtuse."

Danielle smiled. The man had charm and knew how to use it. Her anger evaporated.

"I do have a position open, as I told you at the dinner. I observed your handling of my son and his friends at Zach Ferrell's little get-together at the restaurant. As I said then, I was hoping you might join us as one of our company representatives."

"I'm flattered sir. But I have no formal education other than high school, and a somewhat, er, sordid past."

"I was wondering if you would bring that up, or try to skate over it."

"Let's be blunt sir," she said. "I don't know what your company is or what it does. I was told you are a defense contractor. I'm sure that my recent arrest for narcotics trafficking wouldn't look good on your company's corporate flier. Isn't it unusual for a job interview to be conducted by the president of the company?"

Max Berglin ignored her question. He was smiling. "Yes, Danielle, you have just the kind of sharp intelligence and toughness I'm looking for."

She decided to ignore the unusual nature of the interview. If Mr. Max Berglin was offering her a job, she wanted to know what it was. "What would my duties and hours be, sir, and how much would I be paid? And most important, if you'll excuse me, how am I qualified to be a spokesman for an outfit like this?"

The older man laughed out loud. She could see he was not laughing at her, it was an expression of pleasure.

"My company develops security software for large defense contractors and smaller high-tech firms. Your duties would consist of meeting and greeting potential clients and recommending the company's products."

"You mean I'd be a kind of fancy sales rep?" Danielle imagined an informal party with men drinking and ogling her.

"Yes and no. Your meeting with clients would be in an office setting, strictly business; but your purpose would be to actively promote the company's products. You have a presence, an intelligence, and a certain edginess that would appeal to my clients. I don't doubt you would soon be able to understand enough about our products to admirably represent my company." He leaned over his desk for emphasis. “Your remuneration would be commensurate with your abilities. If you did well you would be very well compensated.” He sat back. “If you did well and you were interested, you might participate at a higher level.”

Danielle sensed an undertone that Max Berglin was interested in her. Was it just her imagination? She watched him closely.

“What I mean is, some of the companies we do business with are engaged in classified work. To participate in that action you’d need a security classification.”

Danielle saw the older man staring at her, gauging her reaction. For some reason she felt an inner excitement at at the possibility.

“You would have to qualify for a three-month training program first. If you don’t pass the tests you will be rejected, of course. Nothing is guaranteed. I’m offering you an opportunity. If you qualified to be a company sales rep you would travel frequently, sometimes overseas. You would become involved in the exciting world of cutting edge technology and security. During your training period you will be paid a minimal salary, enough to get by.”

Danielle sat for a few moments, thinking. The job was appealing. It was better than selling drugs. Besides, she and her father needed the money. Even a small salary would be enough to pay for the necessities.

“I have two questions, sir. I won’t compromise my integrity. If you expect me to be some kind of courtesan or call girl, it’s not happening. And second, I’d like to continue my work with the homeless. It’s something that appeals to me. I don’t want to lose contact with real people.”

Danielle saw the older man lean back in his chair and frown. “You’re shrewd, Danielle. Of course, my clients would find you appealing as a woman, and I admit that’s part of why I asked you to work for us. But you would be protected. You would have to pass a background check but I don’t anticipate any problem with that. As for your latter point, I don’t like it. You see, our contracts involve technology that is, er, on the leading edge and sometimes involves national security. Having an employee of ours on the streets isn’t part of the job description.”

“I think we both have things to consider,” Danielle said, hoping to conclude the interview. “Could I have a few days to think it over?”

Max rose from behind the desk. “Certainly Danielle. Is your work with the homeless a deal-breaker?”

Danielle stood up. “I’m afraid it is, sir.” She knew she was being stubborn.

Max stuck out his hand and Danielle shook it.

“I’ll call you on Monday?” she suggested.

"That will be fine. If anything comes up on our end I'll let you know."

After Danielle left I sat at my desk for five minutes without doing anything. The Menard girl could be a find, but she could also be a disrupting influence. I admitted to myself I was interested in her, but I was too late. She would be wasted on the Ferrell kid.

When Danielle got home she saw her father in his little office off the foyer, reading journals on his laptop. He hadn't used that office since mom died; she took it as a good sign. A six-pack of beer was beside him.

"Dad, Max Berglin said you had a security clearance. Were you ever involved in classified research?"

Pirece looked at his daughter and felt a pang in his heart. She looked a lot like her mother and for a second he thought that Carol had come back to life. "How did your interview go?" he said, ignoring the question.

"I may or may not have a job. The more I think about it, the more preposterous the whole thing seems." Danielle noticed that since her father had come back to life she was much better spoken. She had even stopped swearing.

"In what way?"

"Well, the president of this successful company who does classified work offered a job to an unqualified high school graduate who was recently arrested for drug dealing. I suspect there is an ulterior motive but I can't figure out what it is."

"Is that why he asked you about my security clearance?"

"I have no idea, dad. Did you work on classified projects? Mr. Berglin asked me whether you had blabbed to me about it." Danielle wondered whether her father and Max Berglin were telling her everything.

"Danielle, I suspect that Berglin has been asked by his handler to keep an eye on you, and through you, me."

"Handler?"

"Everyone involved in classified work has a handler, a shepherd, a person who makes sure that you do your job and don't rock the boat."

"Oh, I see. So the job offer was just a sham then. That explains why he would hire an unqualified candidate."

"Don't sell yourself short Danielle. You have intelligence and, I suspect, talent. My advice is to take the job. You should be well compensated, and you'll find out how nice it is not to have to worry about money. When I move out of

Midland you'll discover whether the job is real or an excuse to keep an eye on me."

"So you have definitely decided to leave town?"

"Yes, daughter. There are too many painful memories here. I have a job offer in Boston, contingent on my cleaning myself up by the beginning of the fall term."

Danielle inexplicably found herself feeling sad. Her disgust of him had abated rapidly over the past weeks, as he had made a successful attempt to get his life back together. "I wish you wouldn't go."

Pierce rose from his chair and gave his daughter a hug. "I think you already know it will be better for both of us. You're engaged, you have a job offer, your life seems fair set now."

Danielle couldn't disagree. The more she thought about the job, the more she liked it. The sales stuff, that was OK, but the clandestine nature of "further participation" excited her. Right then she made up her mind. Sham or not, she'd take the job.

— 13 —

Austin Park and his assistant John Rosen were in a frenzy of scientific excitement. Both scientists had abandoned their earlier work to study the notebook provided by Dr. Berglin. They concluded that the photocopied schematics and diagrams were intended to be engineering blueprints for fully operational devices.

"Take a look at this," Austin said to his assistant. He pointed to ten pages of detailed drawings, schematics, and explanations for a complete system to trap and deliver electromagnetic energy from the quantum vacuum. Tesla labeled this system "Receiver for Cosmic Energy."

John was blown away. "Look boss. Here's a diagram of an ingenious multiphase power inverter that can supply 60Hz alternating current from the receiver to an electrical panel."

The two scientists looked at each other in awe.

"My God, this is a practical overunity device: a unit that can power loads without plugging into the electrical grid," John said excitedly.

"My God is right, John." Austin Park's normally unexcitable personality was vibrating with enthusiasm. "This is no perpetual motion machine." Overunity devices – machines that supplied more power than they used – were a joke in the scientific community and were contemptuously called perpetual motion machines.

Austin and John thoroughly examined the rest of the notebook and discovered schematics for a beam weapon.

"This is a scalar electromagetic weapon with tremendous power," John said. He pointed to the schematics. "This technology is dangerous. It's what Tesla called a Death Ray."

The two researchers studied the notebook for two days. They found diagrams for a radiant energy device that could throw out spheres of ionized plasma.

There was a smaller, more portable version of the cosmic energy receiver that could power machinery. This device was labeled "Pierce-Arrow, 1942." Next to it was an old-fashioned receiver with tubes that Tesla had named "Pierce-Arrow, 1931." John was excited when he saw a schematic for an ingenious bladeless turbine. Austin discovered what Tesla labeled a "mechanical oscillator" that could be tuned to operate at the resonant frequencies of various objects. John found diagrams for a high-powered wireless signal transmitter. There were also some unfinished sketches, one of which was marked "superluminal engine."

Both men were puzzled. "Some of these inventions are practical," John said. "They could have made Tesla a very rich man."

When they studied the life of Nikola Tesla they discovered that the great inventor died broke in a New York hotel room.

John shook his head. "It makes no sense Austin. This receiver for cosmic energy all by itself is a world changer. It could power machinery, homes, and factories. Why was it never developed?"

"He was a century or more ahead of his time," Austin concluded. "Tesla's futuristic devices weren't practical for the times."

The two men did a little historical research of the period between 1890 and 1943, when Tesla died. John picked up the notebook, thumbing through its photocopied pages. "It was too great a leap. The world didn't want these breakthroughs. People back then were more interested in toasters, light bulbs, and telephones, not the wireless transmission of power."

"Tesla lost his funding during the early years of the twentieth century, John, partly because he had a combative personality. He called Einstein's Theory of Relativity a beggar wrapped in purple whom ignorant people take for a king. He dismissed Hertz's theory of electromagnetic waves. He hated Thomas Edison and J. P. Morgan, the banker, who cut off his funding. As a result he spent decades after that doing work for others that was far beneath his genius."

John could understand Tesla's attitude. All through high school and even at MIT he met people who couldn't think out of the box, who refused to even entertain new ideas. It was frustrating. "Tesla must have died a bitter man."

Austin took the precious notebook from John. "This must be the result of decades of thought."

"Tesla had an eidetic memory and could visualize devices in his head that would work the first time he built them. As we will hopefully discover as soon as possible."

Austin pointed to the schematic of a large broadcasting tower. "At Wardenclyffe he built the world's first tower for the wireless transmission of power, probably based on this diagram. If his work hadn't been shut down in 1906 because J. P. Morgan refused to fund it, we might be living in a different world now." [5]

John was passionate. "By God Dr. Park, it's up to us to make something of the great man's work." He pointed to the diagrams of the cosmic energy receiver. "This unit makes every electric generation plant in the world obsolete."

"You're right John. The question is, how do we proceed?"

After several hours of discussion the two scientists decided to summarize the contents of Tesla's notebook. Austin would call Dr. Berglin after work and recommend development of the portable receiver.

"It could be used to power homes and factories," Park said. "Such a device would be practical, understandable to normal citizens, and easily commercialized and marketed."

The only problem for John was the theory behind the receiver.

"I don't think even Tesla knew how this thing worked. He was basically a brilliant engineer. It's almost as if he got a working blueprint from heaven and just copied it."

"The man had hundreds of patents; he was a certifiable genius. Let's build the thing and worry about the theory later."

John ground his teeth. It went against the grain of his training in theoretical physics. "We're not amateur basement experimenters, dammit!"

"When it comes to this stuff we are. Let's get to work."

The two scientists, working off Tesla's schematics and notes, got busy building a small prototype receiver. Three weeks later, after several false starts, they were ready to test it with a simple bench experiment.

Austin wired the prototype to an inverter. The inverter changed the direct current coming from the receiver to alternating current and boosted the voltage to normal household levels. A simple switch was wired in. The load was a 1/3 hp one phase alternating current motor that accepted standard AC.

"Is this a smart device?" John wondered.

"What do you mean?" Austin asked.

"The receiver might not have enough power to get the motor going, or the receiver could overload it."

"It probably won't work at all."

"We have to trust to the great inventor."

The two scientists looked at each other and laughed. Both of them felt a little silly. Like trained monkeys, they had built the device from Tesla's schematics without a full understanding of what it could do.

"I feel like a UFOlogist wearing a tin foil hat," John joked.

"Here goes," Austin said, closing the switch that would wire the receiver into the circuit.

Nothing happened.

The two men stared at the motor, willing it to move.

"Look," Austin said. The rotor slowly began to turn. Then it sped up alarmingly for a few seconds and settled down, humming along smoothly. John and Austin were amazed. The prototype took the right amount of "cosmic energy" into the circuit without overloading it.

The two scientists were elated and baffled. "How does the receiver tap into the cosmic energy?" John asked.

"I have no idea." He pointed at Tesla's receiver, happily spinning the motor with no power source. "How does the device know how to regulate the current flow through the circuit?"

The two men looked at each other.

"We have a lot of work to do," John said.

The two scientists tested the device a dozen more times. Each time there was a pause as the receiver "thought" for a few moments. The rotor began turning slowly, then rapidly for a short burst, and then it settled down.

Austin and John looked at each other in amazement. "It's impossible, but we did it!" Austin said. They took photographs and carefully organized their data. Then they thanked the great Nikola Tesla and wondered how they could possibly explain their results.

"That's your job, hotshot," Austin told John. "You're the theoretician around here."

Curious, Austin tested the receiver for electromagnetic radiation, radio frequency emissions, microwave emissions, and even brought out a Geiger counter to measure gamma rays and beta particles. There was nothing. The box itself was cool to the touch. He powered up the device again, watching how the receiver first decided how much energy was necessary to get the motor started, then gradually went higher and higher until it went slightly past the optimum running amps, then backed off. He shook his head in wonder. "John, Tesla's receiver approaches the optimum running amps from above and below. It's almost...sentient."

John nodded and looked up at the clock. "It's past seven Dr. Park; I'm tired. Let's go home."

"All right. I'll leave the switch closed and we'll see if the rotor is still turning when we come in tomorrow." Both men left the lab. John Rosen was so excited he almost ran his car into a stop sign on his way home. Austin Park hoped the motor would be turning when they arrived at eight the next morning, but his more fatalistic personality expected failure.

The next morning when Austin walked into the lab the little motor was still turning. "I don't believe it," he muttered. Just then John Rosen walked in.

John removed the motor from the circuit and Austin examined it. The stator, rotor, and windings all looked normal. He checked the motor for radiation and retested the box that held the receiver. There was nothing measurable.

"We did it!" John exclaimed.

"Tesla did it," Austin said.

That evening John and Austin were still in the lab. John got a call from Vahan Katelian.

"I haven't heard from you in a while, Vahan."

"No John. I want you to concentrate on your work."

John had known Vahan for several years. Before he left for MIT Vahan and his brothers had rescued him from some toughs and the two had struck up a somewhat unusual friendship. Vahan had introduced him to Dr. Park after John had received his PhD.

"What's new?"

"Why would anything be new?" John put the mobile on speaker so Austin could hear.

"C'mon Johnny, don't hold out on me. I heard something happened in the lab yesterday."

"How did you find out about that? You couldn't possibly know anything. It only happened twelve hours ago."

"You forget about my extended family," Vahan replied.

John had forgotten. Vahan's brothers, cousins, and other acquaintances would make up a small city. They constantly networked, looking for business opportunities. "Let me guess," John replied. "You have a friend of the family, or a fifth cousin, who works as a janitor at Octagon, and he overheard something."

Vahan laughed. "Not anywhere near that complicated John. My uncle is assistant research director at your facility. Each day researchers are required to submit a report to the director. My uncle reads every one of them."

"Yeah, I write those reports. Do you mean Old Man Nalbandian is a relative of yours?"

Vahan sighed. "Haven't you learned anything about us yet, John? The families used to fight each other but now we mostly work together. The Nalbandians and the Katelians have been in business together for two generations."

John knew that Vahan never did anything randomly. There was a reason for this call. "So what do you want?"

"We – I – want to know whether this discovery of yours has any commercial application."

"Vahan, we just did the experiment a few hours ago. We don't even know how we did it. How are we supposed to know if it can be marketed?"

"Don't play dumb, John. Of course we know that. We want your opinion – right here at the earliest stages – whether you think this discovery has commercial potential. We trust you. You're almost as smart as one of us!"

It was a standing joke between them: "Who's smarter, Jews or Armenians?" John thought about Vahan's question. Naturally skeptical, he had been feeling an unexplainable inner excitement as they successfully tested and retested the device.

"My guess is that this one is a winner." He began to explain the technical details behind Tesla's receiver, but Vahan stopped him. "I'm not a scientist, John, keep it simple."

"All right. Our discovery is way outside the accepted boundaries of electrodynamics. We won't know how reliable the device is until we do more testing."

"Thanks John. I knew you'd come through."

After Vahan hung up John met Austin's eyes. Austin said, "So, we're being closely monitored."

John didn't reply. He was feeling excited and was looking forward to going back to the lab in the morning. He didn't care who was funding them or whether the investors had hidden security cameras all over the lab.

Austin wondered whether the Katelians knew of Tesla's notebook. That family had a shady reputation. At the end of the day he locked it into a secure cabinet in the lab.

Vahan Katelian and John Rosen

John Rosen worked until nine that night. Exhausted, he went back to his cramped one bedroom apartment on campus in the student section. It was the cheapest apartment he could find, which is why he spent most of his time in the Octagon's spacious lab. After he showered he felt sleepy and decided to go to bed, but his mind was racing. He couldn't sleep.

Vahan's call had disturbed him. He had detected a certain ruthless greed in Vahan's voice he didn't like. He remembered the first time he met Vahan Katelian. It had been during the final semester of his senior year at Midland East High School several years ago, a few months before he left for Boston and MIT. He was walking downtown in late May, going to the hardware store for a new toilet seat for his bathroom. In front of the store a funny-looking little man was talking to a guy in a luxurious dark beige business suit, a fedora hat, and highly polished leather shoes. The well dressed guy was in his late twenties and looked like a hedge fund manager or a hustler. He had a hawk nose, intense black hair, and was constantly turning his head to look about him like a soldier on sentry duty. As John walked to the door he glanced over at Vahan and they locked eyes for a split second. Something passed between them. Vahan motioned for him to wait outside the store and they began talking. John was fascinated by Vahan, who introduced himself and Elmo Tackett, the ugly little guy. John liked Vahan immediately even though there was something prickly about him. While they conversed Elmo stared at him emotionlessly, which made John uncomfortable.

He and Vahan would meet occasionally for coffee at Sweetwaters that summer. One day John asked him about Elmo.

Vahan was evasive. "We use Elmo for...certain work the family needs done." Later John discovered more details about his family and their "business ventures," some of which sounded criminal. John wasn't nosy and didn't pry. He liked Vahan for his quick intelligence, his acerbic sense of humor, and his street smarts. He had never seen Vahan in casual clothes. "I dress well because it gives the family a good image. I like looking good."

As they talked John noticed an obvious strain of vanity in Vahan's personality. John concluded that Vahan was selfish and would only do something if there was money in it, or if there was something in it for him. He wondered if he could count on Vahan as a friend. He found out the day before he left for MIT in late August.

John was coming out of PRC Bank after withdrawing over four thousand dollars in cash. Two men came up to him and demanded his money. John was amazed that he would be confronted in broad daylight outside a bank. But the toughs intimidated everyone around them and people avoided the scene. John was about to lose his summer wages when Vahan, Elmo, and three other guys surrounded them. "Get lost," Vahan said to the robbers. "Leave this guy alone from now on, you hear me?" The toughs ran off and Vahan smiled.

John was shaking from the adrenal rush. "Thanks Vahan. You came in the nick of time."

"Thank these guys." Vahan indicated the three men. "The tall one here is my cousin Sevan, the short guy is my cousin Raffi, and this guy here is my younger brother Zadig."

"Are you guys twins?" John asked. He could hardly tell Vahan and Zadig apart.

"We are. Zadig here is three minutes younger than me." The two brothers grinned.

"I'm very grateful for your intervention," John said, executing a small bow of acknowledgment. "Thank you."

"He's got good manners," Zadig said, and the others laughed. The Katelians walked away as if the entire incident had been as routine as helping an old lady pick up the purse she dropped.

When he got back from MIT six years later, thinking about pursuing post-doctoral work at Carleton, Vahan called him the very first day he arrived in town. "Hello John, it's Vahan."

"How did you know I was back in Midland?" They had kept in touch with occasional phone calls over the past six years, but John was surprised and a little nervous.

"Oh, I know a lot of things John. The reason I called is because I might have a job for you."

"Be serious, Vahan. I'm not a businessman and I don't care that much about money."

"Oh Johnny boy, I'm talking about something that will be perfectly suitable for you. We've been keeping tabs on your progress."

John felt there was something sinister about this statement.

"Keeping tabs on me?"

"Don't fret John. I know a researcher at Octagon Research, in Research Park. He's an applied physicist who specializes in electrodynamics. He is doing some original research into the work of Nikola Tesla and Gabriel Kron. Out of the mainstream stuff. His name is Austin Park and he's looking for an assistant. Does that sound like something you'd be interested in?"

"It does! I've got offers from the NSA and a Washington DC think tank, but none of that interests me. I want to do original research and break new ground."

"If you go to Room 317 of the Octagon building at 8 a.m. tomorrow, Dr. Park will be expecting you. I'll make sure the guards know who you are, but make sure you have ID on you."

"I'm not sure whether to be happy or concerned, Vahan. This is the second big favor you've done for me. I feel that you are placing me under an obligation. It makes me a little uncomfortable."

Vahan laughed. "No obligation my friend. Honestly John, I like you. I'm a very busy man and if I didn't I never would have kept in touch with you. If you don't feel comfortable with my proposal, by all means carry on with your life."

John thought that either Vahan was a really nice guy or he was a master psychologist. Probably a little of both.

"OK then, I may or may not. Do you have time to have coffee at Sweetwaters this Saturday like we used to?"

"I'd like that."

"I hope I won't see that little twerp, what's his name? Elmo?"

Vahan chuckled. "No, you won't see him, I can guarantee that. Electrodynamics is somewhat, ah, out of his area of expertise."

"Good. Looking forward to it. And by the way, Jews are much smarter than Armenians."

Vahan laughed. "All right John. I'll see you at Sweetwaters on Saturday as soon as the place opens."

When John went to the Octagon building the next day it was just as Vahan had described. Park was doing original research, and he hired John on the spot after a half-hour interview.

Now, a year later, they had made a potential breakthrough.

And Austin's boss was none other than Vartan Nalbandian, one of Vahan's connections.

The two researchers worked for a week testing and retesting Tesla's "1942" receiver, trying to pin down the theoretical basis behind it. Austin Park stretched and yawned. "It's six o'clock John. I'm burnt out for the day."

"Let's keep going," John said. "Nobel Prize here we come."

"John, you need to devise a coherent theory to explain this," Park ordered. "You work on that, I'll finish up here. Then I'm going home and sleep for twelve hours."

Park saw his assistant scowl. The two men had become friends, but the younger Rosen had a volatile temperament.

"We both know we don't really know how this works."

"That's where you come in son. I already told you that. You're the theory guy. Get going, figure it out."

"I've already cooked up something. I'll write a paper that hopefully won't make us look like fools. But look out for the men in black."

"Why do you say that?"

"Something Berglin mentioned to me when he was here. He implied that the Tesla sketches might originally have come from a top secret project. If so, we have to be careful."

Zbigniew Byrnes and Stapleton Talk at TAC

James Stapleton's headset began flashing. Probably Byrnes again. The former national security adviser was domineering and micro-managed everything.

The headset consisted of a thin band that went around the head, two tiny round discs that fit over the ear, and a molecule-thin gray visor that looked like it was made out of nothing. To Stapleton it looked like something from a science-fiction movie. He placed it over his head. Instantly Zbigniew Byrnes appeared in a pure white virtual space that looked like a way station between the living and the dead. Byrnes appeared as he was: a man in his 70s with a head of full white hair. He leaned on a cane.

"Stapleton! What's this I hear about Octagon Research?"

Stapleton almost took the headset off. Byrnes' mouth was moving, the twit. He still hadn't figured out that these things operated on thought impulses. He knew Byrnes had understood his derogatory thoughts.

"You're not indispensable Stapleton," Byrnes said, leaning forward on his cane.

Stapleton stood about ten feet from Byrnes in the White Room, next to a virtual desk, while his body was in his office on the third floor of the TAC building. Stapleton thought into the headphones. "We both know that's not true. Nothing is happening at Octagon that you don't already know."

"That's where you're wrong, Stapleton. My contact in Midland tells me that two research scientists are on the verge of a breakthrough in frontier physics."

Stapleton was startled.

"As I say, you're not indispensable. I want you to look into the work of two scientists at the Octagon Research facility in Midland, Illinois. Austin Park and John Rosen. They're working on some kind of overunity device."

"What?" Overunity was the strict property of the unacknowledged special access programs. Absolutely off-limits.

"Keep an eye on Park and Rosen, Room 317, Octagon Research, do you understand?"

Zbigniew Byrnes vanished.

Stapleton took off the headset and the White Room disappeared. He would have to have a word with his man in Midland, Vartan Nalbandian.

Part VI

Midland

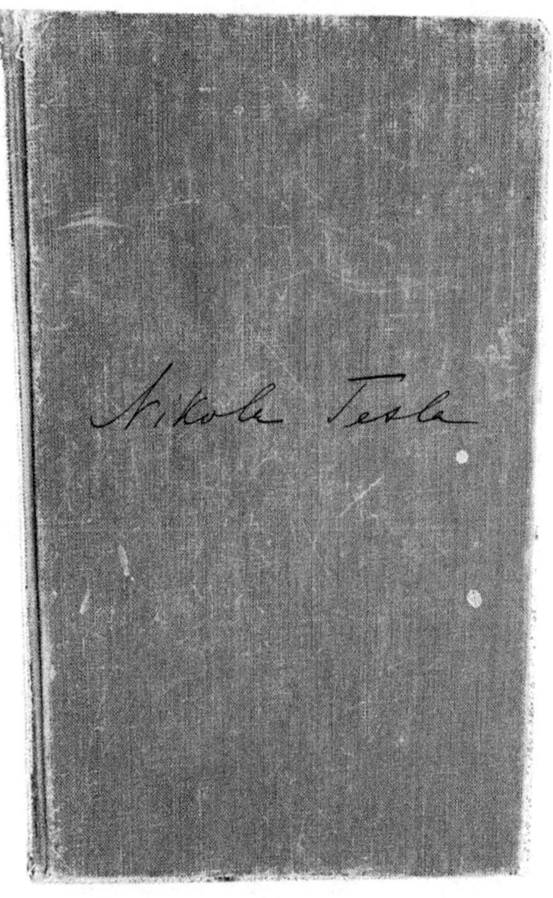

— 14 —

Mark Ferrell delayed calling his son for over a month after Rachel left, but it had to be done. "Zach, it's dad. Rachel left the house. She's having an affair with Don Halloran, the firm's VP."

Zach should have felt something, maybe sorrow or anger, but he didn't. "OK dad. Do you still love her?"

"I think I might, but she made it clear that she was leaving and never coming back."

"OK dad, promise me you won't start drinking like Danielle's father, or put a bullet in your head."

Mark laughed. "I don't think it will come to that, son."

"Good. Just testing. I'm experiencing a little bit of that with Danielle and Pierce, and it's no way to live."

"How are you guys doing?"

"Danielle went for her interview and has decided to start the training. Pierce looks like he's turning his life around – hold it dad, I have to take this call."

"Zach? This is Pierce Menard. I wanted you to know that I received an email a couple of days ago from a wealthy relative of mine who hasn't given up on me. He has agreed to lend me the funds necessary to get me back on my feet. Therefore I will not be a financial burden on you and Danielle."

"That's great Mr. Menard. Are you going to stay at the house?"

"Temporarily. Frank has agreed to lend me enough to refurbish the house so I can sell it. I already have a job offer, contingent on getting myself cleaned up."

"All right sir. You raised an absolutely spectacular daughter."

Zach heard Pierce's voice quiver with emotion. "Thank you Zach, but we both know what a failure I've been in that department. I guarantee you that will change."

Zach switched off.

"Guess what dad, I just got a call from Pierce Menard, Danielle's father. He says he's got money now and he's going to turn his life around."

Mark laughed. "I'll believe that when I see it."

"You sound like mom now."

"Sorry son, bad habit I've gotten into. I'm not sure what will happen with our house now. I may wind up doing just what Pierce is doing."

"You and Pierce could live together," Zach joked. "Then you could have bachelor parties with lots of women hanging around."

"Zach, do you think Danielle might turn out like Rachel?"

"No dad, that's not possible."

Ah, the innocence of youth. "For better and for worse, I guess."

"Don't be maudlin dad. Everything will be OK."

"All right Zach. I'll talk to you later."

Wayne DiPietro Notices a Discrepancy

Wayne DiPietro's job as a CPA at PRC Accountants would have been boring for most people, but he liked it. His job was to audit corporate accounts, and he was good at it. He loved numbers and figures, and making things balance. This morning, as he was auditing the accounts of the PANA corporation, he found something potentially disturbing. Over the past several weeks he had noticed a small increase in expenditures across the board. He checked his figures and discovered an average increase of approximately $7,000 per week without an accompanying increase in revenue. When he checked the ledgers he could see nothing amiss, but it bothered him. He noted the increase in his account log but didn't mention it in his quarterly auditor's opinion.

Larry Potvin went to work as usual on a Monday morning in mid-February. Jenny went to her part time job as a receptionist at the chiropractic office of Leon Kraynek. When she came home at 3 p.m. she was tired and decided to lie down before starting dinner. As she passed Larry's office at the end of the hall she saw a bunch of papers scattered over his desk. That was curious because her husband was meticulous about his accounting and his auto shop.

Larry walked into the kitchen at 5:30, whistling and feeling cheerful. Jenny was stirring a pot of goulash.

"Hello Jenny, how was your day?"

They chit-chatted back and forth about the day. "Larry, what's up?" Jenny asked.

Larry's face went blank for a moment. "About what?"

"Well, you always keep your desk so clean and I noticed how messy it was this morning. You've been buying new equipment for your shop and you told me a couple of weeks ago that you'd rented a new building. I'm wondering where are you getting the money?"

Larry's eyes narrowed. Jenny had asked the question innocently but he knew he had to come up with a good answer, and quickly. He couldn't think of anything. "I've been making some extra money at work lately, that's all, bringing some work home. Just more accounting." It sounded lame, but Jenny's eyes widened in pleased surprise.

"That's great honey. Are we going to be able to move our cars back into the garage this year?"

"I'm planning on it." He was greatly relieved and decided to change the subject. "Is that goulash I smell?"

"It sure is, with a quarter cup of Hungarian sweet paprika."

Larry watched Jenny closely as they ate and talked over dinner. She said nothing more about the money. With the twenty-five grand he'd made so far he had already spent ten grand on a head engine lathe and almost that much on a new engine crane, engine stand, new floor jacks, a large air compressor, and two new paint sprayers. He had already transferred his welder, tool cabinets, chassis stands, and other sundry equipment over to the new place on Ashley, which had two hydraulic floor lifts. Everything was going great! Even so, he wondered how much Jenny knew about his new venture. He had not told her how much extra he was making. She had no interest in cars, so there shouldn't be any problems on the home front.

He was moving faster than he'd planned and felt excited. By the end of March he would be settled in and could afford to hire Zach Ferrell part-time. The only problem was that he couldn't share the excitement of his new life with his son, or with anyone. Karl had no interest in anything but his books. Larry never thought he'd have a son like that.

Bruce Tarpley, Larry's co-worker at PANA, came to his auto shop to see the restored 'vette on a warm day at the end of February.

"I'm going to blindfold you buddy, to get the maximum impact."

Bruce objected strongly. "Just let me see my baby!"

Larry was bigger and stronger and he put a clean rag over Bruce's head so it covered his face, walking him up to the car. When he took off the blindfold Bruce almost wet himself.

"God, it's beautiful." Bruce walked around the restored vehicle, admiring the new paint job (Corvette orange), the new chrome, and the original equipment headlights.

"Brand new sport mirrors and white letter steel belted tires," Larry pointed out proudly. "Wait till you see this." Larry lifted the hood to expose a brand new engine with OEM chrome valve covers. The engine gleamed. "This car originally came with a 210 horsepower V8. The old one was a wreck, but I was able to get a 350 specially built from VetteDreams in Utah."

Larry got down on his knees and pointed to the dual exhaust pipes. "Look at that. Magnaflow dual exhaust, stainless steel, turbo edition. Let's you *hear* the engine." The Magnaflow was another concession to originality and it had been a pain in the ass to mount. But he'd done it for the customer.

Bruce also noticed the painted chassis, which made Larry feel like a superhero.

"It looks brand new!" Bruce said.

"Get in," Larry said, handing Bruce the key.

When the engine turned over it made a growling sound. Bruce's eyes widened with pleasure.

They tooled the car around and the look on Bruce's face was priceless. The man had tears in his eyes when they came back to the shop. Fortunately the streets were clear of snow and slush and salt.

Bruce spoke fervently. "This is the best money I've ever spent in my life." He shook Larry's hand vigorously.

Larry understood that Bruce's look of complete satisfaction and joy was the real reason he wanted to do this full time. At PANA all he did was balance figures on a ledger. It was really, really boring and unsatisfying. To make people happy was as important as the money.

That night before bed Larry got down on his knees and asked God to make everything turn out all right.

Jessie and Heather Decide Their Futures

Jessie DiPietro sat at her desk in her bedroom for a long time. She was still living with Myra and Wayne at the house. It was OK but she was feeling a little stifled.

She had to decide what to do with her life. Her dream of marrying Zach had fallen through. What she really wanted was to raise a family and have someone take care of her. She was quick in her studies but didn't see herself as a career woman. She thought about Zach's friends, and the guys she had met at Carleton. Not one of them interested her, except maybe Gary Cronin. When she thought that, she laughed and called Heather.

"Guess what I was just thinking about?"

"I'll never guess."

"Zach's friend Gary."

"Gary? That fat slob? Are you kidding?"

"He's nice, I love that British accent. And Heather, I happened to talk with a girl he slept with last year. She says he's very good in bed. Very well endowed." She told her friend about her desire to start a family.

"Really!" Heather replied. "How odd!"

"Why would it be odd?" Jessie asked.

"Odd that you, with all your intelligence, should be thinking about settling down and starting a family. Whereas I, Jessie, have decided to begin my career as a journalist. Or possibly a career in the State Department."

"The State Department! Do you want to be a diplomat?"

Heather spoke excitedly. "I've been thinking about the foreign service. I like travel and I love relationships. I'm a good observer of people. I'm a facilitator. I'd love it as a career. And if I don't pass the tests or fail somehow I can always fall back on journalism."

Jessie was amazed. Her friend had her life path all mapped out. "In a way I envy you, Heather. You figured it out."

"I did. And it's not pharmacology. You helped. Our little talks got me thinking; when I talked with my father he was OK with it. He said, 'Sweetheart, I don't think chemistry is your thing.' It was cute."

Jessie heard her friend pause. "Jessie, I want to stay in touch always, OK? No matter what happens."

Jessie was surprised at the passion and urgency in her friend's voice. "Sure Heather. No matter where you are in the world you're just a call away."

"Good, it's settled then. Friends for life, OK?"

"OK."

When Heather rang off Jessie wondered what had prompted all that emotion. Maybe Heather was the unconventional one and she was the dowdy. It *was* odd that she, who was very bright and could have her choice of careers, appeared to have settled for the mundane life of a housewife. Heather was reaching for something she might not be qualified for. Jessie smiled. She'd get Gary's number from Zach tonight.

Part VII

Tesla

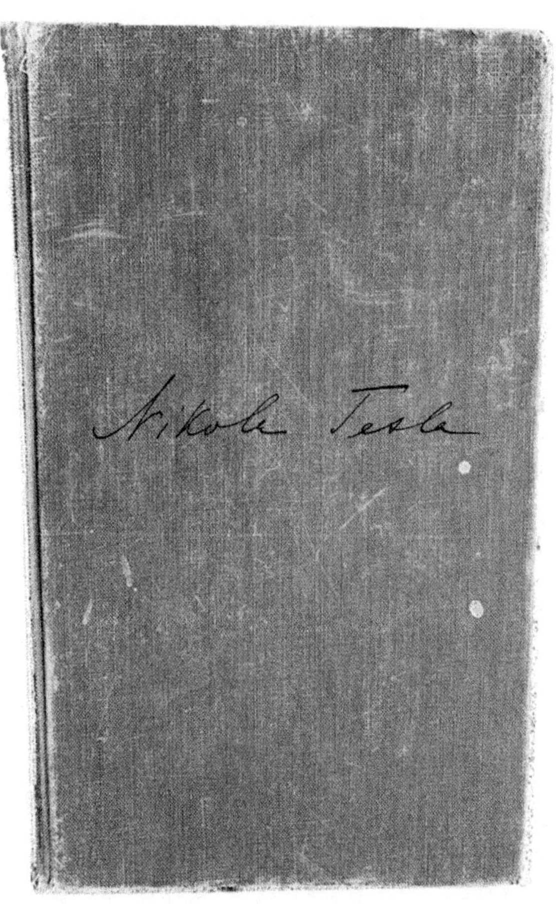

— 15 —

When John Rosen went back to the lab at eight the next morning Austin Park was already there.

"You look like the inside of a sweaty baseball glove," John joked.

"I've been here since five in the morning. Couldn't sleep." Austin straightened from the lab bench and pointed to their simple experiment. John saw that he had clamped the motor, the receiver, the switch, and the inverter onto a half-inch piece of plywood. "Have you made any progress on explaining the theory behind this?"

"I looked at everything available on dark energy, even went into some old stuff on aether theory, mostly a lot of crap. What did Berglin say when you told him about our progress?"

"You didn't answer my question," Park replied.

"That's because I'm clueless."

"Dr. Berglin told us to go ahead with the portable receiver. He was very excited about the commercial possibilities."

"Whoo!" John threw a small sheaf of papers into the air. They scattered all over the floor. "Let's get laid."

The normally serious Austin Park laughed. "What will you tell the ladies? That you invented a device that can turn a motor? I don't think they'll be too impressed with that."

"You're right. But we should get some reward." He went around picking up the papers, groaning. "I didn't sleep last night either." He handed his work to his boss. "I made some notes."

As Austin looked over the papers John made a pot of coffee and tried to wake up. He heard laughter. "It's nonsense all right, work on it some more."

"It's not that bad."

Austin put a hand on John's arm. "John, I don't want you to mention our success in your daily reports."

"Vahan already suspects we have made a breakthrough. He's been on me to do something practical."

"All you've said in your daily reports is that the receiver is still not 100% reliable and that we don't know why it works. Which is almost the complete truth. Let's keep it that way."

"Worried about the men in black?"

"More like Old Man Nalbandian. There's something about that guy I don't trust."

"I don't like him either."

"John, let's keep our hats on this one until we are absolutely sure we know what we're doing."

John considered refusing. Park's career was already established but if he was caught falsifying data on a report his career might be over before it got started. "All right."

"Thanks John. I know it's unusual, but if we ever get to publish this your name will be right next to mine on the paper."

John was pleased. Sometimes grad students and rookies like him didn't get credit at all.

After another month of experimentation and investigation into the receiver John had the outline of a coherent theory.

He handed Park a sheaf of printouts. "I revised my paper. The Tesla diagrams are just engineering blueprints; I've tried to fit what we've done into current theory. Take a look at it tonight. Make any corrections and I'll upload it to the preprint server tomorrow."

Austin shook his head. "You may have forgotten that we can't even disseminate this information John. It's not our intellectual property."

"But we did all the work!"

"It's out of our hands. Technically this invention is the property of Octagon Research Inc. and the investors. Or didn't you read the contract you signed?"

"Fuck the contract."

"We are already outside the lines by fudging our reports."

"Fuck the reports."

"You sound like a kid whose mom won't give him a cookie."

"Dammit boss, we have something here that can change the world and we're hemmed in by petty rules and regulations."

Austin scrutinized John, wondering what kind of a man he really was. "I feel the same as you, but we are legally bound by those petty rules and regulations."

"Maybe we should demonstrate this thing privately to Max Berglin. He knows a lot more than us about how the system works."

Austin was dubious.

"What do you think will happen if we show this to Old Man Nalbandian?"

"He'll report it uplines."

"Correct. Someone else will get credit." John was angry. "We may never see this technology again."

Both men looked at each other. "There's no harm in showing our results to an investor legally contracted with Octagon Research," John suggested.

"I'd like to test the receiver outside the lab."

"Now you're talking!"

The two men gazed at each other for several moments. Park spoke first. "I'll call Berglin."

The result was that on a warm Sunday afternoon in late April, Austin and John went to the home of Max Berglin Sr., a palace in the exclusive Palmer Park suburb of Midland. Austin drove up a long driveway to a black metal gate with an intercom button and gave a password given to him by Dr. Berglin. Park drove his Toyota along an asphalt path, past perfectly manicured gardens that were brilliantly in bloom. They parked in the turnaround and Berglin greeted them at the door, a massive slab of wood that could have stopped a mortar shell.

The three men walked down to Max Berglin's basement lab carrying the experiment on its wooden board.

"You know you guys are off the reservation, don't you?" I asked.

Park and Rosen both nodded.

"There's still time to drive off and forget about this." I knew that I was also off the res if I went any further. My contract with Octagon Research stated that nothing could leave the Octagon building. My responsibility was to take the experiment back to the lab, but I wasn't going to throw my two guys under the bus. Moreover, I wanted to see if the experiment would work outside the lab.

"It's too important to trust to Nalbandian," John said.

I knew by now that Vartan Nalbandian was associated with the Katelians, and that both families were part of the local mafia. If my CEO Al Jordan ever found out, he would rip me. I knew the Board would not be happy with what I was about to do.

"All right," I said. I felt like a guy jumping off a building attached to a harness. First the excitement, then you dangled twenty stories over cement. If the harness held.

John and Austin placed the experiment on my lab bench. "That's it? Looks like a high school science project."

Park smiled. "What were you expecting, Dr. Berglin? This is applied physics."

"The receiver is a white box." A white box is a unit with known components, as opposed to a black box where the internal workings are unknown.

"That's right Dr. Berglin," Austin said, handing me a copy of their work, John's paper, and all of their schematics for building the receiver. "Strictly do-it-yourself." He patted the receiver affectionately. It was a metal cube about eighteen inches on each side. Rosen hooked up the receiver to the AC motor and closed the switch. For a few seconds nothing happened. Then, just as in the lab, the rotor turned slowly, then faster and faster, before it settled down.

"How do you know this isn't the Aspden Effect?" I asked.

"Watch," Park said. "The motor will continue to run, powered by Tesla's receiver, forever."

"The receiving device seems intelligent. It approaches the running current from below and above the optimum."

"That's right, Dr. Berglin."

"But how?"

"We don't know, Dr. Berglin. We don't think even Tesla knew. All we know is that this device, at least in this simple bench experiment, works this way every time."

Austin Park confirmed this. "We've tested the receiver a total of 176 times, and have left it running for 36 hours at a time. It appears to have 100% reliability."

I watched, fascinated, for almost an hour as the motor continued to turn. There were no visible effects whatsoever. The motor just kept turning over, propelled by some invisible force.

"It's a perpetual motion machine," Rosen joked.

"Somehow the receiver knows just how much energy to draw from the aether," Park said. "I'm beginning to think that the cosmic energy, as Tesla called it, is intelligent."

"Austin measured no radiation of any kind, including thermal," John added.

"An honest-to-God overunity device!" I was very grateful to these two scientists. "Thank you for risking your careers, gentlemen. I very much appreciate it."

Austin Park spoke. "Now, Dr. Berglin, we need to know what we should do next."

I sighed. "Take the experiment back to Octagon. Continue your research. I'm going to talk to an old friend and I'll get back with you."

After Park and Rosen packed up and left I called Bernie Hartwig, head of the Department of Physics at Carleton University. Bernie used to work for SAIC in McLean, Virginia, just a hop down I-495 or the Dolly Madison from Bethesda, where I worked at Lockheed. SAIC was known for its secretive and classified research with the intelligence community and the Pentagon. That area of the country was the heart of the U.S. intelligence community. I met Bernie at a conference on cybersecurity three years before I started my company. He was fifteen years older than me and even though his personality was a bit secretive, we hit it off immediately. We would occasionally meet and play billiards at his house, sip single malt, and discuss physics and politics. Bernie had advised me on doing business with clients in the intelligence community. I owed part of my company's success to his excellent mentoring. After leaving SAIC he had moved to Midland, a town outside Chicago, to join the faculty at Carleton University. When I left Lockheed he advised me to set up in business there. It had worked out well for both of us. During Berglin Enterprises' first year I had been quite a pest, calling him several times every week. I hadn't talked to him in quite a while.

When Bernie Hartwig got home to his luxurious apartment in the Tavistock riverfront complex, he sat on his recliner in front of the big picture window overlooking the Midland River.

He opened up a bottle of Merlot and slowly drank a few glasses, enjoying the view. He loved the Merlot's full, fruity flavor and its high alcohol content. As he rolled the wine around in his glass, feeling very mellow, his mobile rang. It was Max Berglin.

"How are you Max? It's been a while."

"I'm sorry I haven't called you for so long old friend, but I need your help again."

"Let me guess: you've gotten yourself into hot water with the authorities."

"Even better than that Bernie. Two of my scientists have developed a proven overunity device based on some old material of Nikola Tesla. The problem is that the experiment is tied up at Octagon Research. How do I pry it loose?"

Bernie was baffled.

"You sell security software, Max. What are you doing with research scientists?"

"It's a little hobby of mine. You know about my interest in Tesla and frontier physics."

"Let's not get into *that* again, Max!" The two had often argued about what was going on in the underbelly of the intelligence community, and about the future of technology. Bernie was sometimes amazed at Max's optimism and his naiveté.

"I'm deadly serious, Bernie, and awfully excited. The overunity device is real, I've vetted it. I want to develop the technology."

Bernie was shocked when Max described Park and Rosen's experiment. An actual, working overunity device – a power supply that created more energy than it used. You read about that stuff on kooky inventor and conspiracy theory sites. "Max, you should know better. Even if you have developed an overunity device – forgive me for my skepticism – trust me when I say that you can't pry anything loose from an outfit like Octagon. I know something about that from my work at SAIC."

"I love ya Bernie. Your skepticism was always something I enjoyed, almost as good as beating you at billiards. I always told you it was your only personality defect."

Bernie laughed, but he spoke seriously. "Max, take a word of advice from someone with more experience in the intelligence game. You can't gain access to that technology without running afoul of the law. You undoubtedly signed a contract to that effect."

Bernie heard a sigh. "Yes I did Bernie. But goddammit, something as valuable as this needs to be released to the world. The man who can develop it will be the world's greatest philanthropist, and wealthier than Bill Gates."

"You have a good heart Max, but I'm sorry I can't help you on this one. I have never been able to make you understand that there really is a deep black underbelly to the military-industrial complex. You are free to do anything you like, Max, as long as you didn't infringe on their territory. Exotic technology is their territory."

"We'll agree to disagree on that one, Bernie."

"Max, you have to tell your scientists to return the experiment. And *you* have to disassociate yourself from this. Besides being in violation of intellectual property law, you're involving yourself in waters that are too deep for you."

"I have already done the former. I'm not so sure about the latter."

They seemed to have reached a friendly impasse.

Max changed the subject. "Do you want to play a game of billiards?"

"That might be fun. Just like old times."

"That's great! Prepare to be annihilated."

After they had arranged a date and time, Bernie hung up. His next duty was to inform his shepherd.

Sipping his wine, he made the call and a voice answered. "Hello Bernie."

"Who am I speaking to?" He always asked that as a joke, knowing the answer he would receive.

"You don't have a need to know. What is it?"

Bernie described Max Berglin's experiment with as much detail as he could provide. "It may or may not be genuine. I'll have to see it myself."

"Good work Bernie." The voice on the other end was a little condescending. "Do so and report. Call if you have trouble gaining access to the facility. If there are further instructions you'll be notified."

Bernie sighed and drained his wine glass, feeling contemplative. After a brilliant academic career at the University of Michigan he had been hired at SAIC to do classified research in quantum vacuum fluctuations. Just before he left SAIC he had been approached by a Captain Sam Lineau, an impressive gray-haired man who had spent 25 years as a naval intelligence officer.

Lineau had spoken in a deep bass command voice. "Bernie, I work for an interagency group connected with the Science and Technology Division of the DHS. Our job is to identify potentially dangerous technologies that could, if they got into the wrong hands, be detrimental to the security of the United States."

"All right."

"Occasionally, brilliant experimenters or researchers in the private sector will develop advanced technology. Unfortunately these people will often sell their research to the highest bidder, which may turn out to be a hostile government, a terrorist group, or a criminal organization with goals ranging from profit to political mayhem. We need someone with the relevant knowledge and expertise to help us improve our ability to identify these potential threats. Do you understand Bernie?"

"Yes sir." He was then only 28 years old and the older Lineau had a compelling aura of command and authority. He made Bernie feel special. When he agreed to participate Bernie was read in to a coded program called PHOENIX, which monitors public developments in cutting-edge technology.

Lineau spoke firmly. "You can say nothing about the program to anyone, do you understand Bernie? You cannot either confirm or deny its existence." After he signed documents to that effect he had been offered a research position in the physics department at Carleton. It had turned out to be ideal – as if someone had studied his personality and found the perfect fit for his talents and temperament. Maybe they had.

Bernie reached for the bottle and poured out the last of it into his glass. He was, essentially, a field intelligence officer in addition to his responsibilities as head of the physics department at Carleton University. His duties consisted of staying abreast of the literature (which he would do anyway) and keeping tabs on public and commercial developments in technology. Every so often he investigated a startup or a privately owned lab to check on some new research, just as he would do tomorrow at Octagon.

Three years after coming to Carleton he had been offered the department chair and a handsome apartment in the plush Tavistock development. He accepted gratefully. Over the years, working with PHOENIX, he developed quite a large contact list and was now well-known in the research and entrepreneurial community. To small startups he was the likable and avuncular academic at Carleton University – a man completely uninterested in business – who wasn't too stuffy to get out of his ivory tower and hob-nob with the masses. He was known as an impartial observer who would give free advice about the viability of their inventions and make suggestions about how to develop them (aided anonymously by his handlers in PHOENIX). He mailed weekly reports to a post office box in Chicago and received a check in the mail every month. He was very well rewarded for his labors and felt he was doing his country a service. But he had no idea who it was he reported to or where they were. Was he even working for a government sponsored program? After all, who was Capt. Sam Lineau? After his commitment to PHOENIX he had never seen or heard from the man again.

Bernie drained the last bit of Merlot in his glass and decided not to open another bottle. The damnable part of intelligence work was that secrecy was so strict and the work was so compartmentalized.

Unfortunately he was now officially butting heads with a man he liked and admired. He could only explain himself in a vague, unsatisfying way.

Bernie Sees Park and Rosen

Bernie Hartwig walked into Austin Park's lab at six in the morning on the first of May, an hour before Director Nalbandian arrived in the building. He had called Dr. Park and asked, as a senior and respected scientist, to observe and evaluate the experiment.

"Who informed you that we had anything worth seeing?" Park had asked.

"Max Berglin called me."

"All right then, but the guards will take your phone or camera if you have one, so leave them in your car. If you want to see the experiment you have to get here early."

Bernie watched as the two young scientists set up the experiment and demonstrated Tesla's receiver. His jaw dropped. As the motor whirred on the lab table without the battery, he looked up from the lab bench. "So it's true then."

"Yes," Austin Park replied. Bernie could see that both Park and his assistant were literally brimming over with excitement.

"It's incredible."

Austin Park smiled. "Based directly on Tesla's work."

"Would you mind telling me where the Tesla material came from?" Bernie asked. He had never seen anything in Tesla's published work that remotely resembled this "receiver."

The two scientists looked at each other. "We can't tell you that Dr. Hartwig," Austin replied. "If you want more information you'll have to talk to Dr. Berglin. He's half-owner in our research."

Bernie stepped away from the table and paced around the lab bench. He would have to report back to PHOENIX that Max's experiment was genuine and may have commercial potential. It wasn't such a big leap from driving an AC motor to powering machinery and even homes and factories. He wondered if Max had somehow gotten hold of classified information. It would be just like his impulsive friend.

Bernie said goodbye and thanked the two researchers. On the drive home he thought: If Max continued, his duties would place him directly in the path of his headstrong friend.

I received a phone call from Bernie Hartwig at home, two days after he visited Park and Rosen at the Octagon. "Max, this is Bernie. Can I come over for a private talk?"

I let my old friend in and we walked into my billiards room.

"Just what do you think you're doing Max?"

"I haven't done anything yet."

"You took an experiment that belongs to Octagon Research right under the nose of Director Nalbandian." Bernie had made some inquiries and was now certain that the shadowy Technology Acquisition Consortium, in Chicago, was behind Octagon Research.

"It was returned, Bernie. I just wanted to see the thing in person, which you have also done, outside the lab environment. I don't understand what Nalbandian has to do with it. I'm told he's just a glorified bookkeeper over there."

Bernie laughed. "Vartan Nalbandian is one of the most dangerous men in the city. He's connected to the Katelians."

"OK Bernie. You mean the mafia families here in town."

"That's right Max. I have some friendly advice: Leave to Octagon the things that are Octagon's."

"Goddamit Bernie, I didn't get where I am by playing it safe. I'm a risk taker."

Bernie couldn't mention his involvement with PHOENIX but he had to warn off his friend. "Let me tell you a little story Max. Once upon a time, in Ann Arbor, Michigan, there was a little startup company called McNeil Technologies. Blaise McNeil and two of his friends made a startling discovery in the field of electrodynamics. They developed a prototype – a drone about two feet in diameter – that was capable of inertia-less flight at tremendous speeds. McNeil put lights on it. They were flying it around like one of those remote-controlled model airplanes and people were reporting UFO sightings."

Max laughed out loud. "That's hilarious Bernie. A freakin' UFO! Are you serious?"

Bernie smiled. "I saw it myself Max."

Bernie could see Max was about to ask him how he knew McNeil and why he drove all the way to Ann Arbor, but Max waved his hand in dismissal. "All right Bernie, I won't ask you. You're involved somewhere, correct?"

Bernie nodded and continued. "Long story short, Mr. McNeil was visited by two members of the national security establishment, who offered to buy their technology. McNeil and his two partners refused. They thought they could commercialize their development and make piles of money. But they were frightened. So, to avoid trouble, they moved their operation out of the US, to the West Indies I think. Anyway, three months later all of them were dead in a laboratory explosion."[6]

"Coincidence, Bernie."

I did remember seeing that story in the *Chicago Tribune* a couple years ago. "McNeil was obviously an idiot. More than likely his people didn't know what they were doing."

"Oh, undoubtedly Max. But I want you to be very, very careful, do you understand? I've grown quite fond of you over the years."

I could see that Bernie was genuinely concerned for my safety, and it disturbed me. I had always trusted his judgment; he had never steered me wrong. Moreover, I detected genuine fear in his voice and body language. "All right Bernie. I won't go any further with Park and Rosen. But I will continue their funding."

Hartwig nodded. "That's the smart thing, Max. You're just an investor, perfectly legitimate."

I had never seen Bernie so passionate. He usually spoke softly and thoughtfully. We both sat there for several minutes, thinking about what had been said. I emerged from my reverie to see Bernie staring out the window onto the garden. I tried to lighten the mood. "Let's play a game of billiards. I'll thrash you like I always do."

"Only if I can have some of that imported Glendronach single malt."

When John Rosen and Austin Park found out that Dr. Berglin was not interested in releasing their new technology to the world, Austin felt resigned and John was angry.

"Calm down John. We are already in violation of our contractual arrangements; I'm glad Berglin called us on it. If anyone found out it would be a stain on our careers."

"At least with Berglin we had a chance to give this to the world."

"Berglin could have done nothing, he was just curious. Besides, his company has already forwarded the funding and this discovery isn't his. It belongs to Octagon Research, in case you hadn't remembered."

John was in a rage now. "You know what's going to happen! The overunity device will disappear, along with the other 5,000 sequestered patents over the past seventy years."[7]

"There's nothing we can do, John. Our discovery was never our intellectual property."

"But we could have at least gotten credit, Austin. We could have won Nobel prizes!" John was grasping at straws now in his frustration.

"You can't fight the system. Besides, we can't continue to lie on our daily reports. There's been too much activity lately and Vartan Nalbandian is getting suspicious. He'll be in here any day now."

"Fuck that, Dr. Park."

"John, don't do anything stupid."

Rosen crossed his arms over his chest and said nothing. He was seething.

"Today is Wednesday. At the end of the day Friday, when you submit your weekly report, tell everything. That's an order."

John, obstinate, said nothing.

"John, do you hear me?"

"I hear you."

"Good. Let's keep working on Tesla's portable receiver. I want to see if we can power heavier loads than a little AC motor."

John agreed to this happily enough. As they worked, Austin Park wondered what was going on in his young assistant's head.

Part VIII

Midland

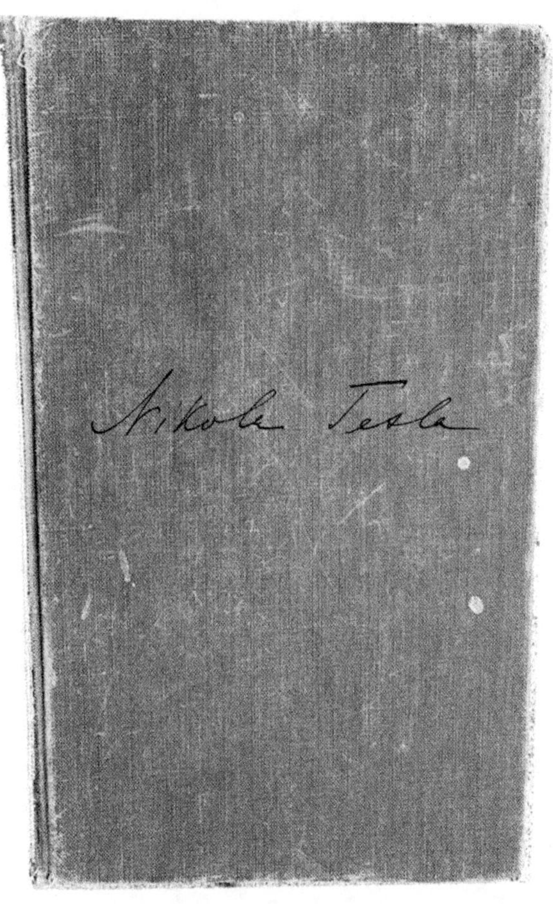

— 16 —

Danielle received a phone call the weekend after her job interview, at the beginning of February. A voice said, "Ms. Menard, this is Wei Lin at Berglin Enterprises. I am happy to inform you that your employment application has been accepted."

"Thank you Mr. Wei. How do we proceed?"

"Report to the personnel department in Room 301 at 8 a.m. Monday morning. You'll have to sign a company contract and then you can begin your training."

That was how her involvement with Berglin Enterprises began. While Zach was in school finishing his engineering degree (and working on cars with the doubtful Larry Potvin) she was learning how to talk to potential clients. She studied the company's products and learned how to sell them to high-profile executives and their staff in simulated sales meetings. She completed her training in only two months.

During that time she and Zach had met for coffee several times. They talked easily, but there was no mention of a marriage date. Was Zach changing, or was it her? He seemed more boyish than ever. She made no mention of it.

In early April she made her first sale to a Boeing rep at a fancy restaurant in Chicago. Afterwards the rep propositioned her. She knew how to handle that from her experience on the streets, and from her training. The client was rebuffed without ruffling any feathers; her handler was impressed. "That was well done, Danielle, and a good sale. The boss will be pleased."

She was in a different world now. She was sometimes flown on the company plane for sales meetings, mostly at smaller hi-tech firms. Her last presentation had been in London for a British firm. At this meeting she knew she was just eye candy but she was learning a lot. She had taken off her jacket and her tattoos had created a sensation. She had to explain each one. After that lucrative meeting she had been able to buy some very nice clothes. She threw away all her old stuff except for one pair of black jeans, a black shirt, and her black boots.

Zach noticed the change in her when she went to see him at his father's house in late May. They hadn't seen each other for several weeks. The semester was over now and he was working full time with Larry Potvin.

Zach was surprised when he saw her. "Danielle, it's almost like you're a different person."

"In what way?"

"You're...more worldly, more sophisticated, you even walk differently. Maybe it's the clothes you wear – I never see you in your jeans anymore."

"I still go downtown on Wednesday nights. The homeless people don't see any change in me." But she knew what he meant. She was looking at the world entirely differently now. No longer was she the poverty-stricken daughter of a hopeless father with no future, but a woman of means.

"You're different," Zach repeated. "How is it that a university educated engineer is working with a small time automobile restorer, while you are traveling the world selling software to big-time corporate executives?"

Danielle shrugged her shoulders. She didn't understand any of it, but Zach seemed dissatisfied. "Do you like the change, Zach?"

He laughed. "I'm not sure."

Just then Mark walked into the room. "Hello Danielle." Zach's father was looking at her as if he had never seen her before. She could almost see his lips form the words "Wow."

"Hello Mr. Ferrell." It seemed funny to refer to Zach's dad as 'Mr. Ferrell.' She thought of him now as Mark, and he seemed different too. Smaller somehow, less important.

"Have you guys set a wedding date yet?" Mark asked.

Zach and Danielle's eyes met quickly. Each saw a startled expression on the other's face. Both laughed simultaneously. Danielle, more experienced in social situations, took the lead. "No we haven't, Mar – Mr. Ferrell," she said. "Have we Zach?"

"Not yet," Zach said with a boyish grin.

"All right, would you like to stay for dinner Danielle?"

"Sure."

They sat down to a plain but wholesome dinner of roast beef, potatoes, and gravy. She and Zach talked like they did in the old days and it was OK. After she said goodbye to Mark and he left the room she kissed Zach, but there was no talk of making love.

In her father's Toyota on the way home Danielle wondered where their lives were going. She saw more of a change in Zach than she did in herself. She used to see Zach as the gregarious leader of a set of brilliant people who were out of her reach. Now she saw him for what he was: just another college student who would probably wind up working at a desk for an engineering company somewhere. He would want to raise a family and take his sons to baseball and football games.

Zach drove back to the rental house feeling like crap. He needed someone to talk to. Preferably a female; preferably the old Danielle. But that was over now.

Zach Meets Jessie

Zach had just walked in the door when his phone rang. It was Jessie.

"I haven't heard from you in a while Jessie. How's it going?"

"I'm kind of at a stuck point. I'm not sure about the direction of my life."

Zach's gloomy mood lightened. "I was thinking the same thing about my life."

"I thought you and Danielle were all set, Zach."

"We were, but during the last few months she's totally changed."

"Really?"

Zach told her about Danielle's new job, how she was flying all over the place and working long hours, how he hardly ever saw her, and how distant she was. "I don't get it Jess. In a few months she's become a different person."

"Maybe she's becoming the person she always was but never had the chance to be."

Zach thought about that. "You may be right Jessie. If so, it's a person I don't know. Maybe all those years living with her useless father suppressed her real personality."

Jessie's purpose for calling was forgotten now. She wanted to ask Zach about Gary, but if Zach was available... "You want to have coffee and talk?"

"Yeah, lets. I can meet you at Sweetwaters at seven for an hour, if that works for you."

Jessie checked her calendar. "I'll see you there, Zach."

When Zach got to Sweetwaters Jessie was already at a table. She didn't waste any time starting the conversation.

"Zach, I have no idea what I'm going to do with my life. That's what college is supposed to be for. Do you?"

Zach thought a moment. "Yeah, I guess I do. I'm going to be an engineer. I like to build things and fix things."

Jessie shook her head impatiently. "No, I'm not talking about that. *Why* are you going to be an engineer, and what's the point?"

"What's gotten into you Jessie?"

Jessie told him about Heather's decision to abandon pharmacology and try for the Foreign Service. "I'm smarter than her but she's reaching higher. It's frustrating because I can't make up my mind."

Zach thought about Danielle and his gloomy mood returned. "I thought I knew where I was going."

Jessie echoed his mood. "Life seems pointless, really. Look at Myra and Wayne. Dad spends all his time at the office taking care of other people's money. What he really wants is social standing – something he has no possible way of getting. Myra teaches science to stupid high school kids who could care less. What she really wants is more people to have spiritual understanding, whatever that is. Both of them admire that scumbag Trevor Clarke. My father even said he wanted to be more like him. How can people think like that? I look at my future and all I see is a blank."

She looked up at the handsome face. "Help, Zach."

Zach saw a new side of Jessie from the frivolous girl he'd known. He thought about his own parents. "Mark and Rachel broke up. When dad told Rachel he was happy as a junior partner, Rachel told him he was a weakling and an underachiever. Now she's shacking up with the firm's VP."

"My point exactly."

"She also said that Mark had made a big mistake supporting Danielle, and that she wasn't good enough for me. The crappy thing, Jessie, is that she may have been right."

They sat silently for several minutes.

"Is happiness or success more important?" Zach asked. "Rachel said that success allowed you to have influence in the world. Mark said that happiness was the end result of *anything* you do. I have no idea which one is right."

"Neither do I."

Jessie took a sip of her latte. "What are you going to do about Danielle?"

"I don't know. I'm just going to let it play out. We weren't going to get married until after I graduated in January."

Jessie smiled sympathetically. "I think it's more on her than on you."

Zach looked at Jessie. She had a pleasant heart-shaped face and a nice smile. She didn't wow people like Danielle but she was comforting.

Jessie gathered her courage. "Do you want a family, Zach? If you think it's impertinent you don't have to answer."

"I've been thinking about that. Yeah, I do, I think. I want to first establish myself in my career, then settle down someplace."

"Do you like Midland or do you want to get out of here?"

"I don't know. Danielle and I were going to leave but now I'm not sure. I want to do what makes me happy, I guess."

"Look at us, we're so indecisive!"

Zach laughed. "That reminds me of a joke. The boss says to the employee, 'Do we have your commitment?' and the guys says 'Yes and no.'"

"That's me. At least you have a goal in life and know how to get it."

Zach thought of something. "Maybe Danielle has a goal too, and maybe she's going for it." He brightened. "That makes me feel better."

"You're a good person, Zach. I'm glad I know you."

Zach smiled back.

Jessie took the last gulp of her latte and looked at her mobile. "This was good Zach. I gotta go – a big paper is due tomorrow."

"Have you decided your major yet?" Jessie and Heather were behind him at Carleton, but she had to commit by the beginning of her senior year.

"Not yet, no." She hung her head.

"Cheer up girl, you'll get it."

"Let's do this every week, OK Zach?"

"Sure."

— 17 —

I was very pleased with the progress of Danielle Menard. She had made several good sales and her performance in London had been superb. That had been a test to see how she would do with one of my more difficult clients. Now I wanted to see if she wanted to step up her game. Doing business with some of my clients in the intelligence and military security area required sales personnel to have security clearances. These customers had government contracts and were my most lucrative (and prickly) clients. I felt that Danielle was tough enough and diplomatic enough to be effective with them. Was she up for it?

I asked Max Jr. to sound her out. My son had graduated the previous semester but wasn't looking for employment. Tara Bolshoi, the receptionist, told me he was hanging around the company a lot, doing I knew not what. I decided to put him to work.

On a warm Tuesday in mid-June Danielle had gotten back from a business trip to New York. She had not been successful and was not in a good mood. She was standing in the lobby at Berglin Enterprises and saw Max Berglin Jr. approaching. She pasted on a smile. "Hello Max."

"Hello Danielle. I'd like to take you out to dinner."

"Have you forgotten that I'm engaged to be married?"

Max Jr. was very smooth. "Not at all Danielle. This is more in the nature of a business dinner."

She didn't feel she could say no to the bosses son. "Very well."

"I'll pick you up at seven."

Max showed up at her door in a limo. "What's this?" she said, her temper rising a little. "A business dinner and you show up in a limousine?"

"Relax Danielle. I thought it might be a treat."

"All right, where are we going?"

"To the restaurant at the downtown Hilton. They have a great chef, I love the way he prepares lobster bisque."

Danielle was learning to appreciate Midland, which had the attributes of a much larger city like Chicago or New York. Carleton University was a draw for some big academic names. A lot of wealthy Chicago executives lived here and commuted. The town had a sophisticated air and society.

Max turned to her as they sat drinking cocktails in the bar. "I lied. I wanted to take you out tonight because you turn me on." He was supposed to have sounded out Danielle for his father, but he didn't feel like it. He should be looking for a job, but he didn't feel like doing that either.

Danielle held out her hand, pointing to her ring. "What's wrong with you Max? I'm engaged to marry your friend Zach."

Max smiled charmingly. "You aren't married yet."

"I didn't think you were this vulgar, Max." He really did have a nice smile. "It won't work. Besides, I don't like you in that way. What will Zach do when he finds out?"

Max leaned forward, trying to look down her front. "He won't find out because we won't tell him."

Danielle slid her barstool backward. "Enough Max. I really do like this drink though. What is it?"

"Raspberry dacquiri. I thought you might enjoy it."

"I do." She looked appreciatively at the tastefully decorated bar and restaurant. "Thanks for the limo and the drink, I really do appreciate it."

"You're welcome."

Danielle drained her cocktail. "Can I have another one?"

"Certainly." He ordered and passed the drink to her.

"Max, what's this all about?"

Max leaned back and looked her over. "You're drop-dead gorgeous Danielle, and I'm really horny. I'm used to getting what I want. I've talked to Zach; I know you two aren't an item anymore."

Danielle was amused. "Do you think you and I are an item?"

He tried his forceful routine. It usually worked with colder types like Danielle. "Hell no Danielle. You're just god-awful beautiful and I want you."

"Well, you can't have me."

Max Jr. looked like a tiger about to pounce. "That just makes me want you even more. The girls I meet are either wallflowers or predators, and they're always after my money."

Danielle wondered whether all rich guys were like this. Some of the clients she met were like Max Jr. "If you have so much money why have you been renting out a crummy student house with five other guys?"

Max grimaced. "Dad wanted me to see how the other half lives. I didn't like it."

"You're a little spoiled, Max." She could see him struggling to contain his anger. He had the look of someone who wasn't used to having his will thwarted.

"You're right I suppose." Max spoke in tones of someone who knows he has to be socially polite. After a few seconds he regained his composure and smiled.

She took another sip of her drink. "This is really good."

"I'm glad you're enjoying it."

The conversation seemed to have reached a dead-end. Danielle finished her cocktail and rose. Max leaned back and looked her over. "You're sure you won't reconsider?"

"Take me home, Max. I think I've had too much to drink."

Max Jr. saw his father over the weekend at home. "Danielle didn't seem interested in an increased role in the company."

"Really?" His father raised his eyebrows questioningly in a self-important way that had always irritated him.

Max Jr. spoke spitefully. "She seems frivolous. If I were in your position I wouldn't trust her loyalty."

"Thank you son. I'll take that under consideration."

Max Jr. knew his father didn't believe him. "Can I have $300?"

His father didn't hesitate. He reached into his wallet and handed over the money.

"There's a job for you in the company if you want it."

"Thank you." Max Jr. was growing to dislike his father more and more.

Danielle Talks to Pierce

When Danielle got home from work on Friday her father was in front of the TV, watching Nova on PBS. She sat down beside him on the couch.

"Dad, tell me about what happened before mom died."

Pierce's face screwed up in anguish. "I'm sorry, daughter, I'm not yet strong enough to face that. I'm stretching myself to the limit recovering from my drinking."

"But dad, why don't you get some help? Uncle Frank said he'd give you the necessary funds."

"Therapy is impossible, Danielle, as you will discover if you get into the intelligence game. Has Max Berglin talked to you yet?"

Danielle wasn't sure what he was talking about, but he was looking closely at her. "Max junior took me out for cocktails a couple nights ago in a limo. I only talk with Max senior when he briefs me before my assignments."

She saw her father nod, as if satisfied with something he wasn't telling her. The implied question of Zach and her impending marriage wasn't mentioned. Both of them seemed to think it was on hold for now.

"Consider carefully before you plunge into the game."

"The game?"

"The intelligence game. You'll find out if you agree to participate, and you can't know what it is until you do. That's the catch." He paused. "Once you're in it is very difficult to get out."

— 18 —

Every quarter, PANA Corp. sent their accounts to PRC Accountants. Wayne DiPietro went over the last audit check and discovered his note. He was curious to see if the pattern of extra expenditures was repeated in the April – June period. When he checked over the ledgers he found the same audit profile: approximately $7,000 of additional expenditure each week for the quarter, with revenue remaining flat. He looked over the ledgers for the past eight quarters. The extra expenditures had only begun at the beginning of this year's first quarter. Was there something amiss? He was required to write his opinion in his Auditors Report, but he would hold off on that for a couple of days until the end of the week on July 7th.

His wife Myra DiPietro, who saw Larry Potvin's wife Jenny socially, told him that Larry had rented a new building for his shop and was buying new equipment. Jenny was a little worried about where the extra money was coming from. Wayne decided to drive over to Ashley Street after work and look in.

Wayne drove by Larry Potvin's shop at 5:45. The garage door was open and he got out of the car, inspecting the outside. The space was significantly bigger than Larry's two-car garage, but nothing grandiose. When he walked inside Larry and Zach Ferrell were moving a body into Larry's paint shop. Wayne decided not to interfere, and let the men work. He looked around the place and saw a new lathe and engine crane as well as three new tool carriers and some other stuff he didn't recognize. He began to mentally add up the approximate cost.

Larry came out of the paint room and said, "May I help you?" Then he recognized Wayne. "Oh, hi Wayne. I didn't know you were into cars."

Larry was a blunt person, so Wayne decided to be blunt. "I'm not, Larry. But I have to be honest with you. I'm auditing the accounts of PANA, where you are the accountant. It's probably nothing, but I noticed an increase in expenditure in the PANA account since the beginning of the year." He nodded his head at the new equipment. "The total amount of increase would about match what you have here."

Larry was furious and afraid at the same time. Who did this jackass think he was, making serious accusations against his character? At the same time he wondered whether Wayne was on to him, the prissy bastard. He decided to be aggressive. "Now listen here, DiPietro, what's your game? I haven't seen you in a year and you waltz in here accusing me of fraud?"

Wayne backed off; Larry's anger seemed genuine. "As I said, it's nothing. It's my responsibility as an auditor to—"

"You're an auditor, Wayne, not a detective," Larry said. "Your job is to examine accounts and issue an opinion." Larry took a step forward. He was smaller and thinner than Wayne, but also an Army vet. "Why don't you stick to your job and stop poking your nose into things that don't concern you."

Wayne looked around one more time at the setup. "All right Larry, have it your way." Without another word he turned and walked out of the shop.

Larry walked back into the paint room, steaming. He didn't feel like working any more today. "Zach, get two coats of primer on that body and you can knock off for the day. I'm going home." Like everything he did, Zach had turned out to be really good with the paint gun.

Zach lifted the mask off. "OK boss."

On the drive home Larry felt a stab of fear in his guts. The scam had worked perfectly for over five months. He had been thinking of going past the six-month time limit. He was up and running, he had almost everything he needed now, and he was getting enough customers to pay the rent and make a profit even though he and Zach were only working part-time. Should he just quit his job at PANA?

It was then he realized that to quit at any time would send the accounting profile back to ground. Why hadn't he thought of that at the beginning? He needed a back door to get out of the scam without anyone tracing him.

That night in his office he racked his brain to think of how to do it but couldn't come up with anything. If he quit his job DiPietro might be able to pin the fraud on him. He would be ruined.

There was only one solution. DiPietro would have to cover for him. If the auditor's report were clean he would be in the clear and no one would be the wiser.

He decided to write a letter to his mysterious benefactor.

In the letter he said

> The six months is almost up, but Wayne DiPietro, an auditor, may be on to me. He said he noticed a change in the accounting profile. A slight increase in expenditure, and he accused me in as many words of embezzling. If you have any bright ideas send them to me. Otherwise I'm going to have to make DiPietro see reason or we are both fucked. I'll wait four days and if I don't hear from you I'm going to deal with this myself.

The next morning before work Larry drove the letter down to the Post Office drop box.

When Trevor Clarke saw the letter on Friday morning, he swore. He didn't trust Potvin; the man was too clumsy. Under no circumstances could he allow any scandal to reach him. Tonight was the opening of the new wing of the Arts Center, and he would be among the dignitaries. He was to meet Bob Justice, the head of the Planning Commission, Judge Roland Massimino, and Craig Ginzburg, a real estate developer, for drinks and a business discussion. A lucrative new riverfront development was being planned; to be even more extravagant than Tavistock. He had not been thinking big enough when he set up his embezzling projects. He was ready to shut them all down if this deal went through.

He wrote in his reply:

> Talk to DiPietro. If he won't cooperate send me another letter immediately.

The mail was clumsy and slow but it was safe.

Larry nodded in satisfaction when he got the letter the following Monday. He would take care of this himself. He would do it today. At 2 p.m. he called Wayne DiPietro after looking up his number in the phone book.

"I'm busy Larry, what do you want?"

"Look Wayne, I don't like the way we left things last Wednesday."

"Neither do I, Larry. But I have to send in my auditor's report by the end of the day on Friday."

"Forget about it Wayne, there's nothing. You are doing a commendable job protecting your client's interests. Your suspicions are groundless."

"Are they Larry? The more I look into this, the more I'm convinced something fishy is going on."

Larry decided to play it nonchalantly. "As you told me on Wednesday, have it your way. But there's nothing to worry about. I've been using my savings to build up my business, that's all." He didn't have much saved, but how could DiPietro know that?

"Nevertheless Larry, I'm going to put in my auditor's report that I think the company is being embezzled. Maybe not by you, but by someone."

"You're determined to do that?" Larry asked.

"Yes. It's going in my report at the end of the day on Friday."

"All right Wayne, but you couldn't be more wrong. Those expenditures are simply routine business matters."

After Wayne hung up Larry drafted another letter. At lunch he dropped it in the mail. As he was driving away from the Post Office he wondered why the instructions were always to submit a handwritten letter. He realized that his handwriting could be traced! The mastermind always sent a computer-printed letter on generic paper. Again, in his excitement about the project he had overlooked something obvious. Whoever was running this scam was smart. Smarter than him, anyway.

Trevor Clarke Plans Big

The Arts Center opening had gone well. After the gala, Trevor circulated at the afterglow party. He had a few drinks and then headed off to a small private conference room. When he arrived the robust Judge Massimino was already there, along with Craig Ginzburg and the steely-eyed Bob Justice of the Planning Commission. Justice was a skinny guy who looked like a marathon runner. Trevor noted with disapproval that he was poorly dressed in blue jeans and a crumpled shirt. Vahan Katelian was seated at the table as well but he was just an observer. His bit would come later, after construction began.

After everyone shook hands, Ginzburg gave a presentation. He was a soft man with a jowly face and a smile like an ambulance-chasing lawyer. The developer pointed to several large glossies of the proposed project framed on large easels for easy viewing. "The exterior and interior designs were done by Delaney and Sons out of Chicago," Ginzburg said.

Everyone loved them, even Katelian. "Beautifully done," the judge said in his loud, blustering voice. "I like the curved surfaces on the exterior buildings."

Massimino was the antithesis of a judge, Trevor thought. Large and bulky, with a voice like a boom box, he was blunt to a fault and spoke to everyone in commanding tones, as if all of his opinions were facts.

Ginzburg looked pleased. "Delaney told me that a riverfront development should have a softer profile. I think he's right."

Trevor loved the interiors. Lots of glass and marble, but elegant designs with high ceilings and plenty of space. After some discussion he took Ginzburg's place at the podium. "All right, let's get down to business." He nodded to Ginzburg. "The developer has come through with designs that are eminently sellable. This project will enhance the profile of the city and the prestige of all who live there. We can market it to investors that way."

Judge Massimino laughed. "Before we all go off into transports," he boomed, "let's think about the rabble opposed to this project." He ticked them off on his fingers. "The mealy-mouthed 'progressives' on the City Council, who will mewl about removing the public park on that land and the homeless shelter on the east side of the property. The environmentalists, who will squeal about building on sensitive marshland used by duckies and birdies. And of course the Tavistock tenants, assisted ably by that bastard Tavistock, who will complain that our project is unnecessary and will interfere with their precious 'view.'"

Vahan Katelian spoke up. "Not to mention the newspapers and the blogs, who will talk about building another play palace for filthy-rich Chicago executives."

Trevor replied to this smoothly and confidently. "That's where I come in gentlemen," he said. He had dressed carefully tonight in a double-breasted dark blue suit, and knew he looked good. His British accent and his charming smile were also on display. "This project is going to be built. The property taxes on this development alone will put over a million dollars each year into the city coffers. That money can of course be used to build more and better homeless shelters and nature parks."

Massimino guffawed; Bob Justice smiled broadly.

Trevor used one of his favorite Americanisms. "Gentlemen, Old Man Tavistock and the Tavistock tenants can go fuck themselves."

Everyone laughed, even Katelian.

"My sentiments exactly," Justice agreed.

"You're good, I'll admit that," the judge said.

Trevor acknowledged the compliment with a slight nod of his head. "I am good, and I know how to deflect opposition and shape opinions." After that everyone was on the same page.

They discussed figures and shares. Bob Justice outlined a plan to get the project approved by the Planning Commission. The judge, a former state representative, would be there to help cajole the City Council and to forestall attempts at an end-run from the state legislature. The environmentalists, the newspapers and bloggers, and any other opposition that popped up were Trevor's problem. He would be the public face of the project. If all went as planned, his shares would amount to close on a million.

At the end of the meeting Trevor summed up. "Gentlemen, let's make some money."

Massimino and Justice went off together for drinks. Trevor hung around and talked with Vahan Katelian for a few minutes. In this town the mafia were Armenian, not Italian American, and Vahan was their spokesman.

"Are you on board?" he asked Vahan.

Vahan shrugged. "We're a long way from construction."

"Certainly. I just don't want your crews to walk off the job like they did at Tavistock."

"That couldn't be helped Mr. Clarke. Our men felt that the developers were ignoring a very reasonable wage increase request."

"Your crews intimidated the entire workforce. One of the workers was killed, which caused bad publicity. We're hoping that doesn't happen again."

Vahan was noncommittal. "Cooperation with the families is essential if a project of this scope is to be successful. Old Man Tavistock learned that the hard way."

Trevor saw Vahan looking piercingly at him, measuring him, calculating whether he was up to the job. The Armenian shrugged. "There's money in it for us even if the project isn't completed." Vahan left the room.

Trevor shrugged off the veiled threat. There was so much money in this project that no one could afford to be recalcitrant.

He was feeling good as he walked past the security guard on his way out. He stopped to talk to the man for a few minutes, asking about his family. There were a few people remaining, talking casually in the hallway. Trevor stopped to chat briefly with all of them, using his charm and his friendly smile. As he did so he was vaguely aware that his self-esteem depended entirely on how others regarded him.

When he opened the front door he saw Elmo Tackett waiting for him outside in the parking lot. There remained the now tedious but very important matter of Wayne DiPietro and his auditor's report. Because he was the public face of the new development it was even more vital to be rid of this affair as quickly as possible. His reputation must remain spotless.

Trevor followed Elmo to where his car was parked at the far end of the lot, next to the grass. A little wood butted up to the parking lot and Elmo stood in the trees while he pretended to take a stroll in the fresh air.

"What is it?" Elmo asked.

"Wayne DiPietro, do you know him?"

"I know of him. He works for PRC Auditors in the PRC Bank building."

"That's him. There is a matter of an auditor's report. One of my, er, projects, has run into a bit of a glitch. DiPietro needs to submit a clean auditor's report on the PANA Corporation. This situation must be handled by Thursday evening, because the report goes out Friday."

"I know nothing of auditor's reports," Elmo said. "However I have an associate who does. Another has access to the company's mail. The report could be diverted, altered, and sent with no one knowing."

Trevor explained the matter clearly to Elmo. "Remember that each of these reports must be hand-signed by the auditor. You'd have to involve a handwriting expert."

"Oh, that's no problem," the little man said in his flat, cold voice. Trevor shuddered involuntarily.

"What happens if the report cannot be altered?" Elmo asked.

Trevor spoke without thinking. "Disposal, if necessary."

That was Elmo's terminology. He knew that if that happened he had forever crossed the line. A thrill of dangerous, electric excitement ran through his body. He loved the risk; he could taste it. Wayne DiPietro was just nothing and would not be missed, even by his family.

"Mr. Clarke, that would cost you."

"I know Elmo. I have worked out a lucrative deal with Massimino and Ginzburg. You could name your price."

Through the trees Elmo Tackett pinned Trevor Clarke with his gaze. He could feel the force of the little man's attention.

"Mr. Clarke, I don't need to remind you that I know everything about you."

"I understand perfectly, Elmo. Proceed."

Driving home, he wondered about Elmo Tackett. That little shit had threatened him! Was Elmo a dangerous man? He considered the idea but rejected it. A useful tool that must be carefully handled like a loaded gun perhaps, but under his control. Trevor knew he had massively overreacted to an auditor's report, but he was terrified of losing his elevated social standing. If that was lost Ginzburg and the rest would throw him out and the bank would find another president. However, Elmo was on the job; he had never failed yet. Disposal would be unnecessary. By the time he got home he had dismissed his fears about Wayne DiPietro's report and was thinking pleasurably about the deal he had negotiated. A *lot* of money would flow through the Ginzburg development. A big real estate project created jobs and was good for local business. Even better, all of the participants were highly motivated after the huge success of the Tavistock development. He planned on living the good life in one of those luxurious suites.

Convinced that his life was on the right track, Trevor Clarke slept soundly.

Danielle Makes a Decision

"Hi Zach." Danielle and Zach were at Sweetwaters six weeks after her "date" with Max Jr. Zach noticed she greeted him without enthusiasm.

"I haven't seen you in a while," Zach replied. She looked great as usual in a tailored business suit, and had somehow assumed an unconscious air of assurance and confidence. "You've really changed."

Danielle's smile was a little melancholy. "Yes, Zach, I have." She told him about her recent work with Berglin Enterprises and the people she had met.

Zach was impressed. "You seem to have gravitated off to another world."

"You might say that, Zach. It's so exciting!" She told him about some of the high-profile clients she had made presentations to, and what she had learned about the world of intelligence and high-tech. "The firm wants to give me a security classification Zach, and I have to decide whether I want it. It would bring me in deeper into the classified world. I would be seeing very high-profile clients." Suddenly she knew what her father was trying to tell her during their conversation several days ago, about getting in the intelligence game and not being able to get out.

Zach knew she would do it, and said so.

"It's so fascinating, Zach, and a little lonely, but I wouldn't give it up for the world."

Zach understood immediately. Danielle looked like a woman who had made up her mind. "So it's off then," he said. They didn't really have a relationship anymore; he hadn't seen her since she'd come to his father's house. It had been infatuation, not love.

Danielle leaned forward. "You wouldn't consider joining us Zach, would you?"

Zach thought it over. "Not up my alley, Danielle. I think the world you are describing is for loners like yourself and your father. I'm too extroverted to spend my life in hotels. I like more normal people."

"It's just what I was thinking." She reached into her pocket and gave him his ring. "You'd better keep this Zach. I don't think it will be too long before some other woman gloms on to you."

Zach took the ring, formally accepting their mutual decision. "Should we make an announcement?"

"You do it. People will think it was my fault, and it mostly is."

They sat for a couple of minutes talking. Finally Danielle got up to leave. Zach stood up and held out his hand. "I'll miss you Danielle."

"I'll miss you too, Zach." She let go of his hand and walked out.

Zach watched her black heels tap the linoleum floor of the coffee shop. She opened the door and left without looking back.

When Zach went home to the rented house that night he felt sad and depressed. Now that his connection to Danielle was officially broken, he realized how much she meant to him. He understood the value of that deep level of intimacy he used to have with her. He felt very frustrated with himself. His old buddy Mike Parsons had been right about him when he said he didn't know a lot about people. He understood now that a relationship would only prosper if you worked at it.

Tiki Aatoa Comes to Carleton

When Tiki Aatoa walked into her engineering class she created an immediate sensation. All eyes turned toward her as she took a seat at the back of the room.

'My first mistake,' she thought. 'I must tone down my aura.' Afterward she was surrounded by her classmates, who were curious about the new arrival. She had taken a Samoan surname because she most resembled that racial grouping. She was not used to thinking in those terms.

As she introduced herself to the group she recognized her targets Zach Ferrell and Max Berglin Jr. Both were on terms with the primary Danielle Menard. The primary was unfortunately not a student, and was on the verge of being sucked in to the Network. It was her job to protect the primary until she attained awareness.

Tiki read Ferrell and Berglin. Berglin was increasing his interaction with the primary, whereas Ferrell's connection was growing weaker. This was not good.

She chatted with each for a minute. Today was just for introductions. At the end of their conversations she read sadness in Ferrell and interest in her from Berglin, with a sexual component. Her instructions were to avoid sex at all costs. But these two young men intrigued her; Ferrell because of his physical beauty and Berglin because of his connection to the attenuated resonances.

"Let me get a picture," Max was saying as she stood next to Zach.

"Now you take a pic of me and Tiki," Max said. Zach snapped the image. "I'll send it to you later," Zach said. "Gotta go."

After that the group broke up and Tiki walked to her domicile about a half mile from campus.

Zach met Jessie for coffee that evening.

"What's the latest with you and Danielle?" she asked.

Zach was still feeling depressed. "I'm glad you asked. She told me that Max Berglin Sr. had promoted her and that she would be working seven days a week for the foreseeable future, and would be out of town a lot. We agreed that it was over. She gave me back her ring."

Jessie took a deep breath, but decided not to pry. "I'm sorry, Zach."

"We just connected so deeply, Jessie. I don't know how it all went wrong."

Jessie didn't like the dreamy look in his eyes. She wanted to hug him and tell him that *she* went wrong, not him. She smiled sympathetically.

"Damn! I forgot to send Max that pic." He opened his mobile and sent the image of Tiki and Max standing next to each other.

"Are you interested in that girl?" Jessie asked.

"Her? I just met her a couple of hours ago."

"Hasn't bothered you before."

"What's all this Jessie? Are you exploring your options already?"

She wanted to hit him for being so blunt (and so right). With Zach you had to be forthright. "Yes. I'm interested in you, Zach, always have been."

Zach's sunny personality couldn't stay down for very long. He studied her critically. "I could do a lot worse."

"Zach! A lot *worse*?"

"I like your spirit," Zach said, soothing her ruffled plumage. "I wouldn't want my kids to be wallflowers."

"Sorry Zach, I didn't mean to get angry."

Zach smiled. This girl was a good sounding board; she knew how to listen. He was feeling better. "That's OK."

They chatted comfortably for a while after that.

Rachel Talks to Don Halloran

Rachel Ferrell and Don Halloran were lying in bed after making love. Rachel twirled the hair on his chest with her finger. "Don, did you send that recommendation to the Board?"

"Not yet."

Rachel sat up on her left side. "Please, Don. There's only two days left before you leave for Platchon and Berger." Don admired her breasts and put a hand out. It was slapped away.

"My my, such a temper!" he joked.

"It's not a joking matter."

"I'll do it tomorrow," he said.

"Promise?"

"I promise."

"Then let's go again," she said, pulling him down to her.

The next night Don decided to tell Rachel that he had decided to stay with his marriage. His wife had threatened to divorce him and when she did, he realized that Rachel Ferrell meant nothing to him except a good time in bed. He'd take her to Escoffier, and then, over dessert, break her off gently.

During a very expensive dinner Rachel was in an expansive mood, making her even more attractive to him. When dessert came he was seriously doubting his decision and had almost decided to say nothing.

"Don, I don't think this relationship is a healthy one."

He almost choked over his aperitif. "What?"

"All we do is sleep together and natter about people at the firm. I need more than that."

She was staring at him shrewdly, looking for a reaction. For God's sake. *She* was going to break *him* off! He put his glass down a little too hard on the table, spilling a little on his sleeve.

"So that's how it is. You just used me to get my recommendation for your presidential bid."

Rachel was all business. "That's right Don. You're a real looker, but a little shallow. I'm looking for a man with more substance."

Never in his life had a woman talked to him like this. Women came to him and *he* decided when it was over. Rachel was smiling openly now, with just a hint of contempt. "You thought to use me Don, but it can work the other way around as well."

Don shuddered inwardly. This woman was as ambitious as she was cold. Suddenly he felt great relief about leaving the firm tomorrow. If Rachel was going to be president he wouldn't want to work there anyway. "I wonder how long it will be before you ruin it?" he said.

He had the satisfaction of seeing her face pinch and her eyes narrow, but Rachel quickly regained her composure. "I wonder," she said, taking a sip of her drink. "Now that you're going we're off to a good start, aren't we?"

Don's face flamed scarlet and he rose quickly from the table. He wanted to throw the rest of his drink into her face but instead gulped it down. As he walked past their table he saw her mocking smile.

Rachel Takes Over

Don Halloran was as good as his word, having recommended to the board of Burgoine Rosenberg and Phillips that Rachel Ferrell was the best candidate for president of the firm. Of course he had written that before their dinner two nights ago, as she had intended. First Mark and now Don: when their masks had been stripped off she had found them sadly wanting. She was determined to show her firm that a woman could be a superior leader.

The previous day she had been voted in as a senior partner. The firm would now be known as Burgoine Rosenberg Phillips and Ferrell. She should feel proud, but she was done with that name. She would have to change it back to DuPlessis after her divorce was formalized. She had stated her preference that for now, the firm's name should remain the same.

On her first day as president she walked into the Creative division and confronted her husband. She spoke with thinly disguised contempt. "Mark, your work is and has been unsatisfactory. You can either submit your resignation and leave in two weeks, or I'll fire you right here."

Rachel had been looking forward to this for a long time. Mark and his coworkers should have reacted in outrage or protest. Instead, all four of them simply stared at her with the same contempt she felt for her husband. Will Flowers, the copy editor, was the first to react. "So she did it then."

"Unbelievable," Sheila Brunson remarked. Sheila was the IT specialist.

Rich Locaturro, the graphics designer, took his pen and placed it upright on his erect middle finger, flipping her off. "The beautiful Rachel Ferrell must have finally achieved her dream."

Rachel smiled her cold smile. "If you don't like it here, Rich, you can go with him. We'll be looking for some new blood in the Creative department."

Locaturro said nothing, turning his chair away from her and toward his monitor. He had three kids and an expensive mortgage and he needed this job.

Rachel saw that Mark was leaning back in his chair, smiling. "You may do as you please, Rachel."

"Oh really. Going down without a fight again Mark?"

Mark Ferrell's eyes flared for a second before he calmed. "When one treats people with benevolence, justice, and righteousness, and reposes confidence in them, the army will be united in mind and all will be happy to serve their leaders. That's Sun-tzu."

Sheila smiled and Rachel laughed. "Oh Mark, that's perfect. Quoting a long-dead and irrelevant man who lived two millennia ago. It reflects your outdated attitude perfectly. I could as easily say that nice guys finish last."

Mark admitted silently that she had a point, but he loved the quote. "You are brilliant, Rachel, and you will either succeed famously or implode quickly. I'm not sure which one I want."

Rachel was silent.

"I have already accepted a position at Platchon and Berger. I'll be starting there in six months."

"So you'll be joining the equally inept Don Halloran. Oh Mark, you are so predictable. When the going gets tough, you get going."

Rachel said this with such confidence and authority that Mark felt a twinge of doubt, knowing that it was clearly a reference to his previous New York job.

"It is well that you remembered the non-compete clause in your contract. I am going to hold you to that."

"Certainly. Now, if you'll excuse me, I'd like to remove my things and say goodbye to my staff."

Rachel turned on her heel without a word and strode off, satisfied.

Sheila turned to Will. "Wow."

Mark grinned. "You guys are in for it now. Keep in touch and let me know how it goes."

Mark entered the parking lot after going through security with his box of office memorabilia. As he drove off he wondered where Rachel was sleeping these days.

Elmo Calls Trevor

Elmo Tackett reported to Trevor Clarke on the Friday after Wayne DiPietro's report had been sent. "Mr. Clarke, I'm afraid we have failed. The auditor report went to PANA unaltered."

Trevor almost lost it. He took several deep breaths in an attempt to calm down. "Report."

"Wayne DiPietro did not place the auditor's report in the PRC mail slot, as is usual in such matters. He hand-delivered it to Larry Potvin's audit supervisor at PANA."

"Do you have any idea why the fool took so much trouble over such a trivial matter?"

"No sir. But an associate, who has had the subject under observation, suspects that it is a simple case of anger against Larry Potvin. Apparently the two had words at Potvin's auto shop."

Trevor's anger died. He realized that he had almost certainly overestimated the danger of discovery. To think he had even thought of "disposing" a non-entity like Wayne DiPietro. Even if Larry Potvin was caught there was nothing to link him to the scheme. He had, as the Americans would say, bigger fish to fry now. "Very well Elmo, you've done a good job as usual. Let's drop the matter altogether. Payment in the usual manner."

The Monday after Wayne DiPietro hand-delivered his audit report, Hassan Bashari found it on his desk when he walked in, among a stack of other business. Bashari was PANA's regional audit manager and was responsible for the integrity of financial audits at all sixteen stores in the state. The report had a note attached to it: "Hand Delivered." He called the mailroom and asked about the note. He was told that the auditor had walked into the building and tried to place the report directly on his desk. "He said he was from PRC Auditors over in the PRC Building downtown."

When Bashari eventually read the auditor's report he wasn't convinced. The fact that the auditor had tried to hand-deliver the report was very unusual, and showed that the auditor may have had a personal agenda. He was inclined to let sleeping dogs lie. However, he would definitely keep an eye on Larry Potvin.

Zach Talks to Mark

"The engagement's off, dad." Zach was at the house for Sunday dinner. He could tell his father was lonely and made it a point to drop by once a week.

"But I thought you had such a strong connection?"

"We did. Apparently it was all on my side and not on hers."

Father and son discussed Zach's situation for a while. "The worst part about it is that mom might have been right about her." As soon as he said it Zach knew it wasn't true.

"No son, I don't believe that."

Zach realized that his father's personality was an honest and open one, and that he had inherited it. "You're right dad. It just didn't work out, that's all."

"Isn't she working for Berglin now?"

"Yeah, and that's the problem. Apparently he has her doing classified work. She can't talk about anything."

"Well, I don't understand how an unemployed street kid with tattoos could suddenly be working in the intelligence area."

"I can't either, except maybe it has something to do with her father."

"Of course. If I recall, Pierce was doing classified research. Maybe he put in a good word for her."

"Danielle said something about that but I can't remember what it was. Something about her father not being able to talk about his work even to his wife or family."

"You're best out of it then son. What are your plans? Haven't you been seeing Jessie Dipietro?"

"Only casually." Zach took out his phone and showed Mark the picture of Tiki standing next to Max Jr. "What do you think of her?"

"She's ... unusual. Very bright and sunny."

"Yes, that's what I thought. Even Jessie noticed it."

"Are you interested?"

"Who wouldn't be? I only met her a few days ago. She might be a real bitch."

Mark studied the image. "It's hard to tell anything much from a photograph, but I don't think so son. She does look intriguing though."

"What are you doing for women these days dad?"

Mark shuddered. "Let's get the divorce over with first, son."

"Will Rachel give you a hard time?"

"She couldn't wait to sign the divorce papers. She told me to stay in the house, so I will. We'll split the profits whenever we sell it."

"What are you going to do with yourself?"

"I'm only 47 Zach. But I have to admit Rachel was right about my tepid interest in the advertising and marketing business. I'm tired of it. I have an offer for a position at Platchon and Berger to start in six months, but I'm now thinking of going in with my friend Larry Potvin."

Zach saw his father's face brighten. "You know, that's not such a bad idea."

"I've always been good with my hands."

Zach agreed. "It's probably where I got my facility with engineering."

Mark started to laugh like a man who has discovered an unexpected opportunity. "I'll talk to Larry tomorrow. Even though the house is almost paid for, I still need to make some money."

Zach thought it might be weird to work with his father, but he didn't say anything. It would only be until he had to go back to school in September.

Mike Parsons Comes Back to Town

On the tenth of July, just before he went into the shop, Zach's mobile rang. "Hey Zach, how are you?"

"Mike! How have you been, buddy?"

"I'm doing well on the tour, and I've even made some money. I'm back in town until the Belmont Open in Chicago."

"You have two weeks, that's great."

"Zach, I wanted to run something by you."

"Sure, go ahead."

"Do you remember our little talk last winter? Did you get anything out of it?"

Zach turned back his memory. "Actually I did. You pissed me off but I thought I made some progress." Apparently not enough to keep Danielle, he thought silently.

"That's what I wanted to talk to you about. On the tour I've had a chance to talk with a lot of the guys, and some of the women. People seem to come up to me and tell me their problems. I seem to have good results helping them. I'm thinking of becoming a counselor full time."

Zach was doubtful. "You'd have to pass exams and get licensed. Are you sure you're up for that?"

Mike expected doubt, and he held his temper. "I'm not as dumb as you think, Zach."

"I didn't say you were dumb, I asked if you were up for it."

"Yeah, I am. The Bulldog says he would be able to pay for any classes I have to take."

"That's great! But you'd probably have to study for several years to get licensed. I think you need a Masters degree to be a licensed counselor."

"I might go for it."

Zach was impressed, and said so.

"I've been studying up on what I'd have to do. It's a long haul, I know. So far, so good."

"Do you already have patients?"

Mike laughed. "No, no patients. I know I could get into trouble doing that. I call myself a life coach. The requirements for that aren't strict in this state. I have everyone I talk to sign a legal waiver, absolving me of any blame for perceived mental problems after my sessions with them. I wanted to ask you if you thought I'd be any good at it."

"Well, you helped me. Who are your clients?"

"Guys on the tour. Mostly sports psychology, you know, how do I get mentally ready, stuff like that. Some of the girlfriends of a couple of the guys on tour, relationship stuff. I like the relationship counseling best."

"You don't hear it from your competitors? Like, you're getting all my secrets from my girlfriend?"

"Nope, none of that. I'm seen as a guy who smooths the waters."

"Good job Mikey boy!"

"OK then. Hey, do you want to play this weekend at Deerfield? I'll kick your ass now. I'm a lot better than I used to be."

That weekend Mike showed up at the Deerfield parking lot with a nascent van Dyke. He was wearing nicer clothes. Zach noticed right away that he had a different air about him. "Fuck me Mike, what's all this?" Zach said, waving his arm toward his friend in the manner of a stage magician who has just transformed an ugly toad into a handsome prince.

"I have a new look, buddy. I can see now why women didn't like me. I was a total loser."

"You got a girlfriend now?"

"I'm friends with a couple of the players on the women's tour. We occasionally go out to dinner and talk, but nothing serious."

"Hopefully not one of your clients," Zach joked.

Mike frowned as they walked up to the first tee. "No, I learned that the hard way."

This peroration caused Zach to stop. "You know, that reminds me of Jessie."

"Are you seeing Jessie now?"

"Sort of, on the rebound. It didn't work out with Danielle."

"Pity. That girl is something special. Definitely not a wallflower or an enabler."

Zach caught his friend's subtle reference to wallflowers and Jessie. The old Mike would have been too dull to do that. "What's your opinion of Jessie?"

"No you don't Zach! I haven't seen Jessie since last winter. I've learned never to talk about people I know to other people I know. One of them might turn out to be a client."

"Yes, but you implied something when you said wallflowers and enablers. I want to know what you meant."

Mike studied Zach for a moment. "OK, here it is. I think Jessie is a nice girl, but she doesn't know where she's going. If you get with her, you will always be the leader and she will always be the follower."

Zach was impressed with this analysis. "That's what I was thinking."

Mike and Zach teed off. Mike's shot went just as far as Zach's, right in the middle of the fairway. "You are better," Zach said. He was still thinking about what Mike said about Jessie as they walked down the fairway. "You know, Jessie has a friend, Heather. She's not as smart as Jessie but I like her. She wants to be a diplomat and work for the State Department. If she doesn't make it she'll go into journalism."

"Yeah, I remember Heather. Kinda like Jessie, an edge to her. Sounds like she has a plan."

"She does."

"It's good to have a plan in life Zach," Mike hinted. "I found that out last winter. Now I have a plan and a goal and it really feels good."

Normally talkative, Zach was contemplative the entire round. Mike didn't say anything. He had learned that by talking to his clients: When someone was thinking about something, let them get through it before you opened your grille. He'd made a lot of progress with people by doing just that. A word here, a question there, a hint here, and you got people thinking. Then you let them figure it out themselves.

They finished the round and walked toward the parking lot.

"I want you to meet Heather and Jessie," Zach said. "We'll go out to dinner together. My treat."

Mike was hesitant. "They don't like me."

"They didn't like the old you. You got a new you."

Mike agreed reluctantly. "I'll let you set it up."

That night Zach called Jessie. "Next Friday when we meet for coffee, bring Heather along."

"Why?" Jessie said, suspicious. "Are your eyes roving again?"

"Of course they are. Heather is a good-looking woman."

"I can never tell if you're serious or teasing."

"Jessie, Mike Parsons is back in town. Now wait, before you hang up. Mike has changed, he's totally different."

"He's a creep. I don't like him and Heather doesn't either."

"You don't like the old Mike. This is the new Mike."

"Why all this interest in Mike Parsons? And anyway, when a creep changes he just changes into a different kind of creep."

"Not this time," Zach said. "It will be good practice for Heather."

"Practice?"

"You said she wanted to be a diplomat, didn't you?"

"What does that have to do with anything?"

"She can pretend that Mike is a visiting dignitary from a disgusting foreign country. Or she can pretend that Mike is an alien life form that the earth has to establish diplomatic relations with."

Despite her irritation Jessie laughed. "God Zach, you do have a sense of humor."

"So are we on?"

"I'll talk to Heather about it. See you Friday."

Jessie immediately called her friend. "Zach wants you to come to coffee with us this Friday."

"What's the occasion? Is a zeppelin going to land in the middle of downtown?"

"He's bringing Mike Parsons and he wants you to meet him."

"Mike Parsons? Eeew, no thanks."

"Zach said to pretend he's an alien you have to establish diplomatic relations with. It'll be good practice."

Heather smiled. "I might be able to do that. But no blind date crap, OK?"

"OK. See you Friday."

On Friday Jessie and Heather got to the coffee shop fifteen minutes early. "I want to control the ground and make them come to us," Heather said. She felt like a soldier about to fight a battle.

"You're making a big deal out of nothing. We'll just have coffee and leave."

To her surprise, Heather found herself getting more and more uneasy as the time passed. "What's wrong with me? I'm as nervous as a little girl on her first date."

Zach and his friend walked in.

Heather said, "Who's that with Zach?"

Jessie looked closer. "That's Mike Parsons!"

"No, can't be. Parsons looks like a turd that grew two arms, two legs, and a head."

When the two men arrived at their table, Mike executed a small bow. "Hi Jessie, hi Heather."

Zach took a seat and observed the two women. Heather's jaw was slack, and Jessie was staring. Instead of his usual dirty tennies, worn out jeans and unbuttoned shirt, Mike had come in wearing casual brown loafers, a nice pair of pants, and a dress shirt. He stood silently in back of his chair, telling the ladies he would not intrude unless invited.

Heather remembered her diplomatic mission. "Have a seat, Mike, pleased to see you again," she choked out.

"Hi Mike," Jessie mumbled.

Mike sat down. "Tell the ladies what you've been up to," Zach said.

Heather was prepared to hear the usual stuttering banalities.

"I've been playing disk golf professionally," Mike said. "I have a life coaching business on the side."

This was too much for Heather. "I'm sorry Mike. I'll believe the disk golf bit, but if you're a life coach I'm a snail hibernating for the winter."

Mike knew Jessie and Heather would see the old Mike. Before he came in he had decided to treat them like clients. He nodded and smiled. "It's all true." Mike studied Heather. She was petite and blond, with large brown eyes and full lips. Sensuous, he thought, with a little shiver of excitement.

Jessie and Heather exchanged glances that said, "Who is this guy?"

"You're sure you're not an alien temporarily inhabiting a human body to study us," Heather quipped.

Zach was beginning to get irritated. "That's not necessary Heather." Jessie had to stifle a laugh.

"It's OK, buddy," Mike said, picking up a menu off the table. "I'm hungry. What are you going to have?"

The talk then centered around food for a while.

Heather studied Mike and she liked what she saw. "Mike, I've never seen a person change so much. Did you get a personality transplant?" She was testing him, trying to see how far she could go.

Mike's eyes flashed for a split second. "No, I got some self-confidence."

"Tell me about this life coaching business," Heather said.

Mike told her a little bit about his life and his clients. "Your clients are *women*?" Jessie asked.

"Some of them." Suddenly, he didn't care anymore what the old gang in Midland thought of him. He was glad he left and he wasn't coming back.

Heather felt him withdraw. "I'm sorry Mike, we really have been pretty rude."

He looked her straight in the eye. "Yes, you have."

Heather was impressed. The Mike Parsons she knew would have said something stupid and left.

Just then the waiter came with their food, and conversation stopped for a few minutes.

During the meal Heather caught Mike glancing over at her from time to time. Was he interested in her? It was a strange thought.

In the back of Mike's mind he concluded that if Heather had no interest in him she wouldn't bother to tease him. He liked her acerbic sense of humor. She was probably someone who didn't accept convention and he liked that. He had been that guy until he got a life.

After dessert Mike and Zach left. The two women sat over coffee.

"I think he likes you," Jessie said. They both knew she meant Mike Parsons.

"Yeah. It's not anywhere near as creepy as I would have thought."

Zach is Confused

Zach talked with Jessie the following week at the coffee shop. He was feeling depressed gain. "Even Mike Parsons has a goal. Your friend Heather, who I always thought was a balsa wood boat in the middle of a hurricane, has got her life together." He looked up at Jessie. "Everybody except us."

"Even Danielle," Jessie said. "Talk about a rudderless ship. She's totally turned her life around."

Zach slapped his palm on his knee, startling Jessie. "Larry Potvin is up to something illegal I think."

"Really?"

"Yeah. He's been acting strange and he has a lot of money now. He had words with your father Wayne a while ago, who basically accused him of embezzling from PANA."

"Dad never told me about that."

"I've been thinking. Do I want to be another cog in a corporate machine? At least Larry is doing something he loves. And he's taking a big risk to do it. So is Danielle, and Heather."

Jessie stared at him. This wasn't the Zach she knew.

"You know Jessie, I understand Danielle a lot better now. She was faced with hard life choices when she was sixteen. She got through it and found something she's good at, whatever it is she's doing for Berglin. Same with Mike and Larry Potvin. I'm just skating through life but not really living."

"I am too."

"Maybe we should be like Bonnie and Clyde."

Jessie wasn't sure he was playing around. "Oh, you mean those two bank robbers a hundred years ago."

"Yeah. They were living large; they went out in a trail of glory."

"And a lot of gore."

"Yeah." Zach fiddled with his empty coffee cup. She watched him rotate the cup back and forth by the handle for a minute.

"Fuck this, Jessie. I'm going to have to do some serious thinking. My last semester starts in a couple weeks. I gotta get my act together. I don't want to end up like Mark and Rachel."

Jessie thought about her own parents. "Neither do I."

They left it at that.

Mark Goes In with Larry

Mark Ferrell walked into Larry Potvin's shop on a hot August Friday, the weekend before Zach was to go back to Carleton for his final semester. The place looked disorganized. Mark could see into a windowed office where papers were scattered all over the desk. The in-basket was overflowing. Three cars on the shop floor were in various states of disassembly. To his right a sleek auto body, painted red, was in the paint shop. He saw his son buffing the car to a smooth, shiny finish. As he looked around the shop pleasant memories of working on his own car surged within him. His hands began itching to grab a tool and get to work. Mark understood that he was ready for a life change. This was the kind of honest work he should be doing now; no more Mad Men for him. It looked like Larry could use some help, at least on the business end of things.

"Dad!" Zach said, putting the buffer on a side table. "How are you?"

"Never better, son." Mark walked over to the paint shop. "What are you working on?"

"'86 Mustang, fuel-injected 5.0 HO V-8, eek-4. Doesn't she look sweet?"

"It does. What's an eek-4?"

"Sorry dad. Fourth-generation electronic engine controller. In its day the very best around. Controls sequential port fuel injection, manages and adjusts the EGR, the fuel curve, the ignition timing, and idle speed."

"You talk like an engineer!"

Mark was feeling inordinately cheerful seeing his son gaining expertise. Zach had always been a kid who learned very quickly. He felt like a proud father.

"Remember when you used to work on our cars?"

"I do. It's why I'm here. Where is Larry?"

Zach pointed to the cluttered office. "In there tearing his hair."

"Thanks Zach. Work! Work!" he joked, raising his hands in the air like a conductor.

Mark walked into the office. The windows were open and the fans were blowing. Larry looked harassed.

Larry looked up; his face showed relief. "So you've decided to help me instead of going to your new advertising job?"

"I have." The two had talked several times during the past three weeks. Mark's divorce had gone through and he was looking for work. Larry's business had stalled in an overabundance of paperwork and he was behind in his jobs.

Larry rose from his desk like a man throwing off a ball and chain. "You're a godsend Mark. I can't work a job and a business at the same time."

"All right then. I'll clean up this paperwork so you can work in the shop. We also need a marketing plan; that's right up my alley."

Mark hadn't felt this cheerful in years and it showed. Larry felt it; his mood shifted from overworked entrepreneur to motivated automobile restorer.

"We've already worked out the details," Mark said. "I signed the agreement you sent over and I'm ready to go."

Larry smiled for the first time in months. "Then let's get to work." He sailed out of the office, whistling, and went over to work on a partially disassembled engine. Mark would handle the paperwork, implement a marketing plan, and work in the shop when necessary. If Mark was half as good as his son, he could clean up his backlog in six weeks. Larry had dreams of being the best automobile restorer in the state, but first he had to wind up his affairs at PANA.

At the end of the day Mark Ferrell felt like a new man, despite the uncomfortable heat.

Before Mark went home he called Don Halloran and explained his change of plans.

The day after Rachel dumped Don, Don had called Mark to apologize and explain what had happened. Mark had related the story of his firing and both men blew off some steam. After that Don had surprisingly offered to recommend him to Platchon and Berger.

"Don't do it because you feel guilty," Mark said. "Our marriage was already on the rocks."

"Thanks for that, Mark, I appreciate that. But honestly, I can't be too mad at Rachel. Because of her I cleaned everything up with my wife and realized that she was the best thing in my life. When Berger heard my story he laughed. He said, 'Don, if you can work with that woman you can work with anyone.' When I told him more about my sordid history with Rachel he just smiled. 'I wouldn't trust anyone who could get along with Rachel Ferrell for an extended period of time.' No offense Mark."

"None taken. Apparently my ex-wife has ruffled a lot of feathers."

"You might say that."

Now Mark explained why he wasn't following through on Don's generous offer. He told Don about his partnership with Larry and his lack of enthusiasm for advertising. Don was sympathetic. "This business can grind you down."

"Thanks for understanding Don."

"Are you going to the Arts Center gala this Saturday?" Don asked. "I have an extra ticket if you'd like to come along with my wife and me."

"I'd like that Don, thanks." He used to go out with Rachel to social events out of a sense of duty to the company. Now he would do it for pleasure.

Mark Ferrell walked out the door of the auto shop – his auto shop – after saying goodbye to Zach and Larry. It's amazing how beneficial a new life decision can be, he thought.

Zach, Gary Cronin, Dharwat Singh, Barry Therion, and Kenny Wang all went back to their rented house for their last semester at the beginning of September.

On Monday night Zach told them about his breakup with Danielle, and received their condolences. "You blew it Zach," Kenny Wang said. Everyone else was sympathetic.

On Tuesday night Max Jr. showed up. "What are you doing here Max?" Zach asked, knowing how much he disliked the ratty campus house.

"I'm out of money and I don't want to go home. Kenny said I could come to dinner."

Zach couldn't understand Max. He knew Max Sr. had offered him a job at Berglin Enterprises but Max had done nothing since he graduated. He seemed sullen and uncommunicative. Zach noticed that Max was barely present as they talked after dinner.

"Do you have a thing going with Danielle?" Zach asked him. For some reason he still thought of her as his.

Max was unhelpful. "I asked her out."

"What is Danielle doing now?" Barry Therion asked.

Zach stifled his irritation. Although Danielle had blamed herself for their breakup he had contributed almost nothing to the relationship. "She's working in the classified area now isn't she Max? For your father?"

Max laughed cynically. "Oh, you don't know the half of it."

The guys were curious and demanded to know what the beautiful Menard girl was up to.

"Even if I knew I couldn't tell you," Max said. He was still bitter that his father had made him live in this decrepit rental house and not at home. He felt a grudge against Danielle's earlier treatment of him. "She's getting in way over her head."

No matter how hard the guys pressed, Max would say nothing more. "It's classified, bozos! I don't know anything about that part of the company."

Later that night, in bed, Zach wondered about Danielle. She was involved in something big and making good money. He thought about his pathetic part-time work with Larry Potvin and wished he could be with her right now, doing something really exciting. But he had dismissed her offer without much consideration. It was something his mother might have done. Zach admitted to himself that there was more of Rachel in him than he would like.

Rachel Meets Trevor Clarke

Rachel saw her husband and Don Halloran and his wife at the opening of Kazkav, a new restaurant downtown. The owner was a noted supporter of the arts and a gala fundraiser was to be held afterward at the Arts Center. It was the sort of event at which Trevor Clarke appeared, and she was glad to see him here. She would, of course, avoid those two pimples seated together at a table against the wall.

As president of her firm she was determined to present the very best image. This was a perfect opportunity to meet potential clients, almost all of whom were men. She wore her best dress, made of dark blue silk with a low silver-laced bodice and a small but revealing slit down the right side.

Rachel enjoyed her meal at Kazkav and talked up the firm to her tablemates. She didn't know anyone here; that would have to be quickly remedied. She noticed that the men accepted her but the women not so much. Well, men run the world mostly, and she would talk to Trevor Clarke at the fundraiser.

When Rachel arrived at the Arts Center she went to the Abuisson Room. She hung back at the entrance, looking for Trevor Clarke. When she spotted him with a drink in his hand she waited until he had turned toward the entrance and walked slowly toward him. Rachel could see that Trevor's companion was Paula Trevellian, whose husband owned Trevellian Imports, the favorite dealer in town for those who owned BMW automobiles.

Paula was eying her with disfavor. Rachel ignored the older woman and walked right up to Trevor, whose eyes had shifted to her. She introduced herself.

"Mr. Clarke? I'm Rachel DuPlessis, president of Burgoine Rosenberg and Phillips."

Trevor turned back to Paula Trevellian and in the most urbane and flattering manner, asked if he could be excused to talk to Rachel. Trevor made it clear in his air and manner that he would have preferred to continue his chat with her, but that social imperatives forced him to greet the (rather vulgar) newcomer. Paula smiled. "Of course," she said, and walked away.

"My, my, Mr. Trevor Clarke, that was well done indeed," Rachel said. She tossed her head, showing clearly her interest in him. Her right leg was slightly apart from her left and she positioned herself so that he could, if he desired, get a good look at her. Rachel noted with approval as Trevor stepped back with an appreciative smile, looking her over from head to toe. This man was comfortable with women, and probably with power as well.

"I am very glad to meet you Rachel," Trevor said, sipping his cocktail. He was looking at her right in the eyes.

Rachel noticed the slight emphasis on the word very.

"I was wondering if you would care to leave a little early and have a chat," Trevor said. "I know a cozy little bistro on Fifth Ave that stays open until two in the morning."

"I'd like that," Rachel replied.

"Very well then. I'm emceeing the fundraiser, which will go until about eleven. After that I'll come for you."

Rachel liked the words, "I'll come for you." It made her feel that he was reaching for her, that she was something valuable. She nodded and turned away, pleased with herself. She would go out with Trevor tonight, talk up the firm, and if he wanted her... she would be willing.

That night Trevor Clarke introduced Rachel DuPlessis to the joys of cocaine, and the best sex she ever had.

Part IX

Tesla

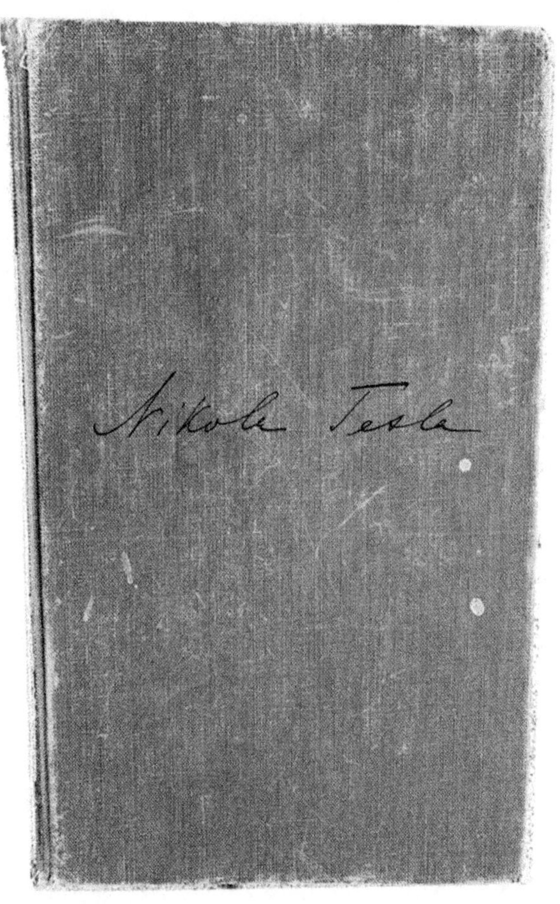

— 19 —

On a Friday afternoon in mid-August John Rosen wrote his usual weekly report. He was getting more and more frustrated.

"Dammit Austin. Are we just going to let this discovery molder away in our lab?"

Austin was calm. "We've discussed this ad nauseum John." He pointed to the Pierce-Arrow receiver with it's little AC motor they had demonstrated to Max Berglin. It was still on the wooden board John had used to transport the experiment to Dr. Berglin's home in Palmer Park last spring. "Dr. Berglin apparently wasn't interested in the little Pierce-Arrow receiver, so we have to hit him harder." He pointed to a cube about three feet on each side, made of half-inch black plastic. "According to Tesla this larger receiver is capable of powering a home or even a factory. Let's perfect that and then blow his socks off."

"When we demonstrated it to Dr. Berglin in April we both felt his enthusiasm. I felt we were very close to releasing the new technology to the world. Someone must have gotten to him."

Austin was fatalistic. "Maybe you're right John, but it doesn't matter. It was probably Dr. Hartwig, the physics department chair at Carleton. He came a couple days after that to see the experiment."

"And right after that Dr. Berglin backed off!"

"There's nothing we can do John, we're just employees. Dr. Berglin has continued our funding so he must still be interested."

"Yes, but every time you've called him he's been uncommunicative."

"That's why we have to finish the larger receiver. I want to have something so impressive that no one can ignore it."

"But it's taking too long. We might never get this thing working!"

It had been a bone of contention between them since April. "We're working, we're getting paid to do cutting-edge research. Have patience John. Eventually we'll have something that will blow people away."

"Eventually! Maybe we will Austin, and maybe we won't." He pointed to the little Pierce-Arrow receiver sitting on its original platform. "That one works. Anyone with an IQ over 100 knows how important this experiment is."

Austin sighed at his temperamental assistant. "Come on John. You've developed your Rosen Aether Theory to explain how this thing works. We're both headed for Nobel Prizes. Let's keep plugging away at the big receiver. We're making progress."

As was usual when they argued, John finally cooled off and went back to work. At the end of the day when Austin was about to go home he saw a look of stubborn petulance on John's face. He recognized that look. "Don't do anything stupid, John."

"Oh, I wouldn't dream of it boss."

Austin was too tired to argue, and left.

John walked over to their little bench experiment and closed the switch. The receiver "thought" for a couple of seconds and the rotor began to turn slowly. It sped up rapidly, then it backed off and began to spin like a purring kitten. It had happened exactly the same way hundreds of times. They had proven Tesla's idea about cosmic energy. Within the fabric of space there was clean, "free" energy that could be tapped into. John gazed at the spinning motor almost in awe. If this little Pierce-Arrow receiver could turn a rotor, the same principles could be used to power a house, or a factory, or maybe even a city. The concepts Tesla used in the experimental receiver were the same as for the larger one. They had already done enough! Besides, the ever-suspicious Vahan Katelian had been on him to do something profitable for months. He was tired of telling him that it was a big leap from an experiment to a product. So be it then. Berglin was too stubborn and Vahan was too irritating. He'd show both of them, and the world too.

John put a plastic cover over the small receiver platform and waited for the guard shift change. He brazenly walked out of the building through the back door and managed to stuff it into his trunk. Then he drove off to his apartment. He would have to return the experiment by Sunday evening or it might be missed.

That night he called Juwan Jackson, his old high school chum. Juwan was now an anchor at Channel 5 News. The handsome and photogenic Jackson had been his buddy in physics and math classes at Midland East. Juwan had always been interested in politics and media. He was the youngest anchor ever at the station.

"Juwan, it's John Rosen."

"John Rosen! What hole did you come out of? Haven't heard from you in years."

"Yeah, well you'll want to hear about this." John explained the overunity device and why it was important.

"Free energy?" Juwan laughed. "That's a load of crap John."

"OK Juwan, I'll call 7 and 3 then. Carmella Johnson over at 7 will send somebody down, I'm sure of that." He was about to hang up.

"Wait John! You're serious about this?"

"Yes Juwan. You know me, I never joke about science."

There was silence on the other end for a few moments. "All right John, for an old friend I'll send a reporter and a cameraman down there. But this better not be bullshit."

John gave him the address. "Make it quick Juwan. This is, ah, sensitive stuff and I'm violating my contract to even show this to you."

Juwan's mood changed instantly. "Now you're talking John. A little controversy never hurt anything."

John quickly unpacked the experiment and unfolded his long work table, placing it in the middle of his smallish living room. Not ideal but the experiment was simple. Only the receiver was complicated and these media guys wouldn't understand it anyway. He could demonstrate it right here.

Several minutes later, as John waited nervously, there was a knock on the door. John jumped, thinking it might be Old Man Nalbandian. That guy scared him. John looked through the peephole and saw a middle-aged, washed-out blonde woman and a cameraman standing behind her. John opened the door, disappointed that Juwan had not come himself.

The woman was bored. "I'm Tina Brooks from Channel 5. This is Pete Hurlovitch. Let's get this over with."

John was irritated. "Do you know anything about science?"

"Science? Are you kidding? I'm at the City desk."

When Tina saw the layout she was aghast. "Is this it? A box and a motor?" She turned to go.

"Wait a minute Tina," the cameraman said. "I think I have an idea what's going to happen here."

"You do?" John said.

"Well, I think so. There's no battery in the circuit, no power source. If this is an overunity device then the circuit should power itself without the battery."

John was amazed at his perspicacity. "That's exactly right, uh, I forgot your name —"

"Pete. I'm a camera buff. I know a little bit about electronics."

"All right then, watch this." John flipped the switch and after a few moments the motor began to turn.

Tina snorted derisively. "That's all you have? A spinning motor?"

John saw that Pete's reaction was much different. "I don't see any wires into the box. Where is the energy to drive the motor coming from?"

"We're tapping into what Nikola Tesla called the cosmic energy."

"Tesla?" Tina interrupted. "Even I know about him. He was that genius inventor." She looked at the spinning motor. "I don't get it. What's so special about a spinning electric motor?"

Pete explained. "Quantum mechanics says that in every cubic centimeter of space there's a tremendous amount of energy. These guys have found a way to tap into that power source." He pointed to the circuit. "You see, there's no battery hooked up. It's like a magic carpet – it gets energy from some invisible source." He looked up at John. "That's right isn't it?"

"Close enough for government work." John looked at Tina and pointed his finger in the air. He'd try his junky theory out on this reporter. "Every point in space is surrounded by tremendous energy vectors that are perfectly in balance. It looks like space is completely empty, a vacuum of nothingness. But that's an illusion. Space is filled with so much energy we would never need another coal fired electricity generator, or gasoline to power our cars, or nuclear power that generates nuclear waste." John pointed to the experiment with it's little turning motor. "If we can develop this concept we could solve the climate problem, the pollution problem, and the resource depletion problem."

Tina got it. "So this is a really big story then, isn't it?"

John glommed on to the "big story" angle. He would need all the publicity he could get! "That's right, Ms. Brooks. And you would have broken, literally, the story of the millenium."

Tina looked at Pete. "All right, let's get going and film this."

At the end of a relaxing Sunday evening Bernie Hartwig was sitting on his couch watching the ten o'clock news.

"There was an interesting event on the scientific front today, wasn't there Tina?" Juwan Jackson said. A headline flashed on the screen that read, LOCAL SCIENTISTS MAKE ENERGY BREAKTHROUGH.

"Yes Juwan, there was."

Bernie felt his stomach tightening. Tina Brooks, in subdued tones, talked about Park and Rosen's overunity device while he almost had a heart attack. Tina Brooks said, "The new technology has as yet no commercial application." However, the spot faithfully detailed the experiment and its potential ramifications. Bernie couldn't believe that the piece had gotten past the station president and their news director. The story ended with Tina Brooks jokingly saying to Juwan Jackson, "Midland Edison watch out. Soon all of us may be able to power our own homes for free."

Bernie knew he was going to hear from his shepherd in PHOENIX about this.

The Technology Acquisition Consortium

Lt. Colonel James Stapleton (ret) was furious. He had just finished reading his briefing papers and reviewing last evening's Channel 5 broadcast. It was a total fiasco. He turned his chair and gazed out from his third floor office to a small parking lot, beyond which was an electrified, barbed wire fence with a guard post. He was the Network's Chief Technical Security Officer, responsible for the six state area of Illinois, Minnesota, Wisconsin, Michigan, Ohio, and Indiana. TAC was a part of that network; a loose collection of patriots working in high-tech, defense, and intelligence companies outside the normal channels of the government, the commercial sector, and the traditional military. The Network's mission was simple: to protect the people of the United States from the weaponization of new technology. It was his job to put out brushfires like the one that had developed in Midland.

Stapleton reached for his speakerphone. "Lieutenant Spieth, please come in to my office." The lieutenant, a recent Air Force Academy graduate and an expert in frontier physics, entered. Spieth was of medium height, with thinning blond hair and a face that was too narrow for good looks. "Lieutenant, what's going on in Midland, Illinois?"

He had done nothing after his call from Byrnes several months ago. His contact, Vartan Nalbandian, had assured him that his research project at Octagon was going nowhere. Now this!

"Our man at Octagon Research says that a working overunity experiment was stolen by one of their scientists."

"When did this happen?"

"Just yesterday sir," Spieth replied.

"Why has there been nothing about this in my briefs?"

Lieutenant Spieth shuffled his feet nervously. "I have just been informed myself an hour ago, sir. Developments have accelerated far beyond our intelligence."

"Have you verified that the experiment is genuine?"

"Yes sir. Dr. Bernie Hartwig, a field intelligence officer, has seen and verified the setup. It's real, sir, and was apparently stolen by a junior researcher at Octagon Research."

Stapleton was appalled. "Get Nalbandian to retrieve the experiment at once."

Stapleton thought rapidly for a moment. Thousands of people in Midland had already heard the news broadcast, but the experiment itself was trivial. This incident could easily be debunked if handled properly.

"We'll set up a debate between Hartwig and the two scientists. He's supposed to be a hot-shot debater, isn't he?"

"Yes sir. Former captain of the Harvard debate team."

"Who's the president of Channel 5 down there?"

"Geoffrey Challoner, sir. Married, two school-aged children, no military service, journalism major."

"See to it lieutenant. I'll call Challoner and set it up, you handle the details. I'll tell him it's a matter of national security and that the station can hype it any way they want."

Spieth nodded. "Should bring in more viewers and it'll be good publicity for the station."

Stapleton thumbed through his briefing papers. "Who is this Max Berglin?"

"Used to work for Lockheed. Owns a company that sells security software to other companies, some of them in the intelligence sector. Has a security clearance. Per our latest intelligence, not a threat to Network security."

Stapleton looked up grimly.

"Keep an eye on that asshole. I've got a bad feeling about him."

"Yes sir."

The older man regarded his assistant. Spieth was a nerd, but brilliant and trustworthy. After seven years in this job he needed someone to talk to. He knew he should call Byrnes right away but decided to give the lieutenant a bone. Spieth was eager for his trust and had earned it.

"At ease, lieutenant. Have a seat."

Spieth looked gratefully at him and sat down. "Thank you sir."

"As you know I served four tours in Iraq. But after 25 years of military service I got disillusioned with the war and civilian interference with the military."

Spieth nodded and said nothing, encouraging him to continue.

"I consider myself a patriot in the best sense; someone who believes firmly in the United States of America and America's role in combating those who would destroy it. Especially after 9/11. I left the military after the al Maliki regime took over in Iraq, do you remember that?"

The lieutenant spoke with distaste. "Yes sir. Maliki and his Dawa party always had close ties to Iran. At least that bastard Saddam Hussein helped us to contain the Iranians."

"That's right lieutenant. After years of war Iraq was battered but the people were still ruled by a corrupt government. I saw the crooked private contractors come in with sweetheart contracts to 'rebuild' the country's infrastructure and steal most of the money. I saw my men killed by insurgents in Fallujah, hiding behind citizens walking the streets. After billions of dollars spent, another mysterious insurgent group then invaded the country. The Iraqi government then called upon Iran to defend the Iraqi city of Ramadi. It was a total fucking joke, a waste of good men and resources, and I couldn't take it anymore. I retired and joined the private sector.

"I found my way here, to a super-secret and unacknowledged program where I could do some good. I saw how phony the war really was. The real power, lieutenant, lies in a technology so advanced it is the stuff of science fiction. At Nellis AFB, out in the Nevada desert, I personally saw the new, fuel-less aircraft that fly independently of the gravitational field."

Spieth looked eager. "You've actually seen them sir?"

"I have, lieutenant. They make every single airplane and fighter plane in the world obsolete. They make war as we fight it now pointless. For the past sixty years, in the special access programs, the technology developed by those two scientists in Midland has been advanced to Star Wars levels. The Network, and not the government thank God, is the home of these unacknowledged programs.

"Lieutenant, the new technology has to be protected because if it ever gets into the hands of America's enemies...it is unthinkable. I have no sympathy for the civilian US presidents, and other busybodies, who have tried to get their hands on it. To release any part of it to the world's public governments would also make it available to terrorists and fucknuggets all over the globe, who would be able to attack America with impunity."

"Yes sir!"

"It would literally spell doom for the United States. The secret programs are unacknowledged for the very best of reasons: the protection of every man, woman, and child in America. Do you understand Lieutenant Spieth?"

"Yes sir. And thank you sir."

Spieth left the room. Stapleton felt better after unburdening himself, although he was astute enough to understand that his explanation to the lieutenant was mere justification. A part of him saw how releasing the hidden technology could revitalize the country's economy and infrastructure. But the dangers outweighed the benefits. There were too many lunatics out there. The country was much better off with patriots holding the keys, the dangerous technology locked safely within.

Sighing, Stapleton put on his headset and called Byrnes, explaining the situation and his solution.

"The local station is eager for viewers. Park and Rosen want to publicize their invention. I'll get Hartwig on them. He'll debunk those two and completely defuse the situation."

"All right Stapleton. But if this blows up I want you to get a team together," Byrnes ordered.

Stapleton was appalled. "Killing civilians is never a good idea, Byrnes."

"Then handle it! I will take care of the fool who allowed this story to go forward."

Swearing roundly, Stapleton left the White Room and grabbed his mobile phone. These fucking things were primitive stuff compared to the headsets. He personally called Dr. Bernie Hartwig. Normally he let Speith handle this operative but the situation was too sensitive. "Dr. Hartwig, your instructions are to handle this situation using standard debunking procedures."

"Who is this?"

Stapleton moved the phone away from his ear, irritated. Hartwig always asked the same question. He gave the standard response: "You don't have a need to know." He heard a sigh on the other end. Hartwig was a dependable operative, recruited by Sam Lienau, a man who was almost as passionate about their work as he was.

"A courier will come to your office at the university at 9 a.m. tomorrow with instructions. Make sure you do a good job on this one. I've already been ordered to assemble a team and you know what that means."

Hartwig gulped. "All right."

Stapleton hung up. Hartwig's reaction reminded him of when he was read in to Black Shield, the code word for TAC's umbrella special access projects. Somebody walked him into a small room guarded by two armed, stone-faced Marines. It was the first time he had met Zbigniew Byrnes, who stood with one hand on his cane and the other wrapped around a weapon. After swearing his oath Byrnes raised his weapon and pointed it at his chest. The two Marines stepped to the side and pointed their weapons at his head. "If you ever dare to violate your oath, colonel, you know what awaits you," Byrnes had said. That was the way it worked. He was in all the way and there was no turning back.

Director Nalbandian happened to be watching Channel 5 the night of the Tina Brooks story, and was coldly enraged. He personally called Austin Park and John Rosen, firing them both. He demanded that John return all items he had stolen from the building.

John Rosen immediately called Max Berglin, explaining the situation.

"Can you duplicate the experiment?" Max asked John.

"Yes."

"Then get your asses in here right now and get to work. Both of you are on the payroll as of now."

At his apartment John took detailed photographs of their work, re-covered the experiment, and drove over to the Octagon building. He was met at the front gate by an armed guard, who recognized him immediately. "Get out of the vehicle," the guard said.

John exited his beat up Corolla and opened the trunk. "Everything is here. Take it."

"No sir. I will escort you while you return to the lab whatever you stole."

John spent the next ten minutes afraid for his life as he carried the box into the lab, with the guard's weapon pointed at his back. When he was done the guard demanded his phone.

"You can't have it!"

"Shut the fuck up and give me your fuckin' phone."

John gulped and dug into his pocket. The guard grabbed the phone and thumbed through the photographs. "Both you and Dr. Park are persona non grata, do you understand?"

"I understand."

The guard crushed the phone with his boot. "Get the hell out of here."

— 20 —

Bernie Hartwig received his instructions the next morning, hand-delivered by a courier. It was to be a public debate; he was to wait for a call from Channel 5. He knew that Park and Rosen's work was genuine and that he would have to lie. It galled him. However, the story on the evening news had excited a lot of interest in this university town, where over ninety percent of the permanent residents had a college diploma. Bernie was a conservative who believed that the release of this exotic technology would cause chaos. It was one of the reasons he continued to do his work with PHOENIX.

After he hung up he received a call from Tina Brooks, a local reporter. She challenged him to appear at a public debate about the new invention, scheduled for the following evening at 6 p.m. "You will be appearing right after the six o'clock news. The program will be moderated by Juwan Jackson, the Channel 5 anchor." Brooks explained that the two scientists were eager to explain their new invention and that he was to be the devil's advocate.

Bernie laughed to himself. The local reporter's voice was eager and excited; he could tell she thought this could be her big break. He was a skilled conversationalist and public speaker and had often presented at scientific conferences and on national media. He knew he could ruin the two young scientists and he would, even though a part of him was disgusted.

He shoved that part to the side and decided to enjoy himself as much as he could.

On the evening of the debate, John and Austin were nervous.

"Why are we doing this again?" Park asked his assistant.

"Because Dr. Berglin wants us to, boss. Besides, we're on the cusp of a discovery that could change the world. People have to know about it."

Austin gazed at his youthful colleague and wondered what had happened to his own idealism. He had a feeling that this debate would turn into a media circus.

"If only the TV station would have allowed us to show the experiment instead of having this stupid debate," John said.

"The public wouldn't have understood its importance and would have reacted like Tina Brooks did. Be glad for the publicity."

Bernie Hartwig was supremely confident.

Max Berglin Sr. had told Danielle to watch the debate and observe. "Watch how Hartwig operates and the keywords he uses. The guy is not only brilliant, but a real media pro."

Danielle flipped on the TV and watched it with her father in their little TV room.

"Welcome to the debate, ladies and gentlemen!" Juwan Jackson said in excited tones. "Presented commercial free as a public service by Channel 5 and ABC News."

A small stage had been set up, with the good-looking Jackson standing at a podium in front of three chairs. "As you probably know, two local researchers have claimed that it is possible to utilize 'free energy.' They claim to have made a substantial breakthrough that could eventually replace fossil fuels, eliminate pollution, and make everyone energy independent."

John Rosen and Austin Park, sitting nervously in their chairs, looked at each other. They had never said that. Jackson continued. "Their names are Dr. Austin Park and his assistant Dr. John Rosen, seated on my left. To my right is Dr. Bernard Hartwig, noted physicist and head of the Department of Physics at Carleton University. Gentlemen, the time limit for answering questions is three minutes. If your responses are longer than that I will have to cut you off. The debate will last for thirty minutes. Without further ado, let's get started."

Bernie sat in his chair in his best suit, looking suave and comfortable. He glanced over at Park and Rosen and almost laughed. His opponents had no idea what was coming.

"Dr. Park, will you please briefly describe what you did," the moderator said.

"Uh, uh, sure," Park stuttered. "We, uh, were able to, uh, show that it is possible to extract energy from the underlying fabric of space, using some research of the great Nikola Tesla back in 1942."

"1942?" Bernie smoothly interrupted, in his opening gambit. "Surely, something that important would have been released to the public a long time ago."

"Not at all!" John Rosen said. "The industrialists of the day hated Tesla and made sure all of his research was suppressed." As soon as he said it he knew he had goofed. Park looked over at him like a parent about to whack his pet dog that had just torn the curtains.

"Was it really?" Bernie said. It was amazing what cameras and an audience will do to your cognitive abilities. "Are you saying there was a conspiracy to withhold this valuable information from the public?"

Austin Park knew they were trapped. "Uh, no, of course not. We just used some of that information to develop our own process. And we demonstrated this concept in front of you, sir, and you verified it!" Park crowed.

"Did I?" Bernie said. "Ladies and gentlemen, I did indeed go to the laboratory of Dr. Austin Park to observe this experiment." He looked directly at Park. "It was an amateurish setup, and all you did was turn an electric motor." On the TV screen Tina Brooks' film of the experiment was shown. A few people in the audience snickered. Dr. Hartwig laughed and saw Tina Brooks in the audience. "Ms. Brooks! You saw this 'free energy' device in person. What did you think?"

Tina Brooks was very happy. She couldn't have cared less about this stupid debate, but she was getting credit at the station for bringing in more local viewers to the station. "When I saw it I told these two doofuses it looked like a child's toy."

Bernie laughed. "We already know how to make a motor spin, Dr. Park. Just plug it in to your electrical outlet."

The audience laughed.

And so it went. Bernie hardly remembered what happened after that. He implied that both Rosen and Park were impulsive radicals and that their experiment was nothing more than a discredited "perpetual motion machine." In his concluding statement he said that Fleischman and Pons had also been convinced that their cold fusion experiment had worked before it had been proven to be a fraud. He looked sympathetically at his two uncomfortable opponents and spoke like a respected teacher lecturing a couple of brilliant but obstreperous students. "I am sure that both Dr. Park and Dr. Rosen mean well, and they are good people. However, legitimate scientific research has been ongoing in this area for decades." He turned to the audience and smiled. "Rest assured, ladies and gentlemen, that when a real breakthrough occurs the scientific community will be most eager to publicize and develop it for commercial use." He then rose smoothly from his seat, shook hands with Jackson and circulated among the audience, smiling and answering questions. The two inventors gathered their notes and hastily left the studio.

Afterward Bernie was upset about how he had discredited the valid work of two fellow scientists. But he was exhilarated with his performance in the debate. He still had not lost his touch. He hadn't even needed to tell the audience that Rosen had stolen the device and that both men had been fired from their jobs. That would come out later, discrediting them even further.

When it was over Danielle turned to her father, who had sat silently with her watching the debate. The house was a mess; contractors were all over the place making repairs. "He's good," was all Pierce would say about it afterward.

She wanted to ask him about mom again but she could see he wasn't ready. They sat there in silence, listening to a commercial. Danielle realized that although her job was satisfying and fun, she was lonely. Max Jr. had made his intentions very clear but he wasn't her type. There were times she wished she had married Zach and lived a boring, normal life.

After the debate Vahan Katelian had words with Vartan Nalbandian. "How did John Rosen get away with stealing our research?"

"I don't know, but something will have to be done about those two scientists."

Vahan nodded. "Park is no problem, he's easily intimidated. You handle that. I'll take care of Rosen."

Vahan Katelian confronted his old friend later that night at his apartment. He was impeccably dressed, as usual. "John, I'm disappointed in you."

"What do you mean?"

"That little device you built is our intellectual property, and you stole it."

"So you *are* the other venture capitalist with Berglin!"

"Yes John. And you walked off with our stuff."

John had never heard Vahan talk to him in this tone. His face was expressionless; John felt like an entry in Vahan's ledger sheet.

"We have great hopes for the eventual commercial success of this discovery."

"And I just made sure it got publicized to the whole city. Vahan, I — "

He was interrupted. "John, don't fuck with me again, I'm warning you." Vahan was steely-eyed.

"Understood. I got fired anyway."

"Yes I know. I suggest you stick with science and avoid any more, ah, impulsive behavior."

After that he left without saying goodbye. John was glad he didn't have to tell him about being hired by Berglin, but he'd find out anyway.

The next morning Vahan Katelian realized that greater forces than even he was aware of were at work. Just after the Octagon building opened, two unmarked black sedans and a van arrived at the building's entry gate. Six armed men got out of the cars. They blew past the security guards, silenced Vartan Nalbandian, and entered Park and Rosen's former lab. The unidentified men took the experiment, every single piece of lab equipment, and all of the experimental notes, disks, and computers.

In the *Midland Courier* the next day, the following item appeared.

> Channel 5, Midland's ABC affiliate, announced today the tragic death of their program director, Geoffrey Challoner. Challoner was on his way home from work when a drunken driver ran a red light on Main and Liberty, crashing into Challoner's car. The driver is listed in stable condition. Mr. Challoner, who leaves behind a wife and two children, was killed instantly.

When Lt. Col. James Stapleton (ret) at the Technology Acquisition Consortium saw that article, a chill ran down his spine.

Part X

Midland

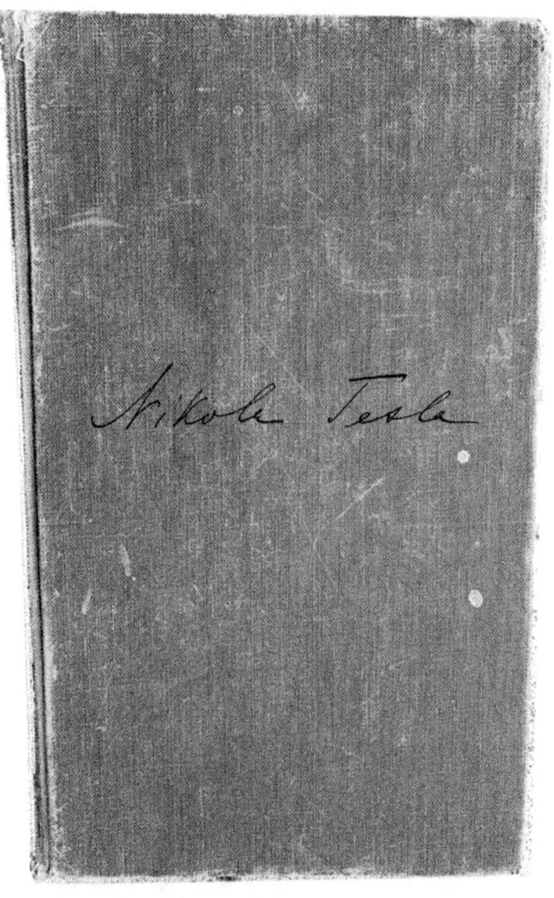

— 21 —

Whenever she was in town Danielle still volunteered her services to the homeless. At ten she would appear on the corner of Second and Monroe, next to the dumpster and the rusted barrel, with two large grocery bags full of food. Her income now enabled her to take everyone who was there to the Fleetwood Diner a block away on First. When she walked out of the diner at midnight she spotted Elmo Tackett on the corner of Monroe, directly on her way home.

"Would you walk with me?" she asked Jamelle, who still showed up occasionally when he couldn't find work.

"Sure Danielle."

As they walked side-by-side past Elmo she saw his eyes on her. As Elmo was about to step toward her a woman, who seemed to appear out of nowhere, stepped between Jamelle and Elmo. The girl was petite and blonde and had a ponytail. Danielle couldn't tell whether she was sixteen or thirty-six. Danielle could have sworn that a golden-white light surrounded her, but it could have been the glare from the street lamp. Elmo looked at the woman in front of him and his face contorted in fear. He stepped back as if he'd run into a brick wall. "Who ... who are you?"

"Hello Elmo, I'm Tiki."

Danielle looked from one to the other. There was something primeval in this confrontation, as if the devil and the angels were testing each other's strength through their human avatars.

Tiki smiled. "I don't want you associating with Danielle, Elmo."

Elmo took another step back and appeared to compose himself. "Get lost Tiki, or whatever your name is. I'll talk to whomever I wish."

Tiki stepped forward calmly and Elmo took another step backward along the sidewalk. Tiki seemed very soft, almost compassionate, in contrast to Elmo's hardness. Elmo took another step backward; then he reached inside his pants and pulled out a knife. Tiki took another step forward and the knife fell from Elmo's hand, clattering to the cement.

"Don't come around here again Tiki. I'll know how to deal with you next time." Elmo was deflating like a balloon that was losing its air.

"You can leave now, Elmo," Tiki said.

Elmo Tackett picked up his knife and slowly walked away. Danielle got the distinct impression that Elmo had lost a battle, but not the war.

Danielle and Jamelle turned toward Tiki. "What was that all about?" Danielle asked.

"You needed help and I was here," she said. Jamelle smiled broadly and held out his hand, introducing himself. "Pleased to meet you," Tiki said. Her smile was like the sun appearing after a thunderstorm. Then she walked off.

"Wait!" Danielle said, but she was gone around the corner.

Danielle looked at Jamelle. "Have you ever seen that woman before?"

"Nah. But she's like an angel or something."

Danielle said goodbye to Jamelle and walked the three blocks home, hoping to see Tiki again. She was a fast walker but could discover no trace of the girl.

Rachel and Trevor

Rachel DuPlessis was thrilled with the public recognition from her relationship with Trevor Clarke. But in private she noticed that behind Trevor's confident and suave demeanor there was nothing very substantial.

"What do you intend to do with your life Trevor?" she asked him one night after making love.

"I don't understand what you mean."

"Oh please, don't give me that injured look. You are basically a front man for the bank, and now for your real estate development. What have you really accomplished?"

"You ask me that?" he said. "What are you but the president of a minor marketing firm in a minor little university town?"

Rachel brushed that away. "The point is I have goals. I want my firm to be the best in its field in Midland, then in the state, and then in the country. I have goals and I'm pursuing them."

Trevor laughed easily. "Well then, congratulations." He did have goals: to live the good life, however that may be accomplished. He did not want to voice them to this woman, who was vulgar and beneath him. He placed a hand gently on her breast. She responded instantly to his touch. "Now that's more like it my dear."

The next night after a concert, Rachel continued their conversation.

She saw Trevor remove his elegant suit coat, his tie, and his shirt, and hang them up carefully. "Trevor, what are your goals in life?"

She could see him control his irritation.

He carefully removed his slacks, folded them, and hung them. "You are determined to be irritating tonight it seems." He smiled but his lips were pressed firmly together.

Rachel turned her head to the side and studied him. "You are a very attractive man, Trevor, but there seems to be something lacking."

Trevor could see where this was going. He decided to cut to the chase. "Rachel, you got rid of Mark because he was unambitious. You then cut ties with Don Halloran because you said he was too shallow. Now you are implying that I am also inadequate."

"It's a simple question, Trevor."

"Could it be that you only attract men that do not measure up?"

"You said it, not me."

Trevor smiled blandly. "Really, Rachel, you are missing the obvious. Perhaps the inadequacy lies in you, not with those you criticize."

Trevor saw a look of astonishment, then disbelief, then rejection cross her face. He almost laughed out loud at her dismissal of his suggestion that she had any responsibility for the relationships she was in. He spoke in his most urbane but distancing voice. "Might I suggest that you stick to your marketing my dear. Let me deal with society and the complex interactions that require a delicate touch."

They did not make love that night.

Nalbandians and Katelians Meet

At the monthly meeting of the families, the most important item on the agenda was the sequestering of their invention. Vartan Nalbandian, assistant research director at Octagon Research, spoke for the Nalbandians. Vahan Katelian spoke for the Katelians. But first routine business had to be attended to.

"Our crews have secured almost 60% of the proposed work to be done on the new Ginzburg waterfront development," Vahan said with satisfaction. "Anticipated revenues should equal or exceed those on the Tavistock project."

There were pleased smiles all around.

"To have two such lucrative developments one after the other will be a windfall for the families," Vartan agreed.

The Nalbandians and the Katelians could trace their lineage back over 1,000 years. Their businesses had family branches on all five continents. The families ran their organizations mafia style. It was a tried and true formula. They used their financial muscle and only when necessary resorted to violence. The goal was to keep out of the newspapers and not run afoul of the law.

Routine business was conducted until the final item on the agenda. The huge, open living room in the Katelian mansion was full tonight as even minor players were here to decide what should next be done with their stolen invention at the Octagon lab. Vahan knew that the families cared little about his risky investment. But when someone steals what is theirs, the situation becomes one of honor and family pride.

"Zadig," Vahan said, "please give us your report."

Vahan's brother was the head of the Katelian's intelligence unit. "Nobody knows who these guys are, but we do know one thing: a man named Bernie Hartwig is connected to them."

"Who is this Hartwig?" Vahan asked.

"Director of Physics at the university," Vartan Nalbandian said. "The guy's a softie, he couldn't have anything to do with those guys."

"Well, he does," Zadig said. "I have it from a strange guy named Elmo Tackett, who does odd jobs for us. I think Tackett is connected somewhere because every lead he gives me pans out."

"So what do we do?" Vahan asked.

The patriarch of the Katelians, Vahan's father Mardig, spoke. "Get Raffi over to Carleton and see what he can find out from this Hartwig."

The next day Raffi Katelian saw Bernie walking out of the Physics building. Not being a man of social affairs, he stepped in front of Hartwig on the sidewalk leading out of the building.

Raffi did not mince words. "We want to know who stole our invention."

Hartwig felt a stab of fear but he stifled it. The man in front of him was short and dark with a black beard. He looked like a criminal. Bernie took an instant dislike to him.

Raffi spoke more harshly. "Zadig says you know who took our stuff and we want to know who it is."

"Not here you fool!" Hartwig hissed. "Come into my office."

Bernie was fearful as the two men marched back into the building. The swarthy man beside him looked like someone who could knife you while eating a hot dog. When they arrived at his office he unlocked the door and gestured. Raffi walked in and stood, while Bernie slumped heavily into his chair. He was feeling every one of his 55 years these days.

"Well?" Raffi asked. "What do you know about this?"

"Who are you?" Kelvenback asked.

"I'm from the people who paid for the discovery you stole," Raffi said.

"I didn't steal anything you fool," Hartwig replied. He studied the man standing in front of his desk. A local guy, probably. "You look like one of the Katelians."

"That's right. I'm Raffi Katelian."

"All right Raffi Katelian. The people who stole your invention are most likely in some deep, dark, black part of the national security establishment that nobody knows about, especially me."

"Why would they steal our stuff?" Raffi demanded.

"How would I know? I'm just a physics professor, not a detective."

Raffi snorted in disgust. Vartan was right, this guy didn't know shit. He walked out of the room.

Bernie wondered whether Raffi's visit was from his handler in PHOENIX. Was this a warning of some kind?

The next morning at 6 a.m. Raffi Katelian was found in an alley off Ann Street downtown with his throat slit. When Bernie saw it on the news headlines he called in sick. Then he called Max.

When Vahan Katelian heard about Raffi's death he immediately thought of Max Berglin. Could their business partner have stolen the invention and killed Raffi to cover up his involvement?

Berglin was supposed to have a security classification. Maybe he used some of his friends to turn on them. It wouldn't be the first time the Katelians had been burned by cheating scumbags.

Pierce Menard Makes a Decision

On a cold, late September day, Danielle came home from work and saw her father's suitcases in the foyer. "Dad? Where are you?"

"I'm upstairs honey."

The house had been fixed up and sold; the new occupants would arrive on the first of the month. She had already secured a nice apartment downtown in one of the more affluent areas just off campus. Her income made that possible now.

Danielle walked up to her father's room at the end of the hallway. She found him in front of a mirror, combing his hair.

"Dad you look great!" Pierce was thin but there was more color in his cheeks and he almost looked healthy again. He was wearing a dark blue suit with a cream colored shirt, a dark blue tie, and his silver cuff links. His thick dark hair, graying now, was brushed back, exposing a wide brow. Danielle was amazed. She hadn't seen him like this for years, before he fell apart. Before mom died.

"I've accepted a research job at MAB Power Solutions outside Boston," he said. "I'll be going back to my old area of expertise."

"And what is that area of expertise dad?" Danielle asked.

Pierce sighed. "All right Danielle." He looked over his daughter and was surprised. In a haze of self pity for years, he remembered her clearly as a sixteen-year-old. But Danielle was a woman now, tall and beautiful like her mother, dressed elegantly in a business suit and heels. Carol's dress. "I haven't really seen you in a long time," he said, feeling guilty.

Danielle waved him off. "That's all water under the bridge dad. I'm proud of you."

Pierce's eyes filled with tears. "That's just what your mother would have said. She was always one to let bygones be bygones."

Danielle was determined to finally get some answers She sat down on the side of the bed, patting the spot next to her. "Tell me about mom and tell me about your research."

Pierce sighed and sat down on the bed next to Danielle. "My area of expertise is electrogravitics – gravity control. This is a subject, daughter, that has no validity in academia or in established physics, which is why I had to go black."

Danielle saw her father's demeanor grow colder. She shivered.

"That's a story I can't tell you about right now Danielle, but I hope to be able to one day. To make a very long story short, I met your mother working on propulsion systems for exotic aircraft. We were both working for one of the deep black programs, which I am not at liberty to tell you about. Do you understand my meaning?"

Danielle nodded. She didn't, but her father was talking to her about stuff she had desperately wanted to know about for a long time.

"Your mother was a brilliant physicist, Danielle. The systems we were working on are very advanced. The technology for them comes from – I'm sorry, Danielle, I can't tell you anything more." Pierce hung his head.

"Dad, what is it?" She could see his eyes tearing up.

"It's about your mother. She ... no, I can't say."

"Father!" Danielle said. She stared at him intently, willing him to respond.

"You see Danielle, we were reverse-engineering a craft...that we think came from, ah, let's say, outer space."

Danielle thought that her father might be slipping mentally back into one of his dazes as he stared past her into the room. But his eyes sharpened and focused. He grew more animated. "Danielle, you should have seen this thing. It didn't have a propulsion system at all. We eventually determined that it generated a spacetime bubble around the craft that rendered it completely independent of the surrounding physics."

The words of the brilliant physicist made little sense to Danielle.

Pierce made a little grimace. "Yes, that's what everyone thinks Danielle. Your mother started talking to people about it. She was very excited to find that there might be, ah, other civilizations out there. Nobody ever told us where this craft came from. However, your mother and I knew that it was beyond any physics on this planet. Well, daughter, that was her demise." He hung his head again.

"You mean that mom was murdered?" Danielle cried.

"I didn't say that, daughter. But I...I just don't know for sure." Danielle saw her father's eyes grow fierce. "Danielle, don't ever, ever mention this subject to anyone, not even as a joke, do you understand? If you were just an average citizen people would just laugh at you. But you are known to be my daughter."

Danielle was in shock. Her mother, murdered! Somehow she knew it would be pointless to ask her father whether he had gone to the police. Her mother's name had never been mentioned in the house after her death.

Pierce looked at her with grave concern. He went to his desk and grabbed a piece of notebook paper and a pen, and wrote for a few moments. "This is the private phone number of Dr. Julian Green, a civilian researcher who is expert in frontier physics and research. If you ever have questions, or get into trouble, call him and mention my name. He's a personal friend of mine."

Danielle raised her eyebrows questioningly.

"I heard him speak at a public lecture in DC eight years ago. Afterwards, we spoke about your mother's death."

Danielle was bitter. "He didn't seem to have helped much."

"It wasn't his fault."

"I'm sorry dad. But I often think about mom."

"There isn't a day I don't think of her."

The two were silent for several moments. "Can you tell me anything about your work?"

She saw her father become more animated. "In the classified areas we have developed really exotic technology. Some of it is similar to what your friend John Rosen and Austin Park are working on. There is a sort of game going on. It's a conflict between those who want to release the classified technology to the world, and those who want to keep the current system."

"So it's about money," Danielle said.

"That's right Danielle, about $60 trillion or so real dollars every year in the current fossil fuel based system. And the power that money generates."

"It's pretty unreal to me."

Pierce was still for a moment, considering. He got up and walked over to the end table next to the wall by his dresser. He hesitated for a second, then opened one of the doors and pointed to a small rectangular box that looked like stereo equipment. He pulled out two of the coolest looking headsets she'd ever seen and handed one to her. It had a thin band that went over the head, a pair of silvery ear pads, and a molecule-thick gray visor. "Here, let's use these. It's a lot easier."

She was fascinated. The visor was literally so thin that when turned on edge, it disappeared. She tried to bend the material, but she couldn't move it. "Dad, what is this thing?"

When Pierce put on the headphone, the band over his head glowed orange. He winked and said, "Consider these a superior version of CAD/CAM. Thought assisted. I can demo with these everything I want to tell you."

"Where did you get them?" Danielle asked.

"I stole them. These things are just trinkets. Nobody will miss them."

Danielle put the headphones on. Suddenly she was in space above the earth, with no boundaries. Her stomach turned over and she felt a horrible vertigo.

Quickly, she yanked the thing off her head. "My God. That was the realest thing I have ever experienced. Was it a hologram?"

Pierce's eyes twinkled. "In a manner of speaking Danielle. It's a recording of a real-time image. I didn't mean to scare you, I forgot I had it loaded."

Pierce gestured for her to put the headset on again. Instead of empty space she was looking at a White Room with no boundaries, like a three-dimensional whiteboard.

Suddenly a lattice of little dots filled the space. "In every cubic centimeter of space, Danielle, there is enough energy to power everything on earth for hundreds of years," Pierce said (thought). "At every point in empty space there is a tremendous amount of energy converging on that point from every direction, creating a balanced null point. Space appears to be completely empty, but that's just an illusion. Over the years we have figured out how to extract some of that energy." Danielle saw energy, which was marked with tiny little arrows of light, streaming in radially to every point in space. Then the point was magnified into a sphere and she saw how each of the spheres was energetically neutral, because the energy that flowed into it came from every direction and balanced itself perfectly. One of the arrows then bent slightly, sending a stream of energy out of the sphere into a device that captured some of it.

"These things are awesome!" Danielle thought. She could hear her father's thoughts in her head, and he could hear hers.

"It's one of the reasons classified technology is so far ahead. Communicating via thought, building prototypes via thought, is infinitely faster and easier than conventional research methods."

"I remember you used to point to the power lines and say that we don't need them."

Pierce smiled, remembering. Danielle caught the image in his mind. She had only been ten then. She saw a whole complex of other thoughts around that incident. Pierce spoke (thought) again. "That debate we saw on TV was about similar ideas, Danielle. Apparently Park and Rosen were able to duplicate the efforts of scientists in the classified area."

"I heard the device, or whatever it was, got stolen."

"Yes, that's what I heard too. Let's continue." Pierce then showed her an electronic circuit. A vast pool of energy surrounded the circuit board but only a tiny bit of it flowed through the wires and components in the circuit. "We use what flows through the wires to power our homes and our electronics. What is outside the circuit is completely wasted, but it is accessible."

"Wow," Danielle remarked. It was so easy to see things with these headsets. It was amazing. If they had them in school....

"That's right Danielle," Pierce said. He smiled and put down his headphone. Danielle took hers off, admiring the sleek design.

"I'm going back in. I'm going to try to release this technology to the world or die trying."

Danielle began to cry. "Oh no father, just when I was beginning to know you and like you!"

Pierce leaned over and hugged his daughter. "Danielle, that's the nicest thing anyone has ever said to me since your mother died. I have often thought over the past five years that I'm anti-social and unlovable."

Danielle put her hands on his shoulders and looked lovingly into his eyes. "No dad, you're not. I'm a loner just like you. That can be hard."

Pierce sighed like someone who has made egregious mistakes and doesn't know how to atone for them. "You have a good heart, Danielle."

Danielle wanted to cheer him up a little. "I'm working with Max Berglin Sr.," she offered. "I think he wants me to get involved more deeply in his business. I'll need a security classification."

Pierce's eyes sharpened. "You have your mother's sometimes impulsive temperament Danielle. Don't make decisions in the excitement of the moment. Tread carefully."

Danielle nodded.

Father and daughter were silent for a few moments. "I have a feeling I will be seeing you again, father," Danielle said. At that moment she was pierced by a feeling that she would never speak to him again.

"I do as well. Be careful, daughter, and trust your instincts. If you get into trouble don't hesitate to call Dr. Green."

As quickly as the feeling came it passed. "All right father."

"Wish me luck, Danielle. I'm going back into the Game. It's in my blood, and it's in yours too."

Danielle smiled. "Yes dad, it is. Instead of being scared I'm afraid I'm very excited to get more involved."

Father and daughter hugged.

"Let's not prolong our goodbye," Pierce said with tears in his eyes. Danielle nodded and kissed him. Pierce took both headsets and placed them inside the little box. As he and Danielle walked downstairs a taxi drove up to the curb and honked. Pierce grabbed his suitcases and walked to the cab. The cabbie loaded everything and Pierce waved to her. Then he was gone.

Suddenly she felt sick to her stomach. This house – she had to leave, there were too many bad memories. She would move into a hotel until her apartment was ready on the first.

The Midland Police Get Involved

The unsolved murder of Raffi Katelian, and the stolen invention that had been so publicly debated, caused consternation within the Midland Police Department. Both cases were unsolved. Everyone remotely connected to Octagon Research had been interviewed. Detective Stan Moyer – soon to be Chief Moyer, he hoped – was in charge of the case. Moyer was convinced that the two incidents were connected.

He had been hopeful that Vartan Nalbandian could provide a lead. The research director, along with the building security guard at Octagon, were the only persons who had actually gotten a good look at the men who had cleaned out the lab in Room 317. The security guard, Hector Cabrera, was so intimidated that he could provide only a general description. Vartan Nalbandian, however, gave a good description of the leader: a tall, muscular man with a square face, bushy eyebrows, and a beak nose. This man had given the orders. Two of the men were of medium height. One had brown hair and a fleshy face with large pores, and the other had jet black hair and refined features. These two men said nothing and were the ones who emptied out the lab. All of the men wore identical black suits with white shirts and polished black shoes. Nalbandian had gotten the best look at the two men who had stood guard at the front door. "Massive men each one, about six and a half feet tall. I was not about to challenge either one. These men had the look of professional killers, of the stone-cold assassin."

Nalbandian had provided a description of each of the six men to a police artist. A check of criminal databases had yielded nothing. He had a friend in the FBI and had requested their involvement. He sent his friend the six police sketches, but so far he hadn't heard back.

It was not much to go on but Moyer was a persistent man; the senior detective in the department.

There were two red flags so far in his investigation. The first was the statement of Vartan Nalbandian, who told him that the leader of the team had offered him money to keep the invention quiet. "He said, 'We know you are the owners.'

When I asked him how he knew that, he said, 'You don't have a need to know.' When I asked him who they were and what did they think they were doing, he said, 'We're from TAC.' Then he gave me this, and handed me a paper. It was something called a Type III Patent Secrecy Order. It said that the invention had to be sequestered for reasons of national security, and that any publication or dissemination of the device or its materials would be met with the direst consequences. This asshole told me that if I sold the invention to him I'd receive twenty million dollars. But if I didn't, and spoke to anyone about it, I'd be in 'grave difficulty.' Those were his words. When I told him that half of Midland knew about it already, he just repeated what he said before. When I told him that this invention had the commercial potential to replace every power plant in the world and was probably worth several hundred billion, not a measly twenty mil, he just said, 'Have it your way.' Then he and his men stripped our lab and stole everything."

This operation had the look of something classified, Moyer concluded. It may be a case where his jurisdiction would end before he could get to the bottom of it. That rankled Senior Detective Stan Moyer.

He had interviewed both Vahan Katelian and Max Berglin. Katelian was enraged that his cousin had been murdered.

"Max Berglin is probably behind Raffi's murder," Vahan said, fuming. "And the stealing of our invention. He wants to cut us out and keep all the profits for himself. It's typical of rich bastards like Berglin with influence. Their word means nothing."

Moyer was doubtful, knowing that Katelian was a hothead. He was unsympathetic toward the local mafia and wasn't displeased that they had gotten burned. When he talked to Max Berglin the man was genuinely mystified about the murder of Raffi Katelian and fatalistic about the loss of his investment. "It happens. You win some and you lose some." Detective Moyer noticed that Berglin said this with a twinkle in his eye. He was up to something, the detective was sure. But after extensive interviews and checking of facts Max Berglin was cleared of both incidents.

The second red flag was one mysterious name that came up twice: a shadowy figure by the name of Elmo Tackett. Nalbandian had mentioned him, and so had Bernie Hartwig. No one knew anything about the man, what he did for a living, or even where he lived. Tackett was his only remaining lead, and he had to discover his whereabouts.

Moyer talked it over with his wife Lou Ann that evening over dinner. "I'm going to pursue this case even if it has to be on my own time outside the department," he told her. "I don't care about Raffi Katelian, he's a known member of the Katelian crime family. But I don't like unsolved murders in my town."

"Do you think the theft and the death of Raffi Katelian are linked?" Lou Ann asked.

"I don't know honey. But the stolen invention has excited my imagination. It must have been legitimate and valuable, otherwise why would someone want to steal it?"

"Be careful darling," Lou Ann said.

— 22 —

Rachel DuPlessis was irritated with Trevor Clarke. His comment about her minor marketing firm rankled. Suggesting that she was inadequate in relationships was insulting. She wanted to find out more about the real Trevor Clarke. Was he truly as shallow as Mark and Don? In her experience, finding people's weaknesses gave her leverage over them. Leverage was power.

Two days later she saw Wayne DiPietro at the supermarket. He was in the wine aisle and she approached him. "Hi Wayne, I haven't seen you in a while."

Wayne turned and saw an enhanced version of the Rachel Ferrell he used to know, a very well dressed woman in designer slacks and a blouse open at the front. A string of pearls hung around her neck. If Wayne thought she was overdressed for the supermarket he did not voice it. "Rachel Ferrell! Wow, you look great."

Rachel preened a bit. "The divorced Rachel Ferrell. It's Rachel DuPlessis now."

"I'm sorry to hear that."

"Thank you Wayne, but it was the best thing for both of us."

"I heard from Mark that you had become president of your firm. Congratulations!"

After some small talk they agreed to have a cup of coffee and catch up. In better times Mark, herself, Wayne, and Myra would go to the Caldwell Coffee Shop and chat. During their conversation Wayne happened to mention Larry Potvin and his suspected embezzling scheme.

"Oh really?" Rachel filed away this nugget. "What was that all about?"

Wayne scowled. "In my opinion the guy was skimming several thousand per week from the PANA automotive accounts. I can't prove it, but where did that loser get the money to open that expensive auto shop he has?"

"That's interesting," Rachel replied. Trevor had casually mentioned Larry Potvin more than once during their conversations. What could those two possibly have in common? "Do you know of any connection between Trevor Clarke and Larry Potvin?"

Wayne put down his coffee cup and thought for a moment. "You know, I had never considered that. Now that you mention it, there was another account I audit that had almost the exact same profile." He looked curiously at Rachel. "The odds of that happening are very slim. Larry Potvin isn't smart enough to run a scam like that without help. I wonder if there was a mastermind behind it."

Rachel recalled something Trevor had said after making love. "Trevor said that Larry Potvin was doing very well and that he never thought a man of Potvin's intelligence could pull it off." Rachel remembered the smug look of pleased self-satisfaction on Trevor's face when he said it. Trevor was a financial wizard; he would be quite capable of running an embezzling scheme. Rachel voiced her thoughts.

Wayne frowned. It griped him that Larry's boss at PANA, Hassan Bashari, had never done anything with his report or even acknowledged receipt of it. Larry had quit his job there so there was nothing he could do now. But it still annoyed his sense of propriety and order.

Rachel saw that Wayne was suspicious. "Perhaps Trevor Clarke is the mastermind?" she suggested.

"Aren't you seeing him?" Wayne's tone was disapproving.

"Yes I am, but that's none of your business."

"Maybe not, but why would you want to get dirt on a guy you're going with? Unless you're trying to bring him down?"

Now Rachel was angry. "Well, it's been nice seeing you Wayne." She drank the rest of her latte and paid her tab. The gall of that man.

Wayne watched her walk up to the cash register. God, she was a good looking woman. Unlike Myra, who couldn't care less now about her appearance. Myra had let herself go and their sex life, which used to be very good, had lost its spark. Wayne sat there after Rachel had left with his coffee cooling, wondering how she was in bed. What she said about Trevor Clarke was a possible lead to Larry Potvin's scheme.

He still remembered the little spat they had last summer in front of Larry's shiny new business. When Wayne DiPietro got his teeth into something he didn't like to let go. He would keep his eyes open for a connection between Potvin and

Trevor Clarke. If he had failed in his duty to catch an embezzler he could make it right and salve his conscience. And maybe even nail Potvin, if he really was a crook.

After Rachel got home she waited for Trevor to pick her up. They were going to the Midland Center for the Performing Arts to see the Bernhardt String Quartet. Afterwards they would do some coke and have some great sex at her place. She didn't even like classical music, but everyone would be there tonight. When they got home she'd try to find out whether Trevor had any connection to this embezzling scheme.

John Rosen and Austin Park Meet Danielle

In early October Danielle returned from a visit to Ann Arbor, Michigan, where she had just made a successful sale to a small high tech company. She had once again underestimated the lucrative nature of these small firms. The owner had just experienced a system breach and was paranoid about security. All she had to do was make the pitch.

When she entered the building from the basement, she walked up to Room 113, Accounts, and saw the Inquisitor. That's what all the salesmen called Wanda Chickere, a very large person who had been born in South Africa. Woe betide the unfortunate who did not have a receipt for every penny on their expense account. All outside salespeople had a company credit card that tracked all purchases, and even if you paid for something yourself you had to have a receipt for it.

After dealing with Wanda she walked out of Accounts and went to the top floor to Briefing. John Rosen was standing in the hallway at the end of the corridor. What was John doing here? She walked down the hallway and approached John, who seemed to be in some kind of reverie. He was staring at the opposite wall, moving his hands around in the air. "Hello John Rosen," she said. "Long time no see."

She was startled to see John jump back and hit his head against the wall. "You scared the shit out of —" Her old Midland East buddy must have expected someone else, because when he turned around his jaw dropped. "No, you can't be...are you Danielle Menard from high school?" The hard-edged, disheveled girl he had known years ago had transformed into a beautiful woman.

"The very same," she said, holding out her hand. John took it gingerly and released it. "Wow, uh, yeah, hi Danielle."

"What are you doing here John?"

"We work here now."

"Do you mean —"

"Yes," John interrupted. "And don't tell anyone you saw me. We're supposed to keep to our room and we even sleep in the back. The boss has got us closeted up here so no one can see us."

"You guys are working on that secret new invention?"

"Yeah. We've got a working prototype now. It's powering everything in our lab."

"Seriously?"

"Yes. But you can't tell anyone, OK? I don't want to lose this job."

"OK John, I never saw you."

John breathed a sigh of relief as he looked her over. In her heels she was taller than he was, and he was almost six feet. He shook his head in amazement, walked back into the lab, and shut the door.

Danielle walked back down the corridor to Room 401, the door marked "Briefing." She walked in and plopped her report on the desk. There was an older man in a crumpled suit seated on the small couch, holding a briefcase. "Oh hi Jimmy, how did it go?" she asked.

"Danmeyer was his usual unpleasant self," he said. "Kept me up until one in the morning and I missed my flight. Had to take the red-eye." Jimmy closed his eyes. Then he opened them. "But I made the sale."

Danielle sat down next to Jimmy Polazzo, wondering how long Jimmy's debrief would take. Every salesperson had to submit a detailed report after every trip, successful or unsuccessful. These reports contained an exact description of every person she saw or talked to and what they talked about. She had to write down her observations about the person's character, personality, demeanor, and opinions, as well as the client's corporate business environment. You didn't get to leave Briefing until someone had read your report, approved it, and interviewed you. Your tech handler also submitted a report, and the two had to match. At Berglin Enterprises honesty was the best policy.

Just then Max Jr. walked into the room. "Oh hi Danielle! Just get back?"

"A couple of minutes ago," she said, covering for Rosen.

"Would you two lovebirds take this conversation to one of the interview rooms?" Jimmy complained. "I'm trying to get some shut-eye."

Danielle frowned at the word lovebirds, but Max Jr. grinned. "Sure Jimmy. Come on Danielle."

Danielle didn't like Max Jr. much but she couldn't say no to the boss' son. They took seats in a little cubbyhole office off the hallway. "What is it Max?" she asked.

"You've been a free woman for a while now Danielle."

"Yes I have Max." She wasn't going to make it easy for him.

"I want to take you out again. Our last date was...too short."

Danielle didn't think so at all. "I'm sorry Max but I'm not interested."

"Do you mean you're not interested in men, or not interested in me?"

Danielle ignored the implied reference to her sexuality and took off her suit coat. She pointed to the tattoo of the unicorn on her right shoulder. "Tell me what you think of this."

Max frowned. "Is this some kind of test?"

"Yes Max, if it makes you feel better. Tell me your thoughts."

Max looked at the tattoo. A golden orb representing the sun sent yellow rays up to her shoulder, illuminating a beautiful white unicorn. "It's a sun and a unicorn."

"Ehhhhhhhh," Danielle said, making the sound of a buzzer. "Was that all you wanted to ask me, or did you come on business?"

"Forget it. I have to see Joe in back." Max Jr. sulked out of the office and Danielle put on her suit coat. That was another thing about Max Sr. You had to look professional at all times while in the building, or when representing the company. Even in the Briefing room. Danielle sat for almost an hour, thinking about her successful sales trip.

She heard her name called and walked back to the desk. An hour later, after a detailed interview, Danielle was about to leave the building when she saw Max Sr. waving to her in the lobby. She walked over to him. They stood in front of a thick glass panel behind a massive marble support column at the back of the building, away from everyone. "Danielle, did you see John Rosen today?"

She considered lying, because she had promised John not to tell anyone. "Yes. I was up at Briefing and saw him standing in the corridor."

"The silly fool," Max muttered to himself. Then he brightened. "Maybe it's for the best. I want to bring you in on this new project we're developing. Absolutely hush-hush, do you understand?"

"Yes. You're talking about the Tesla experiment?"

"Precisely Danielle. I've made a decision." His eyes burned into hers. "We're going to develop this technology and release it, come hell or high water."

Danielle gasped. "But Pierce told me about what happened at Octagon. According to my father, some pretty serious guys showed up and took everything. Are you sure it's safe?"

"I don't know Danielle. Certainly we could put a lot of people out of business with this, and that will likely create a lot of opposition." The older man studied her for a moment and saw her excitement. He grinned. "I thought so. Are you ready for some action?"

Danielle's eyes sparkled and she shook her head rapidly up and down in affirmation.

Vahan Gets Mad

Vahan Katelian discovered that his friend John Rosen had been hired by Max Berglin. He and Austin Park were holed up in the Berglin Enterprises building. So Berglin *had* double-crossed the families! He drove to Berglin Enterprises downtown and asked to see John Rosen. Berglin himself wasn't answering his phone and was "unavailable."

"I'm sorry sir," the receptionist said. "We do not give out the names of our employees."

Normally Vahan would have been interested in this well-dressed woman, but he was abrupt. "You're lying."

Tara Bolshoi didn't respond. Vahan got out his phone and called John's phone.

"Hello?"

"John," Vahan said. "Where are you son?"

"I'm at work. Is this Vahan?"

The receptionist punched the Security button on her console and listened to the conversation.

"You're damn right it's Vahan. Are you working for Berglin now, giving my invention away?"

Vahan heard a click and a few moments later two burly fellows walked quickly toward him from both sides. "I'm sorry sir, but you must leave the building," one of the beefeaters said. Seething, Vahan put his phone away and walked toward the door. One of the men said, "Stop! The boss wants to see you."

Vahan waited for several minutes before a big man walked out of an elevator and approached him. Vahan noticed the man's expensive, tailored suit. It was Berglin Sr. himself, his so-called partner.

"Vahan Katelian." Berglin grinned. "What took you so long?"

Vahan spoke softly. "I don't like your tone. Especially coming from a criminal who apparently doesn't mind violating intellectual property laws."

Vahan had the satisfaction of seeing Berglin's face harden.

"You're a fool, Katelian. I didn't steal your invention, I just hired the guys who dreamed it up."

"You didn't send your goons to steal our stuff at Octagon?"

"Of course not. It's my stuff too. That's something you would do. I just hired the guys you fired."

"We want a cut of the pie. We were the ones who funded the research when people like you were too stupid or too afraid."

Vahan could tell that Berglin was really angry now. He saw the man make a visible effort to tone himself down. "Apparently you didn't read the contract we signed, Vahan. Clause 107 (c): in the event that the project is terminated for any reason, Berglin Enterprises has the right to hire Austin Park and John Rosen. Any discoveries made by them during their employ here is the sole property of Berglin Enterprises. I had my lawyers insert that one."

Vahan was incensed. "You ripped us off! Most of the work was done at Octagon, and now you are going to claim Austin and John made their breakthrough under your employment." Vahan became cold. "If I were you I'd be nicer."

Berglin smiled deprecatingly, leaned over, and got into the younger man's face. "You have no fucking idea who you're dealing with son. If I were you I'd save my threats for the innocents you prey on." Vahan saw Berglin gesture to the security men. "Take this man out of the building and don't let him in again." Then he turned away and walked off.

One of the security guys was apologetic. "Sorry, you pissed off the boss, we gotta take you out."

Vahan was calm now. He had let Max Berglin get under his skin, and he didn't like it. He prided himself on his calmness under pressure; he hated to get angry. "That's all right," Vahan said, straightening his tie as they walked to the front entrance.

Vahan was curious. You can tell a lot about a man by his employees and their attitudes. "Do you like working here?"

"He's tough but fair," the man said. "Doesn't take any bullshit from anyone. I'm satisfied."

Vahan nodded and walked out of the building to the guest parking area. He realized that the families had made a big mistake, letting Park and Rosen go in their anger over Rosen's actions.

They would somehow have to get to Rosen and Park and scare them off. No way this asshole Berglin was going to cash in on their investment. He would ask his father to call a meeting of the families tonight.

At the families' meeting that night, Vahan spoke first. The two heads of family, Mardig Katelian and Vartan Nalbandian, sat on large chairs at a raised dais at the front of a huge open living room that contained several large sofas, recliners, and chairs. A wall of windows with two large doorwalls led out to a massive porch overlooking a large pond filled with geese and ducks.

"That bastard Max Berglin has hired Park and Rosen," Vahan began, rising from a large sofa ten feet in front of the dais. "He's taking our invention and is going to cut us out."

He could see his father shaking his head. "We have a signed contract, son. Relax." Vartan Nalbandian was nodding his head in agreement.

Vahan carefully brushed a piece of lint from his sleeve. "Apparently our lawyers didn't read it carefully enough. Look at clause 107 (c), the item that says Berglin gets to hire Park and Rosen if they are fired or released from Octagon Research. It also says that Berglin gets to keep anything they develop. I went downtown today and saw Berglin. He kicked me out of the building. That *khmbo* double-crossed us."

Mardig Katelian slowly rose from his seat. His eyes were cold as he spoke to a man holding a briefcase, sitting on a couch to his right. The man was furiously digging through some papers. "Is this true, Kalig?"

After a few moments the young man nodded, sweat beading on his forehead. "It's just a contingency sir. How were we to know the invention would be stolen?"

Mardig was dismissive. "Clearly Berglin thought of that 'contingency.'" The patriarch turned toward his son. "Explain."

Vahan described the confrontation. "Berglin denied stealing our invention, but of course he would if he was planning to take everything for himself. I called John Rosen and he all but admitted he's working for Berglin now. He's a sneaky *buhlo*, that Berglin, and I say we get rid of him."

Vartan Nalbandian, head of the Nalbandian family, spoke up. "Vahan's report is confirmed. We have a man in the building who says Park and Rosen are in a special lab. Using our research, they have already perfected a device that can power a lab. That means they've got something that works and that has the potential to make billions."

There were angry shouts from the family members.

"Vahan is right!" Zadig Katelian shouted.

Vahan supported his brother. "If it wasn't for this asshole, Raffi would still be alive today. This is a blood feud. I demand revenge for the murder of my cousin!"

"There's no evidence whatsoever that Berglin killed Raffi," said Aharon Nalbandian, eldest son of the head of the Nalbandian clan.

"Who else could have done it?" Vahan demanded. "It was Berglin who got Rosen to steal the device. It was Berglin who had Raffi killed. Then he hired our scientists out from under us."

There were shouts of agreement.

"If we get rid of Berglin," Vahan said, "Park and Rosen have nowhere else to go. We gain control of the new device and everything else they've developed."

Vartan Nalbandian broke in. "Killing Berglin is stupid. The man is a respected businessman, and socially active. If we were even suspected of the hit, we'd lose most of our business. Nobody would ever hire our crews again."

Vahan was incredulous. "If we get that device we won't need crews. And if Berglin killed Raffi the *Kanun* demands atonement. We are duty-bound to target the culprit and his family. Kin loyalty demands it."

There was loud agreement on the Katelian side, but the Nalbandians were more subdued. The Kanun was the centuries-old code of conduct that made vendettas against those who transgressed sacred.

Vartan noticed that the Katelians had bunched themselves to the back of the room by the large windows, while the Nalbandians had grouped in front, by the dais. He spoke softly in a voice that silenced the shouting and carried across the huge open living area. "It was only after we put aside our differences that we were able to prosper."

"I demand blood revenge for the murder of my cousin," Vahan insisted.

Mardig Katelian walked across the room and consulted quietly with Vartan Nalbandian. Tensions were high. Vahan knew if he made another inflammatory statement the families might start fighting right here.

Mardig Katelian made an announcement. "If it is proven to our satisfaction that Max Berglin killed Raffi, Max Berglin will be killed." A cry of support went up from the Katelian side. "But only I or Vartan can give this order! Is that clear?"

Vahan saw his father look directly at him. Coolly, he nodded his head forward a millimeter in acknowledgment. "It is always the Katelians who are the leaders, and the Nalbandians the followers."

At that, Aharon Nalbandian strode over and put his face inches from his.

Vahan smirked.

"Take that back, Vahan Katelian."

Vahan's insulting grin widened, and he saw Aharon's face flush. Aharon's hand came slowly, deliberately forward, slapping his face softly. Zadig Katelian rushed forward and shoved Aharon to the floor. Suddenly, the place erupted with shouting. Katelians and Nalbandians began slugging it out. Vartan met Mardig's eyes. "Let them blow off some steam."

But when one of the young Nalbandians brought out a knife, Vartan strode to the center of the room. "Enough!" he commanded. "Fasil, put away that knife. Get back to your seats, all of you."

"If you're bleeding, keep off my new sofas," Mardig added in an attempt at humor.

Gradually the noise level subsided and tempers cooled. Mardig looked over at his son. "That was unnecessary," he said, reprimanding Vahan in front of everyone.

Vahan grinned to himself. His eyes met Zadig's. He moved his head slightly, indicating that his brother should meet him at Connor's, their favorite bar downtown. Something would have to be done to remove Mr. Berglin from the picture. He knew Zadig felt the same.

— 23 —

In exchange for services rendered, the families had given Elmo Tackett a small basement apartment in the Tavistock development on the waterfront. The unit used to be a temporary storage area and overnight living quarters for maintenance workers. It was perfect for Elmo's needs.

Elmo liked to look out the big window in front at the water in the Midland River. Sometimes he'd go down to the marshy areas by the riverfront through the underground corridor, which contained a large drainage pipe for the complex. This corridor had a small service door, hidden from view, where he could enter and exit. He would dissect the animals and insects he found there. It was just like being back at St. Mary's Orphanage except that he was his own boss now. He didn't have to listen to other people squawking at him.

His unit was underground, in the first level basement area where workers traveled back and forth picking up supplies. Always casually dressed, he blended in with the Tavistock workers and maintenance crews. No one asked him any questions. Elmo didn't like to talk and only did it when required by the job. He didn't like people, but he liked to give orders to people (even though he was only a messenger) and see them obeyed. He liked to see the fear in people's eyes. It excited him. Of all the emotions, fear and anger showed him that there was something inside living things that made them alive. He wanted to know what it was. But all his attempts to capture that something had failed. That's why he did his dissections; not because he was cruel – Elmo wouldn't know what that word meant – but because he was curious. He had always been curious even as a little child, even after his parents had abandoned him at the Sisters of St. Mary's Orphanage.

Elmo thought of himself as a researcher, an investigator, into the mysteries of life. He was content.

Today, coming back from the marsh, he entered through the underground corridor into his little apartment from the back. Inside a man in a black suit sat on his sofa.

Elmo recognized him as one of the Katelians, one of the cousins to Raffi, the one called Zadig. He had seen him a few years ago outside a bank, along with the funny-looking John Rosen. Elmo had an excellent memory. He wondered whether this was to be a disposal.

The man spoke softly. "We have a job for you, Elmo." The man drew out a paper and several photographs.

Elmo did not like change. His usual contact was Raffi Katelian; he felt nervous around this new person. Elmo walked slowly over to the table next to the sofa. He sat down on the reading chair next to the window, where the light was streaming in. At the top of the paper was a name: "Max Berglin." Beneath was a description of the job and his instructions. Elmo read the instructions carefully, twice. Elmo scrutinized the photographs while Zadig Katelian watched. Max Berglin was six feet one, muscular, with thick, slightly graying blond hair and a square jaw. His eyebrows were curiously thin, almost like a woman's. There were images of him from the front, both sides, and from the back.

"This man is a danger to society, Elmo, do you understand?"

Elmo nodded, even though he was irritated that Zadig spoke to him like he was a child. The instructions said that the target was to be disposed of using a special airgun and special bullets. The bullets contained a fast-acting waterborne barbiturate. The instructions said that no trace of the bullet casing or its contents would be detected in the body, so that no one could trace the disposal to him. That was good because Elmo liked his life and did not want to spend it in jail, or be put to death.

"I understand."

The man smiled. "This weapon is state of the art, Elmo. It's untraceable." He put an envelope on the table in front of him. "Here is thirty thousand dollars. A further thirty thousand will be delivered to you upon successful completion of your duties."

Raffi Katelian had always referred to his activities for them as "duties," as if he were in the army fighting for his country. Elmo didn't like the army. People yelled at you and you were just a pawn following the orders of others, like the wicked Sister Armitage at St. Mary's.

Elmo looked down at the envelope, picking it up. Inside were crisp, brand new $1,000 bills. Elmo took out the bills and counted them. He loved the feel of the smooth paper, slightly abrasive as he ran his fingers over it, and the new money smell. He loved the money smell.

"Max Berglin is an important man," Elmo said. "Influential. Well known in society."

"That is why the price is so high," Zadig replied. "There is no time limit on this disposal. Take your time and do it right."

Elmo considered. Sixty thousand dollars would set him up for a long time. His pleasures were simple: to ride on his scooter, to observe people, to discover the nature of the life force, to solve problems related to his duties. "All right," he said, accepting the job.

Zadig placed a small airgun and twenty small bullets on the table in front of the sofa. "This gun is accurate to a distance of one hundred yards, or the length of a football field." Then he pulled out a small box and fit it into the handle of the air gun at the bottom. "This charger is a small but powerful air compressor that will re-initialize the airgun. It is good for ten charges in the field and will charge the gun within one second. To charge the compressor, plug it in to a wall socket." Zadig showed him how to load a bullet into the chamber.

Elmo nodded his understanding.

"That is all," Zadig said, and rose from the sofa. He opened the door that led to the corridor and left.

Elmo fingered each of the bills lovingly. He smelled each one. Then he put them all back into the envelope and placed it into his safe.

Elmo sat down on the couch, thinking. This job would be the biggest he had ever undertaken. He had slowly built his business as an independent contractor. First he had done odd jobs, and then, as he gained more experience, undertook more sophisticated work. His duties had begun with the Katelians, who normally employed him to track people and to dig up information. This had gradually led to other clients such as Trevor Clarke, who required the utmost discretion. Elmo had become quite good at dressing up in his suit, given to him by Raffi. He would talk to people at their places of business, pretending to be a representative of this company or that, collecting tidbits of information. Sometimes he dressed as a menial and talked to other menials. He knew how to go to bars and meet people the Katelians were in business with, or who the families wanted to do business with. He bought them drinks and pumped them for information.

He had learned to ignore the stares and the contempt when people first met him. He learned to display no emotional reaction, to assume an air of authority and competence, and to be determined. He had learned to dress appropriately and to speak precisely, as if he were an educated man, whenever he dealt with "professionals." He had learned that, after people got over their initial impression of him, they would accept him if he behaved in this manner. Elmo had also learned to move his facial muscles in what passed for a smile. He could appear to be friendly when necessary.

Over the years he had made many contacts within all social strata, including the underbelly of society. He knew he was not liked, but was trusted. Elmo had learned to be meticulous and scrupulously honest. Not because of ethical considerations, but because it was good for business. Elmo saw no difference between professionals and criminals. Professionals were just better dressed and better educated. Therefore he had no qualms about disposing of Max Berglin.

Elmo turned his gaze to the window and thought about how he would dispose of Max Berglin. This one would be much harder than the disposal he had done for Raffi, to a man who was preventing certain family work crews from getting jobs on the Tavistock development. He had been very clever in that disposal, and he would be again. He had tracked the man's movements on the job site. He waited patiently until the man appeared on a small, deserted dirt road at the edge of the construction site. The man was carrying a clipboard and taking notes as he looked into a waste pit that contained metal shards, broken concrete, and other construction materials. Elmo approached and said hi as would one worker to another. He remembered to screw his facial muscles into a practiced smile. No one was around. He pretended to slip on a stone, bumping into the man with the clipboard. When the man fell into the pit he could hear his scream and almost taste the life force substance around him. Elmo wondered what had happened to it as he observed the lifeless and broken body at the bottom of the disposal pit. He had dug his heel into the ground and collapsed a bit of it. He then carefully scuffed away his footprints at the scene, walking out the way he had come to his scooter, erasing his footprints as he did so. Later that afternoon a passing rain shower had obliterated all signs of his presence.

Elmo smiled as he remembered that the Midland Police and the company investigators had assigned cause of death to an accident. They noted that the ground at the edge of the pit had caved in where the man fell. For that disposal he had been paid twenty thousand dollars, which had lasted him two years.

Elmo sat for a long time without moving, thinking about the Max Berglin problem, as the sun gradually disappeared from the sky and the room darkened.

Zach Talks With Tiki

One late October Friday Zach found himself exiting the classroom with Tiki Aatoa. On an impulse he turned to her. "I'm having coffee with a friend of mine this evening. Would you like to come along?"

"I would."

"Meet us at Sweetwaters at 7 then."

When he got to Sweetwaters Zach saw Jessie already seated at a table. "I've invited Tiki Aatoa to have coffee with us."

"What?" Jessie was angry. "I thought these sessions were just for us."

"You and I are in the same boat Jessie. We use these get-togethers to bitch and moan about our lives, but we never do anything about it."

Jessie was about to retort but her fundamental honesty asserted itself. He was right. "I'm interested in you Zach, that's why I come." There! She had said it.

Zach didn't reply to this. "There's something about Tiki you'll like. We've been spinning our wheels and we need someone to give us both a kick in the arse."

Jessie changed the subject. "Heather passed her Foreign Service Officer Test Zach. She passed her orals and made the register. Now she's hoping for an appointment."

Zach was stunned. Heather McCloy a Foreign Service Officer? The same girl who tried to get with him last winter on the disk golf course? It reminded him again of how directionless he was. And the woman across from him. Then Tiki came into the shop and heads turned. She bought tea and a sandwich, and sat down across from Jessie and Zach. Now it was Jessie's turn to be stunned. There was something about her...something Jessie couldn't identify. She had a presence. Jessie found herself responding instinctively to Tiki in a positive way.

Tiki read both of them and was satisfied. Zach was no longer a player, and the girl never would be. If they got together they would both disappear into society and contribute nothing significant to the planetary socio-event matrix. But now that she was here she would help them.

"Why did Heather decide to join the Foreign Service?" Heather blurted. "How could she have gotten so far so fast?" After she spoke Jessie kicked herself. What would this girl, a perfect stranger, know about that? Jessie studied Tiki for a few moments. She saw not a woman her own age, but a wise counselor. Her eyes widened. "How—"

Tiki smiled and the tension inside Jessie dissolved. "That's a good question." Tiki answered in a way that made Jessie feel she was a trusted friend. "You see, Heather found her higher calling, which is to promote harmony within the world's governments. When you find your higher calling things fall into place for you very quickly."

Jessie looked over at Zach and their eyes met. Jessie thought, 'good idea to bring this girl here.' Zach grinned.

"But Heather is incapable of that," Jessie said. "She's just a girl looking to get a husband. She has no ability at all. How did she do it?"

"I don't know. But when you find your higher calling, you gain abilities you never know you had."

"That makes sense," Jessie said. "I've never seen Heather so confident. It's like she's a different person."

Tiki nodded, smiling. "That's right."

"OK, so what's my higher calling?" Zach asked.

Tiki's laughter was like a set of delicate outdoor chimes. "No one can tell you that Zach. You must find it yourself."

"It's too hard," he said. "I haven't got a clue."

"Me either," Jessie said. "What's your higher calling?"

Tiki was startled for a moment and then smiled. "I am an avatar," she said truthfully. "I am here to help the people of earth any way I can."

They should have laughed at her, Zach thought. An engineering student talking like Klaatu from The Day the Earth Stood Still. But they didn't. "Most people never do," Tiki concluded.

"So what's the point of living then?" Jessie asked. "To get married, have children and lead dull, pointless lives like my parents? Billions and billions of us?"

Zach gave Jessie a friendly pat on the shoulder in agreement. It was just what he was thinking.

Tiki took a sip of her tea. "Your planet is on the cusp of finding its higher calling. Or it could continue along as it has. The earth, and both of you, Jessie and Zach, are in the exact same position."

"If enough of us find our higher calling, the whole planet will?" Jessie hardly believed they were having this conversation, but it seemed right somehow.

Tiki smiled in agreement. She was like a light bulb you turned on, Jessie thought. She illuminated everything around her.

"How do you do that?" Jessie asked.

"Oh, you can do it too," Tiki replied. "Heather did it."

Jessie became excited. "Yes! I remember when she decided to apply for the Foreign Service. I was skeptical. I didn't think she could do it, it was too crazy. But she lit up just like you did."

Tiki nodded eagerly. "That's right Jessie! Everyone is capable of doing that. And when you find your higher calling, you literally inspire everyone around you. You—" how should she word this in English— "you contribute a higher note, or vibration, to the symphony of the human race."

Zach got it. "Heather, and you, and even Danielle and Mike Parsons, are in the orchestra. Jessie and me, and most of the rest of us, are sitting in the audience."

"Or outside the building," Jessie added.

"Or nowhere near the building," Zach said.

Tiki was happy. She had gotten these two humans to look inside themselves a little. She could tell that this was the vibrational high point of their meeting and got up quickly, gulping the rest of her tea. "I've got to get home and study." Tiki went over to the register to pay her bill. Jessie and Zach were staring at her. As she turned to walk away she waved to them. "Bye!"

Jessie and Zach, and everyone in their area, also waved and smiled.

When Tiki had gone Jessie turned to Zach. "That was amazing."

"It was," Zach agreed. "I need to find my higher calling."

"I do too."

"Well then, let's get going." Zach grabbed Tiki's untouched sandwich and devoured half of it. "I'm hungry."

Jessie took the other half. "I am too."

Jessie and Zach then engaged in animated conversation.

Part XI

Tesla

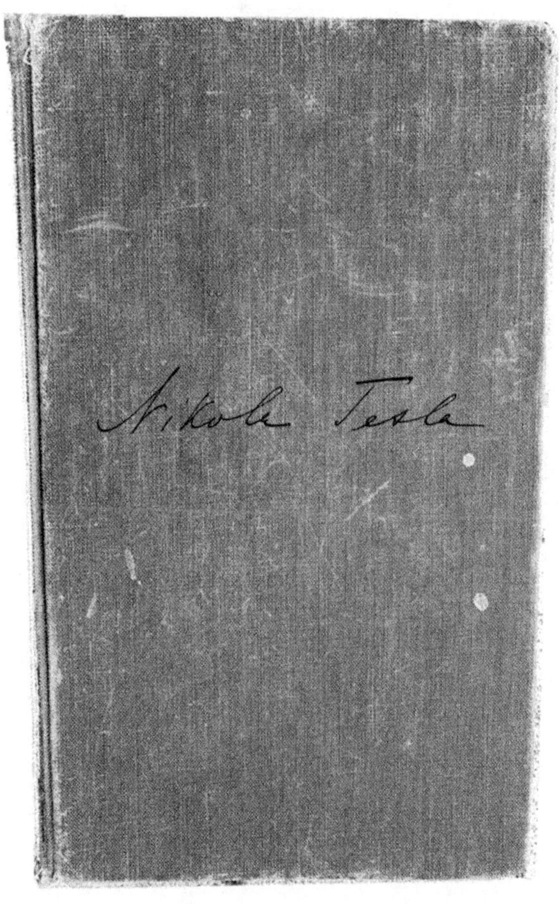

— 24 —

I walked into Room 411 at the end of the hall using a specially coded passkey. My two guys (that's how I thought of them) Austin Park and John Rosen, were working at a lab bench. I looked out at the cold early November morning, a snow shower throwing tiny flakes at the window. I walked over to the device they called the Cube, which was three feet on each side. It had a thick cable protruding from the end of it, to be attached to the electrical panel or the load. Inside the box was Tesla's powerful receiver, the one that had originally excited my imagination.

I pointed to a device on a lab bench that was surrounded by dozens of magnets. All three of us turned to face it. "What's that?"

"I call it the Pulsar," Austin said. Austin and John Rosen explained how they had built it from one of Tesla's schematics in the notebook. Behind us I thought I heard the door to the lab open, but I was too excited to pay attention.

"With the Cube we are just capturing the energy and sending it through a wire to power a load," Austin explained. "Now we're able to remotely send the energy...whatever it is and wherever it comes from, to another terminal."

Park pushed a black box into a slot. Across the room, a very bright sphere of light appeared above a workbench sitting against a wall.

"What do you think of that, sir?" John Rosen said. "It's from the diagram Tesla labeled 'radiant energy device.'"

I looked over the schematics in the notebook. "This is a much more sophisticated device than the one Tesla patented in 1901. I experimented with that one."

"That 1901 radiant energy device is just a child's toy compared to this one," Austin said. He pointed to the notebook. "The great man was so far ahead of his time that no one could understand these things. He just wrote them up and had to sit on them."

John agreed. "We studied Tesla's life. He was like a guy trying to explain electricity to cave men. People back then were morons."

I laughed at Rosen's irreverent attitude. "You guys are making great progress. How reliable is the Cube?"

"One hundred percent reliability Dr. Berglin, just like the Pierce-Arrow receiver that turns the motor," Austin said. "The Cube generates the same alternating current that comes from the power plant."

"It's amazing sir," John said. "The cosmic energy – that's what Tesla called it – outside the circuit seems adaptable to anything. It will flow through a wire or, as we have shown here, travel somehow to any point in space and be usable."

"It doesn't so much travel, Dr. Berglin, as communicate," Park explained. "It's as if every point in space-time is intelligent, a receiver as well as a transmitter. We think that it's not energy that is flowing from here to there, but *information*. Here at the point where we tap into the energy is an invisible matrix of data. That information matrix is somehow transmitted through space to another point in space, releasing energy. It's like a remote computer program being carried invisibly through space itself."

I distinctly remember John, myself, and Austin locking eyes. It was at that moment I realized we were going to change the world. "You've learned how to tap into the cosmic energy and transmit it cleanly through space, without wires."

John nodded his head vigorously. "Like Tesla at Wardenclyffe, only better. This notebook," he said, picking it up from the the bench top, "is the result of decades of Tesla's thought and design."

I was elated, and curious. "Have you tested Tesla's design for that beam weapon?"

"No sir," Austin replied. "As per your instructions we have done nothing with it. But everything else we have tested has worked perfectly." Austin flipped through the pages of the notebook. He pointed to the schematics for the energy weapon, which Tesla had marked with the inscription: 'range: 700 miles.' "I'd imagine this thing would work as well as the Pierce-Arrow receiver, the Cube, and the Pulsar we just showed you."

John shook his head in amazement. "Boss, this guy was the greatest genius humanity has ever produced. All of these designs and schematics are probably operational! We're nothing but glorified technicians, putting things together like a child would piece together a tinker toy model."

Austin smiled. "But these tinker toys will change the course of history."

Just then all three of us heard the door to the lab close. When I turned around I could see no one. I quickly ran to the door and opened it, looking down the hallway. Whoever it was had gone. "You guys don't leave that notebook lying around at night do you?"

"No sir," John replied. "We lock it up in this secure cabinet." John pointed to a special enclosure with thick metal walls and an even thicker door with a keypad on it.

"I'm going to put some security cameras in here, if you don't mind."

Austin and John had no objections. I called Tara Bolshoi, my receptionist and general fixer-upper, to take care of it.

As I walked out of the lab I was thrilled. At the same time I felt a sense of dread. We had just opened Pandora's Box. I had a feeling that the lid was never going back on again.

That evening Bernie Hartwig received a call from one of his handlers in PHOENIX.

"A situation is developing with your friend Max Berglin."

Bernie was going to ask the usual "Who is this?" but decided to forego that pleasure. "Again? What is it this time?"

When Bernie heard about the Cube and the Pulsar he was appalled and astounded. How could two unknown researchers like Austin Park and John Rosen make consecutive breakthroughs of such an astonishing nature in so short a time? The two men were certainly intelligent but not geniuses. He wondered whether Max had gotten hold of some sensitive classified research. That meant big trouble.

"I will call him right away," Bernie assured the caller.

I was sitting in my library reading a boring book, *Fundamental Cybersecurity Concepts*. I had to keep up with the latest developments for my money-making business, even though I was getting more and more bored with the field. My phone rang.

"Hi Bernie. What's up?"

"Max, what are you doing in that lab of yours?"

"How would you know about that?" Then I remembered the lab door opening and closing. Whoever had entered must have heard my conversation with Austin and John.

"I received a call...from someone I can't tell you about," Bernie said. "Just a friendly warning, Max. Be careful with what you are doing. If you go too far you're going to get some people angry that you'd rather not. And Max, if you have somehow gotten access to classified documents, I urge you to return them immediately."

I thought about the photocopied notebook Zach Ferrell had given me. Zach had found it on a shelf in a public library. Certainly something so sensitive would not be treated so cavalierly. "No Bernie, I haven't got anything like that. My guys are operating off some sketches of Nikola Tesla's that were found in one of those old stacks in the Graduate Library."

Bernie was very curious but decided that the less he knew, the less he would have to report back to PHOENIX. That could save Max a lot of potential trouble. "All right Max, let's drop it for now."

I was about to hang up when Bernie said, "You probably have a mole somewhere in your company."

"A mole?"

"Yes Max. It seems that developments in your laboratory reach certain people almost as soon as they occur."

Bernie was being paranoid again, but I thanked him and hung up. This was the second veiled warning I'd received from Bernie about the Tesla research. The original device had been stolen by a bunch of goons, and a man had been killed. What was going on? I decided to call my friend Kenji Hiroto in Japan. Kenji owned a company that specialized in protection services for high-tech companies and high-profile clients in the classified area. I had met Kenji on a trip to Tokyo several years ago at an information security conference. We had struck up a friendship.

"Hiroto-san? This is Max Berglin in Midland." Tokyo was 14 hours ahead of me, so it was 11:30 in the morning there.

"Berglin-san, how are you? It is good to hear from you."

"Kenji, I have a problem and I need your help."

Kenji Hiroto had always liked Max Berglin. He was respectful of other people and cultures, intelligent, and a daring risk-taker.

Kenji listened as Berglin-san told him about the Cube and the Pulsar.

"I'm at risk now, Hiroto-san. I intend to commercialize this discovery and it has a Patent Secrecy Order attached to it."

"Ah, so you are running afoul of your national security establishment."

"I don't know, I suspect so. My building and my people are going to need your services."

We discussed details for several minutes. Kenji said, "All right. I'll draw up the contract today and send it over from my office in Chicago by courier. I'd like to come over and inspect the location myself."

"That would be great, Hiroto-san. We can drink some sake and I'll show you around."

Hiroto Security was known for being discrete, efficient, and totally dedicated. It was a household name in the protection services business with firms in the classified area. His services cost a minor fortune. But I had a feeling that this new discovery, when commercialized, was going to make me so much money I could easily afford it.

Max Sr. Brings Home the Cube

A week later I brought home a device similar to the one that Austin and John had built to power everything in their lab. The Cube's components were inside a matte-black box three feet on each side, composed of non-conducting material. I had been instructed by Austin Park as to its use, which was so simple Pee Wee Hermann could have hooked it up. In anticipation of this day I had already gotten an electrician to modify my main service panel, providing a separate connector for the Cube. Thirty men from Hiroto Security had arrived the day before. I put them in dark gray uniforms with "Berglin Enterprises" decals on the front and on both shoulders.

One of Kenji's men helped me to haul the unit downstairs. Unfortunately the man spoke no English, but with gestures we got the thing into the furnace room. I placed the Cube on the ground underneath the main electrical service box and adjusted the battery powered lamp I had placed around my head.

Kenji's man had no idea what this strange American was doing. He watched as, with a great air of excited anticipation, I turned off the main on my service panel. The basement plunged into darkness. I laughed nervously, for I had forgotten to turn on my lamp. I fumbled around in the darkness for the switch. When I finally got the headlamp on I plugged the thick cable from the Cube into the special receptor on the main electrical panel. I was now almost vibrating with anticipation. On the Cube's top was a little button an inch in diameter. I pressed that button to activate Tesla's receiver, waiting for the big moment.

Nothing happened.

At first I was worried, then I began to get angry. Gradually, I saw a very dim light, as might be seen in the pre-dawn before sunrise. The basement lights slowly became brighter and brighter and then so bright I thought the system was going to blow up my house. After about five minutes, the lights dimmed somewhat and everything looked normal.

I stood there with a sense of awe, knowing that I was completely cut off from the grid. I was now energy-independent! I rushed up the stairs like a paparazzo chasing a famous movie star, followed madly by my security man. I checked to see if the appliances and lights were working on every floor. Slava must have thought I was crazy as I burst excitedly into the kitchen and said, "Eureka!" I ran downstairs again just to reassure myself that the connection to the grid was off and that the new energy source was actually doing the work.

I raised my arms in jubilation. "It works!"

Kenji's man suddenly understood. He said something excitedly in Japanese, which I took to mean "that box is powering the house."

I nodded my understanding. My two guys had done it. I gave fervent thanks to Nikola Tesla, bowing to the Cube in honor of the great inventor. Kenji's man also bowed. We both grinned at each other.

Kenji's man, Katsu Ozama, returned to his post. He told his partner about the amazing new powering device. The news quickly spread throughout the house. Slava, Kenji's security men, and even the house cleaners went down to take a look at the Cube.

After the excitement died down Slava served dinner, which we usually ate together unless my son was home. I knew I had to decide on a plan to release the new technology without causing a furor. I thought of Bernie, who had vehemently warned me not to go public with the new discovery.

I walked up to my home office and talked to my lawyer on face-to-face, an app that came on my mobile. "You're running into the Invention Secrecy Act," he said. "A secrecy order bars the award of a patent and orders that the invention be kept secret. It restricts the filing of foreign patents, and specifies procedures to prevent disclosure of ideas contained in the application."

"That's rather harsh," I replied.

"An inventor can avoid the risk of imposed secrecy if he forgoes patent protection."

"But that means anybody can legally steal the Cube."

"That's right, sir. You can go ahead without patent protection if you want. However, there is still a likelihood that your invention will be suppressed if it is determined that the technology is critical to national security."

It's what Bernie had been hinting at, and basically meant that I had to sit on this forever. That wasn't going to happen. I had my break and I was going for it. I had to discover a way to release the technology under the radar, but I couldn't think of a way to do it that didn't involve an outsider.

I sat at my desk for hours trying to resolve the problem, staring out the window at the wintry landscape. The only result of my mental labor was frustration. As soon as I set up a facility to produce the Cubes it would attract notice from the authorities. If I asked for help from my contacts in the intelligence services, they would be bound to report it. Moreover, the Patent Secrecy Order already attached to Park and Rosen's original invention applied to any commercial offshoot and upgrade of the original concept. Even if I could manufacture the devices in my own building and give them away I might still be in trouble. If what happened at Octagon was any indication I could be endangering everyone who used them. Slava kept bringing me cups of fresh coffee, bless his soul. Eventually I lay down on the bed and fell asleep with my clothes on, the problem still unsolved.

Kenji Hiroto discovered from his men what Max had done. He knew from his experience in the classified area that the American was treading in very deep waters. Fortunately there was a man who might be able to advise his friend. Roka Hatsumi had uncommon knowledge of people, a wide network, and was his personal friend. Perhaps Hatsumi-sama would know what to do.

Part XII

Midland

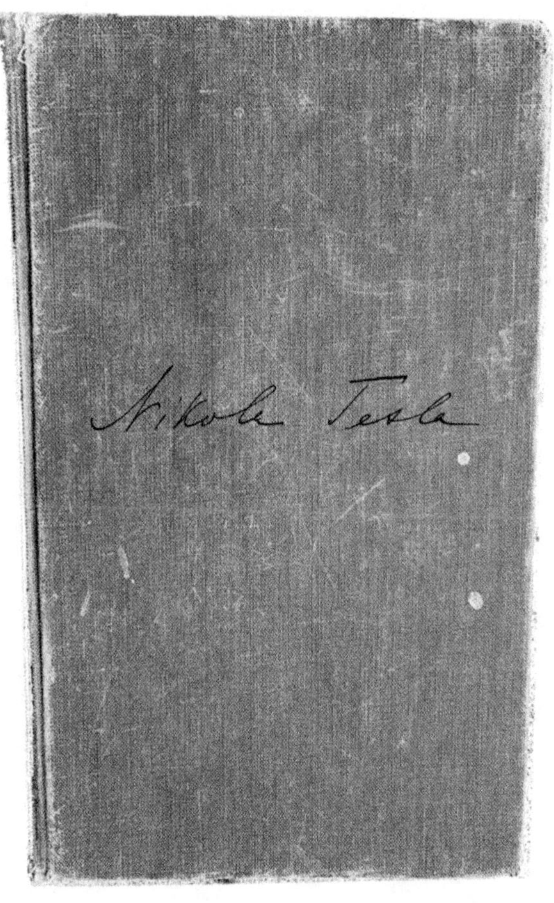

— 25 —

Elmo Tackett had the ability to blend into a crowd. He timed his movements to the people he was around and went unnoticed. Always before, his targets had been ordinary men who led ordinary lives. But Max Berglin was not an ordinary man. For some reason his movements were severely limited. For a week Elmo had been tracking him, but the target went to work in a chauffeured automobile. The vehicle entered the building through a tunnel that went underground into the Centurion Building basement. For the past two days this entrance had been guarded, as well as the front entrance to the building. Elmo didn't like this. Always before he had observed and studied the target until he was familiar with the mark and all of his surroundings.

The target arrived and left work at any time of the day. When he went home he was chauffeured to a gated palatial mansion requiring a keycoded card. Elmo could see that the home was also surrounded by guards.

Elmo could not be said to be a patient man, he simply did his job and looked for opportunities. He had no idea how he was to get to Max Berglin. The thought of a further thirty of those wonderful $1,000 bills made him tingle with anticipation.

Zadig Katelian was keeping an eye on Elmo Tackett. He had seen him monitoring the target for two days now and was satisfied. Elmo gave him the creeps, but the man was machine-like in his attention to his work. All you had to do was wind him up and set him loose.

Detective Moyer Interrogates Elmo

On the twentieth of November Senior Detective Stan Moyer received an anonymous tip from someone who said he was a neighbor of Max Berglin in Palmer

Park. "There's a funny looking little man with ears that stick out from his head riding around Berglin's property on a scooter."

Two days later Elmo received a mobile call from Zadig. "The Midland police are watching your movements. Lay low and do nothing until you receive my call." This was fine with Elmo. He did not like to read, and music held no interest for him. Television and sports were a total bore. Therefore he stopped his observation of Max Berglin. Despite the cold, he went downtown on his little motorized scooter, sometimes during the night, and watched. Elmo loved to observe people. Detective Moyer sent a patrol car to make regular rounds of the Berglin property, but the officers saw nothing unusual.

Three days after the tip Detective Moyer saw a small man on a scooter run a stop sign. He stopped him for a traffic violation. Elmo was enraged but knew he could never cause trouble with the police. He stifled his sense of injustice when the detective insisted he come with him to the police station for questioning. Elmo followed the police car, angry but a little frightened.

Moyer hustled the little man into an interview room. "What is your name?"

Elmo thought about lying but decided against it. Raffi had taught him how to talk to the police. You either said nothing whatsoever or you denied everything, but you never told an untruth. "I am Elmo Tackett. You have no right at all to detain me."

"So *you* are Elmo Tackett!" Moyer cried. "What were you doing surveilling the Berglin Enterprises building and the home of Max Berglin?"

"I have never surveilled, as you put it, Berglin Enterprises or the home of Max Berglin."

"What were you doing outside the gate of his home in Palmer Park? Why did you ride your scooter around the property, using binoculars?"

"I love that property. It's very beautiful. Especially the gardens."

Moyer snorted. The gardens! In mid-November! "Are you involved in any way with the Katelian crime family?" Moyer asked.

Elmo lied smoothly. "Not in the least."

"What do you know about the death of Raffi Katelian?" Moyer knew that the Katelians had been investors in one of the labs at Octagon Research.

"I know nothing about Raffi Katelian, other than what I have read in the *Midland Courier*," Elmo replied. He had been interrogated by the evil Sister Armitage at the orphanage much more severely than this. He had learned to smother his rage and not react in any way.

"Have you ever spoken with Bernie Hartwig?" Moyer barked.

"No sir. I don't even know who he is." Elmo hated calling other people 'sir.' He did it anyway to show "deference," which often worked well in getting rid of irritating persons.

Moyer tried to get Elmo to open up but the man was like a robot who wasn't programmed to give the right answers. He had taken the ETaC course developed by Dr. Paul Ekman, and trained almost every day with the Micro Expression Training Tool. This guy's face was completely flat. There was no leakage anywhere, no facial movement at all. After half an hour he finally gave it up. This ugly little fellow was smooth. Detective Moyer vowed to keep an eye on him in the future.

"You can go, Elmo Tackett," Moyer said.

Elmo got up and walked slowly out of the police station. He knew Moyer was on to him somehow, but the detective couldn't watch him all the time.

Rachel Meets Elmo

Elmo Tackett had the ability to show up at the oddest times.

Rachel and Trevor Clarke walked through Trevor's condo into his garage. A man was standing beside the driver's side door of his BMW.

"What are you doing here?" Trevor asked.

Rachel shuddered. "Who is this ugly little man, Trevor?"

"Did you put the Midland Police onto me?" Elmo asked Trevor in his emotionless voice. "Specifically, a Detective Moyer?"

Trevor was nonplussed. "Why would I do that? All of our business has been concluded."

Elmo smiled crookedly. "Not all of it."

Rachel suddenly understood. "This guy is where you get your designer drugs."

"Goddammit Elmo, why did you have to come here?" Trevor hissed.

"I just wanted to confirm our arrangement and to ensure that you, ah, are not involved in other business that concerns me."

Elmo noticed the look of honest astonishment on Trevor Clarke's face and was satisfied. "All right then, I'll be going."

"How did you get in here?" Trevor asked.

In response, Elmo walked to the side door and opened it. "You should keep your garage door locked Mr. Clarke." Elmo spoke with just the hint of a superior tone which was sure to irritate his client. He didn't like people who treated him with unconscious hauteur, which Trevor Clarke did whenever they met. He didn't like the woman next to him either. She reminded him of a younger and prettier Sister Armitage.

Trevor scowled; he knew he had locked that door. The little bastard must have picked the lock.

As Elmo was about to walk out Rachel said, "Wait." She glanced over at Trevor. "Do you know anything about Larry Potvin's embezzling scheme?"

She saw Trevor's quick intake of breath and knew she had scored a hit. Wayne DiPietro was right. "Oh ma'am I wouldn't know anything about that," Elmo replied with a knowing sarcasm that confirmed her guess.

Elmo left and Trevor walked over to the door, jerking the lock over. He'd have to get all electronic locks with a keypad. "And yes, you're right. He's the turd who arranged a supplier for my recreational substances."

Rachel was satisfied and said nothing about Larry Potvin. She filed the information. She was pleased when she saw Trevor glancing over at her during the evening, wondering whether she knew about his now abandoned scheme.

The next day, having lunch at her desk, Rachel thought about Wayne DiPietro. She must find a way to reward him. She wondered what it would be like with Wayne. He was a well set up man, and handsome, even if his personality was a little boring. She knew that Myra was no longer interested and that she would not see Trevor tonight. Never one to hesitate, she dialed Wayne's number at work.

"Wayne DiPietro, PRC."

"Wayne," Rachel said in her most pleasant voice. "After our talk we weren't in a good place. As president of my firm I can't afford to have bad relations with anyone I might do business with. Could we get together at Sweetwaters this evening and try to smooth things out between us?"

Wayne was right in the middle of a complex ledger and was disposed to be irritated. He remembered how great Rachel looked and sensed an underlying sexual current to her proposal. He was aroused and quickly accepted. "I'll meet you there at 8?" he suggested.

"Eight is fine."

Rachel dressed carefully, putting on a black lace bra and panties under a low-cut blouse and tight-fitting slacks.

Wayne arrived at Sweetwaters wearing a suit but no tie. He had carefully brushed his thinning blond hair after shaving. He thought he looked great and strode into the coffee shop confidently, wondering what the former Rachel Ferrell had in mind. When he saw her he guessed that she might be available.

Rachel could feel his desire for her as they got their coffees and sat at a table in back. They quickly disposed of their earlier misunderstanding. When she rested her hand on the table, Wayne put his larger hand over hers and gently caressed her fingers. It was incredibly sexy. She shuddered, hoping he would be decisive. He was. Wayne leaned over and said, "Let's go to your place."

Wayne carried her to the bedroom and urgently removed her clothes. "So much for those lace panties I put on especially for you," Rachel said.

Wayne did not hear her. He was so horny he couldn't believe it. They made love over and over until Wayne was sweating, and totally exhausted.

"God you're gorgeous Rachel," he said.

Rachel was pleased that his tone contained no trace of the sickly emotion called love. This was pure lust. "I think we should do this again sometime," she suggested.

Wayne smiled wearily. "My wife might disagree."

"You'd better clean up. My scent is all over you."

"It doesn't matter anymore. Myra and I have slept in separate beds for almost a year now."

Rachel cluck-clucked. "Poor boy."

Max Sr. Talks with Roka Hatsumi

A week after Kenji's men arrived I got a call from him.

"How are my men doing?"

"Very well, Hiroto-san. I only caught one man drunk in the bushes so far, with a bottle of Tozai. It's a green bottle."

"No!" Kenji said. "Who was this man?"

"He said it was inferior sake and he preferred the Kirin from Kaetsu Sake Brewery in Niigata Prefecture. He was so drunk I could hardly understand him."

Kenji was laughing now, recognizing the man from my description.

"My foreman only speaks Japanese. You are pulling my leg."

"I am, sorry. Seriously, all is well here. But I have a feeling that this is just the calm before a very big storm."

"Well then Berglin-san, I may have someone who can help you."

"That would be great. I have racked my brains but I can't figure out how to commercialize this discovery without upsetting a lot of powerful people."

"Yes," Kenji agreed. "Starting with the oil companies and the nuclear industry and the utilities."

"And going on from there."

"My friend Roka Hatsumi is in the United States until Christmas," Kenji said. "Is that name familiar to you?"

"I'm afraid not. Is he some kind of Japanese Superman? That's what we're going to need."

"No my friend, but he is very knowledgeable and respected. He is the owner of the Nijinkan martial arts training schools. The Nijinkan have helped to train elite special forces troops for various governments and private military contractors all over the world."

"How can he help?"

"Hatsumi-sama is expert not only at fighting, but also in public relations. He has shifted his focus from martial arts now that he is older. Hatsumi-sama is a personal trainer to some of the world's top corporate executives in the defense and classified area. He knows many influential people and knows what sort of opposition you're likely to face. A good man to have on your side."

I thought about it. My friend was offering help from what he considered an influential source, and I wanted to go ahead anyway. "All right. What do I do?"

"I would like to invite Hatsumi-sama to your home Saturday afternoon for lunch. He is very interested in your discovery. Will that be all right?"

Today was Tuesday, I had nothing going on this weekend. "All right. Let's do it."

"Excellent. We will arrive precisely at noon."

Lt. Col. Stapleton Takes Action

James Stapleton was pleased that Bernard Hartwig, one of his field operatives, had defused the Midland situation in the public debate.

However, Lieutenant Spieth's intelligence reports were becoming more and more alarming. Apparently Berglin had hired the two scientists and they were now holed up in the Centurion building downtown, working on a commercially viable overunity device.

The threat from Max Berglin would have to be eliminated, and he knew just the man for the job.

He would also have to inform Byrnes of his intelligence. He hated talking with Byrnes.

Ralph Zimring sat in his big sunroom with his long legs stretched out, listening to Tchaikovsky's Rite of Spring. His big rambling house was situated in a clearing in the middle of a five-acre wood ten miles north of Northport, Michigan. He kept a small private plane at Woolsey airport, two miles down the road. Ralph was a soldier-for-hire and he liked it.

He was almost seven feet tall and stood out in any crowd, yet no one could positively describe his facial features. He had learned to disguise his identity and hide his height, acting inconspicuously, taking on the identity and the demeanor of the people in his environment. In the business he was known as the Stork.

Somewhere in the recesses of his consciousness Ralph saw a blinking orange light, disturbing the train of his thinking. Immediately he picked up a small headset from the side table and placed it on his head. The device, as if sentient, immediately adjusted itself to his cranium. Instantly he was in the White Room, facing a man he hadn't seen since he left the Army almost ten years ago.

"I can't say it's a pleasure to see you Stapleton."

"The feeling is mutual Zimring, but this is a matter of national security."

Despite their dislike for one another – which arose from a bungled operation in Kahtaniya in northern Iraq – both men understood each other. Stapleton showed Ralph 3D images of Park, Rosen, and Max Berglin Sr., the Centurion Building, and Max Berglin's home in Palmer Park. A detailed briefing followed, all at the speed of thought.

"Max Berglin is the target," Ralph said (thought); Stapleton confirmed.

"He's off the reservation Zimring. If this overunity device gets into the hands of our enemies there's no telling what damage could be done to the United States. It is of the utmost importance that Berglin is made to cooperate, and any new developments sequestered. An Intelligence Community Directive is being prepared. The original device has a Patent Secrecy Order attached to it, so you are on firm legal ground. If the target refuses to cooperate you know what to do."

"Payment to be made in digital currency," Ralph specified. They agreed on a price. "Deal. Report via the White Room."

Ralph refolded the headset and placed it in his pocket. He decided to drive, not fly, and packed his warbag. Then he hopped in his nondescript gray Ford Focus and headed toward Midland, Illinois.

On the trip to Midland Ralph turned up the heater in his car. The cold and gray skies reminded him of a bitter Russian winter three years ago. He had lived on assignment in Moscow for three months, tracking and finally killing Gordze

Khachidze, a viscous psychopath who ran a human trafficking ring for the Solntsevskaya Bratva. Shortly after that his girlfriend had been killed. After Julia's death a dark seed had sprouted and grown to terrifying proportions. He had experienced a severe, life-numbing depression, and had almost committed suicide. But he had made it out the other side.

Ralph didn't fully understood the details of Julia's death. It began when he botched a job to erase Farshid Yazdani, a controversial and inconvenient Iranian diplomat at the UN. At the time he was working for Blackstone, a private military company who had contracted the hit with one of the US intelligence agencies. As he studied Yazdani's movements and found out more about him, he began to like him. Yazdani was a straight-shooter like himself who always told the truth and who couldn't be intimidated. At the last moment, with his finger on the trigger and the shot lined up, he backed out. A resolution backed by the Iranian government and pushed by Yazdani had been passed. The US government had been severely embarrassed and a potential conflict with Iran had been defused. He had also pissed off Jordan Blackwell, the owner of Blackstone. His failure to kill a good man had tarnished Blackstone's reputation in the business. Blackwell was friendly with Duchesne Comstock, an Assistant Director of National Intelligence at the Office of the Director of National Intelligence.

When he got back to Northport he found Julia's body in the basement, her neck snapped cleanly. Ralph recognized the work of another professional, a killer-for-hire named Harriman Drake. Drake was known to be associated with Duchesne Comstock. The grossly obese Comstock was a ladder-climber and a boot-licker. Ralph did some digging and found that Comstock had ordered the hit on Yazdani through Blackstone, seeking to curry favor with ODNI director Herman Putnam. Putnam was a sociopath with political ambitions who had called for the use of tactical nuclear weapons against Iran and North Korea.

It was complicated.

You had to be a fuckin' political scientist to understand the complex relationships within the clandestine community. They changed all the time as alliances formed and dissolved. All he knew was his little part of the story.

Ralph concluded that the hit on Julia was a revenge killing. Blackwell's anger he could understand; he had failed to do the job he had been contracted for. Later he did other work for Blackwell gratis; both men had reputations to uphold. But Comstock? Somehow his refusal to take out Yazdani must have caused grievous harm to Comstock's career. Ralph couldn't imagine why a man – even a misanthrope like Duchene Comstock – would kill an innocent woman just to get revenge on him. However, he wasn't 100% sure about Comstock's involvement in Julia's death. He had not yet been able to locate Harriman Drake who, like himself, was a freelancer. When he did he would snap Drake's neck as he had Julia's.

First he would take care of Max Berglin.

Ralph Zimring Makes His Appearance

When I woke up on Saturday morning at 5:30 I was aware of a presence. Although it was perfectly dark I was sure someone was in my bedroom.

"That's right Max Berglin," a voice said calmly.

I reached for a pistol that I had in the top drawer of the little end table to the left of the bed. "I wouldn't do that," the voice said in conversational tones, as if we were old acquaintances.

I am good in a crisis; my nerves calm and my mental and physical acuity sharpens. "I'm going to flip on the light."

I turned to my right and saw a huge man standing over my bed. "I feel like a lobster who's ready for the boiling pot."

"I am speaking to the so-dangerous Max Berglin?"

"I am he." Whoever this guy was, he had gotten past all of my security hardware, Hiroto's two perimeter guards, and my personal bodyguard. "You haven't killed any of my men, have you?"

"Point for you, Max Berglin. A good commander always thinks of his men first."

I began to get irritated. "All right my good fellow, what's this all about? There's a chair next to the bed, have a seat."

The giant didn't move. "I'm here to sequester your new invention and demand your cooperation. Failing that, I'll have to neutralize you and your two scientists."

I realized that the opposition I had expected had already materialized. I would have to have a word with Kenji: his vaunted security detail had failed on the first attempt.

"Why don't you see what I'm doing here before you jump to conclusions?"

"Orders are orders. I take it that you refuse to cooperate?"

"Hold on a second." I walked slowly over to my dresser and threw on some clothes. "Before you do anything I want you to take a look at something. If we see my housekeeper or my bodyguard I'll tell them that you're, er, an unexpected house guest."

The man's lips curled slightly upward in a smile. "Your bodyguard is unharmed, but he is, shall we say, taking a little nap. Your security detail has been neutralized but is unharmed."

"Come with me." I led the way down to the basement. We saw no one. Slava isn't usually up until 6:30, to prepare breakfast at 7.

The giant moved silently behind me as we trooped down the hall to the kitchen and the basement stairs. As we moved down the wooden stairs I wanted to ask him how he could move without making a sound, but I didn't. For the second time in three days I demonstrated the system. I wondered whether this guy was a real human being or just a sociopathic killer. He surely had the look of one.

"So this is what it's all about." For the first time the giant turned around to face me. He was dressed all in black in some sort of military rig, and wore soundless leather shoes with soft rubber soles. Compared to him I was a little toothpick.

Then ensued the strangest conversation I have ever had in my life. Ralph Zimring introduced himself and for almost half an hour grilled me on my invention and my intentions. Then I told him about myself and my interest in Tesla. Zimring told me about himself. We stood there, chatting like old buddies.

"I was trained as an Army Ranger," the giant said. "Served in the Special Troops Battalion of the 75th. I served my country believing that I was fighting for the cause of freedom. I've done some terrible things, and justified it because of my commitment to the cause. But after an incident in Tikrit, Iraq, I started to get cynical. My counter insurgency team busted into a house of suspected terrorists who turned out to be civilians. Just before he died a bewildered man who had been shot asked me, 'Why do you kill us?' In al Taka, a few months later, I interrogated an insurgent. The guy said he was fighting us because we were invaders. I concluded, eventually, that one man's terrorist is another man's freedom fighter. It all depends on which side you're on."

I nodded. I had never served, but I respected those who did even if they were misguided.

"After I left the military I went into mercenary work, mainly because it pays over $1,000 a day. I like the action and the adrenaline rush of being in dangerous situations."

I was curious. "How did you feel when you killed your first man?"

"A slight pressure on my trigger finger."

I must have looked shocked.

"Sorry. Gallows humor. You joke around like that to relieve the tension. I've seen a lot of men killed. Out of the 50 guys in my Ranger unit 33 of them are dead. I've been to a lot of funerals."

Zimring spoke softly but powerfully. "As a boy I liked to beat up bullies. I started studying the martial arts when I was ten. Kids, even older ones, would come to me when they had problems and I'd take care of it. I always wanted to be a soldier."[8]

I couldn't stop asking this guy questions. "I suppose you must travel a lot."

"Oh yeah. To Iraq with my special ops unit. As a mercenary I started out working for private military contractors. In Columbia fighting drug cartels; back to Iraq, protecting the oil fields; in Russia and Chechnya fighting the mafias; and in China recovering some dangerous stolen technology. I'm lucky to still be alive. After three years I made a ton of money so I decided to work solo. I can afford to be a freelancer now, picking and choosing my jobs. That's how I came here."

The conversation reached a stopping point.

Zimring pointed to the Cube. "Show me how that thing works again."

I demonstrated it once more.

Zimring paused for a moment. Then he spoke like a man who has made a momentous decision. "Fuck Stapleton. I want to warn you, Berglin, that if you don't immediately cease and desist you and your security detail aren't long for this world."

"Really? And who are these mysterious foes ready to take me out?"

Zimring just laughed. "The motherfuckers who sent me are out of your league." He gestured with his hands to the basement window. "I took out all your guys in less than five minutes." His eyes softened and he pointed to the Cube. "I'm a mercenary Berglin, and I have no patience with fools. But this is a game-breaker for me. I'll not interfere if you mean to give this to the world."

I felt guilty. "I'm no saint, Zimring. I want to give this to the world and make a boatload of money doing it!"

The giant guffawed; it sounded like a foghorn in a church. "I have no problem with that. All right then, I am taking you for a man of your word."

With that Ralph Zimring turned away, then he turned back. "One more thing you should know Berglin. You've got a mole somewhere in your organization. Stapleton probably knows what you're doing before you do." With that the giant floated silently up the stairs and was gone.

I had no idea who Stapleton was, but Bernie had also mentioned a mole. As I stood there thinking about the traitor in my midst, Slava came down the stairs. "I've been looking for you, boss. Breakfast is ready and the coffee is hot!"

I told Slava what had happened. We found my bodyguard in a hall closet, tied up with a bandanna around his mouth. Slava and I went outside and found our two security guards immobilized in the same fashion, shivering in the late November cold. The men apologized profusely in Japanese; I couldn't understand a word they said. I bowed and indicated that all was forgiven.

Slava and I went back inside. Before I sat down to breakfast I called Kenji, who was furious at the performance of his men and said that those who had failed would be summarily replaced.

All through breakfast I pondered who might have sent the giant, but I had a lot of work to do before Kenji and Roka Hatsumi arrived at noon. I prepared the table and a meal for my guests. I had been to Japan several times on business, but to me the culture was a bit too straightlaced. However, I did appreciate the culture's traditions, one of which was to honor one's guests in one's home. I prepared miso soup, rice, hand-rolled sushi for an appetizer, tender slices of kobe beef with wasabi and soy dipping sauce, and hibachi slaw. Despite Zimring's warning I felt that this meeting had tremendous significance.

I went down to my cellar and got out four bottles of precious *daiginjo* sake, imported from Japan. Two were for drinking during the meal, and the other two as gifts for my guests. I wrapped each bottle with a thin red ribbon. I remembered to place chopsticks and holders in front of each bamboo placemat, and a covered plate that would hold the *oshibori*, or hot towels. Slava would see to that. I filled a large ceramic *tokkuri* that one of my clients had sent me with both bottles of the chilled sake. I felt nervous, which was very unusual.

At noon the doorbell rang and Slava brought the two men into the kitchen. "Your guests, sir." Kenji Hiroto was a small, rotund man with a cheerful face and a sunny disposition. Roka Hatsumi was an older man, tall and thin, with a mustache and long gray hair that fell to his shoulders. He looked like someone who was in peak physical condition.

I wore slippers, and noticed that Slava had also provided slippers for Kenji and his guest. I bowed. "Thank you for coming to my home. I have prepared a meal for us, then we can talk." I could see that Kenji was pleased with the reception. His American friend had taken the time to prepare everything himself. This was a sign of honor and respect for himself and his guest.

Kenji introduced Roka Hatsumi, who bowed and said, "I am honored."

"Please have a seat gentlemen." First I poured sake from the tokkuri into three *choko* – small porcelain glasses. Then I indicated the food, which was served separately in decorated wooden bowls. "*Itadakimasu!*" I said, and both Roka and Kenji smiled.

Kenji and Roka both reached for the sushi and drank from their choko. I followed suit and remembered to refill the choko for my guest of honor. Kenji refilled my choko, and Roka refilled Kenji's. Kenji had taught me that – at a Japanese meal you never filled your own glass. We made small talk until I said, "Let us eat, gentlemen. I am hungry!"

I remembered to use the wide end of my chopsticks to transfer food to my plate (you don't want to get your cooties on the food) and to use the hot towel to wipe my hands before picking up food. We ate silently for several minutes. Then I leaned back in my chair, put my chopsticks in their holder, and rang a bell.

Both Kenji and his guest said, *"Gochisosama deshita,"* traditional after being treated to a meal. Slava came in and cleared the table, placing hors d'oeuvres of raw fish, rice, and bean sweets on the table. I had sent him out to the Tsai grocery on Friday, a specialty shop that carried a wide variety of genuine Japanese food supplies. We refilled our chokos and Kenji began the discussion.

"Hatsumi-sama, I believe it would be best for you to see what Max here has done."

I rose from the table and (once again!) led the way into the basement, where I showed them Tesla's Cube that had enabled me to get completely off the grid. "My people are developing more efficient systems, but for now this one is perfectly functional," I explained.

Hatsumi looked to Kenji and cried, "*Hana yori dango!*" Kenji turned to me. "Literally, dumplings rather than flowers. Something useful rather than decorative."

After I answered a few questions, we went back upstairs to drink some more sake. I knew that business would not be discussed until Hatsumi felt comfortable with me, and trusted me. So I decided to open up. The sake had loosened our tongues and I began to tell them about my life. My guests also opened up to me a little. It turned out that Kenji was also a bachelor, and all of us were driven men. "I could never find a woman who didn't want me for my money, or just a one-night stand," I said. "I married but it fell apart a couple years later." I opened my arms. "All this I have, it's practically a palace, but there's no one to share it with."

I noticed that the two men were a bit uncomfortable with my personal revelations but I wanted them to know about some of the most important aspects of my life. If Hatsumi was going to help me he should know what kind of man I was.

After several moments of silence Roka smiled. "I have been happily married for forty years. Michiko comes with me on all my trips abroad."

"You're lucky then."

Kenji grunted. "I too have no one to share my life with."

We drank silently for a few minutes, lost in our own thoughts. I looked over at Hatsumi. "Do you know of a seven-footer by the name of Ralph Zimring?"

Kenji glanced quickly at Hatsumi. "Zimring is a well-known mercenary. We call him *konotori*, the stork."

I saw a look of intense focus on Hatsumi's face. "You say this man took out three of Hiroto-san's men?"

I nodded. "He said that the people who sent him are out of Hiroto-san's league – and yours."

I saw Hatsumi's face flush with anger but it was time for brutal honesty. I looked Hatsumi in the eye. "He said there were many others like him."

Kenji listened carefully for a minute as Hatsumi exploded Japanese at him. The older man was obviously very agitated. "Hatsumi-sama says that we have very good men also, but that fighting is not the goal. He says we must be very, very careful, but that with your device the people of the world could eventually become energy independent. He says that we could drastically reduce pollution and possibly even halt the fighting between nations for scarce resources. He says, 'We will help you if you go public.'"

What could I say? Kenji seemed to think Hatsumi's help would be valuable but I didn't believe anyone could protect me from an army of Zimrings. I thanked Hatsumi. "Come hell or high water I'm going to make Tesla's dream come true." Inside I was eager and excited.

Both Kenji and Hatsumi nodded enthusiastically. Hatsumi said, *"Hajime wa shojo no gotoku, owari wa datto no gotoshi."* Kenji translated this as, "first go slowly, then boldly." I nodded as Hatsumi said haltingly in English, "When you decide how to proceed, call me." Kenji handed over Hatsumi's personal mobile number.

"This is quite an honor," Kenji told me. I bowed to the older man as a sign of gratitude and his trust in me. We left it at that, even though I still had no idea how Hatsumi could help. I ushered my guests out of the house and we bowed to each other at the front door.

I didn't tell them about the mole because I wanted to find the bastard myself. I hoped it wasn't any of my trusted people.

— 26 —

During the next week I drew up a tentative business plan for a small commercial venture that would build and sell Cubes. On Thursday I informed my executive board of the success of our little R&D investment. Despite my enthusiasm they were having none of it. "Max, you have to get real," Al Jordan, my CEO, told me. "You don't mess around with patent secrecy orders."

"What if I started an entirely new company?"

"You're still in the same situation. As long as you leave me and the Board out of it, do what you want. But Max, if you go ahead with this you have to keep it out of this building. Your new venture can have nothing to do with Berglin Enterprises."

Of course Al was right. Selling free-energy devices had no points of intersection with the security software business. Fortunately my Board could competently run the company without me. I was the idea man but they didn't need me for day-to-day operations.

On Friday I received a phone call from Roka Hatsumi. Through an interpreter he told me that Nobu Tanaka, a legendary Japanese engineer and businessman, had agreed to send me his right-hand man, Yusuke Shiozawa. "Tanaka-san specializes in building successful engineering firms from scratch."

I thanked Hatsumi. I know a lot about security software but not much about engineering. Kenji's friend had come through with constructive help in a powerful way.

On Saturday I got really excited thinking about the new organization, which I tentatively named UPower. My two scientists would be the backbone of the new organization, but I needed at least a skeleton staff. The first person I thought of was Danielle Menard. I envisioned the eventual merging of Berglin Enterprises with UPower, gradually getting out of the software security business and into the energy industry. Danielle would be the ideal face of a new, cutting-edge company that would change the world. I immediately grabbed my mobile and called her.

"Danielle, there has been a change in plans for your employment. I need to talk in person. You can either come over here or I can come over there."

"What's the urgency, boss? Can't we just talk on Monday at work?"

"No my girl, this is private and I don't want anyone to overhear us. Your place or mine?"

"That sounds like a proposition, Max Berglin."

"I wish it was. But this is just business – unless you want it to be more than that Danielle."

Danielle was startled. Her thoughts had been going more and more to Zach, but that was over now. She was attracted to big muscular men like Zach and Max and she liked older men. But no. It would be too complicated. "Let's make it strictly business, all right? You come over here."

I quickly combed my hair and changed my clothes. I pulled out my tablet with my business plan, got into my BMW with my bodyguard, and drove over to Danielle's apartment as fast as I could. I was hoping for something...but I didn't think it was going to happen. I tried to leave the guard outside but he insisted (in Japanese) that he come with me. We found Danielle's apartment and she let us in.

"Don't worry about him," I told Danielle. "He only understands Japanese." I looked around at the nicely furnished two-bedroom unit in the Atwater complex. "You're moving up in the world Danielle."

"Not as far up as you've moved Max."

I never allow my employees to get on a first-name basis with me, except this girl. Even in an old pair of jeans and a worn-out blouse she looked fantastic. Tall and graceful, maybe a little too thin, but she was wicked smart and she had IT, whatever that was.

I outlined the success of the Cube and told her about my plans to produce them. "I want you to be spokesperson for the new company, which I'm calling UPower, when it gets off the ground. I've decided that you would also make an excellent spokesperson for Berglin Enterprises. Are you up for it?"

I could see her surprise. "This is rather sudden Max, don't you think? Being a sales rep is a far cry from being spokesperson for your entire operation."

I grinned. It *was* a big step up from sales rep but I just had the feeling it was the right move. All reports from my sales staff were that Danielle was good in front of the microphone and that she excelled at interacting with people. I had seen it myself that day at Seva. "Honestly Danielle, it was a decision I made on a hunch. I always act on my gut instincts. I trust myself to make the right decisions and they almost always turn out well." Unspoken was my realization that Danielle Menard was the first person I ran to when I got really excited about the most important thing in my life. That told me something about my feelings for her.

Danielle considered. "It's a public relations job."

"Precisely. Not dissimilar to what you are doing now, but on a larger scale. You'd need to train under Walter Davidson. He's my one-man PR department. "

Danielle thought for a few moments. "I can handle that. Being a sales rep is OK, but I am getting a little bored with it."

"What we're getting into is anything but boring."

I brought out my tablet and gave her a brief description of her new duties at Berglin Enterprises and enthusiastically outlined her potential responsibilities at UPower.

"You seem to be more interested in UPower than Berglin Enterprises."

"Yes, I am. Austin Park and John Rosen have streamlined the power unit to a three-by-three-by-three foot cube that plugs into the electrical panel. I've tested it in my own house and it works perfectly. I've rented that old abandoned furniture warehouse, you know, the Van Allen franchise that folded a couple of years ago. We've already got engineering help lined up to help us set up production. It turns out your old school chum John Rosen has a talent for organizing, so I'm putting him in charge of product development. Austin Park is head of research."

"You're going to need a lot more staff than that," Danielle said.

"Eventually. But we're going to have to start very, very slowly, and very unobtrusively. At the beginning stages we cannot attract any attention. The idea is to get a small manufacturing facility set up and produce just a few units at a time, selling them to homeowners in town. We won't even mention that the new devices use breakthrough technology; we'll just say it's a highly efficient renewable-energy device. We'll practically give them away at first. Hopefully we'll be totally under the radar."

I could see Danielle's look of skepticism. "Give them away? That's not like you Max. You don't need me for that."

"I have been impressed very strongly with the idea that we have to tread carefully, at least at first. But when this thing gets off the ground we're going to need a persuasive and personable spokesperson. You project just the right image I want Berglin Enterprises to have, Danielle. Did you know that you have already become a symbol for the company among many of my clients?"

Danielle was startled. "I have?"

"Let's just say that you've generated a lot of favorable buzz. You're also a perfect symbol for UPower, a revolutionary new company that's going to change the way the world does business."

I could see the wheels turning in her head.

Danielle thought about what Pierce had told her. She was going to beat her father to the punch! "I understand, Max."

"Good. We're going to put it out – you're going to put it out – that Berglin Enterprises needs more space for a new line of security software. You'll say that Berglin Enterprises will require dozens more programmers and support personnel. And we do need more people, Danielle, because our software security business is expanding. I've got construction crews over at the warehouse right now getting the place fixed up. In the front it will look like an extension of Berglin Enterprises, same logo. The top floor of the building will will be given over to a lab and a small production line to manufacture the new units, which we're calling the Cube."

"The Cube," Danielle said, mulling it over. "It has a ring to it. How long will it take to produce each unit?"

"That's the million-dollar question. It took Park and Rosen two full days to put together the one I have in my basement, but it's strictly hand-made. It's going to take a while to figure out how to set up the assembly process. Yusuke Shiozawa, my engineering consultant, is working on a template for that right now. The manufacturing process will hopefully be fully automated. Shiozawa will help us with that. We'll need a cool design for the container; I've got graphic designers on that as well."

As Danielle thought over my proposal I was feeling enormously confident. The Japanese are the world's foremost computer engineers. Roka Hatsumi had brought in a world renowned engineer and his colleague to my project, showing me how highly he valued it. Shiozawa had called me an hour after Hatsumi's phone call on Friday.

"So when do I start?" Danielle asked.

"Right now. There's a press conference on Tuesday morning to announce the expansion of Berglin Enterprises. I'll introduce you as spokesperson for the company. We need a new image anyway, and you've made quite a name for yourself."

"What am I going to say? It's a little short notice."

"That's up to you." I handed her a briefing paper. "Something along these lines. You know our product line backwards and forwards now. But remember, no mention at all of the Cube or anything about breakthrough technology."

She looked a little nervous so I briefly outlined what I wanted her to say. After that I tried to get her to come out to lunch with me. She was having none of it. On the way home I thought that Danielle perfectly represented the cutting-edge "new look" image I wanted my company to have. She also represented the look I liked.

On Monday I had a meeting with my executive board and told them about the expansion announcement. They weren't pleased that an entire floor of the new building was to be given over to UPower, but they did agree that I had gotten the old warehouse for a song. "You always were a good wheeler-dealer," Al Jordan said.

I had Tara Bolshoi, my receptionist, call the local radio and TV stations to announce the expansion of Berglin Enterprises.

On Tuesday morning I walked up the stairs to my office, wondering if I had made Danielle spokesperson for my company because I was interested in her, or because she was the best person for the job. I needn't have worried. She was spectacular and the entire thing went off smoothly.

After that I went to Room 411 to check on my two scientists. When I entered the big laboratory I saw Park and Rosen hard at work.

"Gentlemen, take a break and tell me how you are progressing." I walked toward a large table with a device that was surrounded by magnets. "Have you changed the configuration of the magnetic array for the Pulsar?"

"Yes," Austin replied. "This is a new version that will drastically increase the amount of power we can draw." He paused. "We made some mistakes with the first one."

"Yeah boss, we couldn't follow simple directions," John Rosen said. "We thought we knew more than Tesla."

John turned to me. "Dr. Berglin, in time we could make this building, or any building, a power plant that can send energy anywhere on the planet."

I studied the device.

"There is a geometry to the magnetic array."

"Correct," Park said. "A strong and properly aligned magnetic field allows us to draw more energy from the quantum fluctuation that is present in every cubic centimeter of space. We've been experimenting with different geometries and field strengths. It's dangerous because if you do it wrong, tremendous power surges can result that could literally blow up the entire building." Austin pointed to a blackened, foot-wide hole ten feet above them. "Experimental error."

Austin arranged a demonstration.

"We've learned how to draw a tiny, tiny bit of energy and direct it in a burst. Look." He went over to the bench and typed into a console. I saw a watermelon suddenly explode on a small table on the other side of the room.

I began to have second thoughts, thinking about how this technology could be weaponized. All it would take was one little leak and the DoD could confiscate the new technology. They could claim it was a potential threat to national security. Fortunately the Cube was basically just a fancy renewable energy device, and I would market it like that.

Austin summarized the accomplishments of the two scientists so far. "We've got the Cube, the radiant energy device – "

"Something that throws out plasma spheres, which we can't find any practical use for," John interrupted.

"– and the Pulsar, which is basically just a prototype of Tesla's wireless power generator. So far we can only send a small amount of energy cleanly through space to a distance of about sixty feet, but if this was developed there's no telling how far we could go with it."

John exhibited Tesla's notebook. "Sir, we've just scratched the surface of what Tesla dreamed up. This thing may be the most valuable information on the planet."

I bowed Japanese fashion. "Thank you gentlemen." I was beginning to imbibe some of that culture.

"Carry on. Your first priority is helping the engineers to set up a production line for the Cube. Answer all of their questions and don't worry about doing any more research – we've got enough to keep us going for years."

I pointed to the notebook. "Keep that locked up when you aren't using it." As I walked out of the lab I noticed the security cameras, pleased with Tara Bolshoi's efficiency.

When I got home I set Slava to finding my informer inside Berglin Enterprises. I gave him a pass to go anywhere, even into the lab. It meant my house wouldn't be as efficient as I wanted it, but I wasn't spending much time at home anyway.

Slava was avuncular, completely non-threatening, and he was good at sniffing things out.

Elmo Gets His Chance

On Wednesday I ducked out of the Berglin Enterprises building through a private underground tunnel to my private parking area. Kenji Hiroto had told me never to leave without my bodyguard, but I wanted to see the progress of the construction crews at the new building without drawing too much attention to myself.

As I drove by the back of the old warehouse I saw a funny-looking man walking along the service driveway to the unloading dock. I didn't think anything of it. Probably one of the construction workers.

Elmo Tackett drove his scooter up the long entranceway from River Dr. to the old warehouse building.

Yesterday he had seen a big truck hauling a sign that said "Berglin Enterprises." He followed the truck down a long entrance road to the property and into the parking lot. There were several trucks and construction equipment lying around, but no security guards. Elmo drove his scooter around the place, memorizing the layout. He went home and drew a map on a piece of paper.

This morning Elmo put his scooter out of sight in the bushes off the entranceway. The entrance road turned left just before the unoccupied guard booth and the parking lot. The road was deserted. As he was walking down to the entrance he saw a dark blue BMW with a vanity plate that said "BERGLIN" coming down the long driveway. He realized his luck was in. The parking lot was about two hundred feet from his present position. He ran as fast as he could, hoping to see Max Berglin and fire the silenced airgun before the target entered the building. Elmo knew from his map that the building was shaped like an "L." The main entrance door was to the left, which had the big Berglin Enterprises sign. Another door to the right was on the other side of the "L," straight ahead from the guardhouse and through the parking lot.

Elmo never thought about his body but now cursed his short little legs as he pumped them as hard as he could. Fortunately there was no one around to see him. When he got past the little turn in the road he saw Berglin already out of his car and walking purposefully toward the door on the right. Construction equipment and vehicles littered the area but he had a clear shot. He already had a bullet loaded and, without thinking, aimed and fired. A miss! The bullet screamed past the target's head and clinked off the wall, sending a small chunk of concrete whizzing past one of the vehicles. The target froze for a moment, enough to allow him to reload. He was still in luck because there was no one outside. He fired a second shot just as the target began to turn around. A hit! Zadig Katelian had not exaggerated when he said that the substance inside the bullet casing was fast acting. As soon as the bullet entered the body the target collapsed. Elmo wanted to put another bullet into the target but someone might come out of the building at any moment. He wanted to get closer so he could see from close up the life force of Max Berglin leave his body. It was too risky. Reluctantly Elmo pocketed the airgun and walked deliberately around the turn and past the loading dock. He found his scooter and drove off.

As Max lay unconscious on the cement parking lot Elmo took the scooter onto River Drive, and back to his waterfront apartment. On the way he wondered whether the life force in the frog was different than the life force in a human.

A drywall contractor came out of the building thirty seconds later and saw a man lying about thirty feet in front of the door. He immediately called 911. An ambulance came about three minutes later, taking Max to Midland East Hospital. Max's bodyguard arrived just as the ambulance was about to leave and called Kenji. "Berglin-san has collapsed!" he barked in Japanese. The man told Hiroto-san that he had stopped for a necessary bathroom break. Out of the bathroom window he saw Berglin-sans' car leaving the building. He had scrambled into the Hiroto Securities vehicle so fast that he had not had time to clean himself properly. By the time he found his vehicle and exited the Centurion Building Berglin-san had disappeared.

Kenji groaned. His security force had now failed twice! Foremost in his mind was his concern for his friend, but also a deep feeling of shame. Although a contract had been signed, he would reduce his bill to reflect the poor quality of service he was delivering. Kenji drove quickly to the hospital and negotiated with the staff to allow Max's bodyguard to stay with Max in his room. Kenji then called Roka Hatsumi.

After an hour the emergency room doctor examining Max returned to the waiting room. "I found a small entrance wound in Mr. Berglin's abdomen, and remnants of a brittle material that could have been a homemade or designer shell casing from a bullet. A toxicology screen was negative." The doctor was mystified. "I have never seen a case like this. There was no exit wound and no trace of a toxic substance in the body."

"How is Max?" Kenji asked.

"There was a significant loss of blood," the doctor told Kenji. "The patient is in stable but critical condition."

Max lay unconscious throughout the day. A ballistics expert pronounced that the fragment was probably from a .22 caliber bullet. The substance of the casing was analyzed by a materials scientist. The remnant was discovered to be an ingeniously crafted bio-substance that was hard enough to penetrate flesh but that would eventually dissolve within the body. A splash of something that was analyzed as a water-borne barbiturate was discovered within the abdominal cavity.

Detective Stan Moyer was baffled. At a building full of contractors no one had seen anything! His men could discover no suspects or leads. The area was filled with construction debris and no shell casings or bullets were found, even though a chink in the wall showed that one shot had missed its target.

On Thursday Max still lay in critical condition.

The *Midland Courier* wrote,

Unknown Assailant Shoots Head of Berglin Enterprises

By Tina Brooks

Max Berglin, President of Berglin Enterprises, was shot today by an unknown assailant. He is in critical condition at Midland East Hospital.

Berglin was walking into the old Van Allen warehouse building off River Dr. when he was attacked. The company is renovating the building to accommodate an expansion in business.

Berglin's body was found by a drywall contractor as he exited the building, who immediately called 911. Chief Detective Stan Moyer of the Midland Police Department told this reporter that there are no leads or suspects in the case.

The victim's son, Max Berglin Jr., complained that his father was growing paranoid. "He's hired a private army from Japan, they are all over the house and the business. Most of these guys don't even speak English, it's totally crazy. I think it has something to do with that new invention everyone was talking about several months ago." Max Jr. is a former engineering student at Carleton University. Max Berglin Sr. lives alone in a large home in Palmer Park with his housekeeper, a Mr. Slava Terbo.

Chief Detective Stan Moyer told this reporter that the FBI was also on the case and that an investigation was underway.

Roka Hatsumi postponed his return to Japan and met Kenji at Max's hospital bed later on Thursday. Both men gazed at the unconscious man, whose breathing was very shallow.

"It's not very good," Kenji said in Japanese to Hatsumi in worried tones. "Could this have been a professional hit?"

Roka shook his head. "Industrial espionage gone wrong, perhaps, or a personal grudge. The FBI's involvement suggests that it is more likely what the Americans call a national security matter. I suspect the Technology Acquisition Consortium in Chicago. My source there knows a man named Roger Comfrey, who arranges for little incidents like this."

"It is very confusing," Kenji concluded. He met the older man's eyes. "We must tread very carefully my friend."

After the first thirty-six hours the patient was still in critical condition. Max's doctors thought he might die. His will was examined. To the surprise of everyone, and to the utter shock of Max Jr., ninety percent of Max's shares in Berglin Enterprises had been willed to Danielle Menard. Max Jr. was bequeathed the home in Palmer Park. Max's ex-wife received five percent of the shares, and five percent went to Slava Terbo. It was discovered that Max had no other known relatives.

Max Berglin recovered. After a week his doctor allowed the recalcitrant patient, still weak from his injury, to go home.

When my son and Danielle heard about my will, Danielle was amazed and Max Jr. was angry. When I was sent home my son asked me why I had willed the business to a perfect stranger. "Because in another few years Danielle Menard will be the most competent person to lead this organization if anything happens to me," I said. Max Jr. raged and protested, but finally shut up when I told him that he was brilliant but irresponsible. "You're not executive material son, and you know it. Several times I've offered you a job with the company but you have turned me down."

Max Jr. spoke bitterly. "All that matter to you is business. I'm your son."

"Yes you are, and I love you. But you seem to have little interest in the company."

"The company! You should have willed those shares to me. Apparently blood ties mean nothing to you."

"I'm sorry son, but if you owned the company you'd probably just sell it." I tried to lighten the mood. "Besides, the house is more valuable than the business. It's a tangible asset, whereas the business might fail and be worth nothing." I surprised a look of hatred in his eyes, and I knew: my own son must be the mole. I had no proof of course, but Slava told me that he ran tame around the Centurion Building, including the fourth floor where Austin and John worked.

I told no one of my suspicions except Austin Park, and kept Slava on as a watchdog for my son. I was devastated. I called Austin and told him my suspicions. "Don't worry boss, we won't show him anything or say anything."

I hoped it would be enough.

Elmo Tackett stayed in his apartment for the rest of the week until he found out on the news that Max Berglin had survived.

That night he heard a knock on the door. Zadig Katelian entered. "You did not complete your mission," he said. "Therefore, your second payment will not be forthcoming."

Elmo was very angry. "The fault is entirely yours! I hit the man flush. Either your airgun or your bullets malfunctioned."

Zadig shook his head. "The job was clumsily done. You shot him on a construction site with dozens of people milling about. You should have waited until he left and ambushed him somewhere else."

"I made meticulous plans and executed them perfectly." He suspected that his interview was being recorded by Zadig so he spoke very carefully, using precise English. "The target was being protected by the Midland police and I was being tailed everywhere I went. Moreover, the target had bodyguards. It was sheer luck that the man slipped off to some building no one even knew about. I was offered an opportunity, one opportunity only, and I took it. I successfully made the shot and no one saw me. I hit the target as instructed, using the weapon you supplied. It is not my fault that your equipment is defective."

Zadig shrugged. He had liked Raffi and the buhlo who killed him had to die. Neither he nor Vahan believed it was some mysterious men in black. "Maybe so. We got it from some guy who works for one of the defense contractors. He said it couldn't fail. But the agreement was, no disposal, no money."

After Zadig left Elmo seethed. It wasn't his fault!

But Elmo Tackett was a patient man. He would wait. The thought of more of the crispy new bills motivated him.

The next time he would do it the old-fashioned way.

Danielle came to see me at my home one week after the shooting. She looked very nervous.

When she arrived at the house two athletic men, armed, took her up to my bedroom, which had been turned into a sick room. Both men exited and shut the door. When I saw her I smiled.

"Max, I'm really glad you're all right. But why did you will me most of your business? Shouldn't Al Jordan have gotten it? After all, he's the CEO and an experienced executive."

"Whoa girl, hold on a second. It's nice to see you." My interaction with Kenji and his men had taught me the benefits of first establishing harmony before discussing matters of importance.

"I'm sorry Max," she said, fiddling with her purse string. "How are you feeling?"

"Much better, thank you."

I looked her over. She wore her usual business suit but I could see worry lines on her face. She looked thinner, on edge, but still beautiful. "Have you been worrying about me?" I asked.

Danielle blushed. "Well, uh, a little, and the will..."

"Relax, Danielle. Have you been studying with Walter Davidson in Public Relations as I asked you to?"

"Yes Max. It's fascinating. But I've also been dealing with your son."

"Has he been asking you a lot of questions?"

"As a matter of fact he has. Oh Max, I'm afraid I may have said something about our new project..."

"Danielle, this is for your ears only, do you understand?" She nodded. "I suspect that Max Jr. has been leaking information about our new discovery. Please be very circumspect with him."

"Max Jr.? An informer? It's – no, maybe it's not...."

"My sentiments exactly. But I haven't been a good father, Danielle. I've been pretty much a selfish person my whole life. The way he turned out is partly my fault."

"That's nonsense, Max. Look at me and my life and my father – I'm no saint but I've learned responsibility. I don't whine about my life and make people around me miserable."

"But Danielle, your life was much easier than Max's."

Danielle opened her mouth to object but I cut her off. "Yes you lived in a hovel with a drunk. But I know something about the brilliant Pierce Regier from my time at MIT, and what happened to him and his wife. Your father was brilliant and so was your mother. Before your mom died he was a good father who paid attention to you. Then when he fell apart you learned responsibility because you had to take care of him. My son did not have these advantages, Danielle. I've been so wrapped up in myself all I gave him was the far greater cruelty of affluence and indifference. I was never interested in him as Pierce was in you."

"You're a good person, Max. You've helped a lot of people."

"Perhaps. But I haven't been a good father. So let's give Max Jr. a pass. Just watch what you say to him."

Danielle nodded. "Very well."

"Good. Now, about my will. I am extremely upset all this happened because my will was, and is, an extremely private matter. You may not know that I have no living relations in the world other than my ex-wife. By mutual agreement we have not spoken in twenty years. Your inclusion in my will was a logical decision based on my estimation of your abilities and your character. I intended to groom you as my successor and when the time was right, to inform you and the board. Understood?"

Danielle saw an attractive but lonely man without family who probably had an infatuation with her. She was confident in her abilities, but she thought Max was overreacting. The will change was probably impulsive, and after a time he would probably change his mind again. She dismissed her concerns. "Certainly Max. Thank you, I am honored. Now to change the subject: Do you know who shot you?"

I frowned. "No, dammit. I felt the first bullet go by my head and I froze for a moment. Before I could turn around the second bullet hit me sideways and went through my stomach."

"The FBI says it's a national security matter."

"My two Japanese friends have some ideas about that. They will try to find out who did this."

Slava Talks to Detective Moyer

Slava Terbo was getting bored.

Max had told him to keep an eye on his son but the boy didn't seem to have any purpose in life. At night he associated with a couple of his college acquaintances who had found jobs in Midland, going out to bars and trying to pick up women. During the day the young man loitered around the Berglin Enterprises building, asking about the two scientists holed up in Room 411, and pretending he was on errands for his father.

As Max Jr. left the building late Friday afternoon, Slava followed him. After turning the corner onto Ann Street, a funny-looking little man on a scooter stopped to engage the young man in conversation. Slava tried to listen in, but he was too far away. After a minute the man on the scooter rode away and Max Jr. turned suddenly. Slava ducked back along the wall but he had been seen.

"Slava!" Max Jr. demanded, walking toward him. "What are you doing here? Are you watching me?"

Slava stepped out and faced Max's son, who was even taller than his father. "As a matter of fact I am. Something isn't right and I want to know what you're doing."

The boy was infuriated. "You're father's housekeeper! Go back to your pots and pans and stay out of business that doesn't concern you."

"If it concerns your father it concerns me," Slava replied.

Max Jr. looked him over. "He sent you to watch me, did he? It's bad enough he wills his shares to Danielle Menard, but sending his housekeeper to spy on me? That's the outside of enough, Slava."

"Who was that little man on the scooter?"

"None of your business." Max Jr. walked away, very angry.

As Slava walked down Ann Street he noticed a police car cruising slowly down the street. He heard a soft burst of the siren and stopped as the cruiser pulled over to the curb. A good looking man with graying hair, dressed in a dark blue suit, got out and approached him. "Are you Slava Terbo, Max Berglin's housekeeper?"

Out of the corner of his eye, a block away, Slava saw Max Jr. turn back. He raised his middle finger in a vulgar gesture. "I am. May I ask why you stopped me?"

The man held out his hand. "I'm Detective Stan Moyer." The two men shook hands. "The FBI and the Midland Police have been looking into the shooting of Max Berglin. That little bastard – you'll excuse my language – on the scooter is my prime suspect."

"He looks like a child. That ugly little man shot Max?"

"I didn't say that. But he has connections to the local mafia, a Vahan Katelian. The Katelians and Max Berglin had a falling out."

"Yes, that's true. Mr. Berglin hired the two scientists and Katelian wasn't very happy about it."

"Did you happen to hear what Elmo said to Max Jr.?"

"Unfortunately I did not, Detective Moyer."

"Do you have any idea what that discussion was about?"

"I'm afraid not detective. I am sorry to be so uninformative."

Moyer clenched his fists in irritation. "I can't seem to get a break on this case."

"I've been following Max Jr. around for a week," Slava volunteered, "on the orders of his father, who suspects he might be giving away company secrets."

Moyer nodded. "That explains Elmo Tackett's involvement. Elmo is an independent contractor for the local mafia. He's a little spy who messes about in other people's business."

"Thank you for your efforts, detective. Mr. Berglin and I really appreciate it. If I hear anything I'll call you."

Moyer gave Slava his card, and drove away.

Part XIII

Necker Island

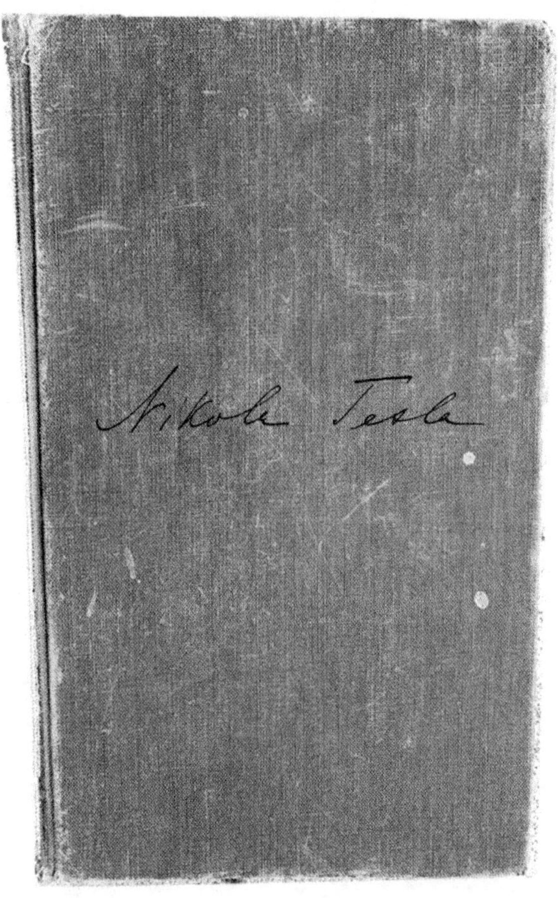

— 27 —

The holiday season began with six inches of snow on the day before Christmas. I was out of bed and back to work two weeks after the shooting, but still weak. My first meeting was with Kenji Hiroto in my fourth floor office. He told me that Roka Harsumi was leaving the day after Christmas to return to Japan. Hatsumi had been extremely helpful, setting me up with Yusuke Shiozawa. Shiozawa was a renowned engineer who was designing our Cube assembly line. Hatsumi had also upgraded my security force with a half dozen elite men, who were lent to Kenji's contingent. One of these men was a new foreman whose name was Goro Kokawa, a thin, intense man about my age and height with burning black eyes and a hawk nose. For some irrational reason the man inspired my confidence. He looked like an eagle about to pounce on his prey.

Kenji recommended another bodyguard, a slight man who never said a word but who hovered discreetly in the background and never got in the way. "This man is one of Hatsumi-sama's best. He will not speak to you, and it is not necessary to speak to him. He will observe and act if necessary, and will be with you twenty-four hours a day."

"I am honored Hiroto-san, but do you think it is necessary?"

"This is no longer just about you, my friend, or your company. You have made something that the world needs – an unlimited, clean source of energy that can make each man energy independent. Until we have won this battle, you will be facing many enemies." Kenji's eyes softened. "I am very proud of you, Max Berglin. Men have been coming forward for decades with brilliant innovations like yours, but their work was somehow suppressed. Not this time. Do you understand?"

I was amazed at the intensity of my friend, who was normally sunny and cheerful. "Yes, Kenji, I do."

"And please, Max, do not go anywhere without protection."

"Certainly not Hiroto-san."

"Hatsumi-sama will be calling on you soon before he goes back to Japan. Please listen carefully to what he says."

When Roka Hatsumi visited me later in the day in my fourth floor office, he was frowning. He apologized through an interpreter. "Excuse the interpreter but my English is not the best. I must be absolutely clear."

"I am at your service. Please take all the time you need."

Roka spoke very seriously. "Max Berglin, I have talked to several of my people, some of whom are working in very secretive, high-tech programs that my friend Julian Green says are unsupervised. These men tell me that if you dare to bring your discovery to the market it will precipitate a war against you. If you do this you are endangering your own life and the lives of everyone associated with you."

"Thank you Hatsumi-sama. The police suspect that the man who shot me is local, hired by the local mafia."

"That may be, but there is another problem. You have never been involved in the military or in the clandestine areas."

"I spent five years at Lockheed."

"*I no naka no kawazu, taikai o shirazu.* A frog in a well cannot conceive of the ocean." After a few more moments of silence he said, "After much thought and discussion with my people I have concluded that in this matter, fighting is futile. *Deru kui wa utareru.* The stake that sticks out is hammered down."

I smiled, understanding his meaning.

"You must take a different approach, Berglin-san. Therefore I would like you to meet a friend of mine, Dr. Julian Green. Mr. Green is an authority on the secretive, hi-tech classified areas and can give you good advice. This is the area where your opposition will come from. Dr. Green is giving a briefing for many of the world's government leaders on Necker Island in the Caribbean after the New Year. It would be a good idea for you to take a leave of absence from town. The conference itself will have military-grade security. I would like you to attend."

I looked out the window at the snow and the cold. The Caribbean sounded great.

"Can I invite two guests? I would like my company spokesperson, and my CEO, to join me. I will have to take one of my bodyguards as well."

"That may be difficult Mr. Berglin," Roka said. "Seating is limited. I will ask Dr. Green and get back to you shortly."

Hatsumi left and went to the lobby. When he came back twenty minutes later I was still sitting in my chair, thinking about what I had started. My distinct impression from Roka Hatsumi was his concern for the Cube, not me. I'd take his help any way I could get it. When Hatsumi came back into the room I rose. "It's all settled," Hatsumi said. "Please write the names of the two people you want to take with you, your bodyguard, and your own name. I will see that your party is on the guest list."

I said thank you and goodbye to Hatsumi. I called Danielle and Al Jordan, telling them to be ready on the Monday after New Year's Day to fly to a beautiful tropical island.

Danielle was thrilled when our plane landed in San Juan Puerto Rico. She had never been to the tropics. The 85 degree heat and humidity was welcome after leaving Midland, where the temperature was 12. Al Jordan and I took everything in stride and were amused by her naive enjoyment. My bodyguard was silent and, like a good referee in a sporting contest, almost invisible. We boarded a private plane and landed within the hour at Beef Island Airport on Virgin Tortola, in the British Virgin Islands. Then we boarded a launch and were taken to Necker Island. On the way I was in a good mood, and seemed no worse for wear since I had gotten back on my feet.

"Necker Island is entirely owned by a billionaire, Richard Branson, who started the Virgin record label." Danielle read from the sleek Necker Island brochure, the wind whipping her hair around her head. "He bought the island from Lord Cobham for $180,000 in 1978, and spent $10 million to build a luxury resort." I could tell that Danielle loved the smell of the ocean and the occasional salt spray that washed over them. When we got to the island we were met by a waiter in a white suit who handed us glasses of champagne. "Here's your Necker water!"

"We're only here for the briefing and a short dinner," I said to Danielle. "The briefing will begin at 10 a.m. and last until around 3 p.m. There are representatives from over 30 countries here."

We reached the Great House, which was essentially a restaurant on the lower floor and an open air bar with seating for about one hundred on the roof terrace. "That's A. P. Ramakrishnan, Prime Minister of India," I said to Danielle as we walked through the restaurant and up the stairs, indicating a short but distinguished looking man with jet black hair.

Danielle's eyebrows raised in inquiry.

"Roka Hatsumi told me all about the people attending," I explained.

"There's Senator Bernice Cohen," I said, nodding my head to a tall woman in a cream colored business suit. "Max Berglin! Nice to see you!" she said as she passed us on the stairs. "I met Senator Cohen in Washington before I moved to Midland," I explained to Danielle as we entered the terrace and found seats at a large crowded table covered with a white cotton cloth. Danielle was to my left and Al Jordan to her left. Danielle leaned to her right as I pointed out some more dignitaries. "That bald man in the other row is Sergei Krolov, aide to President Markov of Russia." I nodded my head to the left and forward. "That black haired man in front to the left is Hun Wen, an important figure within Chinese military intelligence."

Danielle's eyes opened wider. "This is a big deal, isn't it Max?" She was excited to meet Dr. Green, whom her father had mentioned before he left for Boston.

"Apparently it is," Al Jordan said from across the table. I could see he was impressed by the various dignitaries, who all had an official air about them. "Who is this Green guy anyway?"

A minute later a tall, muscular man approached their table. He had a slightly pockmarked face and wore thin, round-rimmed glasses. "Welcome, I'm Dr. Julian Green," he said. I rose and shook his hand, noticing his powerful grip. Green was two inches taller than my six feet two. "Do you lift?" I asked.

"Oh yes," Green replied with a smile. "I am often under a great deal of stress in this line of work. Weightlifting keeps my body strong and able to cope."

I was impressed. The man exuded an air of authority and power. "Please stick around after the briefing," Green requested. "You three are here as my personal guests. Hatsumi-sama wanted me to meet you personally. Don't mind the fireworks. Some of the things I'll say are controversial." He nudged his head over to the far right table in front of a small lectern, indicating a white-haired man with a cane by his side.

"That's Zbigniew Byrnes," Green said. "The man seated to his right is Sos Gulbenkian. These individuals are, er, likely to be opposed to your project."

"You know about the Cube?" I said, dismayed.

"Hatsumi-sama told me. Byrnes probably already knows as well."

Green stood up. The room was full to overflowing and an excited buzz of conversation filled the room. Dr. Green had to excuse himself. "We'll talk later," he said.

The briefing began.

"Ladies and gentlemen, distinguished dignitaries and guests, welcome. I'm Dr. Julian Green, founder of the Disclosure Initiative. Today we are going to talk about the landscape of what are called special access programs and their relationship to the public governments and militaries on the planet. Special access programs contain technology that is at least fifty years ahead of the commercial and military sectors. This technology is planet-saving and it is being withheld from you. I see some new faces so I will begin with a summary and then discuss the latest developments.

"What are special access programs? In order to answer this question we have to understand a little about the classification system. There are, in most governments, three general security clearance levels: confidential, secret, and top secret. However, just having a clearance at one of these levels does not automatically give access to any information at that level. In order to be briefed or read in on a given project or program you have to have a demonstrable 'need to know.' But this system is merely the 'white' side of the security system. There is a massive secret 'black' system as well. This hidden structure has been described as a 'shadow military' existing in parallel with open or overtly classified programs. It is for programs considered too sensitive for normal classification measures. These black programs are called Special Access Programs, or SAPs. They are protected by a security system of great complexity. Many of the SAPs are located within industry and funded through special contracts. Under arrangements called carve-outs such programs and funds become removed from the usual security and contract-oversight organizations. This means that you, as government leaders, may have no idea these programs even exist. You do not have access to them.

"There are also levels of special access programs: acknowledged and unacknowledged SAPs. Black Program is slang for an unacknowledged SAP. An unacknowledged SAP is so sensitive that its very existence is a core secret. Some unacknowledged SAPs are so sensitive that they are waived – a technical term – from the normal management and oversight protocols of government. In the United States, even members of Congress on the appropriations and intelligence committees are not allowed to know anything about these programs.[9] A similar situation exists in many governments around the world."

Danielle saw nothing unusual in this. Her father had essentially told her the same thing during one of their occasional talks.

"Black programs are often covered by white programs (normal classification system) or unclassified programs. In the United States, for example, the U2 spy-plane was covered by a weather-research aircraft program. Such covering allows technology to be relatively openly developed until such time as it is ready for application to a black program. The white cover program is then usually canceled, having accomplished its purpose. This happened to the X-30 National Aerospaceplane project in 1994, for example. It appeared to be an unrealistically ambitious program that was eventually canceled. In reality it was a cover for what is almost certainly an exotic black-world aircraft."

Danielle saw Max's eyes widen a little as Green continued. "Someone read in to an unacknowledged SAP would be required to deny even its existence. Even a 'no comment' would be a serious breach of security." Green looked over at Hun Wen. "Even a general or an admiral would not be briefed on the existence of such a program even if it is within his jurisdiction. If your name is not on the so-called bigot list for a program you will not be briefed, no matter what your rank or responsibility. In the United States, for example, the director of the CIA or the Defense Intelligence Agency would not automatically be on all such lists. Thus a wall of denial of the deep black world can be maintained. If you don't know that a program exists, you will honestly deny that it exists. You don't know what you don't know. Moreover, the number of people with access to multiple SAPs is deliberately very limited. This virtually assures that hardly anyone knows what is going on in another program."

Green paused to take a drink of water.

"Distinguished guests, this next part is crucial. This secrecy applies to the executive or ministerial branch at the highest levels. Let us say that the President of the United States were to ask someone who knew about the existence of such a program. That individual would be required to not tell the President, and to actively mislead him if necessary. This policy is detailed in documents I have obtained, which come from CIA Director Allen Dulles in the 1950s. This applies in varying degrees to every government on the planet."

Danielle sat up in her chair and looked over at Max with a startled expression. She saw Byrnes, the white-haired man in the front row, getting angry. Max was shaking his head slightly back and forth. She looked over at Al Jordan and saw his open skepticism.

Green continued. "It is easier to keep a program hidden in a private corporate contractor facility than in a government facility. Deeply buried programs in contractor facilities are called carve outs. The level of secrecy in some of these unacknowledged programs is so strict that even someone having an intelligence ticket at the highest level would not be considered to have a need to know. All of this results in very effective isolation. After a time, virtually no civilian government official will be aware of this system. Thus, ladies and gentlemen, over the decades a separate and independent network of corporations in the defense, intelligence, and high-tech sectors has emerged. This network is largely independent of the world's governments, even though its funding comes from government budgets." Green paused a moment for emphasis.

"Distinguished guests, political leaders come and go. Don't assume that you, as president, minister, or M.P., have been briefed on every SAP. You, as publicly elected officials, don't necessarily have a need to know. Even in the United States, Freedom of Information Act requests cannot penetrate unacknowledged special access programs."[10]

Green took another drink of water.

"Within the black programs is super-secret, highly advanced technology that is at least fifty years ahead of the commercial sector. These new technologies include the extraction of energy from the active vacuum (zero-point energy). This technology all by itself will go a long way to eliminating poverty due to the inequality of incomes. When people become energy independent, they become more self-sufficient."

Danielle saw that Max had leaned forward in his chair, intent on the speaker. "Other technologies also exist, such as gravity control – electrogravitics – and the safe neutralization of nuclear waste and other hazardous bio-materials. If you are asking why such technology hasn't be released, consider that the nuclear waste disposal industry alone does a business worth several billion dollars every year. Introduction of new technology means loss of jobs and a big economic hit to thousands of people. The clean extraction of energy from the quantum vacuum is held back for obvious reasons. The energy industry on this planet, driven by fossil fuels, does a five trillion dollar business annually. The new technology will make the current energy industry and most of its products and services obsolete.

"Even if you don't believe such technology exists, there is a fanatical level of secrecy behind these programs. Something very massive is being hidden. As government officials you have the right to know what it is. The secrecy behind these unacknowledged special access programs is corrupting the democratic process all over the globe because vital information is being withheld from policy makers."

Someone in the front raised her hand and asked, "How long have these special access programs been in place?"

"This covert classified system has been in place since at least 1961. The amazing discoveries in the classified area began in the early 1950s. The late 1950s is when technological development really began to accelerate, and when reality began to catch up with science fiction. Since the 1960s, events on this planet have been motivated by the struggle to move to this new technology. It was decided at that time that this advanced technological knowledge was too dangerous to release into society – so it was essentially privatized. In January 1961, U.S. President Eisenhower gave his famous 'military industrial complex' speech. What he was really talking about are the special access projects, where this technology has been developed and held. In 1961 the President realized that the United States government had lost control of them. In April of that same year President Kennedy gave his famous speech to the American Newspaper Publishers Association. The President spoke about the military industrial complex in similar words to President Eisenhower, describing it as 'a system which has conscripted vast human and material resources into the building of a tightly knit, highly efficient machine that combines military, diplomatic, intelligence, economic, scientific, and political operations.'[11] President Kennedy was talking about what we now call the Deep State.

"As world leaders it is your right to know what is going on in these unacknowledged special access programs. These programs are rogue, beyond the law. You have every right to expose them if you can, and release this frontier technology to the world. What men like Byrnes here aren't telling you is that this advanced technology comes from non-terrestrial sources, and that we have reverse-engineered some of it. It's the dirtiest and most sensitive secret on this planet."

"Little green aliens are taking over the world!" Byrnes shouted. His voice dripped with sarcasm and ridicule.

Green smiled. "That statement is merely a distraction, Mr. Byrnes. What I'm talking about is the secretive and illegal nature of these special access programs. Why should antisocial personalities like yourself and your buddy Sos Gulbenkian control this technology? It's in the wrong hands."

Green then discussed the latest whistleblower information gleaned from persons who work in the black programs. He displayed a number of classified documents and discussed them. He also displayed several models and images of man-made electrogravitic craft.

Danielle saw Byrnes lean on his cane and get to his feet. "Your 'whistle-blower' documents have been stolen," the man said with a look of unmasked hatred. "Your models are imaginary. You are nothing more than a delusional conspiracy theorist. A thief masquerading as a do-gooder!"

Danielle saw that the face of Sos Gulbenkian, seated beside him, resembled a cobra about to strike. The speaker seemed entirely unfazed. "Be very careful," Byrnes said. His voice trembled with suppressed hostility.

Green responded calmly. "My apologies ladies and gentlemen. Our former national security adviser sometimes becomes overwrought when he hears the truth about the illegal programs he is running."

Byrnes leaned heavily on his cane. "One day you'll go too far!" he shouted, pointing a finger at the speaker.

Dr. Green raised his thin eyebrows just a millimeter in hauteur. "You, sir, are a criminal. So is your associate, and the organizations you represent. You are personally operating at least one illegal, unacknowledged program. Would you like me to tell the audience the code word for that program?"

Byrnes became even further enraged and his body began to shake. "I'd advise you to tone down your remarks." The man was so angry that Danielle thought he was about to have a heart attack.

Byrnes found his seat and Dr. Green continued with the briefing, at one point acknowledging "the brave men and women who have risked their lives to bring the information forward."

Byrnes' voice rose again from one of the front tables. "These people are not heroes. They are scoundrels who have violated their oaths of employment!"

Danielle was amazed at the level of hostility, but she saw that the officials in the audience seemed to accept it as nothing extraordinary.

It was clear that Green had a vast knowledge of the classified areas, discussing at one point the unsuccessful efforts of US Presidents since Eisenhower to regain control of the special access programs. Dr. Green finished his briefing and announced that his group was going to host another Disclosure event at the National Press Club in the spring.

"You all remember the earlier event back in 2001. Well, our speakers will now include several formidable public figures in the military, government, and in the scientific community. We will not announce the speaker list in order to protect those who will be sticking their necks out."

The speaker turned and looked pointedly at Gulbenkian and Byrnes. "We are going to blow the lid off, ladies and gentlemen." The two antagonists angrily left the room.

After a Q and A session Green came over to our table, smiling. In response to a silent inquiry, he spoke to Danielle. "This is normal for a briefing of this kind, which I only do once or twice a year. Normally my engagements are not so confrontational."

Green then directed his attention to me.

"I am told that you have a working overunity device."

"It was developed by two research scientists I stole from the local mafia in Midland, Illinois."

If Max thought to shock Green, Danielle thought, he was mistaken.

"I heard a little bit about that. You know, we have a standing offer of $100,000 to anyone who develops a working and duplicatable overunity prototype."

"I don't need the money Dr. Green. But you are welcome to come to my home and take a look."

Dr. Green's eyebrows shot up. "Do you mean you are using your overunity device to power your home?"

"I've been off the grid now for several weeks. Got shot too, almost didn't make it."

To Danielle's surprise, Green laughed.

"Oh yes, that's part of the territory."

"Have you been shot at, sir?" Danielle asked. Another handsome big man, she thought. Just then an attractive older woman came over. "This is my wife Deborah," he said proudly, putting an arm about her waist. Danielle was just a little piqued. Normally men responded to her when other women were present, but Green only had eyes for his wife.

"In the early days I received a number of death threats, Ms. Menard," Green said. "But I have now accumulated so much testimony and have so much documentation that I'm practically untouchable." Danielle was amazed at Green's seeming unconcern.

"My friend Roka Hatsumi said that you are an authority on these special access programs. Where did all this exotic technology come from?"

Green smiled a toothy smile. "Well, we know for a fact that the UFOs that crashed at Roswell, New Mexico back in 1947 were real. Two alien creatures were captured from that downed ship, and the ship itself was thoroughly studied. That was just the beginning. Other ships have also been studied. I can tell you with certainty that in these programs, electrogravitics – antigravity – was mastered by the late 1950s. Energy from the quantum particle flux was also mastered several years later. The exotic military weaponry – scalar electromagnetic weapons, electromagnetic pulse weaponry – all of this came from studying ETVs."

"ETVs?" Danielle asked.

"Extra Terrestrial Vehicles," Green replied. "In the special access programs these exotic aircraft have been duplicated. Most of the sightings we see nowadays are man-made craft."

Al Jordan looked dubious. Green just smiled and said, "*C'est la vie,* my friend." He briefly explained about CSETI, his ET contact group.

I could see Danielle tune out at that point, but I was fascinated. Green talked prosaically of non-terrestrials as if they were as normal as hot dogs and hamburgers.

"So what you are saying is that we are not alone in the universe," Al Jordan said.

Green's eyes widened and he laughed, but not at the speaker. It was a genuine expression of cheerful mirth. "No Mr. Jordan. Our galaxy, this universe, is teeming with intelligent life."

At Al's quizzically doubtful expression, Green said, "Consider, sir. The visible universe is 13.5 billion light years in diameter, with trillions of galaxies, and over 10^{22} stars. Our own galaxy contains at least 100 billion stars. If even a small fraction of those stars have evolved planets with intelligent life, there are literally millions of planets with intelligent life even in this little sector of our galaxy."

"Then why haven't we seen any of these ETs?"

Green smiled broadly and judged the acceptance level of his questioner. "We have, Mr. Jordan."

Al Jordan's jaw dropped and Green quickly changed the subject. "I'm told you have a private security force guarding your device and your properties."

I nodded.

"Good! Because if your device actually works you're probably going to need them."

"Oh it works all right."

"You'll forgive my skepticism gentlemen. I've heard many claims, and have even been duped of tens of thousands of dollars by several clever marketers. Until I see this device I can't believe it."

"You're welcome to come and take a look," I said. I felt that Green was humoring me.

"No offense Dr. Berglin, I really would like to come up and see you. Would it be OK if I brought my science team along?"

"Bring anyone you want."

Al Jordan spoke.

"You said that we were probably going to need this security force Max has hired, but I think it's just paranoia. You don't really mean there's going to be some kind of war?"

Green's eyebrows rose infinitesimally. "Mr. Jordan, I've been beating my head against the Disclosure wall for thirty years now, with little success. You may be my first big break. What I mean is that right now I'm just another conspiracy kook on the fringes of society, even though I have overwhelming proof for my assertions. I need someone who can actually demonstrate a working overunity device that can be duplicated. You guys just might be the thin edge of the wedge. The fact that Hatsumi-sama has recommended you is almost proof positive of your bona fides, in my mind."

"You didn't answer the question," Jordan said.

"The answer is, Mr. Jordan, that yes there is probably going to be some kind of confrontation. Most of the people opposed to disclosure are simply people that will be put out of business by the new technology. A few are just like our friends Zbigniew Byrnes and his pal Sos Gulbenkian. They are the sort of folks who cannot be reasoned with. If there is going to be a confrontation I want it to be fought on our terms, and on our ground. This may be my first real opportunity in three decades to broadly expose the secrecy and the corruption, and who is behind that corruption. In order to do that we have to bring them out into the open. The best way to do that is to present them with a working overunity device and see what they do."

I could see that my CEO was unhappy. He, and the Board, were not in favor of my new venture. They were practical businesspeople who preferred to concentrate on ensuring that a profitable business continued its successful course. Al had only come along because he was tired of the cold. He gave me a speaking glance and I knew I was in trouble at the next board meeting.

Green looked intensely at me and Danielle. "My advice to you is to keep everything local. It's too late now with your security force, that may eventually cause problems. If you are going to commercialize your discovery, hire only local people. That includes tradesman, administrators, PR and marketers, researchers, and even the janitor. If they want a fight, let it be on your ground."

Danielle, a dissatisfied Al Jordan, and I left on the launch after eating a very well prepared dinner courtesy of Dr. Green and the Necker Island staff.

I was quiet when we got to San Juan and boarded our flight back to the US. On the plane I saw a long email from Dr. Green with links to several of his papers on disclosure and ET contact. Green wanted to come to Midland the very next day to see the setup. I replied in the affirmative.

I tried to sleep but my mind was racing. I thought about the story Bernie Hartwig told me about poor Blaise McNeil and his "UFO." I had dismissed it as another urban legend, but maybe it wasn't.

I fell into an uneasy sleep until the plane landed at O'Hare, dreaming about men in black.

Part XIV

Tesla's Cube

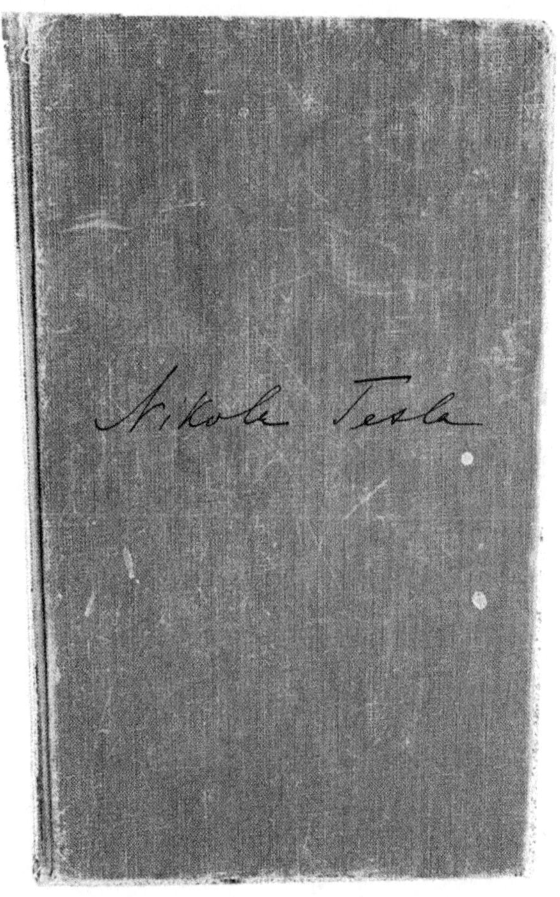

— 28 —

Zach got a call from Mike Parsons on the Friday after New Years. "You want to play a round tomorrow?"

"Sure. What you up to?"

"I've got news, but I'll tell you on the course."

The next morning they met out at Hickory Hills, a course built on a public skiing area, with lots of elevation changes. "Heather got her appointment," Mike said.

"Really? That happened pretty fast."

"Her father is friends with one of the assistant secretaries in the State Department. He pulled a few strings."

"There's more to this Mike."

"Yeah. We've decided to get married. But her appointment is to the consulate in Laos, of all places. Twenty-four months."

"Jesus, Mike. What are you going to do?"

"I don't think it's going to work out, frankly. I passed my Certified Life Skills Coach exam and I'm licensed now. I love what I'm doing. I'm a hometown boy at heart. It doesn't seem fair."

Zach was at a loss for words. "Yeah."

Mike threw his first shot off the tee. "What are you and Jessie doing?"

"Not a thing. The problem is we are both too similar. We can't make up our minds what to do. She would be satisfied with getting married and starting a family. I like her all right, but I want more."

Zach threw a perfect shot over 400 feet down the fairway, which was covered in five inches of snow. "Easy to find that," Mike remarked. "Right down the middle."

"You ever hear from Danielle Menard?" Mike asked.

"I talked to her last week. She went off with Max Berglin to some billionaire island in the British Virgin Islands. Said Berglin had hired John Rosen and his boss Austin Park. You know, the guys that supposedly developed that new energy system."

"What's that all about anyway?"

"Danielle said he's got a unit that is powering his entire house without electricity. Said if they start producing these things it's going to piss off a lot of people in the energy business."

The two buddies marched down the fairway. There was something about Mike that made Zach want to look inside himself and talk about it. "Why am I so indecisive?" he asked.

Mike threw his upshot 200 feet within 25 feet of the basket. "Because you don't commit to anything." They walked 30 feet up the fairway to Zach's drive.

"That's the problem," Zach said, throwing his shot very close to the basket. "Jessie is the same way. We sort of like each other, but we both want to feel more affinity for each other. Love, I guess." The truth was that he was still missing Danielle, and Jessie was just a substitute.

"Commitment is a byproduct of love," Mike said, throwing his putter into the basket. "Love is a feeling of affinity for another person that goes beyond yourself. It's freedom Zach, whereas indecisiveness is a prison."

"Yes, that's right," Zach said, making his short putt. "But I don't know how to love."

"That's because you're too selfish. Jessie is the same way."

They were walking to the second teepad. Zach stopped. "I'm not selfish!"

"Sure you are. I've watched you my whole life. You're gregarious, you like people, but you can't get beyond yourself. That's why you can't feel love, why you don't have the freedom to go beyond your limitations."

"How do you know all this?" Mike's words made sense to Zach like a logic puzzle makes sense, like an engineering problem.

"Because I went through it," Mike said, lining up his tee shot. "I had to get over myself before I could receive those qualities from others that I valued."

Zach thought about that as he stepped up to the teepad. "So you're saying that if you want love, or excitement, or anything, you have to be able to see that in yourself?"

"Yup. If you don't see it in yourself other people won't respond to you in the way you want. Remember how I used to be? A real asshole, with no self-confidence. As soon as I was able to recognize myself as someone who could be loved, Heather started to respond to me. It was like magic."

"It seems unlikely," Zach said. "She hated you."

"Yeah, but sometimes strong negative emotions mask an underlying positive emotion."

Zach turned around and faced his friend. "How does a storekeepers' son know so much? You're like some guru of human relations."

"I found my purpose in life. I pay attention now. I observe people and how they interact with each other. I have to, to be good at my job." He looked Zach in the eyes. "It's the commitment that follows something you love. It applies to people and careers."

Zach thought about the conversation he had with Jessie and Tiki Aatoa about higher calling. "That's right. I need to find my purpose in life."

"Then find in yourself the qualities you admire in others."

"I think you're going to be very successful," Zach said. It was obvious that his old friend had completely shifted his life focus from disk golf to counseling. He wondered how you did something like that. Zach now felt an admiration and a respect for Mike that he never thought was possible.

That night, inspired by his talk with Mike, Zach called Danielle. He wanted to hear her voice and he had an idea he wanted to bounce off her. At first their conversation was awkward, get-reacquainted small talk. Zach could see her nervousness and wondered whether she even liked him anymore. "Rumor has it that you guys have made some kind of breakthrough."

"What gave you that idea?" Danielle asked.

"I heard it from Max."

"Oh, you mean Max Jr." That asshole! Danielle thought. The biggest secret we have and the owner's son blabs it to one of the most extroverted people in town.

"Who else? Anyway, I want to be part of the team."

"Really Zach? You don't even know what we're working on."

"Max said you guys are setting up some kind of manufacturing plant, and you're going to need engineers. I'm an engineer."

"But why Zach? I thought you were all set to get a job, leave town, and settle down."

"I changed my mind."

Danielle laughed and she felt the tension between them break. Zach was unpredictable but good-natured, there was nothing subtle about him. She considered. The company *was* looking for engineers. After they came back from the conference Max Sr. was eager to jump-start the manufacturing process.

"I'm not sure you're qualified, but you can always submit an application. We're looking for electronic systems engineers, mainly, and computer engineers. Haven't you been working in the automotive area with that guy Larry Potvin?"

"Yeah, but I majored in electrical engineering and power systems engineering. I have a knack for putting things together."

"Go ahead and apply then. Go to the new building off River Dr., not the one downtown."

Zach changed the subject. "How are you doing Danielle?"

"I'm now in public relations and marketing. Max has made me the company spokesperson."

"Wow! That's great!"

Danielle could feel his enthusiasm. He was a bit like Max Sr., somewhat impulsive, and willing to push the envelope. But he was also a bit indecisive. However, Max had made a point of wanting to hire only local people for the new project. All of the construction crews were locally hired, and so would the professionals.

After she hung up Danielle thought about her new position. She had not gotten her security clearance but was OK with it. If the secretive world of intelligence was anything like Dr. Green had described at Necker Island, it wouldn't have suited her. She was now on the cutting-edge of technology that could change the world. She hoped her father was happy doing his classified work in Boston.

The next day I went up to Room 411 in the Centurion Building and checked up on my two mad scientists. "We can't keep working like this boss," the impulsive John Rosen told me as soon as I walked in the door. "We love our work but we don't have a normal life. We have to get out of here or we'll both go crazy."

I saw the haggard faces of Park and Rosen and their edgy nervousness. "It's for your own good gentlemen. I wish you could have gone to Necker with us to see the level of hostility we're facing. I want you guys to be safe."

"Thanks boss," John said, "but I'd almost rather be dead than live in this lab for another day."

"All right gentlemen, but I'm assigning each of you two bodyguards. Do not, and I repeat, do NOT, ever go anywhere without them. Otherwise, what happened to me might happen to you."

John thought about his last confrontation with Vahan Katelian and was not averse to accepting Max's order. Austin Park felt similarly.

"I want you guys over at the other building. We'll transfer all the equipment in here over there. Try to stay out of trouble."

"All right sir," Park said. "Anything to get us out of here."

John Rosen couldn't get used to his bodyguards; two silent, no-nonsense Asian fellows who wore gray Berglin Enterprises uniforms and spoke no English. The bigger guy was Yugo. The other, a thin wiry guy with a scraggly black mustache, looked like an evil Bruce Lee. His name was, appropriately, Li.

"It's better this way," Berglin told him. "These guys know exactly what to do and what is necessary in every situation. Just ignore them, they prefer it."

It had only taken a week for Dr. Berglin to set up their lab and transfer all their stuff to the new building. John arrived at the new facility and went to the top floor of the building, followed by his new companions. He walked out into the manufacturing area and saw an old guy with white hair giving orders. One of the men behind him grunted and said something in rapid-fire Japanese to the other guard. John caught the name "Yusuke Shiozawa," probably the systems engineer. One glance around the place and he knew he was useless here; everything was still under construction. He went back to the lab just in time to see Austin drive up. Austin exited the car, followed by his own two bodyguards. The two men laughed when the four watchdogs began grunting at each other in Japanese. John noticed that the men's eyes were constantly moving, aware of every movement around them.

"How is this any different than our previous life?" John complained to Austin.

Park laughed. "At least it's a different lab."

"Can't meet any girls here though. I'm going downtown to the Improv tonight."

"Ought to be interesting."

John brightened. "Yeah, it will!" He pointed to the bodyguards. "I'll tell the women I'm an important celebrity."

The two men had almost completed their schematics for all of the components for the Cube. It was important to have everything nailed down before the manufacturing process began or the engineers would have a fit. The two scientists knocked off at 5 p.m. As John walked to his car in the freezing cold, he saw Vahan Katelian standing behind his car, looking around at the activity. As Vahan turned to confront him he heard something in Japanese. Yugo was suddenly standing between him and Vahan, while Li held Vahan's wrists together. It had happened so swiftly that John wasn't aware of any movement at all.

"You traitor!" Vahan growled.

"What do you want, Vahan?" John said, resigned to enduring Vahan's famous temper.

"First you steal our stuff, then you go to work for Berglin? I thought we were friends."

"Look Vahan. A long time ago you ran off a couple of punks trying to steal my money, and I still really appreciate that. But lately you've made it clear that being your 'friend' means me doing what you want. I'm sorry that I stole your invention and tried to give it to the world but that didn't work out well for me. I returned all your stuff. Then you got mad and fired me and Park. So you only have yourself to blame."

"One day you won't have those two goons with you."

"So that's how it is, is it?" John looked him over. He was wearing a perfectly tailored winter coat over an expensive suit. "You're all front and no substance, Vahan, aren't you?"

Before Vahan could respond John spoke. "You did a good thing funding our research. If you let us alone for a few months, you'll see that your investment will pay off in a big way. Just between you and me, old friend, we did it."

Vahan's eyes widened.

"That's right. We designed a unit that can power a house without electricity. Free energy, totally clean. Think about it. When we start distributing these things it's going to practically cause a war. We may need your help."

John knew that Vahan was totally loyal to his family and their financial interests. His outlook was wholly tribal. But John could tell he had gotten through.

"It will be the bad guys versus the good guys, Vahan. I hope you'll be on the right side."

John appealed to the man's greed. "There's going to be a lot of money in it, enough for everyone."

Despite his dislike of everything Berglin, Vahan was impressed and excited as John's bodyguards marched him away. The men protecting Rosen had moved astonishingly quickly to put themselves in the correct position, like trained military men. Vahan knew instinctively that they were people you didn't fuck with.

As Vahan drove out of the parking lot he realized that the families might have to accept their mistake with Park and Rosen and move on. But Berglin still had to answer for the murder of his cousin Raffi.

Zach Ferrell drove up to the old warehouse building off River Drive. Trucks, equipment, and workers were everywhere. The place was buzzing! Zach liked it. He walked in the side door and down the hall to the back of the building, where temporary offices had been set up amidst the chaos. A harried receptionist was answering phones and directing traffic. "I want to apply for a job," he said to her. Her name tag said Mildred Harrison.

"What are your qualifications?" The woman was a middle-aged brunette who looked like Jessie's mom.

"I'm an electrical engineer, also familiar with power systems."

"Experience?"

"Just graduated. But I've been working in the automotive area as an apprentice for over a year."

The woman tapped her pencil on her chin. "We want experienced people, but Mr. Berglin says they have to live in the area. You might be in luck." She handed him a sheaf of papers. "Fill these out and bring them back here tomorrow morning."

Zach took the papers and looked around for a place to sit. He wanted to get these back as soon as he could to show his interest.

"We can't use people who don't follow simple directions," the woman said. "Bring them back tomorrow, I'm busy."

Zach's innate good humor came through and he smiled. "Yes ma'am, I'll see you right at 8 in the morning."

He could see the woman smiling back. It never failed, that Ferrell charm. It's probably how his father had snared the beautiful Rachel DuPlessis. As he walked out of the building with his application papers he remembered the conversation with Mike Parsons about being indecisive. He realized that charming people was a way to avoid them, and to avoid facing uncomfortable things. He felt the papers almost blow away as a cold breeze ruffled them. He looked down at them, promising himself that if he got the job he would get serious about it even if it turned out to be boring.

The day after Zach visited the new building I realized that I had totally shifted my focus to the new power units. My executive board didn't like it so I called an all-day meeting to hash it out.

Al Jordan opened the discussion. "You're losing focus Max. The suite of security software products we have is the backbone of our business, but you no longer seem interested."

I looked around the conference table at the people who had helped me build a successful company. Al Jordan, of course, the CEO, a balding, flabby man with a serious face who had started a number of successful businesses. To Al's left, Mika Petronen, the COO, a software engineer with a shrewd sense of their market and how to market to it. The man had pale white skin even in the summer. He wore white shirts and a pocket protector, and looked like a mad albino scientist out of the 1950s. To Al's right Barbara Mikhailovich, the CFO. Barbara was a hard-headed mathematician with an eidetic memory.

Al's comment rankled but I was honest with myself. "You are right, Al. That is why I have proposed a new organization chart."

Four heads converged around the printout, which I spread out on the table. The chart now showed two executive boards for two separate businesses: Berglin Enterprises and UPower. I explained that UPower would concentrate on developing and marketing the new overunity power units. First we would sell to residential customers and later, to commercial businesses. I had myself as CEO of UPower and Danielle as head of Public Relations. John Rosen was Director of Research and Austin Park was the Director of Product Development. "I know we're pretty thin at UPower right now. I'm hoping you guys can keep an eye on us so we don't go off the rails."

Al Jordan sighed with relief. "This is exactly what we were hoping for, Max," he said, looking around at the other two. "We like the business we're in and don't want to go off chasing unicorns." He softened that criticism with a wide grin. "We want to keep you guys in the saddle."

"Wow. I called an all-day meeting and we're done."

Barbara, Al, and Mika looked at each other and shook their heads. "No we're not Max," Al said. "We've got you here and we're going to keep you here until midnight if need be, until we iron out every last detail."

I groaned but realized my CEO was right. I had a tendency to go off on tangents. My board was doing the job I hired them for.

The first item was the money I was spending on security services. Even though Kenji had reduced his bill considerably, the amounts were still noteworthy. "Why should Berglin Enterprises pay so much money for a startup that is going nowhere?" Al asked. Barbara and Mika both nodded their agreement. Fortunately Al had been to Necker and had some idea of the significance of the Cube even if he didn't agree UPower was a viable business. UPower had tremendous upside, which I emphasized, but the Board thought it was a total long shot. After several hours I was able to work out a six-month deadline. "In six months, Max, you can either come back to Berglin Enterprises or you can move over to UPower. We can't keep spending this kind of money forever."

"I love you guys; you take care of me."

"And ourselves as well," Barbara said. Al and Mika nodded their agreement. I understood their implied criticism and realized that Berglin Enterprises was now too large for me to control anymore. I kept thinking of it like a pilot does his aircraft or a captain his ship. The company had grown beyond that. "I understand."

Everybody relaxed. The Board had gotten their point across and was satisfied, at least for the present. I knew I would have to go all out now if UPower was to get off the ground. Deadlines were good; they had always motivated me. "OK, are we done?"

Mika, Al, and Barbara looked at me like a parent to a wayward child. "Not yet," Al said. "The company has been expanding rapidly over the past six quarters. Let's update this organization chart for Berglin Enterprises..."

Eight hours later, after innumerable cups of coffee and sandwiches, we were finally done.

"For now," Al warned, poking me on the chest with a stubby forefinger. "I'm going to watch you guys like a hawk."

"Good. That's exactly what I want you to do."

By the time the meeting adjourned it was almost 9 p.m. I saw a smallish woman standing next to the window and another man on the other side. I realized my men had been there all day and they had not even eaten! "Ren, I am so sorry. I hope you have eaten something today?"

Ren bowed. He was a very tall and thin man with an expressive face and long, thin black hair. Ren was one of Roka Hatsumi's men, one of the few in the security force who could understand English. "*Hai!* We have been shuffling in and out of here all day, and have been well provided for."

"That is well. I forget sometimes that you are here doing us a great service."

Ren bowed again. "Hatsumi-sama has given us our orders: to protect the people here, and to do so in a totally unobtrusive fashion. That you did not notice us is very pleasing."

I shook my head. I did not and would not ever understand Japanese cultural norms, but I was glad it was working out. Kenji's men protected the property and Roka's six men were bodyguards to me and my two scientists whenever we went outside the Centurion Building. "Who is this?" I asked, pointing to the petite woman. Ren grinned. "That one we call *bakemono*. Monster."

"Watashi wa bakemono desu," the woman said.

At my quizzical look, Ren explained. "She is small, but a fighter extraordinaire."

The woman bowed. Ren looked over at her and spoke. *"Hana wa sakuragi, hito wa bushi."* Both of them burst into laughter. I later found out that the phrase meant, "As the cherry blossom is considered foremost among flowers, so the warrior is foremost among men." I think it was intended as a compliment.

"What is her real name?" I asked.

"Hiroko, but she hates that name. If you must speak to her, say *bakemono*."

Hiroko smiled.

"Thank you," I said and got up. My knees were stiff from sitting for ten hours. "I think I'll go home now and take a long shower."

On the way home (with Ichiro and Hideki, my two personal guards) I thought about how far I had come. When I founded Berglin Enterprises I was determined to make some money. Well, I'd done it. Now it was time to make a fortune and become a real player in the world. With money comes power and influence. Despite the apparently formidable obstacles, my talk with Dr. Green had inspired me to change the world. I now had the tools to do it.

Dr. Julian Green didn't arrive in town until the day after the board meeting. He was surrounded by three men he called his "science team." I escorted them to the new building and its lab.

"Gentlemen," I said to my visitors, "meet the guys who started it all." I introduced Dr. Green and his team to Austin and John, who then demonstrated the original Pierce-Arrow receiver and the little AC motor, which I had sequestered to a back corner of the lab. "We're making history. I want people to remember how it all began."

Green's science team pronounced the self-powered circuit board to be genuine, and began to congratulate me.

"May I announce your discovery to the world on my website and in my briefings?" Green asked.

"Not until you see what I've got in my house."

I led them to my home in Palmer Park (accompanied by my bodyguards, of course) and showed them the power unit.

"You know what you've got here," Green said after the demonstration. "Pandora's Box."

"Aint it great?"

Green laughed so hard he had to grip the wall to keep upright. It looked to me less like a laugh than a huge release of tension.

Dr. Green sobered. "I'm not so sure I should announce this discovery. Do you have a plan to release this without getting yourselves killed?"

"Somebody already tried that, but I'm still here."

Green nodded, understanding that I was going to go the distance no matter what.

"Hatsumi-sama suggested that I begin very slowly. We're going to handmake a few of these devices and sell them to friends and locals at cost. Meanwhile, we'll go ahead with our manufacturing plant at the new building. The manufacturing area will be sequestered to the top floor, out of the public view. Hatsumi-sama suggested that we build public acceptance of the new devices under the radar. Let demand slowly grow from the grass roots."

"I think that is entirely reasonable. I'm just as 'green' as you are in this area," he joked. "We've had a lot of quacks and slimy marketers try to take us. Never before have we seen an actual, working overunity device." He rubbed his hands in excitement. "Let the game begin!"

The next day was Friday. I went to the new building, entering by the loading door at the back. I talked to Yusuke Shiozawa, the engineering consultant sent by Roka Hatsumi. Park and Rosen were there, working with another engineer to set up and streamline a production line. Everything was in good hands. I felt a sense of great well being.

Midland Edison Investigates

Josh Brackenreed was curious. The largest house in Palmer Park had registered zero megawatts used for the month of December.

His job at Midland Edison was to monitor electric power usage. He reported to his boss in the Distribution and Operations section, which planned for future power needs. The state's utility policy dictated that electric utilities on the traditional power grid must purchase excess electricity generated by renewable energy systems. The company was required to investigate the matter, but there was no record of a solar installation or any renewable resource at the property. Josh checked the energy usage for the home for the past three years. Prior to December the house had been using electricity at the expected rate. Josh decided to go over there on his own time, after work.

When he called the house a man named Slava answered the phone. "Hello, I'm John Brackenreed from the electric company," Josh said. "Would it be all right if I came over to inspect your electric service? We've noticed that your power usage went to zero last month."

"Oh yes, you should see it Mr. Brackenreed," Slava said. "The sweetest little setup you can imagine."

Josh had no idea what the man was talking about, but it made him even more curious. "Would you mind if I stopped by at 5:30 today?"

"That's not a problem," Slava said. "The boss usually doesn't get home until seven."

Josh arrived at the mansion and identified himself at the gate through the intercom. When he got to the door it was opened by a smallish man with thinning gray hair, who reminded Josh of his grandfather. "Mr. Brackenreed?" Slava asked.

"Uh, yes sir, I'm from Midland Edison."

Slava looked the man over and nodded. Brackenreed was nondescript, of average height and average looks. He looked like someone who sat at a desk all day.

Josh followed Slava through the marble-floored foyer and turned right at an open door. They went down two flights of stairs. Slava turned on the lights and the men walked into an enormous finished basement with a theater room and a ball room with a stage. Every one of these rooms was twice the size of his one-bedroom apartment. Slava turned right at a red-painted door and they entered a spotless furnace room with a cement floor. To the left was a sprinkler system unit, and two geothermal furnaces on a separate electrical service.

"Here's the electrical service," Slava said proudly. He pointed to the furnaces. "We're entirely off the grid."

Grandpa seemed to be waiting for him, so Josh humored the old man. "I don't see anything unusual." The setup looked completely normal.

Slava grinned widely, with the air of a man who is going to spring a great surprise on someone who is totally clueless. Slava gestured to the Cube, which was plugged into a specially rigged electrical panel that supplied the other panels. "The Cube does everything."

Josh walked over to the device. It wasn't a device, really, just a featureless box painted black. There was a button about an inch in diameter on the top cover of the unit. A thick cord ran from the box and plugged into the electric service. Josh was totally confused. "Where are the Cube's wires?"

Slava chortled, an old man who was showing the tech-savvy kid a thing or two. "Doesn't have any, other than the cord that plugs into the electric panel."

"What is this? A joke?"

"No sir. Examine this panel. You can see that the main breaker is shut off."

Josh went over and looked. Sure enough, there was no power coming into the house, just as he had seen on the board in his office. Josh scratched his head. "How does this thing work? What *is* it?"

"I don't have a clue."

Josh walked around the Cube again. It was just a smooth, featureless black box. It wasn't plugged into anything. Where was the energy coming from? "Do you mind if I talk to the owner?" Josh asked.

Slava considered. The boss told him not to tell anyone about the new power unit. But this man was on official business from the electric company. "Let me call him. He likes to show the thing off, and I don't know anything about it. Except that it works," the older man said after a pause.

Slava grabbed his mobile and made the call. He was not supposed to call except in an emergency and he hoped Max wouldn't slap him down for it. "Boss? This is Slava. I have someone here from Midland Edison. He says he is required to investigate our electric usage in case we have surplus energy that could go back to the grid."

Josh heard a man's voice say, "I never thought of that. The Cube could probably supply a lot of power back to the grid. I'll be right over."

Josh shook his head. Was this guy some kind of kooky inventor who thought he could save the world? As he waited he built up a mental image of the owner. On the one hand his house was a palace and everything was meticulously clean, so he couldn't be too crazy. He pictured a tall thin man with a scraggly beard, burning blue eyes, and a fanatical look.

Fifteen minutes later Max walked into the basement in a nice suit, looking like Coach Barnes of the Carleton University football team. Two men wearing uniforms preceded him.

"I know you!" Josh blurted. "You're the owner of Berglin Enterprises. I've seen your picture on the news."

I smiled indulgently. "That's right. Now what is this all about?"

"Well sir, I'm here because I need to know if this device is a renewable energy system. Can it send power back to the grid?"

I considered. "Right now it is tuned to only deliver enough power to run the house. But I suppose it could be adjusted to send energy back into the grid."

Josh was pleased. Berglin was a respected citizen and he had made a good contact. His boss, Ruth Vandenberghe, would be pleased that he had found another renewable energy resource. The State of Illinois required a certain percentage of its electricity generation to come from non-fossil-fuel sources. "Do you know how this thing works?"

"I have a PhD in physics, but I haven't a clue. I don't think even the guys who developed it are completely sure."

Josh was now displeased. "It could be dangerous. What if it blows up?"

"My friend, this thing doesn't work on any power equation you know of. It's an overunity device."

Josh snorted. "A perpetual motion machine."

"Test it out for yourself sonny." Josh saw Berglin grab a flashlight that was sitting on top of one of the furnaces. "Here's the main breaker. Push the button on the Cube, then use the flashlight and turn on the main."

Josh pushed the button on the Cube and they were instantly plugged into darkness. "OK," I said. "Now turn on the breaker."

Josh did and the place lit up. "OK, everything normal here," Josh commented.

"That's right. Now switch off the breaker, then depress the button on the Cube again."

Josh pressed the breaker switch and the lights went off. Then, using the flashlight, he pushed the button on the Cube.

Nothing happened. "Another lunatic," Josh muttered.

I grinned in the darkness. "Just wait a few moments."

Josh saw a faint glow in the light fixtures. Gradually, the lights grew brighter and brighter, then a little too bright, and then faded slightly. Everything looked normal. "But it's not connected to anything!"

"Now you've got it son. The world's first, demonstrable, working overunity device."

Josh was stunned. He walked around the Cube once more, shaking his head. He put his hand on the device and could feel nothing. "There's nothing in here. It's a trick! This is just a black box."

"A white box," I corrected. "The Cube's components are known and are available for inspection."

Josh stared at the unit. "I still don't believe it. It's impossible."

"Get your technicians out here then. They will measure standard alternating current at 60Hz, no different than the feed from Midland Edison."

Josh was flabbergasted and still skeptical.

"I can see you're a man who does not believe the evidence of your own senses. You have observed the Cube, you have seen that it works, yet you doubt its validity?"

Josh was stumped. "No sir. But can I tell my supervisor that this...thing, whatever it is, is a renewable energy source?"

"Hold off on that until I ask the developers," I replied. Slava gave me a speaking look. "All right, I'll call Park now."

Park, Josh thought. He should remember that name from somewhere....

"Austin, this is Max Berglin. I have a man here from Midland Edison. He wants to know whether the Cube could be modified to send power back to the grid. Oh yes? All right then." I turned and said, "It most certainly can, but that would be down the road a little way."

Josh felt like a man who has discovered that all his training has been superseded by a man on a flying elephant waving a magic carpet, on which several monkeys were brandishing light sabers. "Uh, yes sir, I'm sorry for inconveniencing you."

Slava gleefully showed Josh out, making deprecating comments about outdated technology. Brackenreed wondered just what in God's name he was going to put on his report.

Trevor Clarke and Rachel Hear about the Cube

Trevor Clarke went home from the bank to change his clothes. It would be another night out in society, the Brinson's party. The Brinsons were a major investor in the smallish PRC Bank and his attendance was mandatory. It would more than likely be a tawdry affair but despite the bitter cold, Rachel would want to accompany him. He used to think that society parties were fun. Lately he had been getting more and more weary of them, even with the attractive Ms. DuPlessis at his side. Claudia Brinson was a dead bore; a vulgar woman who thought that her husband's money was a substitute for intelligence and social understanding. Midland society was nothing like London's, but it did have a sort of pecking order. Here, as in London, money could only get you so far. Trevor thought Midland was more honest than in England, where even the stupidest peer of the realm could gain access at the highest levels.

The Brinsons were tolerated but were never invited to the more exclusive social gatherings.

When Trevor walked in to the showy Brinson home with Rachel on his arm, the first person he saw was Danielle Menard. Trevor stopped short. Rachel, irritated, began tugging on his arm and frowned when she saw the object of his attention.

"Who is that woman?" he asked her.

"Oh, that's just Danielle Menard," Rachel said. "The poor little drug dealer whose daddy turned out to be a loser, and she no better."

Trevor responded sharply. "I think not." He normally deferred to Rachel because of her beauty and her domineering personality. But he could hardly believe the change that had come over the girl he had only seen once, and had once been afraid would expose his drug use. She was dressed smartly in a clinging, sleeveless black dress with pearls around her pale white neck. Danielle looked like a beautiful swan, gliding along smoothly in her high heels, taller even than most of the men. And those tattoos! On anyone else they would be inappropriate, but on her they were a statement.

Rachel, miffed, walked with him toward the striking young woman. Trevor noticed Danielle's composure, and approved. Rachel's tone was dismissive. "Well, there's the Menard girl. Did you know, Trevor, that she spent a night in jail for dealing drugs?"

Trevor was very interested to see Danielle's reaction and approved when Danielle simply nodded her head toward Rachel and turned to him. "I have never seen it so cold in February!"

Trevor was pleased. The young woman had dismissed his self-important companion with aplomb. Moreover, she had behaved as though the two were perfect strangers, silently telling Trevor that their past history was completely forgotten. Trevor smiled broadly. "Ms. Danielle Menard, I believe?"

Rachel flounced off and Trevor began to make polite conversation with Danielle. Eventually he surmised, by subtle questioning and attentive listening, that something big was happening at Berglin Enterprises. It had to do with that moronic demonstration last summer. From Danielle he learned that the invention – which had been the topic of conversation in society for a week after the debate – had been developed. Max Berglin was using it to power his home! Trevor was stunned. He had always considered the demonstration a publicity stunt.

Danielle,was satisfied. She left the man for whom she had previously supplied designer drugs. Max had told her to mention the new device to Trevor, for reasons he had not explained. She had done it casually, without making the information seem intentional. She surmised that Max was playing some game.

Danielle had completed her assignment. She said thank you and goodbye to her hostess. She found her car on the street and immediately messaged Max. "Mission accomplished," she texted. "Trevor bit and he'll probably tell everyone of importance in this town about us."

I was pleased with Danielle's report. I knew we had to go very slowly with the Cube, but the electric company was already on to us. Besides, I was excited and my blood was up. My scientists, my company, and my reputation had been embarrassed at that silly public debate. I wanted to show all of my doubters in town that our invention was for real.

Rachel was still pouting about Danielle when Trevor saw Claudia Brinson walking toward him. It was a social necessity to talk to her, but he gleaned some interesting information from the noted society gossip. His Rachel and Wayne DiPietro, an accountant at PRC Auditors, had hooked up one night. They were seen by one of Claudia's friends at Sweetwaters, who overheard their conversation and Wayne's proposed liaison.

That night Trevor called her on it after making love. Her dismissive attitude upset him.

"Are we married? We're having an affair, Trevor. And really, you've been awfully boring in bed recently."

"Is it time for you to move on then? I am no longer useful to you, apparently."

She didn't disagree. "To be seen with you in social situations lends a certain cache to my image," she said in a perfectly self-absorbed way. "Your accent, your adroitness...but really my dear, you should try harder to please me."

Trevor pushed himself up on one elbow. "You know, Rachel, you are the most self-centered person I have ever met."

"If you mean I know what I want, I'll agree."

Trevor could hardly believe her conceit. "You are very beautiful, my dear, but too crude. Your lack of nuance and sophistication will eventually cause you to fail."

Trevor saw that his sally hadn't penetrated the armor of her self- importance. He sighed, acknowledging to himself that Rachel DuPlessis was the perfect woman for him. They were both selfish and had no interest in a long-term relationship. However, her abrasiveness and her tendency to use people detracted from her social aura. He had talked about that quite extensively with Don Halloran and Mark Ferrell at the opening of Kazkav last month. Trevor made a decision. He might, in the near future, have to relieve himself of her presence. It would not do at all to be associated with a tawdry ladder climber.

"I just remembered something, my dear, that might be useful to you." They had both gotten into the habit of calling each other "my dear," which had a distancing effect they could both hide behind.

Rachel sat up eagerly, her breasts moving attractively. Trevor moved his hand toward her and she slapped him away. "You are like a dog my dear, when offered a succulent bone."

"What is it, Trevor?"

He knew he had her. "Apparently Max Berglin has developed a new renewable energy device and he plans to market and sell it. According to what I've heard, it's going to be a huge money-maker."

"Who told you that?"

Trevor was irritated. "What difference does it make?" Danielle Menard was probably credible, and he resented Rachel's tone. The Menard woman had spoken authoritatively, and was now the spokesperson for Berglin's company. Why would she lie? "Let's just say that the information is reliable. You may regard it as factual."

Trevor smiled as Rachel's face assumed the eager expression of greed he recognized in the vulgar. As the sheet fell from her as she turned over on her back he thought: To hell with vulgarity. This woman was gorgeous and he'd hang onto her a little while longer.

When Rachel arrived at her office at 6 a.m. the next morning (satisfying herself that she was the first one in the building) she thought about Max Berglin and his new device. She always sat alone at her desk from 6 to 7, planning her day and ways to advance herself and her company. Berglin had always rubbed her the wrong way so she had avoided him. However, to market a valuable new product would be a boon to her firm. After pondering the problem until almost 7 she decided to make an appointment to see Max Berglin. She would do it in person, inquiring about one of Berglin's software security products. During the interview she would gradually turn the conversation to the exciting new invention.

— 29 —

Two days later a sedan with tinted windows pulled up in front of the Berglin Enterprises building at 8 a.m. Four men in business suits walked in to the lobby, pausing to look around. Rachel DuPlessis was there, checking out the premises. She wanted to get a feel for how Max Berglin operated before she made her appointment to see him. The lobby was beautiful, a two-story affair with large plate-glass windows, two supporting marble columns, and a nice looking spiral staircase leading to the second floor. A smart-looking blonde with short hair in a light blue business suit sat at the front desk, fielding calls. The place emanated a feeling of prosperity and professionalism.

Rachel walked up to the desk and introduced herself. "Is it possible to make an appointment to see Mr. Berglin?" Rachel feigned interest in one of Berglin's security software products for her company and the appointment was made. She engaged the woman in chit chat, drawing her out. "Have you been with the company long, Tara?" Rachel got her name from the tag attached with a gold pin to the front of her suit.

Tara Bolshoi was aware of the four men who had just entered the building. "Yes, since the beginning. Before I came here I worked in Fortune 500 companies for almost fifteen years." As Tara explained that she had met Max Berglin at Lockheed, she wondered what Rachel DuPlessis was up to. In addition to her duties as a receptionist, she had been hired to manage the front end of the business, including the security detail. She was Max Berglin's eyes and ears on the company floor.

Rachel completed her business. She was about to leave when both women heard the sound of footsteps. Rachel turned around and Tara focused her attention on the four men as they approached the desk.

Rachel watched with a sense of excitement as the suits spread out at the reception desk, completely ignoring her. The men at the end faced outward, the other two faced inward, confronting Tara. Rachel sensed an altercation and walked slowly away. She eased her back against one of the windows where she would have a good view.

"We're here to see Mr. Max Berglin," said a hard-looking man with a square jaw and a chiseled face that bespoke hard exercise.

"Do you have an appointment sir?" Tara asked.

"No. But I suggest that you tell your boss to make some room in his schedule."

"I'm sorry sir, but no one speaks to Mr. Berglin without an appointment. If you'd like I can set one up right now."

"We represent a capital investment firm, and are prepared to invest in Mr. Berglin's, ah, new product."

Tara smiled and turned on her considerable charm. "That is well, gentlemen. However, Mr. Berglin is not looking for investors at this time." Max had instructed her how to field any official inquiries about the Cube. She had a rote procedure to follow.

Chiseled Jaw's face hardened. He leaned forward and looked at her name tag. "It would be in Mr. Berglin's best interest, Ms. Bolshoi, to see us immediately."

Tara had been instructed by Max not to provoke an argument. She looked at her computer screen. "Will 9 a.m. tomorrow be suitable? Mr. Berglin has no openings today."

Chiseled Jaw frowned impatiently.

Obviously these men were used to getting their way. They looked like military men, not businessmen. Tara was intrigued, for Max had told her to expect an inquiry like this.

"We'll be back here precisely at 9 a.m. tomorrow," he said with a hard edge to his voice. "And Tara, Max Berglin had better be here."

Tara watched as the men swiftly turned toward the door and marched through it like soldiers on their way to the front. She emailed Max about the men and the appointment. She then accessed the security cameras and sent Max the feed of their conversation. Tara was burning with curiosity about what would happen tomorrow.

Rachel was just as excited as Tara and decided to show up at 9 a.m. the next morning, even though her appointment wasn't until next week.

Precisely at 9 a.m. the next day Chiseled Jaw and his three companions, all carrying thin briefcases in their right hands, walked into the lobby. Tara saw that Rachel DuPlessis had placed herself against the side window at the end of the lobby.

"Please write your names clearly on the register," Tara said, smiling. "Mr. Berglin wants to know who he is talking to."

Chiseled Jaw and his entourage ignored her and began walking toward the elevator. Tara pressed a red button on her console. Immediately four of Kenji Hiroto's men appeared. She loved the look and the mannerisms of these men who moved so lightly and gracefully. There was something really sexy about them. Chiseled Jaw seemed startled, Tara observed, and his men spread out in a line to face the guards. Pit bulls confronting ballet dancers, she thought.

A small woman spoke. "Please place your briefcases on the ground, gentlemen, and do not move forward." Tara recognized the woman the other security people called *bakemono.*

Chiseled Jaw laughed. His men did not obey, but neither did they move. "Is this really necessary?"

Monster bowed. "I'm afraid it is, gentlemen. By not signing the register you have deliberately ignored business etiquette and have shown disrespect to our company."

The three suits looked to Chiseled Jaw, who nodded reluctantly. The men placed their briefcases on the floor. While Chiseled Jaw and Monster exchanged pleasantries, her men went through the four briefcases. After a quick inspection one of the security guards spoke swiftly in Japanese: "The briefcases contain only papers, no hidden compartments. The men are unarmed." Tara couldn't understand them, but she saw Monster bow again to Chiseled Jaw and his men. "Our apologies gentlemen. If you will come this way."

Seven men and one woman entered the elevator together.

Rachel decided to stay around and see what happened when the four suits came back down to the lobby.

I sat in my well-lit corner office with Ichiro and Hideki on duty outside. I had seen yesterday's images and watched the drama downstairs on the security cameras. I was ready but a little nervous. I was pretty sure I was about to receive an offer to sell the Cube, just as Vartan Nalbandian had at Octagon Research. Bernie and Julian Green already told me what to expect. I knew what I was going to do.

Just then the elevator door opened and eight persons began walking purposefully down the hallway. I recognized Monster and Manabu, a severe looking man with a van Dyke, who were in front. My guests must be the guys with briefcases. Two more of my men trailed behind. I stood up as Monster and Manabu went to the back of the room and faced forward. "Gentlemen, please have a seat." I pointed to four comfortable leather chairs that had been placed in a semicircle in front of my large steel and glass desk. My visitors, dressed in black suits, made no move to sit down. They stood just behind the chairs like statues. Each one held a briefcase.

Chiseled Jaw smiled dryly. He reached into his briefcase and threw a sheaf of papers onto my desk. "I am James Mosfet. I represent Bluefin Technologies, a capital investment firm. We want to buy your new device, which I am told is called the Cube. We are prepared to pay handsomely for it."

Julian Green told me when he came to my house that this would probably be the opening play. "There must be a misunderstanding gentlemen," I said. "I believe Tara told you yesterday that I am not looking for investors. This operation will be completely in-house." I paused and smiled ironically. "I have never heard of Bluefin Technologies."

Mosfet's face hardened. "I'm afraid you don't understand, Max Berglin. On your desk is an agreement to purchase your invention and all intellectual property associated with it, for the generous sum of twenty million dollars."

I gulped. It was a considerable sum. "The Cube is potentially worth billions, as you well know." I took a shot. "If I do not cooperate, will the same thing happen to me as what happened at the Octagon building?"

I saw Mosfet's eyes blaze, and knew I had my answer. These were probably the guys who stole Katelian's original invention.

Mosfet motioned to the man to his left, who threw an official-looking document onto my desk. I glanced at the heading, which read "Intelligence Community Directive 1773." Underneath that was "Director of National Intelligence."

"On your desk is an Intelligence Community Directive (ICD). It has been signed by Director James Stapleton and approved by General Herman Putnam, the Director of National Intelligence. I suggest, I very strongly suggest, Mr. Berglin, that you read it carefully and sign the agreement. The Cube is now a national security matter." The man to his right opened his briefcase and took out another paper, handing it to James. "This is the Patent Secrecy Order, Mr. Berglin, associated with this development, in case you were going to commercialize this product. It forbids you from publicly releasing any of the technology associated with the Cube, or any offshoot of it." Mosfet placed the paper on the desk next to the others.

I was familiar with the PSO and had discussed it with my lawyers. I scrutinized the ICD carefully. Mosfet had said, "signed by Director James Stapleton and approved by General Herman Putnam, the Director of National Intelligence." The signature at the bottom of the ISD did indeed show the signature of a Lt. Col. James Stapleton, but identified him as "Director, Technologies Acquisition Consortium." Gen. Putnam's signature was nowhere on the document. I breathed a sigh of relief. These men were here under false pretenses.

I looked up and took another shot in the dark. "I see. Did you send a mercenary named Ralph Zimring to my house three weeks ago?"

I surprised a look of incomprehension on Mosfet's face. The man to his right frowned. "A mercenary? Really?" Mosfet frowned him down. "That is irrelevant. You have our offer, Mr. Berglin. We know your associate Bernard Hartwig, and we know you aren't an innocent." His face softened and his voice assumed an almost pleading tone. "Take the offer Mr. Berglin, for all the reasons you probably well understand."

I caught his more conciliatory attitude and wondered whether I should accept the offer. Twenty million was a lot of money. I could save myself a whole lot of potential trouble. But I just couldn't do it.

"I'm sorry gentlemen, but I intend to commercialize this development myself. However, I will sign anything you'd like that says I will never sell the Cube to anyone, or militarize it, or endanger national security."

Mosfet's face drooped a little. "That's not good enough, Max Berglin. Of course you understand that I and my team are merely representatives. Act sensibly, Mr. Berglin. Don't do anything stupid." He pushed the agreement under my hand. "Sign the agreement."

"If I sign, will the technology go into a special access program?"

"Assuredly. For very good reasons which I also think you understand."

I gathered the papers together. "I'll think about it." And I would. "But I'm almost certain I won't change my mind."

"You have 46 hours. I have to report success or failure by 0800 on Friday morning."

My security people had relaxed and the tension in the room had vanished. "Would you guys like to see the Cube and verify its validity?" I suggested. "My offer is genuine. If you come with me to my house I can show you how it works."

James nodded, knowing that his mission had probably failed. However, he could salvage something by getting a first-hand look at the new device. "I'd like my men to also see the demonstration."

"Of course."

"Stand down," he ordered his three companions. "We'll see this Cube of Berglin's and report directly afterward."

"You won't mind if my men escort yours to the door?"

Rachel saw the men, including Max Berglin, come out of the elevator. She was hoping for another confrontation but the tension between them had been defused somehow. She left after they walked out, almost grinding her teeth in her impatience to talk with Berglin. But that wouldn't happen until the following week. She was certain something big was in the works and she wanted to be part of it.

Nine persons left my office, the documents on my desk forgotten. Along with Monster and Manabu in the back seat, I drove "Mosfet" over to my home. The sedan carrying his men followed, and another car with three of my security men in it bracketed the sedan from the rear. I realized on the way that Mosfet was a fake name, based on the MOSFET transistor. When we got to Palmer Park we all trooped downstairs and I demonstrated the unit (again). "We're going to make this baby look really slick," I said. "When we're up and running we won't be able to sell them fast enough."

One of Mosfet's men spoke. "Christ, Murray. I want one of those."

"I can't believe it, Berglin," James said. "Your product is genuine! You have aligned with the one outfit in the entire world that will scare the shit out of Byr—, er, my people."

Apparently James knew about my alliance with Roka Hatsumi and his Ninjikan organization. "Ah yes, Zbigniew Byrnes. I saw him on Necker Island last month."

James' eyebrows rose in surprise. "So you know Julian Green too?"

"Yes, my management team had a nice talk with him. I demonstrated the unit for him."

"Be careful Berglin. Even though I personally sympathize with your project, Byrnes won't look favorably on this development."

"Neither will that psychopath Gulbenkian," said another of the men. Mosfet's face grimaced at that name.

I was irritated. "Who the hell is this Byrnes anyway? What gives him the right to interfere in my affairs?"

"It's not just your affair Berglin. That's why I'm here. Zbigniew Byrnes sits on the boards of at least a dozen influential and powerful companies, all of whom have a vested interest in the status quo. All perfectly legal and above board. But he is also connected within the deep national security state. His group is fanatical about preserving their status in the world."

"How would he know about the Cube?"

"Byrnes' group has a network of informers in companies connected with the sciences or in the defense area." James gave me a speaking look. "There are probably one or two in your own company." Of course. My son, and maybe others as well.

He pointed to the Cube. "I don't have to tell you that this device makes energy generation via fossil fuels archaic. It also makes energy distribution within the current system obsolete. If your device comes to the market there will be a significant drop in oil, gas, petroleum, and coal use. Clearly, many companies in the Fortune 500 will take a big financial hit. Not to mention the millions of jobs that will be lost in the traditional economy if your device becomes a commercial success. You'll have the whole world against you Berglin."

For the first time I truly realized the position I had put myself in. Kenji, Hatsumi, Bernie, and Julian Green had tried to impress upon me how serious my little box was, but I had ignored them. "Of course I expect opposition, that's why I hired a private security force to protect me. I just thought that people would embrace it. I mean, that argument was used against the automobile by the makers of horse-drawn carriages."

James gave me a quizzical look. "You really are a dreamer aren't you Berglin?"

"I guess I am. A practical dreamer though. And I love to take risks."

This sparked a spontaneous laugh from James.

"When you laugh you look like a real human being."

"I got into this business because I wanted to do some good in the world," James responded a little stiffly. "You see, Berglin, people like you are dangerous. This Cube of yours is going to create an awful lot of unnecessary conflict. Too many people are going to suffer."

I considered this. "You may be right in the short term. But in the long term this technology has to be introduced or we're simply going to run out of resources. Better to get it over with as soon as possible. The economy will eventually readjust and we'll be better off."

James shook his head. "Byrnes is a sociopath but he's right in this case, even if it's for the wrong reasons. You can't introduce technology this powerful into a world of lunatics."

We were silent for a few moments. I thought of the Cube and the Pulsar, and their ability to draw energy directly from the quantum vacuum. I considered the potential militarization of them. Then I thought of the millions of poor people on the planet who had trouble paying their heating bills; who could use that money to buy more food or warmer clothes or better medical care for themselves and their children. I concluded that even if James was right, I was still going ahead. "How does Byrnes' group operate? There's no way a small group of people can be so secretive. It's human nature to fight and compete."

James was irritated. "The Manhattan Project began in 1936 and lasted until 1944. It employed over 130,000 people, and not one of them squealed, Berglin. Get real! In the classified area everything, and I mean everything, is compartmentalized. You know that! Nobody knows what anyone else is doing. All I can say is, don't turn your back. When Byrnes' group hits you, you might never know until it's too late."

"Green said that my device could potentially be worth trillions of dollars."

"Every dollar that goes to you will be taken away from someone in the system."

"No. Sure, I plan to get really rich, but eventually I'm going to give it away."

"That's not what I meant. I meant that Byrnes and people like him think that way. If you keep going they'll see you as the enemy."

— 30 —

Elmo Tackett rode his motorbike on a freezing late-February afternoon to the old Van Allen furniture warehouse. The building was only a mile north from the Tavistock development along the Midland River, off River Dr. He hated riding when it was this cold, but he hadn't given up on getting more of those crispy banknotes. Berglin had announced the expansion of his facility to this backwater, but it didn't fit the pattern of his life. The target was a wealthy man who liked affluent surroundings. Why was he building his new addition in an old warehouse? Something fishy was going on.

Elmo did not like Max Berglin, primarily because he had thwarted his mission. He felt a great grudge. This rich and privileged professional had prevented him from collecting his remaining thirty one thousand dollar bills. Elmo came to the asphalt road that led to the building. He turned left from River Drive ontoand tooled his bike until he saw a sign that said "Berglin Enterprises. Please present your ID."

Drat! This wasn't here before when he had put one of those bullets into Berglin. Elmo motored up to a guard who was standing in a small enclosed booth with a sliding window. Would he be recognized? "What's going on here?" Elmo asked.

"Who are you?" the guard asked. "Please present your ID." The man was a foreigner, Elmo decided. He looked Japanese. Elmo pretended to fumble in his coat pocket, and lifted his head to see the building around a slight bend in the road. There was still a lot of construction equipment, trucks and loaders and such, lying about, but the place was beginning to have a more finished look. A large sign was being hoisted that read "Berglin Enterprises" over the front entrance.

"Uh, sorry, I was just curious about what Mr. Berglin was doing in there."

“I can’t let you in, sir, without a badge.”

Elmo didn’t know why people smiled. It made their faces look funny. “All right then, thank you.”

“Wait.” The guard reached into the booth and handed him a brochure. “This will tell you all about the new building and what we’re doing.”

“Thank you.” Elmo was feeling nervous now. He took the flier and put it in his coat pocket. A sharp wind rose, cutting into his face. Elmo hastily turned his scooter around and got out of there. He hadn’t been recognized in his winter clothing.

Zach Gets Going at Berglin Enterprises

Zach Ferrell’s application was accepted. The first thing he did was to study the layout Yusuke Shiozawa had devised for the production line. The idea was to build a fully automated “zero error” production process that would be computer controlled. This required a lot of electrical engineering as well as specialized workstations that would assemble the various components for the Cube.

Zach didn’t understand the theory behind the Cube and he didn’t want to. His job was to help engineer the workstations and he hopped to it with gusto. In contrast to the automotive job he used to have with Larry Potvin, this work was like designing fine jewelry compared to cleaning out gunk from carburetors. All he knew was that when they were done he would be part of something that would literally change history.

Right now they were still in the design phase. Yusuke Shiozawa, advised by Park and Rosen, laid out the geometry and the placement of each workstation in the most efficient manner. They had already torn the thing down once and were about to do so again, but Zach didn’t care. He was busy building the workstations that would actually assemble the Cube. It was heady work.

One day Danielle Menard walked into the facility. Zach saw her as she walked down the corridor to Max’s temporary office. After she came out Zach placed himself in the hallway in front of her. “God you look awesome, Danielle.”

“We haven’t seen each other in five months and that’s what you come up with?” she said, the ghost of a smile around her lips.

“It’s the first thing that popped into my mind,” Zach said.

Danielle giggled. “So you’re working for us now?”

Just then Max Sr. came out of his office. A frown creased the older man’s face. “Oh yes, you’re Zach Ferrell aren’t you.”

Zach stood a little straighter and Danielle almost giggled again. The two men she was attracted to most were facing off.

"Yes sir," Zach said, a bit aggressively. Then his expression lightened. "I'm really excited about the work we're doing here, sir."

Max's expression brightened and he looked eager. "Isn't it? This is the best gig in the world right now."

Zach caught his excitement. "I've only been here for two weeks but I'm getting impatient to get this thing up and running."

Danielle saw that the two men were physically much alike. Zach was built like Julian Green. Max was more muscular, but two inches smaller. Both men had outgoing temperaments. Max, forty now but looking ten years younger, had urbanity, confidence, and a more mature charm as compared to Zach's more youthful exuberance.

"All right Ferrell, get back to work," Max said. Zach caught the undertone that said, 'and keep away from my woman.'

"Yes sir, and no sir," Zach replied. He saw the boss grin, and marked him down as a man who didn't take himself too seriously. Probably a good guy to work for, he thought.

The older man began possessively guiding Danielle down the hall. "C'mon Danielle, let's get back to the office." Zach stayed to see whether Danielle would look back. She did. He was satisfied. Since they broke it off he hadn't found anyone he liked nearly as much, male or female.

That night Zach had coffee with Jessie. Heather McCloy was also there with Mike Parsons.

"Heard you got hired at Berglin's," Mike said after they got their drinks and sat down.

Zach bit into a doughnut. "I did!"

"I haven't seen you in two weeks Zach," Jessie complained.

Zach saw the quick glance from Heather, silently telling her to back off and not whine. Mike picked up on it instantly.

Zach spoke to Mike. "I can see you haven't lost your touch."

Mike and Heather looked at each other with shared understanding.

Jessie looked bewildered. Zach felt sorry for her. "It's nothing Jess. Just an old joke between me and Mike."

Zach contemplated Heather and Mike. They looked like a couple in perfect agreement, with an implicit understanding and approval that good friends have.

"That's right Zach. Don't settle," Mike said. Again Heather glanced over to him and they both smiled.

"Is this some sort of mind-reading demonstration?" Jessie asked. She didn't get it, and felt that Zach was moving away from her. The closeness between Heather and Mike irritated her. She remembered what a dork the guy used to be, and couldn't understand how Heather had fallen for him. "So when do you leave on your assignment?" she asked Heather, trying to keep her voice level.

Heather's face fell. "In three weeks. I'm going to Laos!" Zach could tell that she was really excited to go, and at the same time sad that Mike couldn't go with her.

Mike spoke proudly. "She's learning Lao. Boning up on the culture and traditions of the country."

"Yeah," Heather said. "A real prize. A communist dictatorship run by generals. I've also been studying Vietnamese, they have a lot of influence there."

The conversation drifted to various topics. Zach noticed how tight Heather and Mike were and wondered whether they'd still be together after her 24-month assignment was over. He glanced over at Jessie, who was moping and staring into her coffee. He tried to engage her and include her in the discussion, but she didn't seem interested. It was as if she liked him better when he was indecisive. She was getting to be tiresome, Zach decided.

Max Distributes the Cube

After the appearance of "James Murray" and his men I got nervous. I had told him privately that with a phone call I could summon several hundred of Hatsumi's men to defend my property, but that was just a bluff. Roka and Kenji both told me to keep under the radar, and Hatsumi said that fighting was futile. I believed him. So far a seven-foot mercenary and a team sent by a fanatic named Zbigniew Byrnes had already made an appearance. I was pretty sure that was just the beginning if I didn't stand down. I found myself thinking in confrontational terms and I didn't like it.

I called a meeting of UPower. Danielle reported that inquiries were coming in from all over the city. "Looks like that ploy of mine worked. I mentioned the Cube to Trevor Clarke at the Brinson party last month. He must have told everyone in Midland."

"Let's give credit where credit is due," I said. "That was my idea."

Danielle stuck her tongue out playfully.

"We're far from being operational at this point at the new facility," Austin said with a worried frown. "Shiozawa and I are doing our best to develop a production line, but it's slow going. We're not ready yet."

I thought for a moment. "Build Cubes, by hand if you have to, and satisfy the immediate demand. I want to get these things out to the public as fast as possible. The more people have them, the harder it will be to prevent the introduction of our new technology into the local economy."

"How much should we charge?" Austin asked.

"Profit isn't important at this point. Charge something affordable and pump them out as quickly as you can."

"People will need help setting up the Cubes," Danielle said.

"I have just the guy to do that. Your old boyfriend Zach Ferrell."

I saw Danielle start. "How is he doing, Max?"

"He's as energetic as a one-legged buttkicker." Mildred Harrison, my former office manager and now counterpart to Tara Bolshoi at UPower, told me that he was doing very well. "Yusuke Shiozawa says that Zach is a very competent and creative engineer."

I turned to Austin Park. "Austin, you and John get going on this. Hire more people if you have to, but only locals." I turned to the group. "Try not to distribute the Cubes more than a few miles outside the city limits." Everyone nodded. "Austin, get the Ferrell kid installing these things as fast as you can make them. I have a feeling we don't have much time left before things get hairy around here."

Two weeks later, twenty-seven hand-made Cubes had been installed by Zach Ferrell at private residences all over the city.

The production line was still snagged. Shiozawa hadn't yet worked out the bugs, so in the meantime I put the kid to work doing something productive.

That night Bernie came over for a game of billiards and I told him about UPower's progress. I thought of my son, who had turned out to be an informant. I wondered who he was informing. I hadn't seen him in weeks so he must be getting money from somewhere. "You know Bernie, I'm growing more fond of Zach Ferrell. He's turning out to be the kind of person I wish Max Jr. could be."

"You shouldn't let Max Jr. run tame in your business, Max. Either put him to work or tell him to find a job elsewhere."

"I've warned everyone to be circumspect when he's around, and I've got security cameras now. I love Max even though I know there's a streak of darkness in him."

"Some people are like that," Bernie said. "I've known a few of them in my work."

"Not Zach. He's got a sunny, engaging personality and he's learning responsibility. In order to install the Cubes an electrician has to come into the home and either modify the existing electrical panel or put in a new one. Zach interviewed every local electrician in town and lit a fire under the one he hired, giving him all the wiring jobs. The electrician is now talking up the Cube to all of his clients and his fellow tradesmen."

"You're a sly one Max," Bernie teased. "Get the young man out of the shop so he can't compete with you on company time."

I burst out laughing. So Bernie knew about my interest in Danielle. "Damn right Bernie. He's twenty years younger than me and I'm going to use every advantage I have!" I was honest with myself; I could see why Danielle had wanted to marry Zach. His youth and his outgoing nature probably appealed to her more introspective one.

"In another month, Bernie, the electric company is going to be in for a big surprise as more and more homes go off the grid."

Bernie frowned. "That's bound to attract more attention from the authorities, Max."

"It's not ideal but it can't be helped."

Bernie studied the table, leaned over, and executed an amazing five-cushion shot. "I hope your UPower enterprise works out as well as *that!*"

"Admit it Bernie, that was total luck."

"Well yes. But it still counts."

We both laughed.

After Bernie left I found myself thinking of Zach Ferrell and Danielle. Those two were probably a complementary pair. I stifled that thought and went to bed.

John Rosen made sure that one of the Cubes went to the home of Vahan Katelian. When Zach entered the grounds of the gated Katelian mansion, he was met by Rosen's old friend and antagonist. The boss himself had a run-in with this guy, Zach knew.

After Zach was done, Vahan grunted. He had been brusque throughout and seemed to hold a grudge. "Tell your boss that this little trinket doesn't make up for what John did."

Zach was irritated. "Are you still on that?" He knew the back story on it from Danielle. "You fired Park and Rosen and Max hired them. You made a mistake. Get over yourself."

Katelian, in a well-tailored business suit, raised a finger to Zach. "There's still the matter of my brother Raffi. We still think Berglin was behind that." Vahan knew that Zach used to be the Menard girl's boyfriend, and still talked to her. He must know something.

Zach was astonished. He was supposed to be nice to customers but this guy was an asshole. "Look, Vahan Katelian. Max had some guys visit him a few weeks ago, offered him twenty mil for the Cube. Does that sound familiar?"

Vahan started.

"The same guys who stole your experiment got your brother too." Zach was just speculating but as soon as he said it he knew it was true.

Vahan was much struck. "Who are they then?"

"I don't know, but we've got a whole security crew trying to protect us from those guys."

Vahan relaxed. Perhaps his father was right. At the last meeting of the families, Mardig and Vartan had formally declared an end to the Raffi situation. Even so, he knew that Zadig disliked Max Berglin even more than he.

Who Are These People?

by Tina Brooks

City Desk

An influx of Asian employees at Berglin Enterprises has been noticed and commented upon by many in Midland. Almost exclusively men, the employees speak no English and are usually accompanied by an interpreter when they go out in public.

The men wear gray uniforms with a "Berglin Enterprises" decal sewn on both sleeves and on the chest. Two of the men are always seen around Max Berglin Sr. when in public. The two famous (or shall I say infamous!) scientists, Austin Park and John Rosen, are also followed closely by two of the men. You'll recall that Park and Rosen caused a sensation last year with their now-debunked "free energy" device.

When this reporter asked Max Berglin about the men, he just smiled and said evasively, "New employees over from Japan. Cultural exchange visit. We've sent some of our people over there. One of their top guys is over here helping us to get more efficient in our business operations." I don't buy it. Berglin Enterprises is in the software security business. Why do they need men who speak no English to guard a bunch of office computers? Something strange is going on.

This paper has received photographs and videos of the men, who patrol the new Berglin Enterprises facility at the old Van Allen furniture warehouse. A dozen more have been spotted at their downtown headquarters building. All reports indicate that they look like military people, or trained bodyguards.

A Berglin Enterprises employee relates this story: "I was coming into work last week when two unmarked black sedans drove up and parked right next to the front entrance. Four men dressed in black suits got out in a hurry, carrying briefcases. A few minutes later some of our security people confronted the strange men. I saw them march the four briefcase guys into the elevator. It was bizarre, like something you see on TV."

Trevor Clarke mentioned that "something big" was up at Berglin Enterprises. Mr. Clarke, the well-known society figure and president of PRC Bank, said he had it from Danielle Menard, now the Public Relations spokesperson for Berglin's company. Last year, Ms. Menard spent a night in jail for drug dealing and possession. If that isn't strange enough, I also talked with Josh Brackenreed, a systems analyst for Midland Electric, who volunteered the following information to the Courier. He said that Max Berglin actually has a working "free energy" device that powers his large home in Palmer Park, and that the electric company has officially classified the new unit as a "renewable energy device."

So what gives, Max Berglin? What are you hiding? And who are these people, who look more like a private foreign army than legitimate employees?

When I saw the article I knew that Julian Green had been right about not using foreign security people. But I didn't trust anyone I knew in the US. It was ironic: The people I truly relied on came from a culture I didn't understand, half a world away.

Elmo Gets Wise

Max Berglin had bodyguards now. Whoever they were had spotted Elmo one cold, dry March day when he was staking out the house in Palmer Park on his scooter. Suddenly two men came out of the bushes by the gate and ran him down as he got on his little motorbike. The men grunted in some strange language he had never heard before. One of them held his hands behind his back. The other punched him in the stomach, knocking all the wind out of him.

He called Zadig Katelian. "There is an army surrounding Max Berglin. I got beat up today and I won't try again until those foreigners are gone."

"Poor boy. You took thirty bills of our money to do a job and you didn't do it."

Elmo sneered. "You are a crook who doesn't keep his word. Our deal was thirty one thousand dollar bills after the shooting. I got a bullet in Berglin using your weapon, but he recovered. It's not my fault." Elmo had no patience for people who lied. He never lied, not because he cared about people, but because it was the best way to do business.

"You fucked up, Tackett. You either kill Berglin or give us our money back. Otherwise we're going to come for you on that fuckin' little scooter of yours. A cripple could run you down."

"Fuck you Zadig. You forget you have family members all over town. If you even touch a hair on my head you'll be the loser, do you understand me?"

Zadig shuddered. He understood Elmo's implied threat and he knew the little bastard wasn't kidding. He could get one of their boys to burn this guy, but the risk was too great. Elmo Tackett was a slithery motherfucker with the devil's own luck. He was the type of motherfucker who would set a bomb to your house and kill everyone in it, then go home and watch TV. The guy was twisted in a way that scared even him. "We'll be watching you Tackett. And remember we got our own brand of justice."

Elmo heard the phone click. He paid no attention to Zadig's threats. The one thing on his mind was the thirty bills he had yet to collect. Elmo went into his safe and got them out, running his fingers through the crisp notes and smelling the money smell.

He would bide his time and wait.

After his conversation with Tackett, Zadig brooded. His brother Vahan hadn't been close to Raffi, but he had been. Vahan already told him that Berglin probably didn't have Raffi killed. Zadig wasn't convinced. Did not Max Berglin have a security classification? He was part of the same shadowy network as the guys who had stolen their work at Octagon. Zadig went downstairs and observed the Cube. There were no wires connected to it. The thing took power magically out of the air; enough to power the entire Katelian property! He understood suddenly that Berglin's device (*their* device) was a paradigm shifter. He realized how completely the families had been duped. Their invention was going to make Berglin fabulously wealthy. And with wealth comes power. If it wasn't for Berglin the Cube would belong solely to the families, who could have dictated terms to the whole world! It was clear: Max Berglin was a cheater and a con man who had come in at the last minute to snatch away the prize. Zadig ground his teeth and hoped Tackett would be successful next time. He had called Elmo just to light a fire under that little bastard.

Byrnes Orders Stapleton

James Stapleton sat in his office at the Technology Acquisition Consortium outside Chicago, looking out the window at another snowy day. This frozen, godforsaken climate was depressing. Suddenly the door burst open and slammed against the wall. Stapleton whirled around in his chair. "What the HELL —"

Zbigniew Byrnes walked into the room, arrogant, dominating it by the force of his personality. Stapleton felt his anger dissipate. As he looked into the old man's face it was replaced with cold fear. He quickly looked away. There was something terrifyingly sinister about this man.... Stapleton leaned back in his chair and tried to relax. He knew this was serious because Byrnes never saw anyone in person.

"That's much better old fellow," Byrnes said. He maneuvered himself into a chair facing the younger man. Just then two guards burst into the room, holding guns. "Oh, it's you sir," one of them said to Byrnes. The other, a beefy fellow with hard black eyes, trained his gun on Stapleton. At that moment James Stapleton understood where the real power lay in TAC. "Fuck."

"My sentiments exactly colonel," Byrnes said. "Put on your headphones."

Before he put on his headphones Stapleton saw that the guards still had their guns on him.

The two men entered the White Room.

"Now listen," Byrnes said. "That outlier Berglin and those two buggery scientists of his have been making dozens of overunity devices. Those maniacs have been putting them in homes all over that rubbishing town of Midland. Do you understand what that means?"

"I don't believe you. My man in Midland says there's only one, in Berglin's home."

"You're wrong. If you had any intelligence at all you'd have gone to Midland Electric. There's a man there who said that 28 homes are now off the grid. He's been to every one of them, and they all have those Cubes, or whatever that maniac Berglin calls them."

Stapleton was shocked. "I—"

"Silence you fool! Here is what you do. There are only two men in the whole world who understand this device and how to build it: those scientists of his, Austin Park and John Rosen. They are the evil geniuses behind the whole project."

"What about Berglin?"

"Berglin is a businessman, he knows nothing about it."

Stapleton gathered his courage. "You're wrong, Byrnes. Max Berglin is a respected physicist in his own right."

"He certainly is. But my man Murray says that Berglin has as much of an idea how that device works as my dog knows how to build the Large Hadron Supercollider. The two scientists are the key to the entire project."

Stapleton leaned back in his virtual chair. Byrnes had settled down now, and he tried to meet the older man's eyes, but had to glance quickly away. He, who had seen men ripped apart by land mines in Iraq, could not face this man. Byrnes' eyes were a brilliant blue and behind them was a powerful, almost hypnotic intelligence and the uncompromising conviction of a fanatic. The son-of-a-bitch was always right. Where was he getting his information?

Stapleton wiped drops of sweat from his face with a clammy hand. "Berglin is trying to build a production line but it isn't going well. Park and Rosen are making the devices by hand. You may be right."

"Of course I'm right! If you had any brains you'd have taken care of those two at the very first. But it's still not too late. My sources tell me that the entire operation is local to the City of Midland, by design. The problem is already contained."

"Both of them are surrounded by elite, special forces bodyguards."

"Take care of it Stapleton, that's why you're in charge here."

Stapleton realized that Byrnes was right. Berglin was the moving force behind everything, but only the two scientists had the knowledge to keep the project going.

"That's right, colonel," Byrnes said. "Take care of those two and the threat can still be eliminated. Until this incident in Midland you have been very successful. Don't let the side down."

After Byrnes left Stapleton considered his position. Dangerous technology such as Berglin's and that fool Blaise McNeil's had to be sequestered. But he was little more than an errand boy, himself sequestered within the bowels of the Network. The United States was not the only country that had special access programs; they also existed in Germany, several other European governments, Russia, and China. All of these programs denied access to their governments and the traditional militaries. Rumor had it that humans had already established bases on the moon and on Mars, and that the new fuel-less craft were interplanetary. He shook his head, disgusted. The United States should be leading the development of this new technology, safe from attack! For the first time the colonel began to doubt his commitment to the cause. Zbigniew Byrnes was, he had to admit, completely anti-social. If sociopaths like Byrnes ran the Network his country, and the entire human race, was in trouble.

It occurred to Stapleton that men like Byrnes ran the world. Narrow-minded people who were rigidly focused on only one thing. People who never changed their ideas and who always acted the same way, regardless of circumstances. This gave them a powerful mindset and a conviction of rightness that others automatically responded to. When Zbigniew Byrnes was national security adviser, his commanding personality and inflexibility overcame the opinions of everyone in the cabinet, including the president. He was still a powerful and even feared figure within the national security establishment.

But Byrnes was right about Berglin: this new technology could not be allowed to hit the market. Stapleton sighed and did his duty. He called Roger Comfrey up to his office. Comfrey – most inaptly named – was in charge of operations. He gave his instructions. Where he had failed with Berglin he would not with Park and Rosen.

After Zbigniew Byrnes left the facility he smiled grimly to himself. He had caught Stapleton's astonishment at the accuracy of his intelligence. Oh colonel, if you only knew where my information comes from. All successful overunity devices have recognizable footprints within the zero-point energy field. That field is monitored all day every day. Every successful overunity experiment has been, is, and will be known wherever it is conducted on the planet.

Part XV

Attack

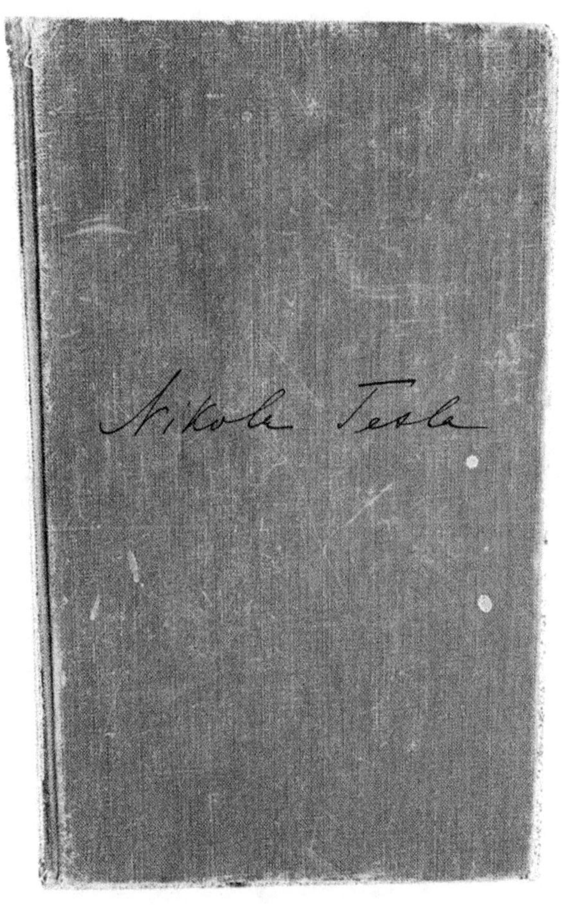

— 31 —

After work Austin Park and John Rosen walked into Sweetwaters. Austin ordered a latte, John ordered hot honey-ginger tea and a sweet roll. They found seats at the back.

"Finally, we got rid of those bodyguards," John said.

Austin sighed. He was very, very tired and stressed. "It's been almost a year, John. I don't know how much more of this I can take."

"That's why we're here," John said, looking nervously over at the wall of windows. It was almost dark. Suddenly he began to laugh. "The only place in town where we can be seen no matter where we sit!"

Austin giggled nervously, looking around. The entire front, back, and the west wall of the coffee shop had floor to ceiling windows. They were sitting ducks, but he didn't care anymore. "You know John, I used to think technology was the answer to everything."

"Isn't it? Just look what it's done for us!"

"That is the point entirely," Austin replied. "I used to be excited about life and my work. Now I wake up in fear, with two guys outside my door."

"Yeah, but look what we've done Austin. We built an overunity device that works. We have almost perfected Tesla's system for wireless transmission of energy to anywhere in space."

"It's not worth it. I'm going back to my family in South Korea."

"What? You're abandoning the project?" John was shocked and dropped his roll. It fell onto the floor and he looked at it in disgust.

Austin nodded decisively. "I just made up my mind right now. I've had it with all the secrecy and the tension. I feel like I'm serving a prison sentence."

"We ARE in prison Austin! Haven't we talked about that? We're all of us in a corporate prison run by crazy people who want to keep us working and slaving in their fossil-fuel empire." John slammed his glass down on the table and glared at this friend. "Now is not the time to quit when we're almost at the goal line."

"You do it John. You have more energy than me. I'm out."

John steamed silently. He knew it would be pointless to argue with Park; the man was as stubborn as a mule. He tried again. "Think of all the people you're abandoning, Austin. The entire human race! We need to finish this."

"I don't care anymore."

Just then Austin's mobile rang. He heard a burst of guttural Japanese and Austin's face hardened. Park put the phone away from his ear, a look of profound irritation on his face.

"Sounds like Matsui," John said, smiling. Japanese, to his American ear, sounded like John Belushi at the Samurai Delicatessen. Matsui was one of Austin's bodyguards and spoke no English.

"Why are you bothering me Matsui?" John heard some more Japanese. "Because we can't take it anymore. We climbed out the bathroom window and ran out through the loading door when the guards weren't looking."

John laughed. It was the first time they had both been alone since the boss hired Kenji's firm. Just then his own phone rang. It was Yugo, his bodyguard. "You are both in great danger!" he said in strongly accented English. "Stay where you are, don't move! I am on the way."

John rang off. He grabbed Austin's phone, which was still spewing Japanese, and shut it off. "Maybe you're right. I feel like a hamster about to be put back in his cage."

Austin didn't reply. He grabbed his phone and went to a travel agency site. After a few moments he slammed his mobile on the table. "I've done it John. I ordered a ticket and I'm leaving in a few hours, at 8 a.m. out of O'Hare."

John saw the confirmation page. He looked up and saw Mike Parsons and his girlfriend, and Zach Ferrell and another girl, walk in. Zach looked up and saw them. He hurried over.

"What are you guys doing here? Where are your guards?"

"Austin just quit," John said.

Zach was dumbfounded. "You quit the greatest undertaking in the history of mankind?"

Austin's stubborn face grew harsher. "Yes, I did. And it's none of your business."

"The hell it isn't. Without you we might not make it."

"Thanks for the vote of confidence," John said. He wasn't too surprised. He'd seen the signs in his partner of weary discontent for the past several weeks.

John looked up at Zach. "Not to worry. I know almost everything he does now."

Zach looked at Austin and saw a man who had completely disengaged.

"I'm going to a hotel and stay there until my plane leaves," Austin said. "And John," he said, glaring at his assistant, "you're not to say a word to the boss about this."

"You must be overworked Austin," John said. "Zach here works for UPower now. He is best friends with Danielle Menard, who often works with the boss."

"Whatever."

When John thought about his inevitable return to the lab and endless days of drudgery all of his anger at Austin evaporated. For too long they had both been living like circus animals. "I'll come with you," John suggested. "Maybe I can meet some girls in the hotel bar."

Zach was flabbergasted. He saw Austin and John walk hurriedly out of the coffee shop.

When the two scientists got out of the place they both looked at each other and laughed. "Whoo!" John said, and started running. Austin followed, feeling like a zoo animal who had been released from his cage.

Zach went slowly over to the table occupied by Jessie, Mike, and Heather. "Those two guys are the heart and soul of UPower. They both just quit."

Jessie smiled. "Well, you're strong enough to stop both of them."

Zach gave her a startled glance. "I am!"

He ran out of the coffee shop and saw the two men a block away, walking rapidly toward the hotel. Should he go after them? John and Austin were friends now and he didn't want to accost them on the street.

He started running. The boss wouldn't appreciate him abandoning his precious pair of scientists, even if he had to physically detain them.

When Zach reached the intersection of First and Main, a block from the hotel, a black sedan with its lights off sped silently to the curb. Two men ran out of the vehicle and grabbed Austin and John. Before Zach could reach the car the men had muscled the two scientists into the back seat. The car accelerated down the street and was gone.

Zach reported the abduction to the Midland Police Dept. and texted Danielle, who would tell the boss.

Ralph Zimring Gets a Job

The day after Park and Rosen were abducted Ralph Zimring received a mobile call at nine in the morning. He was relaxing in his Northern Michigan home, wishing he could get one of those devices of Berglin's. He had a glass of wine in his hand, looking out his living room window at a forested winter landscape. His thoughts kept returning to Julia.

"There's a job for you if you want it," a voice said.

"Yeah?"

"There's an escalating national security issue in Midland, Illinois. A private foreign army is protecting a man who is endangering national security. Your job would be to work with a special detachment that will be sent in to eliminate the threat and free the city from their presence. Your participation will be under an assumed name."

"The target wouldn't be Max Berglin, would it?"

"How the fuck do you know that?" the voice asked.

"I already dealt with him. He's not a threat." This duplication of effort was typical with clandestine work. Everything was so compartmentalized the left hand never knew what the right hand was doing.

"You're not qualified to make that assessment, Zimring."

Ralph was bored now. He didn't know who this guy was, but he didn't like him. "You have to do better than that."

"I already told you. A former Lockheed employee, a guy named Max Berglin, has hired foreign mercenaries from Japan and China, a fucking private army, and more are coming."

Ralph didn't know that. "A private army?"

"That's right Zimring."

He had only seen three of Berglin's foreign mercenaries, two guarding the perimeter of the house and one personal bodyguard. That was OK, but if Berglin was bringing in an army...the thought galled the patriot in him. Could he have misread the man? He'd have to check out the situation again.

"All right," Ralph said. "I'm in."

"You'll be paid at the standard pay grade for enlisted personnel. The detachment will be ad hoc."

"I don't want any money. This is for my country, I'll do this one gratis." He had plenty of money. His contracts were lucrative, except when he did pro bono work.

"Your patriotism is commendable. Today is April 4th. Report to Commander Duggan this Friday, April 6th, at 0800."

Ralph knew that Duggan commanded an elite unit at Fort McCoy, Wisconsin, which trains over 100,000 troops every year. The detachment would be totally invisible there. But after he reported to Duggan he would do a little reconnaissance. He'd go to Midland a couple of days early and scout the place. He'd check out this private army.

If Max Berglin had lied to him....

Ralph had an incentive. This operation was "ad hoc," and appeared to be something Duchene Comstock would have his filthy hands in. He might have a wonderful excuse to avenge the death of Julia if that obese slob showed up. The thought of his hands around Comstock's neck was incentive enough.

Ralph packed his bags and was on the road in half an hour. On the way he stopped by a tailor's shop in Traverse City, owned by an old Army vet. He remembered the uniforms worn by Berglin's security detail. After paying extravagantly, he was outfitted with a Berglin Enterprises uni. He grinned, thinking about the fun he would have masquerading as one of Berglin's guards.

Max Calls in Some Chips

I heard from Danielle that Park and Rosen had gone downtown without their bodyguards, and about their capture. I was angry; but I had done the same thing a few months ago. At 6:15 I left my bedroom on my way to the kitchen. Ichiro showed up, babbling Japanese at me until Monster came in. She said that her men were scouring the city for the two scientists.

My gut froze because without them, UPower was almost dead. We might be able to figure out what they had done with the Cube but it would take a lot of time I didn't have. I was almost four months into the six-month deadline given me by the Board. Now everything was falling apart. Without financial support from Berglin Enterprises, UPower would quickly collapse.

At breakfast I reread last week's article in the *Courier*, fuming. I'd left it on my desk to motivate me. Even if I got Rosen and Austin back that piece had been turning public opinion against me just when I needed time to set up production for the Cube. Didn't these people understand that I was going to make everyone energy-independent? I went down to the *Courier* offices on Third Street and talked to Tina Brooks, the author of the piece. Later I had a conversation with Clive Barnsley, the paper's chief editor. Brooks was angry that the "big story" she'd been promised had turned out to be nothing. I suspected that the article she wrote was a revenge piece. I explained everything to both of them and even offered to take them home for a demonstration, but they were adamant.

Barnsley was a prissy sort of fellow. "Those scientists of yours were destroyed by Hartwig in that silly debate, which was nothing but free promotion for you and your company. As far as I'm concerned, this Cube of yours is just a marketing gimmick. And those men of yours are causing problems in the community. Why can't you just hire local people?"

I replied angrily that I was hiring lots of local people in my new facility. But Barnsely couldn't get the idea of "foreign troops" out of his head, which was some kind of buzzword that had inflamed opinions. Barnsley smirked when I told them to talk to Josh Brackenreed at Midland Edison to verify the validity of the Cube. "We already did that. His boss, Ruth Vandenberghe, said that Brackenreed 'was too excited about a simple renewable energy device.'"

I gave up on that line. Of course the utility company wouldn't want to promote the Cube. It would cut into their business.

I told them that Park and Rosen had been kidnapped. Barnsely was insultingly unconcerned. "They probably went out for a spree. According to what I've heard, you've had them cooped up in that lab of yours for months." Tina Brooks called her contact at the Midland Police Department who said that the men hadn't been missing above twelve hours. "The only person who saw it was Zach Ferrell, one of your employees. It's low priority for now, both men are adults," she said.

I was frustrated but decided that getting on the bad side of the media wasn't a good thing. I apologized for any upset I'd caused, and left.

I talked the situation over with Danielle. We decided not to publicize the abduction of our two researchers. We'd keep it quiet for now and hope we could get them back. Danielle was to call a press conference the following morning in response to the *Courier* article. (I hoped that at least somebody would show up, even if it was only the campus newspaper, *The Daily*.) Danielle would say that the new security men would stay out of the community except when traveling with myself, Park, and Rosen, who had all received unspecified threats. Danielle would explain that until they had identified those who were issuing the threats, the company would have to remain on alert, with security men guarding both buildings. As soon as the threat was over the security men would leave the country. I would also talk with the Midland police and explain the situation as best I could.

That evening at home things went from bad to worse. I received a call from a number I didn't recognize, but I picked up.

"Max Berglin?"

"Speaking."

"This is Julian Green."

"I want to thank you again for the invite to Necker. It was great."

"I wish this was a social call Max, but I'm afraid I have some disturbing information. I have learned that a team is being sent to Midland, the purpose of which is to 'neutralize' the Cube. The attackers will be filtering in from Fort McCoy in Wisconsin. According to my informant this is an elite group put together specifically to take care of the 'Max Berglin problem.' Be careful."

"Thank you Dr. Green, but how do you know this?"

"Let's just say that a lot of people send me sensitive information, including whistleblowers, and that my network is large. The information I have just given you is valid." Green checked his watch. "Today is Saturday, the 5th of April. By the 10th the unit is expected to be in the area and ready for action. Get set!"

"But why, Julian? This is an absurd overreaction to a couple dozen renewable energy devices."

Green was amused. "Oh my dear Max you are such an innocent, and I say that as a compliment. Consider that the GDP of this planet in the current fossil fuel system is trillions of real dollars every year. What do you think will happen if your technology becomes broadly disseminated and developed? If you were in Byrnes' shoes, would you allow someone to destroy your painstakingly constructed business empire?"

"But —" I began to see, again, the opposing point of view. I was honest enough with myself to see that whenever I got onto a project I pursued it with zeal, ignoring divergent opinions.

"Are you sure Byrnes is behind this?"

"Byrnes, TAC, and a loose coalition of people with the same interests. My best guess is that this operation is sponsored by his friend Herman Putnam, the Director of National Intelligence. Putnam calls himself a patriot. I'm told that Commander Duggan at Fort McCoy is sympathetic."

"So Byrnes wasn't kidding at Necker then."

"I'm afraid not Max. Sociopaths are by definition irrational, so don't try to understand them. Byrnes has got it into his head that you are dangerous. He's got enough money and influence to buy enough people to squash your invention. Your only advantage is that this operation is probably unacknowledged, outside the chain of command, and therefore illegal."

"That's probably not going to help me if bullets start flying."

Green laughed. I got the impression that he had been through something like this himself. "Probably not Max, but it shouldn't come to that. These guys will want to avoid complications."

"All right, thank you Julian. We'll be ready." I hoped. "Oh, one more thing. Our two scientists were abducted last night. Please put your feelers out for me; I want to know who did this."

"Wow, Byrnes must be in panic mode. Let's hope they're not TWEPed, but I doubt that will happen. Their knowledge is too valuable and will probably be their salvation."

"What's TWEPed?"

"Termination With Extreme Prejudice."

— 32 —

Driving down Main St. the previous evening, Vahan Katelian saw Austin Park and John Rosen walking together. They were alone, without their guards. On an impulse, he swerved his Mercedes and made a U-turn. He was determined to speak with the scientists who had made the breakthrough, funded with the families' money. At that moment a black sedan raced by him on his left. When the scientists were forced into the sedan, Vahan acted quickly. Following the sedan as it raced up the street, he called his brother Zadig. "Get Bobby and the boys up here quickly, Zadig. Back me up. Park and Rosen have been snatched. I think it's by the guys who killed Raffi and stole our experiment."

As Vahan quickly gave directions he followed the sedan, which had slowed down and melded itself into the traffic flow. After five minutes he saw Zadig's Mercedes and a van driven by Bobby Popp, with his men from the families' security service. The sedan made a right turn onto Airport Drive, one of Midland's two primary roads out of town. As he pulled in behind the vehicle Vahan motioned to Bobby and Zadig to follow the sedan. Vahan took a silenced airgun (exactly like the one Elmo used) and leaned out the window. He put two bullets into the back tires of the sedan, sending it screaming out into traffic. Airport Dr. was a two lane street in both directions, and traffic was light. The sedan came to a stop in the center turn lane. The three Katelian vehicles surrounded the black sedan. Two armed men came out firing from the sedan, but Popp and Vahan were old hats at this game. Vahan saw that the two assailants resembled the description given by Vartan Nalbandian of the men who had stripped their lab at the Octagon. Popp and six of the boys surrounded the kidnappers, cutting off their escape and giving the kidnappers too many bogeys. Vahan Katelian got out of his car and approached silently from the passenger side, using his vehicle as a shield. He calmly shot one of the kidnappers in the side of the head. Suddenly, the two scientists ran wildly out of the sedan toward the van. Vahan saw Bobby jump to cut them off. Three of their men caught the other kidnapper in a crossfire and gunned him down using the airguns. Bobby threw the two scientists, who were both babbling, into the back seat of Vahan's Mercedes. As Vahan got into his car he noticed that the two bullet casings in the sedan's tires were already starting to dissolve. Bobby and his men entered the van and all three vehicles drove off slowly, blending into traffic, as if nothing but a traffic accident had occurred. Popp, with the van, turned left and went a different route down a side street.

On the way to the Katelian mansion Vahan, followed by his brother Zadig, experienced a savage joy. They had finally avenged the killing of Raffi! Moreover, the airguns with their untraceable bullets had proven themselves in battle. The cartridges with their five dissolving bullets fired off flawlessly at one-second intervals after the guns had charged up. The guns had just enough power to penetrate the steel belts of the tires. The two assassins had also used silenced weapons. The entire skirmish had unfolded like a silent movie, lasting less than one minute. A few gawking citizens had slowed to see the incident. He had seen one of them on his cell before they left the scene, but Vahan laughed as he thought about the impending police investigation. The cops would find nothing to trace back to the Katelians. The two assassins had been completely surprised and had not even hit their vehicles, or marked any of their men. It was a one-in-a-thousand operation where everything had gone right, proving that the gods favored the Katelians.

Vahan grinned as he turned to see Park and Rosen in the back seat. Park was cowering in the corner. That crazy Rosen with his goofy-looking clown hair was shouting and gesturing angrily. Vahan thought John was funny. He wasn't afraid, just angry. Vahan liked that.

All three vehicles drove to the Katelian mansion. Later Vahan, Zadig, and Bobby Popp congratulated themselves on getting a little of theirs back and satisfying the blood feud. An eye for an eye. It didn't bring Raffi back but Vahan felt nothing but hatred and contempt for the malignants they left bleeding out on the street.

Now the families had a big bargaining chip with Max Berglin.

Five hours later, Detective Stan Moyer was baffled. The bodies of the two dead men at the crime scene had no identification on them. Their vehicle had no VIN number and no identifying marks of any kind. Later, at the hospital, the cause of death was officially listed as death by unknown projectiles. One man had a hole in the side of his head and the other had two holes in his chest and one in his back. No bullets had been found in the bodies or at the crime scene. The case resembled the Max Berglin shooting, which was still unsolved. Angry and frustrated, Moyer had nothing to investigate except a couple of shell casings, which would probably lead back to untraceable weapons. This had all the fingerprints of some kind of covert military or national security operation. Just like the break-in at Octagon Research.

It was out of his jurisdiction and he decided to wash his hands of the entire affair. Something very sinister was going on in his little town, but he was powerless to do anything about it.

My phone rang in the middle of the night. It was Vahan Katelian.

"What do you want Katelian?"

"My my, what heat Berglin! I have something of yours."

"Were you behind the abduction of Park and Rosen?" Even at two in the morning this bastard looked like he was going to a gala at the Ritz.

"We were not, you stupid shit. Me, Zadig, and our security service rescued your guys. They were being abducted by a couple of men in an unmarked black sedan."

"Are they all right?"

Vahan laughed. "They look like Bill Burr at a fundamentalist meeting, but they are unharmed."

"Put them on."

"Fuck you Berglin. Not until we get a piece of that action."

I calmed myself from unreasoning anger. "Listen Katelian, it's gone way beyond that now. There's a special forces group coming to Midland on the tenth. They are here to take the Cube and anything else they can get their hands on."

Vahan swore eloquently in Armenian. "Are these the same guys who tore up our lab at the Octagon? The guys who took your scientists" – he kicked himself for calling them Berglin's – "were driving a black sedan and were wearing suits."

It was my turn to curse. "My guess is yes. According to my source they are part of the national security apparatus. And they aren't fucking around."

Vahan thought for a moment. "The enemy of my enemy is my friend," he suggested.

"I'll think about it. Put them on."

Park and Rosen appeared, looking disheveled and weary. Austin looked sullen and Rosen antagonistic. "We didn't bargain for this, Dr. Berglin," Park said.

"Chin up Dr. Park!" I replied. "The situation has escalated beyond us both."

"I'm going back to Korea," Park said. "I —"

"That's enough," Vahan interrupted. He turned toward the screen. "OK, I've got your scientists. How do you want to play this?"

I pondered for several moments. "We're in the dark, Vahan. I'm going to protect my new assembly line with my security force, you protect our two scientists. Understand that your two prisoners are the most important asset we both have. Do you need help? I can reinforce your force with some of my men."

"No, that won't work. The families will supply men and weapons, and we can get more from outside the city if necessary. The families will not want foreigners in their midst."

Despite my dislike of the man, I saw Vahan's determination. Katelian was obviously a good man in a fight, having rescued my two scientists. I softened somewhat. "Well then Vahan, prepare for war. If at all possible I will try to defuse this situation without fighting. But if it comes to that, good luck. We have to cooperate now even though we don't like each other."

The next morning was the 6th of April. Over coffee, I read the headline in the *Midland Courier:* "Local Business Hires Foreign Mercenaries." The story was by Tina Brooks again. She said that Berglin Enterprises had hired foreign troops to prevent a lawful seizure of dangerous, untested high-tech devices. I could hardly believe my eyes. I called the paper and explained the situation, but Barnsley wasn't buying it. "Our sources tell us that some of your men are mercenaries. Do you deny it?"

I couldn't. When I tried to explain that a military unit was coming to Midland to take the Cube and the Pulsar, Barnsley cut me off. "My source tells me it's a national security matter and you are in violation of a Patent Secrecy Order. If I were you, Berglin, I'd stop whatever you're doing and obey the law." Barnsley hung up before I could ask him who his "source" was.

Later, I called a meeting of UPower to plan strategy. We met in the basement of the Berglin Enterprises building. The Board was also there. Al Jordan had one of the Cubes now. He had converted Mika and Barbara in favor of UPower, at least until the six-month deadline was up. Monster and the two foremen were also present. Goro looked after the Centurion Building and Matsui supervised the warehouse contingent. Monster was in charge of the entire detail. Surprisingly, Kenji Hiroto had also showed up a couple of hours before.

"What are you doing here Hiroto-san?" I asked.

"Hatsumi-sama has asked me to discipline his bodyguards, who have failed in their duties. We are both very sorry, Berglin-san. This is the third time we have failed you. We have both realized there is a big difference between fighting and guard duty. My men, and Hatsumi-sama's men, are fierce fighters in combat. But normally Hiroto Security provides protection in military settings. I will have to diversify my training for purely civilian operations."

I waved my hand in the air dismissively. "What's done is done. You might as well sit in on our strategy meeting."

We agreed that protecting the people at the warehouse making the Cubes was the highest priority, and then the equipment to make the Cubes and the Pulsar. Kenji said he was going to pull most of his men from Berglin over to UPower.

"That is the threat now, Berglin-san. I'll keep a skeleton crew at the Centurion Building though." Kenji left with a scowl on his face to see to his men and their deployment.

I thought of something, brought about by a remark Julian Green had made at Necker Island. Although Byrnes and Green were enemies there was a "hot line" where each could communicate with the other, as during the Cold War between the United States and the Soviet Union. "Al, call Danielle right now and have her put together a packet of everything we know about the Cube. I'm going to call Green and have him contact Byrnes. We'll tell him that if they attack us, we will release everything we know in one burst all over the net to every newspaper and blog we can think of. Maybe we can avoid a confrontation."

"Good idea Max," Jordan said. He left the room talking into his mobile.

An hour later I heard back from Dr. Green. "Byrnes is all worked up about this thing. He says to go ahead and release your information, and I'm afraid he's right. The Cube uses heretofore unknown and unproven technology. You'll look just like your two scientists in their debate with Dr. Hartwig."

"Then it's going to come down to a confrontation."

"Almost certainly. I don't know how to advise you, other than to have a well understood plan in place."

I rang off. After several minutes of thought I concluded that we were screwed.

The next morning, April 7th, I wondered what the *Courier* was going to publish.

In the online edition Tina Brooks – who knew absolutely nothing about physics or our operation – said that we were building an untested, experimental device that could be dangerous to the city:

US to Send Security Detachment to Midland

Local Business Violates Patent Law

by Tina Brooks

The Berglin Enterprises group, according to *Courier* sources, is building two experimental devices utilizing unknown technology that could adversely affect public safety.

The Cube and the Pulsar, as they are known to Berglin Enterprises employees, both utilize an untested, potentially dangerous new technology. The Director of National Intelligence, supported by the Department of Defense, is sending in a detachment to ensure the safety not only of the citizenry, but also company employees.

Duchesne Comstock, Assistant Director of National Intelligence in Washington DC, said that "the new inventions are untested and potentially hazardous. They are being developed by unsupervised amateurs who have no idea what they are doing. It is necessary for public safety as well as national security to sequester these devices," Comstock said.

"We're being framed," I told Slava when he came into the kitchen to clear away the breakfast dishes. "Byrnes is going full throttle." There was just enough truth in the article to be believable.

That evening one of Hiroto's men walked in with Park and Rosen. Austin spoke sardonically. "Vahan told me to tell you that he couldn't stand us anymore and you were to take us back."

John Rosen grinned. "I'm having the time of my life boss. What's next?"

Austin looked like a washrag that had been scrubbed too much, but John Rosen was ready to go. "Welcome back gentlemen. I want you over at the new building as usual, some questions have come up. Proceed as if everything is normal." Monster personally escorted the two scientists, Park protesting that he wanted nothing more to do with Berglin Enterprises or UPower.

Monster put two hands on Austin's chest. "Stop your whining. The safest place for you is with us. You're a marked man, do you understand?" Park nodded glumly and the three left.

In three days, if Green's intelligence was correct, the special forces unit would arrive. I wondered how far Byrnes would go if it came to fighting.

That night Zach called Danielle after work.

"How are you doing?"

"I'm great Zach. This work is exciting, isn't it?"

"It certainly is. I'm so juiced I can't wait for the detachment to come."

"You know how serious the situation is, don't you?"

"Yeah, and I wouldn't miss it for anything."

The two former lovers talked for several minutes until the conversation halted awkwardly. Zach was encouraged because he felt Danielle's tension. If she didn't care about him, he reasoned, he would just be a casual acquaintance she could blow off without feeling anything. He was starting to think more and more like Mike Parsons now when it came to people and relationships. "I've been thinking about you."

There was a pause at the other end. "Have you really Zach?"

"Yes. I realize that what you said last year was right. I wasn't ready for a long term relationship. I am now."

Danielle gazed at Zach through the mobile. He did look more decisive, but maybe he was still just a happy-go-lucky boy.

Zach picked up on that right away. "That's OK Danielle. I just wanted to let you know I'm still interested."

Danielle's breathing became more rapid. "OK Zach. Do you realize that Max Berglin is also interested? He hasn't been pushy or anything, but he's made his feelings plain."

Zach felt like saying, "He's just an old man!" Something stopped him. "I get it Danielle." He looked her in the eyes like he used to do, sending as much affection as he could over his crummy mobile device.

Danielle felt it. "Oh Zach. It's almost..."

"Yeah. Like old times."

Danielle nodded.

"I won't push you Danielle. I just wanted to make sure you hadn't written me off."

"I haven't done that Zach."

Zach was satisfied. "Ok then, do you have any idea what this security detachment is going to do?"

"No Zach. Max is in the dark too. He's pulling most of Hiroto's men over to UPower, but no one knows what to expect."

Zach didn't like her referring Berglin as "Max" but he let it go. "I've got two more Cubes to deliver and set up tomorrow. I hope I don't get captured like Park and John Rosen." Zach was making a playful bid for sympathy.

Danielle laughed. "Take care of yourself Zach."

"Don't worry. I have two bodyguards with me whenever I do deliveries." Zach wanted to ask her out but decided not to. "Maybe I'll call you again," he suggested.

"I'd like that."

Ralph Zimring arrived in Midland at dawn on a cold April 8th, snooping around. The unit was to gather, in civilian clothes, on April 9th. He had already been briefed at Fort McCoy about his duties, but he was free until 0600 tomorrow. Several men from the detachment had been sent in to scout the territory and apprise Major Bates, the team leader, of the situation. There were 24 men in total, six of whom were, like him, mercenaries. He had met four of the mercenaries; standard issue guys. Another was to join them in Midland. The other men were from a special forces detachment stationed at Fort McCoy on temporary assignment to Major Bates, who conducted their mission brief.

Despite his great height he attracted little attention dressed in his Berglin Enterprises uniform. Ralph knew how to blend into the background, walking slightly hunched over and keeping his eyes lowered. He affected the apologetic mannerisms of a nerdy employee who was embarrassed that he had grown so tall.

The mission objective of Bates was the new building by the river, where the two scientists and the devices were, and secondarily the Berglin Enterprises building downtown. The goal was to sequester the devices and all of the documentation and computer paraphernalia. The unit was to use force if necessary to get Max Berglin and the two scientists to cease and desist. Failing that, to detain the three men and take them back to Lieutenant Spieth at a classified facility in Chicago.

Ralph Zimring didn't give a shit about their mission, or Bates. He was looking mainly for a private army Berglin was supposed to have, and whether they were a danger to the security of the City of Midland.

At 9 a.m. Ralph went to the Centurion Building downtown. He saw two Oriental men walking the perimeter and wondered how many men were inside. After walking through the lobby he presented himself to a good-looking woman at the reception desk. He told her he was one of the Berglin security detail making a routine check.

"I've never seen you before," Tara Bolshoi said. "I manage the detail and you're not on my list." She pressed her red button underneath the desk.

Ralph smiled easily, seeing the movement and knowing what was coming. "I'm known to Max Berglin."

"Oh you are, are you?" Tara was pretty sure that the giant had no harmful intent. "You wouldn't be from the security detachment that's being sent here?"

Ralph grinned. "And what if I am?" He noticed that two men had quietly entered the lobby.

"If you know Max you could tell me how many men are coming and what they are going to do."

Ralph was perfectly amiable. "First tell me how many foreign military men you have in Midland. I'm told Berglin has hired a private army."

Tara laughed. "A private army? You're joking, Mr...."

"Zimring, Tara. Ralph Zimring. And I'm not joking. Major Bates thinks so, and that's part of the problem."

Tara decided to be completely open and honest. That was Max Berglin's way. "The total number of men here is thirty. There are six men from the Nijinkan, personal bodyguards for Max Berglin, Austin Park, and John Rosen. There are an additional twenty-four men, all of whom guard the property and the other employees."

Thirty men. Not exactly an army, but a strong enough force. Ralph didn't like it. "Thank you Tara. The detachment being sent to Midland consists of twenty-four men, of whom six are mercenaries like me."

Tara's eyes widened. "You're a mercenary? You mean, you kill people for a living?"

Ralph's eyes brimmed with amusement. "Oh, not every day. I like to relax on weekends."

"Your weekdays must be busy then." Tara saw the giant's responsive grin. She looked over to the two security guards and nodded her head. The men left. "When is the detachment to arrive?"

"Early in the morning on the tenth. Do you mind if I walk around the building?"

Tara got the distinct impression that if he wanted to, Mr. Ralph Zimring would go wherever he wanted, guards or no. She sighed and turned her chair to the console. Tara called the duty foreman, who understood some English. "Goro. A *kyojin* about seven feet tall will be walking around the building for a little while. He's wearing a Berglin Enterprises uniform that's a little too small." Tara giggled. Ralph's pants were three inches too short. "Don't disturb him but monitor his movements. *Misumasu.*"

"Hai." Tara turned her chair to face him. "Well, there you are. Take a tour but don't be overlong."

Ralph bowed as stately as could a man almost seven feet tall wearing a uni that was a little too tight. He would have a word with Sergeant Tracy, his tailor, when he returned to Northport. "Thank you Tara," he said, his eyes twinkling.

Tara waved him away, liking the man's swarthy good looks and his demeanor. But he was too tall, much too tall, for her taste.

Ralph made a quick tour of the building and counted only the two men he'd seen in the lobby. Counting the two outside, there were four here at the Centurion. The bulk of Berglin's forces must be at the other building.

Ralph took a bus to Berglin's other building, gauging the reaction of the passengers to his Berglin Enterprises uni. He received a number of disgusted glances but nothing overtly hostile. Ralph walked casually into the parking lot of the building from the narrow two-lane road off River Drive. The first person he saw was a petite woman leading a patrol around the building. There were six men total on the perimeter. The woman spotted him immediately. Their eyes met and Ralph knew that she was very observant and would not let him pass. She barked something in Japanese and her five men formed a semi-circle about ten feet away from him. Ralph quickly glanced at all of them and smiled. The men moved with an easy grace, and had the look of fighters who had seen some action. Monster's eyes widened almost imperceptibly when she saw his height. Other than that she returned his smile coolly. Ralph silently approved her unflustered reaction to him.

"What is your business here?" she asked in perfectly accented English.

Ralph answered in tones of someone who has probably been discovered but who still has hope. "New employee reporting for duty ma'am."

Monster smiled a smile that said, 'the bigger they are the harder they fall.' "I think not, *kyojin*. You will come with me please."

Ralph Zimring laughed out loud. He liked this woman's attitude. Her men were in a defensive posture. There was no hostility; these men were clearly on guard duty. He shrugged. He was a day early and under strict orders not to create trouble, although he was bored and itching for a fight. "All right then, cutie pie," Ralph said. "Take me to your leader."

Monster walked him toward the back entrance, the other five men trailing him. They went into a small office along a narrow corridor, but not before Ralph got a glimpse of the production area. Clearly these guys were intending to manufacture Cubes but weren't ready yet. The place had the look of having already been set up and torn down. Ralph remained standing, and so did the other men. Monster sat down and placed a call to Max Berglin. "It's begun," she said. "Do want to talk to this man? He's seven feet tall!"

"You will wait here," Monster said, rising. "The boss will be here shortly." She left.

Ralph leaned against the back wall and watched the five men who circled him within the small room. They stood at ease without fidgeting or displaying nervousness or awkwardness. He wanted to pit his skills against theirs and almost took a step forward. Immediately his guards moved very slightly and came more alert. Just then Monster reentered the room with a muscular man Ralph recognized as Max Berglin, who turned to face him.

"Just what are you people up to?"

Ralph answered with the bullshit Major Bates had told everyone to say. "We're here to ensure public safety."

Berglin said nothing. Ralph grinned. "Not buying that, are you?"

"I thought we had an understanding."

"We did, until you brought a private army into Midland. A foreign army." Ralph was genuinely angry now. "What do you think you're doing Berglin? Trying to start a war?" He indicated the men surrounding him.

"I'm protecting my investment from people who want to steal it."

"You didn't answer my question. You could and should have used Americans for the job."

"What difference does it make? Kenji Hiroto and Roka Hatsumi are personal friends of mine."

At Hatsumi's name Ralph gave a start. "You know *Hatsumi?*"

"We had dinner together. He's helping me to build Cubes and advising me not to fight. Fat lot of good that's doing."

Ralph pondered for a moment. After his stint with the Rangers and to hone his skills for mercenary work, he had trained ninja-style in one of Hatsumi's Nijinkan academies in New York.

"There are two dozen men in total from Hiroto Security, plus six bodyguards sent to me by Roka Hatsumi. If you want to call that a private army, go ahead."

Ralph nodded. Berglin had confirmed Tara Bolshoi's figures. He had never heard of Hiroto Security but these thirty men wouldn't stand up to the detachment if it came to a fight. He relaxed a little.

"My men are wearing Berglin Enterprises uniforms. We have not caused any trouble in town." Berglin spoke bitterly. "The local newspaper is doing a good job of stirring up emotions against us."

Ralph remembered the looks he had gotten on the bus. "Yeah, they do that. Create opposition."

"Who's they?"

"Fuck if I know. I'm just a foot soldier. It's stiffening the backs of the locals against the bad guys. You know, win the hearts and minds of the population and get them on your side. Win the game before you even fight the battle."

"Yes, but who's doing it? Somebody took a shot at me. The two scientists who developed the Cube were abducted. I had to resort to defending myself. Your appearance here again is proof that I'm not paranoid."

"You're lying to me Berglin." Ralph spoke ominously. "There's something else that has military application. It's supposed to be very dangerous."

Ralph saw Berglin think for a moment. "Oh that. The Pulsar. It's not a weapon, it's a means of transmitting power without wires."

"That's bullshit Berglin. I'm told it's a weapon."

"You were told wrong. It *could* be weaponized, but only if you were a psychopath."

Ralph still didn't like it. Either Berglin was lying or Bates was. He studied Max Berglin carefully. What he saw was an ambitious man who wanted to make money, but one with no hostile intent. Unlike Duchene Comstock, who had apparently ordered the detachment to Midland. The men he had observed were defensive, not offensive, unlike the detachment. Ralph decided that Berglin was straight and that Duggan and Bates were either lying or were dupes of Comstock.

"All right, I'm out. But watch your step Berglin. There are 23 other guys coming here in less than two days. Some of them enjoy killing."

"Hatsumi mentioned you when we talked one day. He said you trained at the Nijinkan. My men have as well. There aren't any sociopaths here, Zimring. What do you say?"

Ralph understood the implied attempt to recruit him. Oh hell, I want some action and why not be on the side of improving the lives of the ordinary guy? "On one condition."

"What is it?"

"I want one of those Cubes. It's cold in northern Michigan."

"If we get out of this I'll have one made for you."

"OK, you got me. Now tell me what I'm supposed to do." It was typical of Ralph Zimring that he assessed situations quickly and made up his mind just as quickly. It was a requirement for field work or you got dead fast.

Ralph saw Berglin make a call. "I'm sending Ralph Zimring to see you." He told Ralph, "Report to the woman they call Monster."

"She's the leader of all these men?"

Berglin nodded, and Ralph laughed. He was going to enjoy this gig a lot more than the other one.

Ralph went to a hotel room downtown. He had chosen a suite on the top floor of the Sheraton because he liked being able to see out a long way. The shower heads at the Sheraton were almost tall enough for him.

Just before he got into the shower he called Lieutenant Colin McEachern, Major Bates' liaison at Fort McCoy. "I just met Max Berglin, this guy who is supposed to be a terrorist. All he has is a self-powering box and about thirty guards."

"It's not your fuckin' job to worry about what he's got and what he doesn't. As long as you are part of this team you'll obey orders. Stay the hell away from Berglin until the group forms tomorrow morning. You'll get your orders then."

"That's just it, lieutenant. I'm out. I just called to let you know."

"Goddamit Zimring! I recommended you to Major Bates on the insistence of Duchene Comstock, the assistant DNI."

"Comstock recommended *me*?"

"He did. I'm going to catch hell from Commander Duggan and Major Bates if you don't show up."

"Sorry about that lieutenant, but Comstock and I have a history." Ralph hung up.

So Comstock recommended him to Duggan, did he? That POG probably wanted the other mercenaries to put a bullet in his back during the fighting. It would be a convenient way for Comstock to dispose of an irritant. To Ralph his recruitment was more evidence of Comstock's involvement with Julia. He began to get excited. If one of the other mercenaries was Harriman Drake, that would be the final proof. Drake's way of snapping the neck was his signature, and he had seen proof on Julia's body. He would eliminate two scumbags at the same time.

Ralph looked forward to the fighting like a little boy does to Christmas day.

After Zimring hung up Lieutenant McEachern swore. Goddam mercenaries! The plan was to let them do the wet work if it came to that. If any civilians were killed, the major could say that the deaths were due to a rogue element unassociated with the government.

The headline in the *Midland Courier* for the April 9th early edition read, "Rescue Force to Face Local Group." The subhead read, "Citizen Advisory." I was beyond being surprised now. The story was the lead, above the fold and center of the page. Written by Clive Barnsley, it read:

Rescue Force to Face Local Group

Citizen Advisory

by Clive Barnsley

The rescue force, sent by the Director of National Intelligence liaising with the Department of Defense, will arrive in Midland sometime today.

The team, according to Lieutenant Colin McEachern at Fort McCoy in Wisconsin, will be collecting an experimental device that the DNI has declared "a danger to national security and the public health," and will not use force unless threatened.

Citizens are advised to stay away from the Berglin Enterprises building on Main, the old Van Allen furniture warehouse by the river, and the residence of Max Berglin in Palmer Park.

The article reminded me of my two scientists, who were again holed up in the back of the new building. On the evening of April 5th Vahan had given Austin and John back to me. I could see that Austin Park had completely checked out. When Monster escorted the two scientists to the lab I accompanied them. John Rosen put his hands on Austin's shoulders and shook him. "Wake up boss. Stop your moping and let's get to work."

John let the older man complain for a few minutes, and then stopped him. "Are you really lonely for Korea and your family? You haven't been back there for years." He tried to add some levity. "The only thing you know how to do is lab work!"

Despite himself Austin grinned. "I suppose you're right."

"Think of the Pulsar and the breakthrough we could make Austin. Both of us will get Nobels. We continue in the great tradition of Nikola Tesla, a man whose frontier physics was ignored throughout his life." John was passionate now, and some of it rubbed off on the older man.

"If we live that long."

"You're supposed to be the wise Asian fatalist who cares nothing for death."

Austin thought of Bruce Lee. The contrast between him and that gentleman was so stark he laughed out loud.

John saw his boss perk up. "I've just had an idea," Austin said, becoming more animated. "Bring the Pulsar over here..."

I was satisfied. Austin had returned to the project, at least for now. John Rosen was a keeper.

During the past several months the two scientists – inspired by Tesla's notebook – had continued to investigate the phenomenon behind the Cube and the Pulsar.

It became obvious that both devices were a subset of a much greater phenomenon. Their experiments showed that, amazingly, every point in space was intelligent. Space itself could be programmed. They had already discovered an invisible substrate that was perfectly balanced at each point in space. This substrate contained a tremendous amount of energy. They had tapped into that with the Cube, somewhat like a boy collecting the misty spray coming off a huge waterfall. But the Pulsar was able to do much more. Austin estimated that the amount of energy in every cubic centimeter of space would yield values in the yotta eV range. Which did indeed make the Pulsar a potentially dangerous weapon.

John didn't care about that. He was too excited about where the science would take them. "We both understand the potential of this discovery Austin. Instantaneous communication to any point in the universe, and maybe even space travel!"

Both men read the *Courier* and knew that a military force was being sent to sequester their invention, but who was sending it? They had argued about it ad nauseum. "The only way to kill this thing is by killing us," Austin said.

"Nobody's going to get killed," John said.

"Just like the boss, right?"

John had no answer for that, but he had an idea. When he told Austin the older man's face lit up. "I can't believe we haven't thought of that before." Both men grinned.

It was April 10th. Myself, Austin Park, and John Rosen were in the warehouse before dawn, along with all of Kenji's and Hatsumi's men. Zimring had disappeared, but told me he was waiting eagerly for the fight and would appear when he was needed.

We had gathered in the lab on the fourth floor, hoping to protect the experiments and the half-finished assembly line. There were no men outside; I wanted to maintain an entirely defensive posture. I had given all of my employees the day off. The Centurion Building downtown was empty. The night before I told my house staff to stay home and told Slava to get a hotel room at my expense. He refused. Slava insisted on staying in the house and brought out his pistol. "I'll know what to do when those guys show up," he said. I told him he could do nothing. I was worried about the old guy; I had grown to like and depend on him.

Somebody plunked down a hardcopy edition of the *Midland Courier*, interrupting my reverie. I was sick of the paper but couldn't help glancing at the headline.

Rescue Force to Safely Sequester Dangerous Weapons

Confrontation?

By Clive Barnsley

What will it be, Max Berglin? Will you and your men obey the law, or confront the law?

The rescue force, under the auspices of the Department of Defense, is here to sequester potentially dangerous new weapons developed by the two infamous scientists, Austin Park and John Rosen. Our sources tell us that the two scientists have developed potentially dangerous new technology that could be a threat to public safety. Are these two mavericks competent to develop exotic new technology that should be safely in the hands of competent scientists?

The goal of the detachment is to peacefully secure the illegal and unsafe new weapons without conflict. If violence occurs it will be on the head of Max Berglin.

These stories were preposterous, I thought. First the *Courier* told us that Park and Rosen had been discredited and debunked, and portrayed them as incompetents. Then they say they've developed exotic new technology. Despite Julian Green's and Zimring's intelligence I couldn't believe that an armed force was coming to my building. That stuff happened in other countries, not the United States. We drank instant coffee and waited. By eight o'clock nothing had happened. I was ready to tell everyone to go home.

"Military vehicles approaching." That was Hideki, one of my bodyguards. Several of the men had placed themselves as lookouts at the windows. "They're entering the parking lot."

The warehouse was surrounded by hills on three sides, fronting a line of trees and brush that led down to the river. The tops of the hills were flat and covered with grass. The entrance was a narrow two-lane road a quarter mile from River Drive. The guard gate was unoccupied because I didn't want to present a confrontational appearance.

Twenty-three men, including five mercenaries, quietly walked to the front door.

Major Bates and his aide, Lieutenant McEachern, were in front. All that could be heard were faint footsteps on the cold pavement, and the occasional rattle of metal. Bates noticed that several members of the public had gathered on the grassy, low hills that overlooked the parking lot. He pointed with his thumb and hissed. "Lieutenant McEachern, what are those citizens doing up there?"

"I don't know sir. Barnsley and I told everyone to stay away."

Bates stopped walking and everyone silently pulled up. "You fool. Telling everyone to stay away was an invitation to have a party!"

Colin McEachern gloomily surveyed the public gathering on the rise. More people were arriving. "I'm sorry sir. I thought that if we presented the possibility of violence it would scare everyone off."

Bates scowled and muttered something about idiots just out of West Point. He ordered four men to cover the building exits and walked toward the door. "I thought you said that this place was heavily guarded?"

"It was, sir, as of yesterday evening."

Bates stopped ten feet from the entrance and gestured to the five mercenaries. "You know what you have to do!" He stepped back to see what these morons were going to do, envisioning the barbarians at the gates of Rome. Mutumbe, Carlucchi, and Donovan were known to him. Mutumbe was tall and gangling with an old-fashioned Afro, and excelled in hand-to-hand combat. Carlucchi was dark Italian, a moody and morose fighter, but disciplined. Donovan was expatriate Irish, from a family that had been sending its men to wars all over the globe for 300 years. The other two joined the unit at the insistence of DNI Putnam himself. Drake and Bayless were unknown to him.

The five mercenaries were ready. This was the kind of good old-fashioned action they liked, and it was all under the auspices of the gummint! Drake and Bayless glanced quickly at each other. Drake, a beefy man with a barrel chest and a face like a Neanderthal, put his gloved fist through the window. Glass smashed over the tiled hallway. Bayless, a swarthy man with a black stubble of beard, turned the knob and the door opened. He grinned at Drake. "The door was unlocked!" The two men both guffawed and rushed in, followed by their three companions. Bates held up his hand, not allowing his men to enter. "Let those whores tell us what we have to face."

Drake and Bayless ran down the empty hallway and into a very large, open room filled with new desks and computer workstations. The room, which looked like an office under construction, was empty. "What the fuck?" Drake said. He turned to Mutumbe. "There's nobody here!"

Bayless was confused. "Somebody go tell that fuckin' idiot major that the place is deserted."

At that moment Major Bates walked into the room with his men. Outside, some of the more curious people on the hill had filtered down onto the parking lot with their mobile phones.

"They're upstairs you morons. We'll cover the stairs and all the exits. You guys get your asses up there."

That was fine with Drake and Bayless. The two mercenaries ran up the first flight of stairs to the second floor, which contained administrative offices. Mutumbe, Carlucchi, and Donovan followed more cautiously. Everything was dark. "We aint never going to see no action," Bayless grumbled.

"Fuck this," Drake said. He grabbed a Makharov PB-71 pistol from beneath his belt in a beefy right hand and ran through the exit to the stairs. "I want to smell some blood."

Bayless was behind Drake as they climbed the stairs."Christ, where did you get that?" Bayless said. The Makharov held a clip of twenty murderous .35 caliber bullets. He saw that Bates' men were already in position on the stairs.

"Took it off a dead Chechen back in '15 in Ekazhevo, Ingushetia," Drake replied. "A sweet shooter but you gotta have a strong wrist."

Drake and Bayless burst through the door to the third floor, followed by the other three mercenaries. It too was dark and empty. "Goddammit!" Drake shouted. He brandished his weapon. "Cowards, show yourselves!"

Bayless laughed. "We only got one more floor to go. Get ready."

Drake felt his blood boiling and he had a hard-on. Drake and Bayless ran up the stairs and crashed through the door into a huge laboratory. Austin Park and John Rosen stood inside a small room at the back behind a large plate glass window, in plain sight. Bayless saw men up against the walls and looked for Max Berglin. Drake, without thinking, raised his gun and fired at a tall, nerdy looking asshole with curly hair. Glass crashed as the two faces disappeared just before his shot went off. At that moment Bayless saw Max Berglin standing at one of the lab tables, surrounded by two bodyguards, but he couldn't get a good shot. The bodyguards didn't interest him. His orders were to get Berglin, preferably alive.

Donovan, Mutumbe, and Carlucchi saw Berglin's security force and fanned out to meet them. "Get your fuckin' asses in here!" Donovan shouted to Bates' men on the stairs. "There's a couple dozen of these fucknuggets!"

Bates' men rushed into the room just as the mercenaries charged into Hiroto's men, screaming battle cries. Suddenly a huge man appeared from out of the drop ceiling above and landed on top of Drake, knocking him to the floor. Ralph saw Bayless aiming his weapon at Berglin. With a huge hand he lunged and grabbed hold of the mercenary, executing a chop to the temple, knocking the man out. Drake, sputtering, got up and quickly drew his Makharov, but the giant was expecting this. The pistol was knocked from his hand and he stood, facing Zimring. Hand-to-hand combat was going on all around them. Drake grinned. "C'mon you big asshole, lemme see what you got."

Ralph was happy. Ralph saw the killing hatred in Drake's eyes and the blood lust. "Julia Pence," he said just loudly enough for Drake to hear. The man's eyes narrowed in fear and hatred and then he exploded into action. Drake came at him with a hard kick to the groin with his left leg but Ralph dodged it smoothly, snapping his stiffened left hand hard against the right side of Drake's neck. He felt something crack as Drake fell, unconscious, to the floor. Bates' men, weapons out, began marching toward the two scientists at the back of the lab.

Then something happened that Ralph would never forget as long as he lived. An orange ball of light about four feet in diameter suddenly exploded above the heads of the fighting men. The hostilities in the room abruptly ceased. The men suddenly stopped what they were doing in the middle of a blow, stunned. Many of the fighters fell to the floor. Everyone looked upward toward the twelve-foot ceiling at the orange ball, which was slowly dissolving. A glowing mist spread slowly across the room, engulfing everyone. Gradually, the light faded. Hiroto's men, Bates' men, and the three mercenaries who were still conscious looked around in confusion. All of the fighters had forgotten their purpose for being there.

Donovan was the first to speak. "Aren't we supposed to be doing something?" He spoke like a man with a very important errand who has suffered temporary amnesia. Hiroto's men were babbling in Japanese to each other, equally at a loss.

Ralph Zimring gradually got himself together. He saw John Rosen and Austin Park standing at the entrance to a little glassed-in room at the back, amidst shattered glass. Ralph walked toward the two men on legs that were a little shaky.

John and Austin looked around at the ruins of expensive lab equipment, and several valuable experiments. Ralph felt like laughing, and he did. These two nerds were responsible for stopping a roomful of fighters!

"What did you two guys just do? I feel like I just a got a psychic cleanse."

The two scientists looked up at the giant in awe. "I'm not really sure," John said, recovering first. "We used the Pulsar on a very low energy setting, hoping to knock everyone out." He raised his arm and indicated Bates' men, who had dropped their weapons and were standing around without purpose.

Major Bates wanted to raise his hand and bark out orders to these drooling idiots, but he just didn't feel like it. A pleasant lethargy was overtaking him, as if he had just finished a grueling workout and was now in need of rest. He found a place on the floor, curled up, and went to sleep.

"Wait a minute," Ralph said. "You mean that the weapon you used was the Pulsar? I thought that thing was dangerous."

"It could be *made* dangerous," Austin replied. "What you saw here was radiant energy from what Tesla called the luminiferous ether."

Suddenly Ralph understood. It was like nuclear energy: you could use it to power electric generators or you could use it in bombs to kill people. "Well for fuck's sake. That ball of light seems to have defused the conflict. How did it do that?"

Rosen and Park looked at each other. "We don't know," Park said. "We generated energy that Tesla called radiant energy. It is supposed to have healing properties.[12] We tested it out last night and were hoping it would work here."

"We need to do more research on that," John added.

Ralph was able to think straight again. He saw the petite little woman Berglin called Monster leaning against the wall and he walked over to her. Donovan, Mutumbe, and Carlucchi were still standing with jaws dropped, unable to understand what had happened to them. For now they were harmless until this potion, or whatever it was, wore off. Bayless was down and bleeding out. Ralph knew he had killed Drake and for some reason felt sorrow.

Lieutenant McEachern, who had fallen to the floor unconscious after the burst of energy, woke up and got to his feet. He rushed over to his commander. Bates was breathing evenly and looked like a man having a good rest. McEachern assumed command. He knew that his orders were to capture Berglin, the two scientists, and take everything out of the lab into the vehicles. But Berglin clearly had developed an unknown and very dangerous new weapon that his detachment was powerless against. His mission had failed. In the back of his mind he wondered why his brief had been so sketchy. Had Major Bates had been lied to? Was the detachment expendable? Maybe Commander Duggan already knew about the new weapon! The lieutenant fought his weakness and got Bates on an improvised stretcher made of lab coats tied between two metal poles. He got his men to help the wounded or incapacitated men and got them ready to leave. As far as he could tell there were no fatalities except for two of the mercenaries. As he turned to march them out he saw several people standing at the door, holding up their mobiles and chattering excitedly. He knew he should order the civilians out of the area but the pleasant lethargy had settled into every cell of his body, as after a long hot bath.

"What just happened?" Donovan asked Mutumbe and Carlucchi as the last of the detachment departed.

"Fuck if I know," Carlucchi replied.

"Let's get out of here," Mutumbe suggested. "There's something wrong about this place. It feels like a church instead of a battle zone. It's not right."

Carlucchi pointed to the bodies of Drake and Bayless. "What do we do with those two?"

"Leave them," Mutumbe said. "If anybody asks we'll blame it on them."

Donovan spat. "Good idea. Never liked 'em anyway."

The three mercenaries slowly left the room. The onlookers, seeing that everything was safe, burst in.

Ralph observed that Monster and Berglin were unhurt and no one was in charge. He began to herd the public out of the lab. "Who are you?" a voice asked. "What happened here?" People were firing questions at him as if he was the President.

Ralph had no patience for publicity seekers and the vulgarly curious. He rose to his full height. "This building is under military quarantine. All citizens are to leave immediately!" The crowd was completely intimidated by the angry giant. They went silent and began to run, frightened, from the room. This reminded Ralph of a scene from an old Japanese monster movie with himself as Rhodan destroying Tokyo and he laughed. He gestured toward two of Monster's men, who seemed to be aware and in good shape. "See that these people leave the building and lock the doors. Post guards at the exits and don't let anyone in here."

Ren and Hideki had never seen a human being as large as Ralph Zimring, and were awed and amused. "Yes sir!" Ren said, pretending to be frightened. He executed an exaggerated bow. Ralph laughed; the two men smiled.

Ralph asked Monster if she was all right. She looked woozy, had a cut on her forehead, and her shoulder was bleeding. Several of her men lay unconscious on the floor. At the sight of him she seemed to return to her senses, barking out orders in Japanese. Eventually Monster got her men together, examining the wounded, and called the hospital. The two nerdy scientists came out of their little bunker, inspecting the lab and taking inventory of the damage with Berglin. Once Ralph saw that Monster was all right he walked back with her to the small office where the two scientists had sprung their surprise. To his amazement, he still felt a sense of well-being. He searched inside himself for the seed of darkness but it wasn't there. He felt like a man possessed by demons who had just been exorcised. It must have been that orange light.

Intensely curious, Ralph walked to the back room. He saw an open black box with components surrounded by a circular array of magnets, and a laptop. Someone had written "Pulsar" in red magic marker on the side of the box. "This is it?" he said, incredulous. "This piece of shit is the dangerous new technology?" He took out his phone and snapped a pic.

Monster smiled. She was amazed by this giant who moved so gracefully. The top of her head didn't even reach the button on his shirt pocket. "It's not what's on the outside, but what's on the inside," she said.

Ralph understood her immediately and laughed. He had never in his life laughed as many times as he had today. "Do you want to go out for some coffee?"

Monster gave the big man a considering look. She waited, drawing out the moment, and then smiled. "Sure, but later. I have to finish up here and talk to Max Berglin first."

"Call me?" He felt like a pimply nerd asking the prom queen out for a date.

"As soon as I have completed my duties."

Ralph saluted. "Yes ma'am," he said, and walked out of the room. Daiko, a fighter she had trained with in Japan, grinned at her. Monster blushed. "Back to work!" she commanded. All the men smiled mischievously.

Half of the city, it seemed to Tina Brooks, was converging on the Berglin warehouse. She and her cameraman fought the traffic and finally got to the parking lot in the Channel 5 van. Police were already present, refusing entrance to the public and trying to keep the entrance road clear. She saw people arriving on foot from the woods by the river and hiking up to the little hills above the parking lot. Cars were parked along the entrance road on the grass; people on foot were getting out and walking. A police barricade was being formed to stop the inflow from reaching the building. Tina could see that several people had already made it inside. The officer at the gate accepted her press credentials and let them in. She found a place to park the van close to the entrance, on the grass. Just as she got out she recognized Zach Ferrell's beat-up Mazda drive up to the gate. The officer accepted his employee ID and she followed with her cameraman shooting the scene. Tina knew all about the operation. She and Barnsley had been briefed by one of Major Bates' men as part of the paper's cooperative effort to ensure public safety.

Tina ran up to Zach, followed by her cameraman. "Zach Ferrell! What's happening here?"

Zach recognized the reporter at once and began to walk faster. Why didn't she just observe and report like she was supposed to? He had heard all about the fink from Danielle, who said that she was an irritating bitch and not to be trusted. Just then the front door to the building slammed open. Military personnel began exiting the building.

The rescue force! Tina thought excitedly. She walked up to a man she recognized as Lieutenant McEachern. She and Barnsley had been briefed by one of Major Bates' men as part of the paper's cooperative effort to ensure public safety. She saw that Bates was lying on a stretcher. "Lieutenant! What happened in there? Have you confiscated the device? What happened to Major Bates?"

The lieutenant ignored her, as did his men. McEachern's mind was still fuzzy. His pleasant feeling of lethargy was, if anything, even stronger. Tina saw the detachment stumbling silently toward their vehicles like a bunch of confused zombies. By this time the police had shown up in force, but none of Midland's finest knew anything about the confrontation. What a letdown! Instead of trained fighters who had successfully completed their mission, they looked like a bunch of tired high school football players leaving the practice field. She walked over to McEachern and put her mike in his face. "What happened here?" The lieutenant suddenly snapped to attention like someone who just woke up from a dream. "Uh, you know, we were fighting, hand-to-hand combat, heading toward the back of the lab where those two scientists were. Then all of a sudden there was this orange light...and then we didn't feel like fighting anymore."

Tina lost it. "What??? You didn't *feel* like *fighting* anymore?"

The lieutenant's training screamed to him to put his game face on, but he was feeling very tired now. "Sounds strange, doesn't it? But that's exactly what happened. Everybody in the room just stopped fighting. We couldn't figure out what we were doing in there." He pointed to the stretcher. "The major just fell asleep on the floor."

Tina was incredulous. She walked over to the stretcher and saw that sure enough, a man in uniform was sleeping as peacefully as a baby. "Are you men fighters or cowards? Get back in there and do your duty!"

The lieutenant turned around and ordered his men to their vehicles. The detachment looked like they had all suffered concussions. Some force – an orange light? – must have knocked them out.

Tina turned to her cameraman. "Can you believe that? Did you get it all?" The cameraman nodded. "I want to find out about that orange light. I'm going up there right now." Tina walked quickly toward the entrance. Before she could get there, two Japanese men in Berglin Enterprises uniforms posted themselves in front of the door.

"You two! What happened up there?" The men shook their heads; they understood no English. Tina was about to walk to the side entrance but that door was guarded as well. Suddenly a gigantic man, ducking, burst through the door. The two guards barked something in Japanese and chuckled. The walking mountain said something in Japanese to them that sounded like *bakemono*, and the men laughed.

Tina thrust a microphone in an outstretched arm up to the giant's face. "All right you. Tell me what happened in there!"

For the second time in five minutes Ralph Zimring was confronted by a small woman. Tina Brooks looked like a rage-aholic ferret with a hairpiece. She furiously demanded "some answers."

Amused, Ralph explained everything.

"So there *was* an orange light?"

"Yeah, it came from that device, what do they call it, the Pulsar? And then everybody just stopped what they were doing. It was a great fight, but then nobody felt like fighting anymore."

Tina was beside herself. "What do you mean, you fool? Dozens of combat trained fighters just suddenly put down their weapons? This isn't a Disney movie!"

Ralph scratched his head. "It does sound kinda goofy, doesn't it? But that's the way it was."

"Did you sequester that Pulsar thing?" Tina asked. "It's supposed to be dangerous."

"Coulda fooled me. I actually got a look at it and snapped a picture with my phone. Here it is."

Tina looked at the image. "*That* thing is a threat to public safety?" She realized that she and Barnsely had been duped. That Pulsar thing was no different from that silly little spinning motor of Park and Rosen's. They had been fooled by the smooth-talking Duchene Comstock from the ODNI.

"Well, you can see the array of magnets around it. Maybe that's the dangerous part."

Tina looked to see if she was being made fun of, and saw the big man's lips twitching. "What's your name?"

"Ralph Zimring, ma'am," the giant said, executing a passable bow. "*Je suis entièrement à votre service*."

Tina sighed, all the anger going out of her. "Were you part of this rescue force?"

"Actually I quit the force, but I was part of it originally. I switched sides." Ralph told her about his involvement in the fight. "As far as I can tell, these new inventions are harmless. Although one of the scientists did say that the Pulsar could be weaponized. If you were a sociopath."

"All right Mr. Zimring, thank you."

She turned to the camera, which was panning the parking lot. A few of the soldiers were still milling around the parking lot. People were starting to come down from the grassy knolls. Everyone was snapping pictures with their phones. The Midland police were trying to restore order to the chaos.

Tina saw Max Berglin come out of the building. A funny looking little man walked up and started to draw something out of his pocket.

Elmo Tackett kept an eye on the movements of Max Berglin. The Midland Police only occasionally tracked him now. On the morning the rescue force arrived he got up before dawn, on a hunch, and got on his scooter. He knew the police would be busy today; it said so in the paper. Berglin usually left the house at 7 a.m. but today the military was coming to confiscate his inventions. He was hoping Berglin would leave early and be distracted. It was worth thirty more bills if he could get him.

Elmo drove around Palmer Park and saw no activity. After an hour of fruitless waiting he checked the Channel 5 news site and saw Tina Brooks' live report. Abandoning Palmer Park he headed off on River Drive to the warehouse. In the chaos he was able to park his scooter and enter the parking lot. Just then Max Berglin came out of the main entrance. Elmo automatically began to draw his pistol. For a split-second he had a clean shot at Berglin, but a woman with a cameraman was marching toward him. Police were all over the place and people were snapping images with their phones. Elmo hesitated; it was too risky. The target was now out of the line of his fire. He took his hand out of his pocket. Frustrated, he rode his scooter back to his apartment, madder than ever at Max Berglin.

— 33 —

Jessie and Heather were hanging out in the coffee shop.

A voice in the back said, “Check out what’s happening on Channel 5.” Someone switched on the TV.

The two women saw Tina Brooks, some military people, the police, and a seven foot tall man in a military rig. “Hey look, there’s Zach,” Heather said.

“Look at that guy,” Jessie said, pointing to Ralph Zimring. “Zach looks like a midget next to him.”

A dozen people excitedly ran by with their mobiles raised. “Must be that public safety unit,” Heather remarked.

Mike Parsons walked in. “What’s Zach doing there?”

“He told me that he and Max Berglin were going over to the warehouse to help those two scientists,” Jessie replied. “Zach said the invaders were going to get a big surprise.”

“Crazy fool.” Mike secretly wished he was there.

Wayne and Myra DiPietro watched the broadcast live. Myra was angry and Wayne’s sense of the orderliness of things was grossly offended.

“They didn’t get the weapon,” Wayne said. “Who does this Berglin think he is?”

Myra agreed wholeheartedly. “I have no patience with greedy persons like Max Berglin. The man is a criminal and should be thrown in jail.”

“If it wasn’t for that foreign army he probably would have.”

“They should have taken those two scientists too. I am a compassionate person, but the authorities have been too lenient. Max Berglin is endangering the entire city.”

Husband and wife looked at each other. They hadn't been in such close agreement for a long time. Wayne picked Myra up in his arms and took her to the bedroom.

Hassan Bashari, PANA's regional auditor, watched the unfolding events. The fighting reminded him of his experiences on the West Bank. The detachment was like the Israelis when they attacked occupied Palestine to make room for their settlements.

Hassan had come to the US after tiring of the harassment by Israeli occupation forces, and the unending inter-Arab disputes between Hamas and Fatah. Hassan learned at an early age to deal with the Israeli military occupation. Not a day had gone by when there wasn't a skirmish with the Israelis in the West Bank. He had experienced the helplessness associated with intimidation by a superior force. His sentiments were all with the defenders and against the detachment.

He saw the detachment walk out of the building and knew they had failed. He couldn't understand why. Say what you want about the Israelis, they were well trained and they knew exactly what they were doing. They were efficient and persistent and didn't lose focus. The detachment sent in to save the city could learn a few lessons from them.

Hassan shook his head. He knew he was much happier here, but sometimes he missed the old days. The excitement, the passion, and the camaraderie with his fellow freedom fighters had been exhilarating. Back then he was fighting for a cause; now he was in a boring job at PANA. Max Berglin was bravely standing up to the government, and that took courage.

He wondered whether Berglin Enterprises would have work for a good accounts manager, or maybe even a security guard. He knew how to handle weapons and was no stranger to conflict.

Larry Potvin and Mark Ferrell couldn't believe what they were seeing. One of their customers was in the shop and saw what was happening on his mobile. The men had stopped work and were watching Channel 5 on the TV.

It was clear to Larry even before Tina Brooks' comments that something unusual had happened and that the mission had failed. God, he wished he was there. His hands itched for a weapon. He didn't like Berglin's foreign security detail but he suspected that the *Courier* was exaggerating the threat to the city. Zach told Mark they were making renewable energy power units. He wanted one himself. This little town, for some reason, had been targeted by the national security establishment. He wanted to know why.

Mark Ferrell couldn't believe it when he saw Zach at the scene. There were military and police all over the parking lot. People were running around with their mobiles, taking pictures. Mark saw Zach being questioned by a police officer. He hoped his son hadn't gotten into any trouble.

This Isn't Over

The detachment returned to Fort McCoy. Commander Duggan debriefed Major Bates. The major couldn't explain what had happened to his team, or to himself. "Commander, there was this orange light that made everyone want to stop fighting. It knocked everyone out." Bates felt that whatever the orange light was, its effects were still with him. He felt different, not like himself anymore. His anger at terrorists and malcontents who would harm his country had evaporated. Berglin's weapon had changed his personality! Maybe it was some kind of mind-control device. Before he left for Midland he wasn't convinced of Berglin's danger to the city. Now he was convinced that whatever Max Berglin had developed was a threat. He voiced these thoughts to the commander.

Bates' story was confirmed by McEachern and all of the fighters. The three mercenaries, who showed up to collect their money, also agreed with Bates. Commander Duggan could see that his men were in a state of total confusion. They looked different. They were softer somehow, no longer fine-edged fighting men. It was unacceptable.

"An orange light!" Duggan barked. "Was it a laser?" If Berglin had developed some kind of beam weapon, things had gone much further than anyone thought.

"No, it looked more like a plasma sphere," McEachern replied. "There was a silent burst and the thing just appeared out of nowhere."

All the men nodded their heads.

Commander Duggan was appalled and angry. Somebody must have leaked very sensitive information to Berglin. Clearly, his men had gone up against something they couldn't handle. Had General Putnam lied to him? His detachment might have been expendable; collateral damage in some bigger game. That thought made him even angrier.

"Bates! Your report is unacceptable."

Bates and McEachern nodded. "Yes sir, it is." Bates said. "Something happened down there we can't explain. There is definitely a threat to national security in Midland. We failed and we are sorry."

"What happened to Drake and Bayless?"

"Dead," Donovan said. "Pieces of garbage, both of them." Duggan agreed silently, as did the other mercenaries.

"Zimring took both of them out," Mutumbe said.

"Zimring! Well, at least the bastard did something useful." Drake and Bayless had been foisted onto the detachment by Comstock. Commander Duggan was glad those two shitbirds were dead.

Commander Duggan dismissed the team. He thanked them for their participation and sent them back to their units. He told the three mercenaries to fuck off, they weren't getting paid. Strangely, none of them reacted with hostility. They walked out of the room and were never seen again.

Duggan then reported to DNI Putnam, who was furious. Putnam ripped him for an incompetent and said a lot of other unpleasant things. After his colloquy with Putnam, Duggan reached into his drawer and drank half a fifth of Jim Beam. He vowed never again to participate in anything outside the chain of command. It's what happens when a patriot sticks his neck out, he thought bitterly.

When DNI Putnam reported to TAC, his contact was appalled. "I'm not giving *that* report to Byrnes," Lieutenant Spieth said. "And neither will the area director."

"You're a fucking coward, whoever you are," General Putnam replied.

"Have it your way general," Spieth said, and hung up.

General Putnam was now so infuriated he did not hesitate to call the mad dog himself, who had personally recruited him to TAC. To his surprise Zbigniew Byrnes was icily calm, as if he had expected something like this to happen.

"We're going to take care of this situation once and for all," Byrnes said.

Putnam got the idea that some mysterious, overwhelming force was involved. "What the hell are you planning Byrnes?"

"You don't have a need to know, general."

"I'm the fucking Director of National Intelligence! What do you mean I don't need to know?"

"You heard what I said. But general, you're going to be very pleased when you see what happens. We are going to fight fire with fire."

General Herman Putnam's politics were slightly to the right of his mentor, General Curtis LeMay, who once called for nuclear weapons to be used in Vietnam. He got the impression from Byrnes that something world shattering was going to happen in Midland. He also received the impression that Zbigniew Byrnes was going mad.

The confrontation with the detachment should have decided things in our favor. Unfortunately, it had as much effect as a pebble in a lake.

Chief Stan Moyer (who had gotten his promotion) called me, asking if I had any information about the attackers. I said I didn't and that I was starting to get really angry. "Who are these people?"

Moyer sounded exasperated and defeated. "I don't know anything Mr. Berglin. But my guess is that this isn't over."

I agreed. The people on the hill never videoed anything useful; they didn't have access to the inside of the building until the battle was over. No one filmed the orange light. The whole thing just resulted in a lot of excited talk on the internet. The only useful element was the Pulsar's projection of Tesla's radiant energy, which seemed to have a pacifying effect. We were right back where we started.

Max Talks to Kenji Hiroto

That night I got a visit from Ralph Zimring, who showed up at Palmer Park escorted by a blushing Monster. Zimring had an affectionate arm around her neck as they stood side by side. "I don't think this is over, Berglin."

"That's what Chief Moyer said," I replied.

"Whoever is after you failed. They are clearly motivated to prevent the release of your new technology and will try again. My advice is to get your security detail out of Midland immediately. Don't give them an excuse to attack you. You're just a good citizen going about your business."

"And leave ourselves open to attack?"

"I've been in the military or a mercenary my whole life. I know how it goes. Get Hiroto's guys out of here, now, and leave yourself wide open. You've got nothing to hide." The big man looked down at Monster and smiled. "But she stays."

"What do we do if another force is sent?" I asked.

"Word is that it's going to involve some exotic technology. Your Pulsar did them in, so it's tit for tat. They think you have some kind of frontier science weapon and it scares the shit out of them. I'll stay on as a military adviser if you like."

"I like. OK, we'll do it." I got out my phone and called Kenji. "My friend, we won the battle but we didn't win the war. Take your men out and send me the bill, and thank you so much for your help."

"What is your plan?" Kenji asked.

I pointed the phone at Zimring and Monster. "These two will be our military advisers. We're going to play it like we're the victims of the big bad government."

Kenji smiled. "I think that's wise. Hatsumi-sama would agree, I'm sure."

The next day I hired a local security firm, who supplied four standard-issue security guards, two for each building. Zimring was visibly relieved.

I concluded that we had been very lucky so far.

"Prepare for War"

Before Kenji's men left town I interviewed every one of them involved in the battle, with Monster as interpreter. The Pulsar's radiant energy apparently made people softer, depending upon your exposure to it. The mercenaries and some of Kenji's men had been in the middle of the room at the center of the burst. These men seemed to have lost all desire for fighting. Monster and myself, who had been against the wall, were less affected. I felt a temporary euphoria but nothing beyond that. Kenji told me that several of his men had quit his service. I noticed that Ralph Zimring had lost a very hard edginess to his personality. Down the road we would definitely have to explore the effects of radiant energy on biology and consciousness.

I visited the lab two days later and checked with Austin and John about the Pulsar. "We'll need several more months of testing it to even begin to understand its capabilities," Park said.

"Could you generate another burst of radiant energy?"

"I think we can, but the device is unreliable at present. It would only be effective within a limited radius, maybe a hundred feet." Park's face displayed frustration and excitement. "The Pulsar has so much potential but our knowledge is incomplete."

I called Julian Green and told him what had occurred. Green told me about a near-death experience he had as a child. "I'm convinced that Tesla's radiant energy comes from an invisible substrate that is totally benign, and that the quintessential nature of the universe is benign as well."

"That's great Julian, but I need your advice about what's coming next. My military adviser tells me Byrnes isn't going to give up. Another attack is likely on the way."

"You can't fight these guys, Max. You were very lucky this time. I'll send you an info packet about how to proceed next. You have to broadly disseminate the technology. Make it open source, get as many people involved as possible. Create so many targets it will be impossible to stop."

"Thanks Julian, but I didn't risk my life and a significant portion of my investment budget to give this gratis to the world."

"Max, your best option would be to have webcams in your lab. Broadcast your research live over the internet. Get so many people interested that Byrnes can't contain it."

"You told me to keep everything local, now you're telling me the opposite."

"Keep your team local, broadly disseminate the knowledge behind the technology. Byrnes and TAC are part of a trans-national security state that doesn't want your discovery to be commercialized. But they can't stop the entire world."

"I can't do that Julian. I'm not an altruist like you."

Green laughed. "Well then, my advice is to get as many Cubes in as many homes as you can. Give them away if you have to. The more people who use them, the harder it will be to contain."

"That was our idea too."

"Good! Remember Max, you're not the problem. Byrnes and his Network are the problem. They're going to escalate the situation because broad dissemination of the Cube means the end of their fossil-fuel empire. Get ready for media blasts from unexpected quarters. More than likely the next stage will not be military. Get ready to have your people lured away or frightened."

As the end of April approached, nothing happened. Hope returned to UPower. Al Jordan and the Board busied themselves with normal business routine, convinced that our little skirmish was a one-off. By the beginning of May I was almost convinced that we were in the clear.

I told Clive Barnsley on a video chat that Hiroto's men had left town, but that didn't abate his hostility.

"You aren't in the clear," he said one warm day in early May. "My sources still tell me that your device, whatever it is, will be confiscated. You're a criminal, Berglin, and I hope they throw you in jail."

"One of those sources wouldn't be Duchene Comstock, would it?" Zimring had told me all about him.

"You'd better watch your step Mr. Berglin. You think you're in the right, but you couldn't be more wrong."

After his conversation with Max Berglin Clive Barnsely considered. Tina had shown him the image of the Pulsar. He was shocked by the device's amateurish appearance. Of course he knew nothing about physics, but he wondered if Duchene Comstock had exaggerated the threat. Was the Pulsar really dangerous? Comstock had assured him that the *Courier* was cooperating with a peaceful operation to guarantee public safety, and that Max Berglin's devices were a threat to national security. But he was uncertain now.

Kenji Hiroto decided to stay on, in one of my guest bedrooms, saying that my fight made him feel ten years younger. I gave Park and Rosen a week's leave. John Rosen went bar hopping, telling his story to all who would listen. It was good PR for the company after all of the bad publicity from the *Courier*. Most of the people were disdainful of the security detachment's failure, but the sentiment was that Berglin Enterprises was responsible for the trouble. A few good words were being said by those who had Cubes.

Austin Park went to Korea to see his family under an assumed name, credentials courtesy of Kenji. He was back after five days.

John picked him up from the airport. "You were right John. My father and mother are angry that I have not married. My brothers and sisters think I'm too American. The only thing I know how to do is lab work."

"I told you."

"Have you made any more progress with the Pulsar?"

"I haven't thought about work for almost a week. I've been yukking it up at the bars, meeting some girls, and I even did a routine at the Improv last Wednesday."

"Did you tell any science jokes?"

"I told the one about the statistician, the engineer, and the physicist, who go out rabbit hunting. The physicist sees a rabbit, calculates its trajectory, and fires long by five feet. The engineer calculates a fudge factor and shoots five feet short. The statistician yells, 'We got him!' "

"Did you get a laugh?"

"Nope. They booed me off the stage."

Austin laughed. "You're the life of the party my young friend, but have you fried your brain cells so badly that you've forgotten your physics?"

"No way, Dr. Park. Are you ready to get back to work?"

The two scientists drove straight to the lab.

We were on our own now. Kenji's security men were gone. Yusuke Shiozawa, our Japanese engineering consultant, also went back to Japan. He wanted no part of a hostile confrontation with our government. That meant our assembly line project had crashed, even though Zach Ferrell had absorbed some of the engineering design concepts. I was beginning to like the kid a lot, except for his interest in Danielle. They seemed to be a lot closer these days. I got busy hammering the Ferrell kid to piece together more Cubes, supervised by Park and Rosen. UPower hired two local engineers, young kids just like Zach, to assemble them by hand. To keep the cost down we were charging enough to cover materials cost and a little more. The large outlay for security was gone, which made my executive board very happy.

My six-month grace period for UPower from the Board was almost up now, but I couldn't see how I could stop. I didn't want to. I had started something and I wanted to finish it. Fortunately Al, Mika, and Barbara were very upset at the way the authorities had acted. I was pretty sure I could get another extension. Every day I wondered when Byrnes would put the squeeze on. Green told me that he would know everything we were doing, so why was he waiting? Four weeks after the skirmish we had almost fifty Cubes in private homes all over Midland, and a couple to VIPs in Chicago.

The day after Austin and John went back to work Bernie Hartwig showed up for a game of billiards. Bernie told me he had tried to back out of his agreement with his handlers. "Which I can't tell you anything about. They told me I would lose my job at Carleton, which was part of my contract with them. I still have my position there for now, but I might not be employed much longer if I back out."

I remembered Bernie's skillful work at the debate last year. "What would you think about helping us in public relations? We need more people skilled in that area. The *Courier* is lambasting us. If we ever get UPower off the ground we'll need someone brilliant to help present this new technology to the public. Your doctorate in physics and your status in academia are all pluses."

Bernie's face suddenly lightened and it looked like a huge burden had been lifted from his life. "I've always been good at it. At Harvard I was captain of the debate team, but my parents pushed me into science. Then at SAIC I was trapped into – well, into intelligence work that I no longer want to do."

"It's a quantum leap from head of the physics department at a respected university to public relations director at a floundering startup, Bernie. You've always been rather reclusive. Why the change?"

"I'm sick to death of academia, Max. As I've gotten older I've been getting more and more sour on life. My...other job isn't interesting anymore. Seeing what you've done with UPower has completely changed my perspective. If I don't change course I'm afraid I'll turn into a mistrustful and grumpy reactionary. I need a life change."

"You were very good last year in that debate, even though you made me very angry."

"I was high as a kite for several days afterwards, even though I felt guilty as hell about sabotaging your scientists. There is something exciting about being able to lead a group of people and move their opinions so subtly they don't even know it."

"So get rid of the guilt, then, and join the team of good guys."

"I'll take the job now," Bernie said. "On one condition."

"Condition?"

"Yes Max. I want to work with Danielle Menard."

"All right. Go to Personnel tomorrow morning at the Centurion Building downtown and talk to George Schultz. I'll set that up today. When you get up to speed on our businesses you'll be UPower's Director of Public Relations. When you're done with Personnel report to Danielle; she'll tell you what we need." Walter Davidson, Berglin Enterprises' PR guy, was leaving the firm. Bernie was a godsend.

"You won't feel insulted working with someone who's thirty years younger than you, Bernie? Danielle has no formal education. You have a respected and prestigious position at the university. Don't give that up if you aren't sure."

"Max, for the first time in my life I'm going with my heart instead of my head and I admit I'm a little bit frightened. But I need to change more than I need job security. I'm well off now."

"You'll get change if you work with Danielle. She'll knock your socks off." I looked searchingly at my friend. "Do you think you can handle her Bernie?" The older man was clearly anxious, but I now sensed an underlying excitement.

"I don't think so Max, but I can teach her a thing or two about how to deal with media types like Tina Brooks and Clive Barnsley."

"That's what I'm counting on old fellow."

On Monday the tenth of May the entire board showed up in my third floor office at Berglin Enterprises. Al Jordan threw some papers on my desk. "Look at this," he said. The documents contained very lucrative offers from various companies to every member of my board, for three times what I could afford to pay.

"Well?" I said, looking up.

"It's a lot of money Max," Mika said. "I've been thinking about starting my own company." When I looked at Al, he shifted uncomfortably and said nothing. It was a clever move to take away the most valuable executive assets within Berglin Enterprises, my money-maker. I sat back in my chair, determined to keep the anger I felt off my face. "It is, Mika. I won't hold you to your contract if you'd rather leave."

I could see the relief on the thin man's face. He took out a handkerchief from his back pocket and wiped his forehead. "I can't turn down this kind of money."

I managed a thin smile, determined not to burn any bridges. "Top executives are lured away all the time," I said.

Mika noticed the implied compliment and nodded. "Max, I always said you were an understanding man."

"Legal will send you the appropriate documents for termination of your employment contract. There will be a bonus check for good service."

Mika's almost albino face brightened. "Thank you Max," he said in his thin, high pitched voice. "You've shown the highest character and I appreciate it."

As Mika left the room with a bounce in his step (thinking about all that money, I'd imagine) I turned to Al. "What say you, friend Al? I can probably find someone to replace Mika, but you know my business inside and out." I had to test his loyalty. "I can't use a hesitant CEO, Al. It's all in or nothing."

I could see Barbara staring him down. Al looked at the document, then back at me. "We're in a very unstable financial environment, Max—"

I waved my hand dismissively. So Al Jordan, who I thought was a good friend, turned out to be just another employee. "There's no need for that Al. You'll get a bonus but I'm going to hold you to your non-compete clause. I'm sure you can find something to do for a year that won't interfere with my business."

The roly-poly CEO smiled gratefully. "I've never been completely comfortable with the direction UPower is going in. That's the main reason."

I tried to smile. "The money doesn't hurt."

I looked over at Barbara. "Could you get on to assembling a new Board, Barbara? I know it's a lot to ask."

"On one condition. I want to be CEO."

Well I'll be damned, I thought. She's probably wanted that job for years and I never even noticed. "Done. With a raise."

"I'll get going right now."

Barbara left the room. Al was still standing in front of my desk. "Just like that eh? Looks like you were looking for an excuse to get rid of me."

I stifled my anger. "Not true Al. You've kept the business going and expanded it. I'm taking a risk with Barbara because she's unproven."

Al stepped forward toward my desk and gazed into my face searchingly. I was thinking that although Barbara was fiercely loyal, I had no idea whether she was capable. After several moments Al nodded, satisfied. "I believe you. But the truth is that practically any competent executive could have done it. That's why I don't feel so bad." He stuck out his hand and I shook it.

There were no hard feelings. But I was down two good men.

Rachel DuPlessis received a phone call in her office. A pleasantly modulated male voice said, "I'm looking for a good marketing firm here in Midland, and you were recommended to me."

"You've come to the right place. What can I do for you?"

"I represent a firm that develops computer security software. We would like to hire your firm to develop a marketing campaign that will compete with Berglin Enterprises."

"Who is this?" Rachel asked. The man sounded distant but with an air of command, as if he were used to giving orders and having them obeyed.

"I'm from McKenzie Security Systems. I will send a representative to you tomorrow with a proposed marketing campaign and a budget. Are you interested?"

Rachel made up her mind quickly. She had never had that scheduled meeting with Max Berglin, but this sounded promising. Berglin probably would never get his product off the ground. She didn't like him; he was too arrogant and holier-than-thou. And she loved competition. "Yes. When can I expect you tomorrow?"

"Eight a.m. sharp." The call ended abruptly. Rachel was irritated at the dismissive attitude of the caller, but she shrugged it off. She was never one to doubt herself: once she made a decision she stuck to it and didn't look back.

Trevor Clarke, bored out of his mind at his office in the PRC building, was waiting for his supplier. The Ginzburg Development Project proposal for the Planning Commission was well on its way to completion. Bob Justice was doing his job there, and Judge Massimino was talking up the project to his contacts on Council and in the state legislature. Trevor had already made a good impression on George Bancroft, the *Courier's* publisher. He had spoken to every member of Council and thought he had enough votes lined up. There were no public functions until next week. At times like these he missed his former life of high-stakes trader and the busy social life of London.

His supplier was a local chemist who had a small distribution business on the side. His drug of choice was ecstasy, but his supplier would not allow him to even mention the word or any of its derivatives. He called it 3,4-methylenedioxymethamphetamine. When Trevor wanted to order he had to write a short note with the numbers 3 and 4 in it. The man was intelligent, used the drug himself, and apparently had his own special formula. As a bonus he also advised his clients about addiction and how to get high. He told Trevor that "E" had originally been developed by the Merck pharmaceutical company in 1912.

Trevor loved the drug and the feeling of energy, especially the sexual arousal. Taken orally, the pills were made to look like aspirin and were packaged in an aspirin bottle. The high lasted several hours. He always used it when he felt bored, and sometimes when the alluring Rachel came over. The woman was insatiable; a predator really, but if he didn't perform to her satisfaction he knew she would throw him over.

There was a knock on his office door. A thin smallish man entered the room. He was well dressed, with round wire-rimmed glasses and thin lips, an aristocratic nose, and thinning blond hair. He pulled out a small package. "Here is the information you asked for, sir."

"Thank you Davis." The man sat in the chair and they discussed public relations and finance for fifteen minutes, as if the supplier was a bank client. Trevor wrote him a check. Then the man stood up and walked out of the room, closing the door. Eagerly, Trevor ripped open the package and took two of the small pills. Within fifteen minutes he felt the familiar rush of well being and energy. He would call Rachel tonight and shag her brains out.

Judge Roland Massimino was in his chambers at the Midland District Court when he received a phone call. "Roland Massimino," the voice said.

"Speaking."

"You are involved in a project with a Mr. Ginzburg, a Mr. Justice, and a Mr. Clarke."

"Who is this? I'm writing my case notes and can't be disturbed."

"Your question is irrelevant. Suffice it to say, Roland, that your development project is going to meet with, shall we say, stiff resistance at the state level."

"Listen, you. Cut the nonsense and identify yourself."

The judge heard a sigh on the other end. "Mr. Massimino, please call the Illinois Attorney General's office and ask for Assistant AG Brad Petersen. He'll explain the situation and what you are to do."

Judge Massimino was angry now. "You're an arrogant prick, aren't you? I have friends in the legislature—" The judge heard a beep that signaled a broken connection. Furious, he dialed the number and asked for Petersen. His imposing physical stature, an ingrained belligerence, and some natural luck had accustomed him to success and the overcoming of obstacles. When he did meet with resistance, like a bull he put his head down and moved forward.

"Brad Petersen? This is Judge Roland Massimino, former state representative. I —"

For the second time in sixty seconds he was rudely interrupted. "Yes, Judge Massimino." The voice was irritatingly smooth with a hint of contempt. "I'm afraid that your proposed riverfront project in Midland is a no-go. A state environmental impact statement has discovered...impediments...to its execution."

"Nonsense," the judge replied. "I already have a favorable environmental impact statement from the state. Moreover, the proposal hasn't even been submitted to the planning commission." But they were almost ready to submit. Bob and that Clarke fellow had finally overcome the opposition from old man Tavistock. The votes were there now.

"Nevertheless, Roland, you and your friends Ginzburg, Clarke, and Justice will discover shortly that there are insurmountable environmental barriers to your project. When you are convinced of the truth of my words, call me back and I'll tell you how you can get back on track."

Again the caller hung up. The nerve of that asshole, calling him by his first name! He would have a word with Bob and Craig about this. They must have an unknown but influential enemy with some pretty powerful connections.

After several minutes of agitation, during which he knocked his case notes on the floor, the judge calmed down and leaned back in his plush leather chair. He knew how these things worked. Someone on high wanted a favor and their little group would have to come through. But after that the "impediments" would magically vanish. So be it.

Vahan Katelian was sitting on a white sofa in front of a massive plate glass window that overlooked the grounds of the family mansion. He saw ducks frolicking in the pond but his mood was not pleasant. His father and father-in-law had just informed him that the Ginzburg project was temporarily on hold. This was very bad timing. Without the Ginzburg development the families, and he personally, would suffer a major income shortage. He had promised his crews lucrative employment no later than mid-summer, and if the Ginzburg project went down they'd move on to another. He not only needed skilled workers, but men who didn't mind throwing their weight around. He and Bobby Popp had hand-picked these guys.

Vahan fastidiously adjusted one of his cufflinks and pondered the matter. His thoughts turned to that little skirmish at Berglin's warehouse a couple of weeks ago. Those Asian bodyguards were all out of town now, and Max Berglin was more vulnerable. With a shock he realized that he and Zadig had never called off the hit on Berglin! That little scum Elmo might "dispose" of him any time, and Zadig still favored it. For some reason his twin brother just hated Max Berglin.

Vahan got up and paced the spacious room with its fine paintings, gorgeous view, and plush carpeting. It had been a stupid thing to do, and dangerous for the families if Elmo was caught. But his blood had been up along with the younger generation. He knew from his source in Homicide that the new chief of police, Stan Moyer, had no evidence against Elmo. The police had investigated the Max Berglin shooting for months without success, and had filed the case. Vahan was satisfied, especially after they burned those suits out on Main Street last winter. He and Berglin were working against a common enemy now. Moreover, Elmo had spilled Berglin's blood and the man almost died. It was enough. He would have a talk with Zadig.

Zach Ferrell wanted to put a Cube in his father's auto shop. He and two other engineers were turning out two hand-made Cubes every day, under the supervision of Austin Park.

When he went over there Mark and Larry greeted him warmly. "How are you doing kid?" Larry asked, pumping his hand enthusiastically.

"I've got a present for you." Zach went out to his car and rolled in a Cube.

When Larry saw the unit he wasn't impressed. "It looks like a high school science experiment."

Zach laughed. He could see that his father was hesitant, but he now had a well of experience dealing with customers to draw from. "This thing is jerry-rigged but it's completely harmless. It will get you off the grid and save a lot of money in utility costs. Are you up for it?"

Mark looked at Larry. "My son wouldn't steer us wrong."

"OK then Zach, go ahead."

Zach could see Larry's skepticism as he set up the Cube. Zach wondered whether the device would handle the load when Larry had all his machines running.

When the power came back on Larry was dumbfounded. "This thing violates the laws of electricity."

"How does it work son?" Mark asked.

"Hell if I know!" Zach pointed at the unit. "The Cubes will power a large house, or a small shop like this. It adjusts itself to the connected load."

Both men were amazed but Larry was still skeptical. "We'll see what happens when I use my big lathe. That thing draws a *lot* of power."

"If you have any trouble call me," Zach replied.

Hassan Bashari was astonished after receiving one of the Cubes. Accustomed to struggle and hard work, he never expected favors. A week ago he had gotten a phone call from a young man named Zach Ferrell, who had heard of him from Larry Potvin. Potvin...suddenly Hassan remembered. The suspected embezzler! Why would Potvin want to do him a favor? Unless it was to "grease the skids" a little, as these Americans would say. Maybe Potvin was still worried about exposure, even though it appeared that he had shut down his little scheme.

"Why me?" Hassan asked Zach.

"It's a long story. When you see the product you'll understand."

"But you're charging me less than what the product is worth. If your machine does what it says it's worth a lot more than that. Only someone who later wanted a big favor would do such a thing. You can't do business by giving away your products."

"This is a pre-marketing loss leader," Zach explained, as instructed by Danielle and that older guy Hartwig. "The Cube is a monumental breakthrough in renewable energy and we want as many people as possible to benefit. We're looking to make massive profits in the long run if we can establish a base of satisfied customers in the short run."

Hassan was skeptical, but satisfied. "In that case, I accept with my thanks."

Zach Ferrell came to Hassan's house on Saturday morning, setting up and demonstrating the unit. Hassan's jaw dropped. "You are now officially off the electrical grid," Ferrell said. "Here is a list of Cube customers. There are over sixty now. Call any one of them if you have any questions or want to discuss the unit."

Zach Ferrell left Bashari's small ranch house feeling high as a kite. Providing a list of Cube customers had been their most successful action, and he had thought of it. It helped to know you weren't out on a limb and that others were also using it. Especially after that military unit tried to confiscate it, and all the bad publicity. People were so excited about the unit they were calling their family members and friends. Demand for the Cube had skyrocketed. He was making a difference in the world!

For the first time in his life Zach felt passionate about something. He loved his job. Berglin had hired people to assemble the units so he just had to test them and make sure they worked. He could do that at the lab and then make his deliveries. Zach really wanted to get back to engineering the automated production process, but the boss told him they didn't have time now. Apparently the company was being harassed again.

Best of all, he would see Danielle tonight at the coffee shop. As Zach got into his old Mazda he grinned. The boss had told him to stay away from her but he was having none of that. It was the young buck versus the old-timer, and he intended to win.

— 34 —

I had been wondering where the next attack would come from. On Monday I found out. I got into my office at 8 a.m., in the UPower building. Five minutes later my phone rang. "Mr. Berglin, this is Representative Patricia D'Antonio. I'm told you have a dangerous device that uses exotic technology, and that you are in violation of a Patent Secrecy Order."

"Hello Ms. D'Antonio, it's good to talk to you." I had learned never to volunteer information when talking to anyone in authority, particularly a politician. We chatted for a few minutes and I deflected all of her questions.

"You don't seem to understand the seriousness of your position, Mr. Berglin."

"Perhaps you should concentrate on improving the lives of your constituents instead of harassing honest businessmen," I suggested.

The Congresswoman was angry. "Legislation is being written as I speak that will outlaw exotic and untested devices such as yours in the civilian sector."

"Ms. D'Antonio, I think your best bet is to actually see these devices and have them demonstrated to you in person."

"I was just going to suggest that Mr. Berglin. Can you be in my office at 9 a.m. tomorrow?"

I wanted to laugh at her transparency. "I'm afraid not. The Cube must be demonstrated in a home electrical system, and the Pulsar is just a bench experiment right now. But you are always welcome to stop by my office. I will personally show you how harmless these things are."

"Another time, perhaps." She hung up before I could suggest that we install a Cube in her home.

An hour later I received a call from Senator van Weston. All this attention! I felt flattered, but van Weston was known as a hard-ass conservative.

I let him threaten and bluster for a while.

When he was through I said, "There is no problem, senator. You are free to stop by at any time and I will personally show you these so-called 'destructive and dangerous' devices, one of which is a simple renewable energy device. The other is just a promising experiment." I referred him to Midland Edison and Josh Brackenreed, even though he was only mildly sympathetic.

"Mr. Berglin, you have already been contacted by your state representative. I would advise you to turn over these devices to the proper authorities."

"Thank you for calling sir. We've already had an armed unit in here trying to steal my invention."

"I had nothing to do with that."

"I appreciate that sir. I would like to repeat the offer I gave to Representative D'Antonio: come to Midland any time. I will personally show you how harmless the Cube and the Pulsar really are."

Van Weston hung up. I decided to go upstairs and talk to Austin Park about the Pulsar.

"It's getting better. Reliability is around 60% or so."

"So the experiment will either work, or nothing will happen."

"That's right sir. It's all or nothing."

I thought about how lucky we had been on April 10th when the plasma sphere had reduced the threat from the military detachment. That time the Pulsar had worked. "Is there any harmful radiation or other anomalous effects?"

"Nothing. It's like the Cube; completely silent or you get a burst. We haven't been able to rigorously define the triggering mechanism."

I studied the device silently.

"In its present form the Pulsar is very limited," Park offered. "John and I need to perfect its operation before we explore its capabilities."

"So right now it *is* harmless."

"Yes Dr. Berglin. At present."

I was comforted by that knowledge.

That evening I called Julian Green, looking for guidance.

I told him about the phone calls from Representative D'Antonio and Senator van Weston.

"They are scared out of their gourds," Green said. "TAC knows you are distributing Cubes all over the city and are working on your Pulsar device. They need to act, and act quickly. They've already tried to contain the technology using conventional methods but that didn't work. Their next step is likely an all-out, national media attack. That scares the hell out of them because it risks exposing their illegal special access programs if somebody gets too curious. On the other hand, they view Midland as the thin edge of the wedge."

"Any ideas?"

"They'll paint you as anti-American, unpatriotic, and if necessary, mentally unstable."

"What can I do?"

"Absolutely nothing, except keep making and distributing Cubes. You're going to have to go national with this now Max. The more people who have them, the less effective their innuendo will be." Green again suggested making their work public. "Put it on GitHub. Put webcams in your lab, show the whole world you have something that could benefit everyone."

"It's too risky Dr. Green, we don't have time for that now. We're starting to get requests from all over the country. We can't even remotely keep up with demand."

"I understand. Then it's a race against time, Max. Do you want me to send you some of my volunteers?"

"I can use all the help I can get. Try to send me some engineers and technicians."

"Bunk everyone in your house, it's huge. They can sleep on your basement floor, it's big enough to hold a small army."

"Thanks Julian, you're a real friend."

"This is way bigger than you or me, Max. This is a fight to see who controls the planet."

Three days later my volunteers arrived, thirteen of them. Six of them were engineers or engineering students, one a computer scientist, and the rest young kids looking for a cause to support. I sent them over to Mildred at the warehouse, as if she didn't have enough to do. Bernie and Danielle were busy with a new media campaign for Berglin Enterprises. I had to make sure we kept selling software products. If Berglin Enterprises went under so would UPower.

That evening I went down to the basement to say thanks to Green's volunteers. We had distributed ten more Cubes today but it was just a drop in the bucket. Everyone was crowded around the big screen in the theater room.

"This is 60 Minutes. You might not know it but artificial intelligence is in your phone and in many other electronic devices. The goal of AI is to become smarter than humans, and immortal....Brian Waldrop knocked around Hollywood for thirty years before he got his first major role. Coming up, the Brian Waldrop story...There aren't many jobs more dangerous than being a gorilla doctor. These veterinarians travel deep into the jungle and sometimes risk their lives to protect the rapidly dwindling gorilla population...and finally, brilliant inventor or dangerous lunatic? Sixty Minutes exposes the folly of Dr. Max Berglin, who claims to have invented a 'free energy' device that experts say endangers public safety. That's all coming up on 60 Minutes."

"Hey Zach. Turn on your TV!" It was Gary Cronin, Zach's old college housemate.

"Anjou! How are you?"

"No time Zach. Turn your TV to CBS, you won't believe what's on 60 Minutes."

"Who cares about them? More people listen to alternative news now than those old network programs."

"Plenty of people still watch, Zach. Turn on your TV."

Zach saw an expose of Max Berglin and he was in it. The program described Zach Ferrell as a "well-intentioned but naive young engineer who wants to save the world." Max Berglin was portrayed as the antagonist in a national security drama. The narrator implied that he was a subtly evil man and said that he was illegally defying a patent secrecy order. The program said that Max Berglin had stolen two research scientists away from a respected research firm.

"It's nonsense Gary. A bunch of lies. Some guys in black suits stole the original invention. Park and Rosen were fired from the Octagon. Max just hired them after they were already unemployed."

"That's not what the program says. Why would they lie? Max Jr. confirmed it."

"He did? That scumbag! Max is insanely jealous of his father, Gary. He's just a vindictive and spoiled rich kid."

"So you say."

"All right then, come over to the lab first thing tomorrow morning. I'll show you this so-called 'danger to national security,' and what I'm really doing."

"Deal. Mind if Barry comes along?"

"He's still in town?"

"What did you expect from a French Lit grad? He's helping me with my practice; reads Baudelaire to my patients to cheer them up."

Zach laughed. "That's Barry all over. By the time he's through they'll need more therapy."

Barry Therion and Gary Cronin showed up at the Van Allen warehouse at eight in the morning, each holding a temporary pass Zach had given them. When they got to the fourth floor the two young men saw a woman walking down the hall.

"Oh my God, it's Danielle Menard," Gary said, nudging his beefy friend. Zach popped his head out of a door on the left of the corridor. "Come on in boys. The malevolent Zach Ferrell is here, along with the notorious Austin Park and John Rosen."

"Good words," Barry said. "Malevolent and notorious!"

Zach was smug. "I'm improving my vocabulary. Danielle prefers it."

"Are you working with Danielle?" Gary asked. He watched as she turned the corner. "She's hard to keep your eyes off of."

"Enough of that Gary. She's off limits around here."

The three Carleton friends caught up a little, standing in the hallway. Then Zach showed them a Cube that was running the lab. Austin demonstrated the Pulsar, which just sat there like a doofus and looked about as imposing as George W. Bush at a Mensa meeting.

"That's it?" Barry said. "The thing doesn't do anything."

"It's just a bench experiment, like the boss said. Sometimes it works and sometimes it just sits there." Zach explained about radiant energy and about their research being based on Tesla's work. "I want you to spread the word that this 60 Minutes thing is bullshit."

Barry and Gary poked around the lab until Austin got mad and told them to leave. After they left Austin said, "Don't bring your friends around here anymore Zach." He was obviously irritated that the Pulsar didn't work.

"Best that it didn't do anything anyway," Zach said. "Barry and Gary will spread the word that it's harmless."

"We need the word of people who are more influential than those two," Austin said.

Zach straightened and pointed his finger into the air theatrically. "Back to work!"

"Fuck you Zach," John Rosen said, grinning.

The next day I received an Intelligence Community Directive via courier. It was signed by Duchene Comstock, Deputy Director of National Intelligence for Acquisition and Technology. The heading said "**Unauthorized Disclosure of Classified Information.**" The document warned companies in the classified and computer security areas that "it has been determined by the ODNI that the policies of Berglin Enterprises are compromising to national security." When I showed this document to Legal they said it was just harassment. When I showed it to Bernie he said, "This document has no legal force outside the intelligence community. It's a scare tactic, Max, but no one wants to be on the wrong side of the DNI. It's clearly an attempt to scuttle your company." Over fifty percent of my business was with the intelligence community, and those contracts were lucrative.

Just as I was about to go home Ralph Zimring, ducking his head, stepped into my office.

"I'm told you got something from Comstock."

"Yes I did." I didn't say, "What are you doing in my office?" but I wanted to. Zimring had the run of the place.

"Look, Berglin, you hired me as an adviser. I'm advising. I'd like to take a look at that document."

"Is this personal?"

Ralph's gaze was hard. "It is. But I've seen these things before and I'd like to read it."

I shrugged and pushed the paper over. Zimring squashed himself into a chair two sizes too small and read the document. "It's bullshit Berglin, but it's typical of that worm Duchene Comstock." He told me the story of Julia's death and his suspicions of Comstock's role in it, and added, "This is some kind of rogue operation, just like the invasion team last month. It's illegal, but it can cause you problems."

"It's hard to believe that so many people are so worked up about this."

Ralph looked at me strangely. "Fucknuggets like Comstock don't need a reason for what they do, and some of them exercise a lot of influence. If you don't back off, these guys won't mind starting a war right here in little old Midland."

"Do you think people could get killed?"

The giant stared at me. "You just had a special forces unit in here Berglin! If your Pulsar didn't fire you and your two scientists would probably be in a detention center right now."

Ralph saw my disbelief. "Berglin, I've been a mercenary and before that an Army Ranger. I've killed people in the name of national security; a couple of them were American citizens. You seem to think this is some kind of game. It isn't. Comstock and people like him won't mind making an example of this town if they think your little toys endanger the security of this country." Ralph leaned his huge arms on my desk and brought his swarthy face to within inches of mine. "And neither would I."

I laughed nervously. Zimring was a force of nature, immovable and unstoppable. "That's absurd. Something you read about in novels and see on drama shows."

After a couple of seconds studying my face, the giant backed off. "All right," he said, shrugging his massive shoulders. "But you'd better be prepared to go all the way. You're going to get people killed."

"I'm not backing off." But I was feeling a little overwhelmed.

Zimring grinned with the attitude of someone who thought that people dying was mere commonplace. "That's why I'm still here. That and Michiko. Otherwise I would have already terminated Duchene Comstock and gone back to my little palace in Northport." Zimring straightened to his full height, his head brushing the ceiling. "You're going to need me before this is over, Berglin, believe me."

I believed him.

The next day two of Green's volunteers were killed in an automobile accident. Their vehicle was struck by a truck barreling down River Dr. from a construction site at the proposed Ginzburg development site. Chief Stan Moyer called me personally with his condolences and asked me to come down to his office at the police station. When I arrived he told me the fatalities appeared to be accidental.

"The driver of the truck was speeding and ran a yellow light, but the driver of the other vehicle was texting and moved into the intersection before the light was green." He shrugged. "It happens. We're holding the truck driver for reckless driving and we might be able to get him on involuntary manslaughter. Do you want to press charges?"

"No," I said, knowing I'd have to tell Julian Green. I would also personally call the parents of my two volunteers. "Please find out if it was truly an accident."

Moyer's face hardened and he gave me a warning. "Mr. Berglin, you have been the focus of a lot of trouble for this city, and my department, over the past year. I have nothing against you so far, but I'm responsible for keeping the peace here in Midland. Do us all a favor and end your dispute with the government. I have a feeling that if you don't, events are going to escalate in the wrong direction." I wanted to protest my innocence but I could see it from Moyer's point of view. He was just doing his job.

Moyer took my statement. "Watch out for a funny little man about five feet three, running around on a motor scooter." He described him to me. "His name is Elmo Tackett. I think he's the guy who tried to plug you last fall."

"Thank you detective, I'll be as careful as I can." On a hunch I asked, "Would you like to get off the grid?"

"I've talked with your young man Zach Ferrell about what you are doing, but I never gave it much credit."

"I'll have Zach drop off one of the Cubes to your house this evening. When are you getting off work?"

Moyer's face drooped. He was obviously very tired. "Oh hell, I'll go home and have dinner with my wife for the first time this week. Ferrell can come over any time after 7."

I explained that Zach would arrange for the modification of his electric service and that he would have to pay an electrician. I told him the price of the Cube. "You will make that up quickly."

As I walked out of the police station I kicked myself. We should have been installing these things at the homes of every member of the city council and other local officials. And at the houses of some of these rich and influential Chicago executives. On my last trip to the *Courier* offices I had offered to install one in Clive Barnesly's home. He had flatly refused. "Midland Edison is good enough for me," he said. His voice was slightly fearful.

"I'd rather err with Galen than be correct with Harvey,"[13] I replied. Barnesly didn't get it. I do not understand such obstinacy, and never will.

I grabbed my phone and called Danielle. "Get Bernie Hartwig in here first thing tomorrow morning to my downtown office. I've got a job only he can do."

It was the third week in June now. One by one local officials and businesses turned against Berglin Enterprises. I couldn't blame them. Negative stories appeared in the *Courier,* on local TV, and on the national news. McKenzie Security Systems, one of my biggest competitors, hired a local firm that placed ads in local business media. We even made the *New York Times's* Science section. It was a thorough and contemptuous presentation of our work, which was after all based on the great Nikola Tesla. There was no mention of the great inventor in the piece! We also made NPR's Science Friday, which was a little more understanding. The *Chicago Tribune* had a negative article as well, citing the Intelligence Community Directive. The *Tribune* called Berglin Enterprises "a danger to public safety." A story went out over the Associated Press that slammed our activities. Danielle said most of the national dailies ran the AP piece.

After several weeks of this, software sales were down almost 100%. Not even Danielle's presence could stop the slide. Misinformed people began harassing us when we went to the supermarket or the hardware store. I was spending more and more time at home these days.

My people were cracking under the strain and I thought seriously of giving up. I could see that Julian Green had been right. The squeeze was being put on steadily, inexorably, and unmercifully, like a slowly turning vise.

The only people unaffected were Ralph Zimring and Monster. Both were battle tested; for them, conflict was natural. They attended social functions together, went out walking, and played tennis on the public courts as if nothing was unusual. People called them Betty Ross and the Incredible Hulk. The two were becoming more and more popular around town, even as Berglin Enterprises and everyone who worked for me were frowned upon.

John Rosen went out to see one of their tennis matches on a Sunday. Their play was attended by dozens of public spectators. John described the scene. "There were at least thirty people watching. Zimring was so tall and his arms were so long he covered the court almost without moving. He could hit the ball with terrifying force, but Monster was incredibly quick. She would run down a lot of Zimring's shots and usually won the matches after the giant got too tired. He just couldn't keep up! People were cheering Monster and booing Zimring. It was crazy."

"I'd like to see one of those matches."

"I think it would be a good idea. Everyone knows they are working for you but there's no stigma attached to them. After the match they sat around and talked to the spectators for almost an hour."

Well, maybe it would go a little way to negating some of the bad publicity.

There were a few bright spots. Bernie had gotten Cubes into the homes of several big name Chicago executives. Zach had gotten one into the home of Trevor Clarke, the suave and popular socialite who worked at PRC Bank. The Ferrell kid and Green's volunteers were pumping out Cubes like idiot savants, directed by Park and Rosen, as fast as we could make and test them.

Instead of doing groundbreaking research the two scientists had been reduced to line technicians. Work on the Pulsar, and all other research using Tesla's notebook, stopped.

There was one big problem: software sales were crashing and the company was losing money. Barbara Mikhailovich (my new CEO) told me that in six months, if present trends continued, I could no longer continue operations.

— 35 —

Lieutenant Spieth walked silently into the office of Lt. Col. James Stapleton. He placed a paper on his desk and walked out. Thinking it was a summary of the latest intelligence, Stapleton pulled it toward him along the desk's oaken surface. "Byrnes wants to talk to you," it read.

Stapleton immediately reached into his desk for a headset. Using a mental code he unlocked the White Room. Byrnes was standing there, leaning on his cane. The mad dog had been even more brusque and demanding than usual lately. Today he had the impatient look of someone who had long ago issued orders that were dictated by unpleasant circumstances and was waiting with bad grace for preparations to be made.

"Stapleton, I want you to talk to Berglin right away, personally."

"That's impossible sir. You know very well Ralph Zimring is working with Berglin. He and I served in the army together. Zimring is a nosy bastard. He could ask a lot of uncomfortable questions that could compromise our classified work."

"It can't be helped Stapleton. That Berglin – a fanatic I tell you, after all that's happened to him – continues to manufacture Cubes and distribute them. He's working on some kind of exotic weaponry, colonel, which is even more dangerous. That other fanatic, Green, is supplying him with volunteers."

"Yes I know. Green is worse than Berglin. I'd like to take them both out."

"Both of them have had the devil's own luck," Byrnes growled. "Until now. Take Comstock along with you and half a dozen men. Berglin has sent his security force back to Japan and he's completely vulnerable now. Our media campaign seems to be working; his company is hemorrhaging money. Morale is low and Berglin is thinking of quitting. You know what to do. Now is the time for one last attempt before the Big One."

The Big One?

Byrnes was fantastic at keeping his mind closed. Stapleton could find no sidebands of thought about it. "Yes sir. I'll use my General Northcott identity, shave my head, and wear sunglasses. Zimring may not even recognize me."

"Good show Stapleton. Whatever you do get Berglin and those two scientists to stand down. Take his lab apart and let's end this once and for all."

"Yes sir! I've been dying to get out from under this desk."

For once both men were in complete agreement.

"What do you want to do about the Cubes that are already operational?" Stapleton asked. "Lieutenant Spieth has confirmed over sixty of them. The police chief down there, Stan Moyer, is really pissed off."

Byrnes grimaced. "You take care of Berglin, Park, and Rosen. I'll handle Chief Moyer and the rest."

There was a pause.

"That is all Stapleton."

"Wait! There's something you're not telling me."

Byrnes smiled grimly. "If you fail this time, I'm going to bring in the reserves."

After Byrnes exited Stapleton found himself staring into a misty white space that seemed to continue to infinity. Their communication was absolutely impenetrable and untraceable. Each mind was unique and the configuration space for their discussion could only be accessed by the two minds involved. As always after speaking with Byrnes he examined the White Room with his mind. He tried to detect residual sidebands of thought that may have been left by the older man. There was something about radically new aircraft with exotic weaponry, but he couldn't pin it down. Was that the big surprise? Stapleton concluded that Byrnes had some kind of "final solution" to the Max Berglin problem. His mission was a last-ditch attempt to solve it by conventional methods.

Stapleton took off the headset and examined it. As always, he was fascinated with a technology that literally did not come from this planet. He wondered what secrets were being kept from him. Civilians like Max Berglin and Julian Green had no idea how far the technology had been developed. There were weapons now in the special access programs that could literally vaporize the planet. If they got into the wrong hands...the possibility was unthinkable. If the reports from Duggan of this "orange light" could be believed, Berglin and his two scientists were already onto the weaponization of dark energy. They – and others like them – *had* to be stopped for the good of human civilization. Stapleton leaned back in his chair and sighed the sigh of one who does a difficult duty for the sake of those who could never appreciate it.

The sequestering of exotic technology into the special access programs, and their absolute secrecy, were an absolute necessity. Patriots like himself were demonized by uninformed persons like Julian Green as evildoers who were preventing a golden age on earth. That was nonsense. He and his fellow "conspirators" were the saviors of this planet. We do our duty without thanks, castigated unfairly by those we are protecting. Stapleton sighed again. A true patriot did not need thanks or acknowledgment, but sometimes it was a hard, lonely life.

His only problem was with Zbigniew Byrnes. The man was going off his rocker.

Max Gets a Visit

On Saturday the 27th of June I received an ultimatum.

At 9 a.m. I was talking with Ralph Zimring and Bernie in my downtown office at Berglin Enterprises. I said we should capitulate and hand everything over to the government. Zimring and Bernie were against it. Bernie and I had switched positions.

"You're not dealing with the government Berglin," Zimring said. "Or at least not the real government. Even though this operation appears to be legitimate, it's not."

"That's right Max," Bernie chimed in. Ever since Ralph had joined the team my old friend had gained confidence. "Regardless of appearances this is a deep national security state operation, outside the legal purview of the United States government. It's probably being run from one of the unacknowledged special access programs, who have sympathizers within the established government."

"What difference does it make? To all appearances this *is* a government initiative, and we're being made to look un-American. Perception is reality. We are slowly but surely going out of business."

Suddenly my speaker squawked. It was Tara Bolshoi in Reception. "Party to see you sir. They blew by the security guards and are on their way up."

We heard footsteps down the hall. A two-star general walked into my office surrounded by two men in suits. Not again! Trailing them was a grossly fat man dressed in a crumpled suit that looked like it had been lived in. Tara sent me the camera feed from outside. Two unmarked vehicles waited at the curb before the front entrance of Berglin Enterprises. On the monitor I could see that two more vehicles covered the back entrance.

I was getting really tired of this, but my reaction was nothing compared to our friendly giant's. When Ralph Zimring saw the fat man his eyes blazed and he stood up quickly, almost banging his head on the ceiling. "Comstock, you fucking bastard!" he blazed, totally intimidating everyone in the room.

The fat man slunk against the front wall, which was glassed in. "Who are you?" he squeaked.

"I'm the friend of Julia Pence, the woman you murdered, you bootlicking, contemptible worm!"

Comstock's face went white and his forehead beaded with sweat. "I don't know what you're talking about."

"When I've confirmed it I'm going to kill you, Comstock." Zimring spoke in a terrifyingly cold and emotionless voice. "And there's nowhere on this planet or any other you can hide."

The fat man almost fainted from fear and I didn't blame him. The general spoke. "It's over, Max Berglin. You are either going to stand down and hand over your devices or I'll take you to a classified detention area in Chicago for questioning." He didn't have to add, "Where you'll never be seen again." That was implied in his voice and his demeanor. The general was ramrod straight, about medium height, with a head shaved in a very short crew cut. He had an uncompromising and hardened face that looked like it had seen many battles. A man of fixed ideas, I thought, with whom it was impossible to reason.

Ralph was unimpressed. "Who the fuck are you?" Zimring spoke in a voice implying that the two stars and the decorations on the general's uniform were merely theatrical.

For a moment the general was nonplussed, but he recovered. "I'm General Robert Northcott from the DoD's Special Operations Command. That's SO-COM to you, son." He glanced at Ralph as a king might to one of his servants. "You are way out of line, whoever the hell you are."

Zimring laughed. "You may be from SOCOM but you are not in the chain of command."

I saw Northcott flinch ever so slightly.

Comstock had recovered his composure and was looking malevolently at Zimring. I got the impression the fat man was making plans.

The general spoke into a small device attached to his wrist. "Bring the men up. Berglin is here but he has some seven foot tall fucktard who thinks he's James Bond."

My desk speaker went off again. It was Tara in reception. "Sir, four more men just got out of the vehicles. There's also a Channel 5 truck and some citizens who are outside making a lot of noise."

The general turned to me. "Berglin, I'd advise you to come with us. I've got four combat trained marines with weapons to make sure you do. Then you are going to take us to your lab or facility and we're going to remove all evidence of your lunacy. Then you're going to sign a statement promising to abandon your attempt to undermine the national security. Do you understand?"

I looked bleakly into Northcott's face and saw conviction there, and purpose. I could see the man was genuinely convinced that we were a threat to the United States. All my confidence vanished. Maybe the general was correct. If I was in the right why was there so much implacable opposition? I knew the Pulsar could be weaponized. What if some nutcase or terrorist group got hold of it?

"All right general, you win," I said. I was exhausted from dealing with these uncompromising military types. They would just keep coming, endangering my people. "Tell your men I'll come quietly and give you everything you want."

"Don't do it Max!" Ralph advised. "After they take everything you'll disappear into the bowels of the Network." Four men appeared, holding weapons, in the lobby of my private office. LaShawnda, my new personal secretary, was having a fit in the anteroom.

"We fought the good fight, Ralph, and we lost. Now it's time to accept the consequences."

I was marched like a prisoner out of my own building down the stairs and through the front door, while my employees watched and the media filmed. The general led the parade. He looked the part: a patriotic military man detaining a dangerous criminal in the public interest. When we came out the front door I saw Tina Brooks and her two cameramen. When they tried to approach me the marines motioned with their weapons to stay away. Tina shouted questions but nobody was answering. I was shoved into the back of one of the sedans and we drove away.

Now I know what a debriefing is. I couldn't tell where we were going because the windows were tinted on the inside. I was placed in the back seat with a tinted window that blocked my view of the front. The trip took about twenty minutes. I was hustled blindfolded out of the car and down a long corridor. My possessions were confiscated. I found myself in a windowless room with a table and two uncomfortable wooden chairs, lighted by a single light bulb that hung from the ceiling. Somebody pricked me with a needle and I felt a sense of complete lethargy; I was completely spaced out. My mouth was opening and I knew I was talking but I don't remember what I said. For hours and hours without rest or food, I was taken over in excruciating detail every incident since the adventure with Tesla's notebook began. I was forced to go over everything dozens of times until I wanted to scream with frustration.

After a while the drug wore off but they kept grilling me. When I told the general about the Pulsar he went nuts. He told me I was a traitor and that he would kill me right now. As his men raised their weapons I closed my eyes and thought, 'this is it.' Just then somebody came into the room and addressed the general. "Stapleton!" the voice said. "Byrnes wants you to leave this asshole and get down to that warehouse."

Northcott kicked me in the shins. "We've gotten everything we need anyway." And he had. I had been forced to tell him the names of everyone I could remember who had the Cubes. Moreover, they knew now that Zach Ferrell had the complete list.

"Sign this, asshole," Northcott said, shoving a piece of paper in front of me. I was too tired to go over it carefully but it said something about me handing over the rights to my inventions to TAC. I signed; I was too exhausted and depressed to think anymore.

Everyone left the room; I wondered what was next. Nobody else came. I lay my head down on the table and tried to rest, but I couldn't relax. I felt like a quarterback who had just been creamed by a 350-pound lineman. I was desperately hungry, tired, and thirsty. After half an hour or so I walked back down the corridor. There were several unlocked doors off the hallway and each one contained a small windowless room. The place was deserted. I managed to find my keys and my mobile in a small storage cabinet in the hallway. I was too exhausted to be angry and wondered how I was going to get home. I had no idea where I was.

Two sedans, followed by three large vans, went to the Van Allen warehouse. They were followed by several media trucks from the local stations. The whole thing was broadcast live, interrupting the soap operas. Men dressed in suits went through the building and stripped it. They were surrounded by armed men, who kept everyone away. Several enterprising cameramen got snatches of film through the windows, including some of the conversation. From the top of the hill, a few curious people filmed men in suits carrying everything away to the vans. Ten minutes later Chief Moyer arrived with a dozen police cars. Behind them citizens in their vehicles followed.

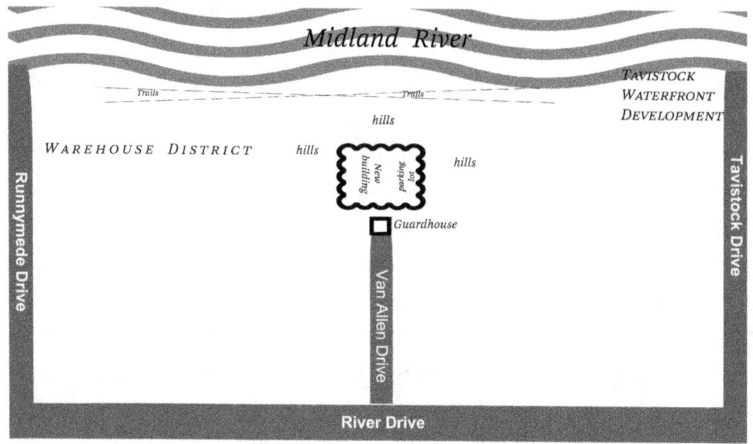

Chief Moyer sent a dozen squad cars past the guard gate and surrounded the intruders, whose vehicles were in the parking lot. They were so busy stripping my warehouse they hardly noticed. Moyer then blocked off the entrance with several black and whites, cutting off access to and from the warehouse. Moyer could have saved himself the trouble because the entire road became blocked with curious onlookers. People were on their phones, observing the live news broadcasts and the streaming video from dozens of excited residents up on the hill. People were parking their cars on Runnymede and Tavistock and walking or running on foot on the trails to the hills overlooking the warehouse. The privileged Tavistock residents were outraged because the canaille were blocking the road in and out of the development.

I walked out of the building and onto a dirt road. I heard car noises and stumbled about a mile until I came to a paved two lane road. Deciding to hitchhike, I stuck my thumb out. The very first car I saw was a sheriff dept vehicle. I jumped up and down and, fortunately, he stopped. I must have looked like a desperate character. Long story short I convinced the officer to drive me down to the warehouse. By the time we got to within a mile of the place it was a madhouse, with cars and people everywhere. The sheriff was getting dispatch reports and he decided he didn't want me around anymore. I didn't tell him who I was and he didn't recognize me. I got out of the vehicle and started walking. I found a fast food place on River Drive and wolfed down two tacos as fast as I could stuff them into my mouth. I passed dozens of people all racing on foot to the warehouse. I kept going until I found the entranceway. Nobody even noticed who I was.

When he arrived at the warehouse Chief Moyer was very angry. Two dark blue sedans were parked near the building's entrance, along with three large vans. Men were loading equipment from inside the building while Berglin employees protested. He recognized Zach Ferrell and several of the volunteers Berglin had recruited. Danielle Menard was also there. A half dozen armed men surrounded the vans and the sedans and protected the interlopers. One of them was roughing up the Ferrell kid, demanding something.

This was *his* city goddammit. First the Octagon, then the shooting on Main Street, and now this. Moyer walked up to a tall man in a dark suit who seemed to be in charge. "What are you doing here?"

"We already cleared this with you Moyer. Get out of our way."

"No one cleared anything with me."

Suit looked confused for a moment and Moyer stepped closer. "Cease and desist immediately. Put down your weapons."

"Chief Moyer, this is a military operation sanctioned by the ODNI to protect the national security. It's out of your jurisdiction."

"That's not good enough. Break out some ID."

Moyer noticed that the man was wearing a very unusual headset. He seemed to be concentrating and then motioned to several armed men who were guarding the vans. The men surrounded him and suit said, "Chief Moyer, take your police and vacate the area. We cannot tolerate civilian interference in this important matter."

Moyer, almost always even tempered, lost it. He grabbed his mobile from his pocket but one of the soldiers knocked it out of his hand. Two dozen of Moyer's men ran out of their black and whites and surrounded the soldiers. Too late the intruder realized that he and his men were encircled and outgunned. Although they had superior weapons, they were sitting ducks. It was an armed standoff, with hundreds of civilians looking on. A total clusterfuck. He used his headset to notify the general, who was still in the building supervising the removal.

Tina Brooks from Channel 5 was in the parking lot, streaming the whole thing. She had finally got her big story! Something was going on here and it had to do with that lunatic Max Berglin again.

Zach was in the back of the warehouse when he saw several vehicles about a quarter mile away coming up the road to the building. Something told him to get out fast so he ran out the front entrance and onto the parking lot. On an impulse he called Mike Parsons, who was sitting in Sweetwaters with Jessie and Heather McCloy. "Mike, get down to the warehouse right now!"

"What's happening?"

"No time to explain Mike. The entrance is being blocked so come down River to Runnymede and park your car. Come over the hill."

"I'm bringing Heather too," Mike said, but Zach had already disconnected.

Zach saw two sedans and three large white vans. Six soldiers precipitated themselves out of the lead van and surrounded several men in suits, who walked briskly toward the door. One of the suits saw him and screamed. "You! Ferrell! Don't move!"

Zach felt an urge to run but stayed put. He saw clearly that he was in the presence of an armed force.

I arrived at the warehouse, disheveled, and looking nothing like myself. I had seen myself in a mirror at the fast food joint; I looked like a homeless person who had just run a marathon. I pushed myself through the crowd, trying to get to the front door. I was just in time to see the police rush to the aid of Chief Moyer, guns raised, shouting angrily. A police sergeant with a large megaphone shouted, "Drop your weapons! Down on the ground!"

There were at least two dozen spectators in the parking lot and almost all of them were screaming, but when the guns were raised they all fell to the ground. I noticed that Moyer's men were in a semicircle so as not to fire into their own men. Several officers were still in their vehicles by the gate entrance. Everybody on the hill fell onto the grass except for Tina Brooks and her two cameramen, who were in plain sight of the soldiers. Instead of dropping their weapons the soldiers raised them menacingly toward the police. Several of the officers looked nervous. The soldiers appeared almost bored, as if this were just an incidental skirmish.

I held my breath. People were still coming down the entrance road on foot, trying to get into the parking lot. More were coming over the hills, unaware of the standoff. If the nerve of any of the police officers broke there could be a lot of people dead on the ground.

Mike Parsons, Heather, and Jessie parked their cars on Runnymede and had to run almost a mile to reach the woods in back of the hill. They forced their way up the hill and saw Zach shoved up against a brick wall at the front of the building. "Zach!" Mike cried, shoving forward.

"Don't go down there Mike," Heather pleaded. "There's nothing you can do."

But Mike wasn't listening. All he knew was that his friend was in trouble.

I saw one of Zach Ferrell's friends walking down the hill toward the police cars and the officers with their guns. I couldn't believe it. I had moved against the building out of the range of fire (I hoped) but this guy looked like he was out for a Sunday stroll. I saw Danielle standing outside the front entrance and frantically motioned for her to go back inside. She was watching Zach get interrogated a few feet away, against the brick wall. She looked concerned for him.

On the hill, Jessie and Heather were screaming. "Mike! What are you doing?"

A couple of the officers in the rear turned around and saw Mike Parsons. One of them was about to pistol whip the kid. "I think I can help," Mike said.

"Get the fuck out of here asshole."

"It's time for everyone to put down their weapons and start a dialog."

The officer, a burly barrel-chested man, looked Mike over. "Are you an experienced negotiator?" he demanded.

"You might say that." He felt a little nervous, but to his surprise also felt an inner excitement. Mike noticed that the attention of the combatants had moved somewhat to him. He hoped that would happen. "Maybe we can start by lowering our guns."

The officer smiled nervously. Moyer and the suit were standing about fifty feet away, glowering. "What's going on back there?" Moyer said, without taking his eyes off his antagonist.

"Some guy who says he wants us all to lower our weapons," the officer replied. "Might be a good idea."

Moyer relaxed a little. It was probably Dekeyser from the department's HNT. "Let Louis come through." When Moyer saw Mike Parsons he almost had a heart attack. "You're not Louis DeKeyser! I thought you were from the Hostage Negotiation Team."

"I'm Mike Parsons," Mike said, introducing himself. "I am a licensed counselor and have experience in crisis situations." The latter wasn't precisely true. But he had been involved in some pretty dicey and verbally violent confrontations in his practice.

Mike turned to the suit. Five soldiers surrounded him, one of whom had his weapon aimed at his heart. Mike held out his hand. "I'm Mike Parsons." He knew suit wouldn't take it but he wanted to get his name and make the situation a little more personal.

"Fuck off," suit said, but knew he was in a hopeless position. Just then Northcott came out of the building.

I saw Zach being led into one of the vans. Just then a girl came out of the crowd and tried to go through the barrier of police, screaming hysterically at Mike. The tension immediately heightened. The policemen raised their weapons, the soldiers did likewise. I saw one of the officers behind his vehicle stand up, ready to fire. At that moment the general came out of the front entrance. He walked past me without even seeing me and gave an order to the suit. "We've got the two scientists and Ferrell and his list and all the equipment. Get these fuckin' people out of here and clear the driveway. We're going to pick up every one of those Cubes and then get out of this piss-ant town."

"Yes SIR!" suit said, turning to Moyer. "You heard the man. Clear the area or people are going to get hurt. We're leaving." Without waiting for Moyer to respond, he returned to one of the sedans. The soldiers followed him and got into one of the vans.

Moyer stood there with his mouth open. The intruders were in their vehicles like nobility waiting for their servants to do their jobs.

"My work here is done," Mike Parsons joked. Heather ran to him and broke down, crying and laughing. "You stupid fool!" She threw her arms around his neck.

Moyer understood that his job *was* to clear the area. But he'd be damned if he would let these guys come to his town and break the law. They had stolen private property and kidnapped Zach Ferrell and those two scientists of Berglin's. Moreover, they didn't clear their operation with him first. That was a serious breach of law enforcement etiquette and it pissed him off.

Moyer turned to Lieutenant Wojnowski. "Clear the driveway lieutenant. Escort these gentlemen and make sure they stay out of people's houses. Use force if you have to but don't get anyone killed."

Wojnowski pointed to the sedans and the white vans. "Who are these guys?"

"I have no idea. The general there claims to be from SOCOM but I have my doubts. Keep an eye on them." Just then a gigantic man and a small lady showed up. "Ralph! Just the man we need."

"Would you like me to monitor the situation Berglin?" he asked.

Stan Moyer looked up at the giant. "Moyer," I said, "this is Ralph Zimring, former army Ranger, and his fiancée Michiko Kagawa, a highly trained military security officer."

Despite the seriousness of the situation, the enormous man next to the tiny woman almost made Moyer laugh. She looked like a toy he was playing with. Then she looked at him like he was a piece of soft bread about to go into a toaster. Zimring himself was an overwhelming physical presence combined with a Zen-like calmness. Moyer laughed again. "I have a feeling you two could handle our friends all by yourselves."

Ralph shrugged like a man who has heard the obvious; the little woman bowed. Moyer made up his mind. "If you two can fit into my vehicle I'd like you to lend me your assistance. I want those vans in my impound facility and we have to make sure these fellows – whoever they are – don't commit mayhem."

Zimring grinned. "Now you're talking, Moyer."

Moyer relaxed. His confidence and his spirits were returning. "Let's go then." He turned to Wojnowski. "I'll take the lead. You know what to do, standard crowd control."

Before I knew it Moyer, Zimring, and Monster got in Moyer's vehicle, which began to slowly inch forward. The policemen efficiently began clearing the entranceway. The two sedans and the vans with all my stuff, along with two dozen police vehicles, drove down Van Allen Drive toward River Drive. I realized I'd miss out on everything if I didn't get a ride. I was very tired but angry at how I'd been treated by the general.

Out of the corner of my eye I saw an ugly little man on a motor scooter ride up. The parking lot was a confusion of people and cars and excited media with cameras and microphones. Too late I realized Moyer's warning about Elmo Tackett. The little man was holding a weapon in his hand, trying to conceal it underneath his shirt. He was only twenty feet away and I knew he couldn't miss. In the pandemonium nobody even noticed he was there. I wanted to duck but realized if I did the shots would hit people behind me.

I was trapped.

Part XVI

The Final Solution

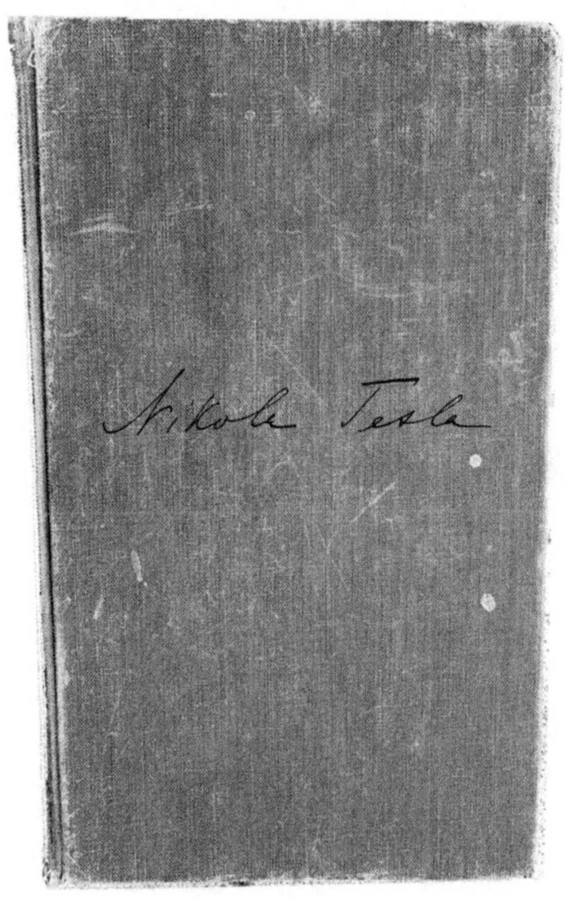

— 36 —

I stood there frozen, knowing I was going to take a bullet. Just then a young girl (or was she an older woman?) stepped between myself and Tackett. There was some sort of light emanating from her. It looked somewhat like the radiant energy coming out of the Pulsar, and it surrounded her body for about twenty feet. She walked slowly toward Tackett. Everyone within her radius stopped what they were doing and looked at her. I could see Elmo's finger underneath his shirt closing on the trigger.

"Do you understand now Elmo?" the girl/woman said. Elmo's face, normally emotionless, took on a look of bewildered comprehension. His finger slackened on the trigger. "Do you mean —"

"Yes Elmo," she said with the air of an all-knowing oracle.

Elmo's jaw slackened and the gun slipped from his fingers to the asphalt. "Do I have it too?"

"Yes, Elmo."

For the first time in his life Elmo Tackett smiled genuinely. "You'll have to explain."

"Very well. I have a vehicle over on Runnymede, a blue Ford Escort. Meet me there in fifteen minutes."

Elmo nodded and turned his scooter toward the entrance. I was transfixed by this beautiful woman, who looked like an angel. Slowly the light surrounding her body began to dissipate; the people within it began to become aware of their surroundings. We had been in some sort of radiant energy bubble, just like the one John and Austin had generated with the Pulsar. I looked for an electronic device on her but she was just wearing shorts and a blouse. Out of the corner of my eye I saw Danielle. On my left Mike Parsons and his girlfriend had also noticed our little drama. The other people who had been in the light bubble were staring at this remarkable woman.

I was excited. Somehow this girl was self-generating a radiant energy field without instrumentation! I needed to find out how she did it. Just as I was about to open my mouth she glided quickly away. This woman had saved my life and I needed to thank her, but she was apparently running off with the scumbag who had tried to kill me.

The entire incident hadn't taken more than half a minute. I saw the last black and white leaving the parking lot. At that point I saw Vahan Katelian, dressed as usual in a tailored suit, with his twin brother Zadig and two of their men. They were standing by the side of a burgundy red Lincoln Continental. I walked slowly over. I felt a wave of exhaustion and stumbled; but I got myself together.

"Katelian! We've got to follow those squad cars. The same guys who stole your invention cleaned me out and are about to confiscate all the Cubes."

"Fuck you Berglin!" Zadig shouted. He had seen that rat Elmo Tackett line up a shot on Berglin and then drop his gun and walk away. "Why should we risk our asses to save you?"

"Because their plan is to go to every house with one of the Cubes and take them, by force if necessary! That means *your* house."

"Did you hear that Vahan?" In contrast to his well-dressed brother, Zadig wore blue jeans and an old shirt.

"Time's a-wasting Vahan!" I said.

"What do you say, Bobby?" Vahan said to a short, thin man with a pock-marked face, who looked like an MMA fighter.

"Yeah boss. Let's go."

Zadig nodded. "They must be stopped."

"I'm coming with you," I said.

"You're dead weight Berglin," Vahan said.

"You need me to identify these guys. I was interrogated by them for four hours."

Bobby Popp nodded his head, looking at my disordered condition. "Looks like he's been worked over all right. Besides, he's good buddies with Moyer."

Vahan was irritated. "All right Berglin. But stay out of our way, understand? We're going to handle this the Katelian way."

By this time the entrance road had been cleared and the sedans, the vans, and the police had all left. People were getting in their cars and the road was clogging up again. Vahan swore. "These citizens are slowing us down. Those guys are getting away and we'll never find them."

"Relax Vahan," I said. "It's going to take them a long time to get all sixty Cubes. Besides, they are being followed by half the Midland police force."

I was sitting in the back seat of the big Lincoln Continental. Vahan turned around, a look of total surprise on his face. "You mean the cops are on *our* side?"

"Not exactly on your side Vahan, but on the side of justice."

Vahan looked bewildered. "It's the same thing."

I had never met a more self-centered person in my life, but I replied diplomatically. I told him what Moyer had said about impounding the intruders' vans. Zadig, Vahan, and Popp looked at each other. "Fuckin' Moyer, unbelievable," Popp remarked. I explained about how angry Moyer was. "He thinks these guys aren't from the government, but some kind of rogue operation."

The three men were filled with unholy glee. "We're free and clear then."

"Just don't do anything stupid. Moyer is a stickler for police protocol."

By this time we had made it out to River Drive, which was still crowded with cars and the curious on foot. Popp, who was driving, asked, "Which way?"

I switched on my mobile and turned to the site of Channel 5 News. "Right. Looks like the police are following those guys down Main."

Vahan was on his mobile. "Go right to Ashley Street and then left to Main. Cut them off from the front."

Popp grinned and gunned the Lincoln to the right of the road, onto the dirt shoulder, amidst honking horns and shouts and curses. "Watch out!" I shouted out the window as three pedestrians about 100 feet away were about to get creamed. Popp pounded his horn and three young men threw themselves to the grass as the Lincoln grazed one of their backsides. He looked over at Vahan. "This is fun!"

"Yeah," Zadig agreed. "And there aren't any cops around to stop us."

I sat in the back of the big Lincoln, watching Bobby Popp almost commit several vehicular homicides. I wondered what had happened to Park and Rosen.

Stapleton was furious. They had gotten away with every piece of lab equipment and most of the makeshift assembly line when the Midland police showed up. Berglin had signed a document turning over the rights to his inventions to TAC. He had scared the crap out of those two scientists, Austin Park and John Rosen. For good measure he had taken them in one of the sedans. But now the entire Midland police force was mobilized against them. He looked out the back window of the sedan and saw two dozen black and whites on their tail. Some crazy in a Continental was speeding toward them from the front and was swerving across the yellow line toward them. Stapleton concluded that this situation had been cursed from the beginning. If Byrnes wanted to contain it he'd have to do something right now.

Stapleton put on his headset and reported to Byrnes. He left his mind wide open when the old man appeared in the White Room. In less than a second they exchanged thoughts and Byrnes knew everything that was happening. He also knew what was in Byrnes' mind.

"There's only one way out now," Byrnes said (thought).

Stapleton saw that Byrnes was going to launch a military intercept on a massive scale.

"An intercept? On the entire town?"

"The infection must be contained."

"Byrnes, Berglin has also distributed several of these Cubes outside the city of Midland. There are a couple in Chicago, one in Detroit, and at least two overseas. We're too late."

Stapleton felt Byrnes' mind harden just before he broke the mental connection. The former national security adviser had always been a hardliner, but Stapleton knew that Byrnes had made a terrible decision – an appalling one that no true patriot could ever agree with. He was sure now that Zbigniew Byrnes had gone over the edge from zealot to insane.

Their situation was hopeless. Stapleton noticed an empty gravel lot ahead, in front of a little park. He pointed to it. "Pull over into that lot to the right," he told the driver. "Get the cars and the vans in there."

The driver, accustomed to implicitly obeying orders, slowed down and messaged. "We're pulling into that parking lot ahead," he said over his radio. "Get everything in there."

"We'll be trapped!" a voice responded. "There's two dozen black and whites following us."

"That's an order goddammit!" Stapleton shouted.

In five minutes their team was in the lot, the entrance blocked by the police. Dozens of civilian cars had followed and were gawking. The madman in the Continental had pulled up in a little cul-de-sac off the gravel lot.

Bobby Popp saw the police cars and swore. Vahan was about to jump out of the Continental but I reached over the front seat and put a hand on his arm. "Remember, the police are on our side. Leave your weapons in here."

"We'll see about that," Vahan said, but stayed inside. He gestured toward the two sedans parked in front of the vans. "Let's keep an eye on those guys," he told Popp.

Zadig spoke harshly. "They look like the same guys we burned out on Main Street. Stay alert."

I opened the side door and got out just as the general got out of his vehicle. His men emerged, carrying their weapons lowered. When Zimring and Monster came out from Moyer's vehicle, all six guns immediately snapped onto the big man. The police were out of their cars, waiting for something to happen.

Zimring spoke to the soldiers, who were staring up at him in awe. "Don't worry boys, I'm just an observer in this one." I almost laughed. In his military rig the giant looked like a superhero from a comic book.

"For the time being," Monster muttered, and the big man grinned.

Chief Moyer was beyond anger and felt a sense of total disbelief. What were these nutcases doing? He was glad to be out of the warehouse but they had just exchanged one venue for an even more public one. He ignored the armed men and stalked over to the general, who was walking slowly toward him. "You people are crazy. What are you doing?"

In response the general reached into his pocket and pulled out two of the headsets. Moyer stared at the sleek, elegant headset in the general's outstretched hand. It emanated a soft, lambent orange light around a molecule-thick headband. The visor that protruded from the headband was so thin it looked like it would float away.

"Take it you stupid yokel. Put it over your head."

Moyer gazed suspiciously at the headset. It was beautiful and looked harmless, but was clearly a device far in advance of anything he'd ever seen. He put the band around his head, which immediately molded to fit his skull. Instantly his mind was connected to the general's and Moyer knew everything the general knew about Byrnes, TAC, and their mission. It was like a sophisticated multimedia presentation complete with script downloaded into his mind, but a million times better.

"But...but . . ." Moyer stood like a mannequin, his eyes locked on the general's. "It's impossible," he said.

"You think into these things you moron. You don't have to open your mouth."

Moyer now knew that the general was really Lt. Col. Jim Stapleton, who was regional director for the Technology Acquisition Consortium. TAC ran an illegal, unacknowledged special access program that sequestered dangerous technology. So these guys *were* rogue.

Stapleton jerked the headset off his skull, but not before Moyer understood that the man wanted to switch sides. However, he was also bound by his oath to TAC. Moyer understood that James Stapleton was a man who honored his word and understood loyalty.

"Wake up Moyer," Stapleton said. After wearing one of those headsets it was irritating to have to speak verbally. "Did you catch what Byrnes is going to do?" The chief of police had taken off the little device and was staring curiously at it, completely absorbed.

Moyer glanced up. "Are you with us or against us Stapleton?"

"If I come over to you some of my men might mutiny."

"You didn't answer my question."

Stapleton looked up at the huge man standing six feet behind the detective. "You're Zimring, aren't you? Mercenary."

"That's right Stapleton. What's your game here? And why is that murderer Duchene Comstock in town?"

"Moyer, give your headset to Zimring."

Moyer watched as Zimring put the little device on his head. After a moment his face displayed complete astonishment. "Zbigniew Byrnes, General Putnam, and Comstock! All three are traitors." He took off the device and locked eyes with Stapleton. "Comstock is mine." Zimring spoke in a voice that would freeze-dry hell.

Stapleton shuddered. He saw what a waste his life had become. In his zeal to protect the national security he had allied himself with a bunch of rogue elements that were about to do something as bad as the terrorists who had brought down the towers. "I used to think you were a rat, Zimring. But I'm going to do the same as you. Fuck Byrnes."

Zimring held out his hand respectfully, knowing that Stapleton was now a dead man walking. "Welcome aboard."

Zimring's huge hand swallowed the colonel's. "We need to get out of here," Stapleton said. "In less than twenty-four hours this town is going to be a battleground."

"You are totally off the reservation now Stapleton," Zimring said.

The colonel was glad he quit even though he knew it meant a bullet in his head: you didn't switch sides in this game. But he felt good to be on the right side again. He addressed Moyer and Zimring. "First we'll drive all this stuff back to the warehouse and I'll send anybody who doesn't want to be here back to base. I think you can use a few more good men."

I walked over and explained the situation to Vahan. "You mean Moyer and that big guy got the general to return your stuff?" Bobby Popp asked. Vahan and Popp couldn't believe it.

"That's right. The general is on our side now." I was feeling expansive, even after that debriefing I had just gotten from that asshole. I wanted to give the general a kick in the shins before the day was out, just as he had done to me. "Don't worry Vahan, you'll get a cut if we ever get out of this."

Vahan looked at me searchingly. I had never known anyone so suspicious. "C'mon Bobby. The families will have to hear about this." Popp gunned the Continental into traffic, leaving me standing there in a cloud of dust. I got a ride with Moyer back to the warehouse, surrounded by police cars. The black and whites had their sirens on, clearing away the gawkers who were clogging the road. On the way Moyer told me about the headsets and what he had learned from Northcott/Stapleton.

At the UPower building Stapleton put on civilian clothes and briefed his men about what was coming. Two of the men immediately joined us; the others were unconvinced. One of the soldiers aimed his weapon at the colonel's head. "You're dead meat Stapleton." They left in the two sedans.

Park and Rosen came out of one of the vans. John Rosen was laughing and Austin Park looked determined. I had totally forgotten about them, but thanked God they were safe. I saw them go into the loading area with the two soldiers and the lab equipment, giving directions for unloading our stolen property. Just then Zach Ferrell came walking slowly up to me. He had the demeanor of a young man who had just discovered how unpleasant the world of grown-ups can be.

Moyer and I were standing by his police vehicle. I heard Moyer put every officer in the department on alert, and call off-duty personnel back on the job. He turned to me. "Stapleton told me a guy named Zbigniew Byrnes has sent in a team of operatives to Midland. They are going to demand the return of Cubes from every homeowner. They are going to justify this by saying that the devices were built in violation of an Intelligence Community Directive and a Patent Secrecy Order and that the Cubes are a danger to national security. It's insane."

"I've seen Byrnes at a conference. The man is a fanatic." I described briefly what had happened at Necker Island.

Moyer shook his head in disbelief and spoke into his dispatch mike. "All of the renewable energy devices in town are going to be confiscated. I want an armed officer at every one of those houses with Cubes. I'll text you the list."

Moyer told me that almost everyone in the department knew what the Cubes were by now. He turned to Zach Ferrell, who was standing in back of me. "Do you have the list of Cube owners?"

"Right here on my mobile," Zach said. Moyer and Zach exchanged information and Moyer realized that his name was on that list.

Moyer turned to me. "Looks like you were in the clear all along Berglin. My apologies."

"You were just doing your job."

Moyer knew now that the problems in his city were being caused by a maverick military element outside the chain of command. As a law enforcement officer he felt he was in the clear to protect and defend his jurisdiction against them. He got in his vehicle and began to arrange the deployment of his men around the city.

One of the black and whites approached me. A friendly face popped his head out of the window. "The Chief says you get a ride anywhere you want. I'll even turn on the siren."

I had the officer drive me to my home in Palmer Park; Zach decided to stay at the warehouse and help put the lab back together. I should have been at Berglin selling software security products, but I didn't feel like it. The publication of the Intelligence Community Directive by Duchene Comstock had tanked my company and helped to scare off qualified candidates for the new Board. I felt like a man on death row waiting for the inevitable. I just wanted to get it over with.

I went to bed that night certain that my Cube would be the first to be confiscated. Chief Moyer had called me two hours earlier. "It's going to happen tomorrow morning. I'll be there at 7 a.m. if you don't mind. Your house is first on the list. Something big is going to go down and I want to see it."

"How do you know that?"

"You saw those headsets. They enable mind-to-mind communication. I know everything Stapleton knows now."

Moyer told me to leave the gate open and assigned two of his best officers to guard my house.

Tina Brooks had called me earlier and asked if she could come at 6 a.m. with a cameraman to film anything exciting. I told her she could. I wouldn't be sleeping much anyway.

I was up at five in the morning with Slava, drinking coffee. At eight a.m. sharp my doorbell rang. Two official-looking men were flanked by a security detail; two armed men in combat gear. I was getting really, really tired of this. I had seen way too many military types during the last few months. Tina was behind me with her cameraman, filming the whole thing. "Are you Maximillian Steven Berglin?" one of the men asked formally.

"I am."

"We are here to confiscate your so-called Cube, which you have constructed and distributed in violation of a Patent Secrecy Order. Mr. Berglin, you have already been advised of the consequences of your actions, yet you have persisted in defying proper authority. I am here to demand that you obey the law."

I was taken aback. I thought the men would come in with guns drawn and forcibly try to take my device. Then Moyer and his men would confront them. Tina would film it and we'd show it on the internet, the good guys vs. the bad guys.

Beside me Tina Brooks spoke. "You understand that Berglin has just built a little furnace that can take people off the electric grid?"

The man was very polite but firm. "I have my orders, ma'am. Mr. Berglin, and everyone who has one of these devices, is breaking the law."

I could see the look of consternation on Tina's face, and her doubt of me. Then I had an idea, based on advice I'd gotten from Julian Green. "Show me some ID. You can't break into my home without establishing your credentials."

Both men pulled out badges that identified them as officers of the TAC Group, affiliated with the Technical and Acquisitions Dept. of the Department of Homeland Security.

"Come here Tina, and film these badges," I said.

I spoke formally. "Robert Hintzman and Blake Remminger, both of you are members of, and are acting under, the auspices of an illegal and unacknowledged special access program. Your actions here are unsanctioned and unknown to the legal government of the United States."

Both of the men's faces went red with anger.

"Chief Moyer, come forward," I said.

Moyer approached, facing Hintzman and Remminger.

"Tell your men to drop their weapons," Moyer said. "I am arresting all four of you under the authority vested in me by the City of Midland."

Hintzman and Remminger laughed. "Give it up Berglin. You are a criminal. In a few hours you'll be in jail where you belong. Moreover, you signed a document yesterday that turns over the rights to your invention to us."

"That document was signed under duress and is invalid."

"Get out of our way Berglin, we're coming in."

I played my last card and spoke the code word that described TAC's USAPs that were known to Julian Green. "Gerboise Bleu, Light Hammer, Ghost Walker, Plume Shield, Senior Dagger, Majestic Wave."

Hintzman bolted forward and got in my face. "Where did you get those codewords, you scumbag?"

I held my ground and repeated the words taught to me by Green. "Gentlemen, you are members of an illegal and unconstitutional program without executive or Congressional oversight, outside the legal framework of the United States government and the chain of command." I brought out what Green called a Non-participation Statement. "This document has been filed with the State of Illinois, the Patent Office, and the DHS. It declares my intention as a free citizen of the United States not to obey commands or orders from operatives of illegal programs, and thereby frees me from prosecution in all matters concerning them. You, Mr. Remminger, and your men, are the criminals. Chief Moyer is here to arrest you. It is your choice whether anyone gets killed."

HIntzman's face turned purple. He swiveled on his heel and gave an order to his men. Just then the two police officers advanced from behind the squad car in the driveway to the left of my front door. Their handguns were raised. "Drop your weapons!" one of the officers shouted. "NOW!!"

One of Hintzman's men turned; I was sure he was going to open fire. I fell to the floor, knocking over Brooks and her cameraman. I heard gunshots from outside and inside the house. Glass smashed and bullets were flying. I heard a thud as a bullet buried itself into the wall a foot above my right shoulder. Suddenly the gunfire ceased. When I raised my head from the floor both of Hintzman's security detail were down. One of the officers was on the grass, bleeding out. Hintzman and Remminger were wounded. I grabbed my phone from my pocket and called 911. "Get an ambulance to 337 Park Place right away! A police officer is down. There are two dead men by my front door. Two others wounded!"

Two minutes later an ambulance arrived. One of the police officers was dead, as were both of Hintzman's men. Hintzman and Remminger, both wounded, were taken in the ambulance along with the other police officer, who had a bullet in his shoulder. The surviving officer was shouting at them, I could hear him through the closed ambulance door.

Moyer called his dispatcher, making them aware that other attacks might be forthcoming, and to stay on alert at the other homes. "We've got two reports of domestic violence and one robbery," the dispatcher said. "There aren't any squad cars available."

"Can't be helped," Moyer said. "On my authority. If I lose my job over this, so be it." There were over sixty Cubes in Midland now, and he had ordered his officers to cover those homes. But what was the surprise planned by Byrnes? His reading of Lt. Col. Stapleton's mind indicated that something appalling was about to occur.

Fifteen minutes later, everyone in Midland found out what it was.

— 37 —

A dozen triangles and boomerangs showed up over the skies of Midland.[14] Most of these craft were about thirty to fifty feet from stem to stern; but they didn't look like any aircraft I had ever seen. They floated in. There was no exhaust; the craft moved silently. One of them, a circular-shaped craft, was very large and looked to be about two hundred feet in diameter. The command ship? It had lights surrounding it and was totally awesome. It was coming in very slowly, the other craft surrounding it.

Moyer was appalled. "What are those things?"

"They're man-made electrogravitic craft," I said. Green told me that this kind of craft had been perfected in the special access programs. For me they were living proof of Tesla's work.

Several of the exotic craft began to slowly move off. Moyer's mind was a whirl, but he had his duty to perform. His dispatch radio blared. "Chief, this is Officer Dougherty! I've got a UFO over a house at 1457 Pine. Two armed men are coming to the door and the homeowner is scared shitless. So am I. What should I do?"

"Hold your position but do not fire unless fired upon. Get your phone out and film everything. Do not allow anyone to entire the domicile, is that clear?"

"Yes sir. But what are those things?"

"They're not UFOs, officer, they're made right here in the good old USA. Keep your head Dougherty, protect the property and the homeowners."

I noticed that one of the triangles was moving closer, over my property. A tightly focused beam of intense white light came out of it and slagged down my wall. It moved back and forth, clearly searching for something. I grabbed a speaker phone from the wall. "Slava! Get out of the kitchen and avoid the basement! Come to the front door!" The kitchen was right above the basement. Suddenly the power went off. The craft then ascended and slowly moved off.

Moyer's dispatch radio was a confusion of voices. "It's fucking Independence Day out here Moyer! We've got Martians destroying houses all over the city!"

Moyer told the dispatcher to calm down, that the craft were terrestrial and not alien. I didn't stay to listen because I hadn't seen Slava in half an hour. Terrified, I ran into the kitchen but Slava wasn't there. I opened the door to the basement. Everything looked normal except for a perfect circular hole about four feet wide in the wall leading down the stairs. A clean, laserlike beam of energy had simply sliced through the wall, vaporizing everything in its path. A few wood shards and some scraps of metal lay strewn about, but the destruction was minimal. The door to the basement was still intact and so were the stairs. Strangely, the metal door handle was cool, cold even. There was no heat – as if the destruction was caused by cold fire. Suddenly it hit me. Radiant energy! Had TAC and Byrnes already weaponized it? That's what Tesla had feared and even proposed back in the 1930s. I grabbed a flashlight from the kitchen counter and ran down the stairs as fast as I could. Where the Cube used to be, and the furnace, was another hole about four feet wide that penetrated into the ground for several feet. Dust was everywhere. I threw the flashlight beam to my left and saw what was left of a body, just a head and part of a torso. Slava! He had died trying to protect the Cube, loyal to the end.

My body began to spasm, and tears flowed uncontrollably down my face. I felt as the Viking berserkers must have felt before a great battle. My Nordic blood was boiling and I wanted to get my hands on the throat of Byrnes and the people who had killed my friend.

I ran up the stairs and saw Moyer getting into his vehicle. "Berglin! Get in that squad car and follow me."

I ran to the police car and called 911 again. I would cremate Slava and place his ashes in a place of honor on the mantle in my living room. I got into the black and white, now abandoned by the two downed officers; the keys were in the ignition. I gunned the engine and followed Moyer. I wanted to get the hell away from my house as fast as possible.

Moyer and I drove out of Palmer Park and onto Main. The streets were crowded with hysterical citizens. Parked cars were everywhere along the side of the road and people were staring up at the sky, pointing.

Moyer and I drove for half a mile and turned right on Pine, in a residential neighborhood. The sidewalks were crowded with frightened people. When we drove up to 1457 we saw a four foot wide smoking hole leading directly to the basement. A woman and two children were on the grass, blood running from the stump of what was left of a small boy's finger. The woman was frantically trying to stem the flow of blood. "They cut off Bradley's finger!" the woman wailed. Just then an ambulance drove up and whisked the child and his mother into the vehicle. The ambulance took off, siren wailing. Moyer and I ran up to the house and down the stairs. The place looked exactly as mine did: a clean, perfectly circular hole in the brick wall that led to the basement. I saw a man standing next to his slagged furnace, frozen in shock. There was a strong smell of gas.

"Get out of here, now!" Moyer screamed, shoving the man up the stairs. Moyer and I carried the fellow out of the house and on to the street. Moyer turned on a switch inside his vehicle, activating two speakers on the outside of the car. "Evacuate the area! The house at 1457 Pine may explode from a gas leak!"

Most of the neighborhood was already out of their houses and moving toward Main, trying to get a glimpse of an exotic boomerang-like aircraft hovering silently overhead. "Did you see what happened?" a woman shouted. "That thing fired a beam weapon just like in Star Wars!"

"Yeah, wasn't it cool?" a young boy's voice responded.

Moyer and I moved our vehicles toward Main, herding people along. The smell of natural gas was getting stronger. Moyer kept shouting for people to get out of their houses. Both of us worked frantically to get people away from 1457.

Suddenly the house exploded in a yellow and red blast of flame. Material was hurled over one hundred feet into the air, damaging houses within a two hundred foot radius. People were screaming and crying. Moyer called Midland Consolidated and told them to shut off the gas to the main from the plant.

"Mommy, what happened to our house?" a child's voice asked.

Moyer and I didn't have time to do anything else because another call came in over his dispatch radio. "Three more laser weapons have destroyed more property sir!" the voice screamed. "5779 Traver, 8060 Seventh, and a suite at the North Tavistock building, number 57."

Moyer and I went to 8060 Seventh, which turned out to be the home of Larry Potvin, Zach's former employer. "Look at that!" he screamed, pointing to another four-foot hole in the side of his brownstone. In his other hand he held his Army rifle. We didn't smell gas and trooped hurriedly downstairs. Whoever was directing these beam weapons was obviously getting more accurate: the Cube had been vaporized but the furnace next to it was untouched. No danger here.

As we hustled up the stairs Potvin was shouting at Moyer and me, demanding to know who was targeting civilians. "I got Jenny out of the house when those thugs came. They laughed at me when I asked them why they were attacking civilians instead of upholding their oaths to support and defend the Constitution of the United States."

And so it continued throughout the day. Men in uniforms came to homes with Cubes, demanding that they be turned over. If the homeowner objected, one of the exotic aircraft would vaporize it. People were both fascinated and horrified. Fascinated at the futuristic craft in the skies, and horrified at the damage they were causing. The young people could hardly believe it. They were excited but worried that evil aliens had come to destroy earth.

The attack lasted five excruciating, frantic hours. Moyer and I went around to as many crisis areas as possible, informing people that the UFOs were just exotic new air force planes. It was as good an explanation as any and certainly better than Martians or evil ETs. We assisted wherever we could without getting in the way. Chief Moyer earned his rank during the crisis, keeping his men and even the dispatchers from freaking out.

At around two in the afternoon all of the craft disappeared from the skies. The huge command craft caused more property damage as its rapid movement caused a massive column of air displacement. Windows were shattered for a mile radius around the city center.

After it was all over, the media in Midland went crazy. Clive Barnesly was as apologetic as a man can be, claiming that he had been duped. I forgave him. Tina Brooks threw her arms around me. "You made me famous. I have just got the story of the millennium!"

Amazingly, there was little mention of this blatant attack on an American city anywhere in the national media. It was covered it as a "mass UFO sighting." When Bernie Hartwig came over to play billiards and drink scotch the next day, he was not surprised. "I have dealt with a number of these Network fellows over the years. This planet is essentially a corporate state run by private groups in the defense, technology, and intelligence sectors. They don't answer to the public governments or even their own militaries. Until people wake up nothing is going to change."

"Well," I said with a twinkle in my eye, "do you think I'm just going to give up?"

"Are you serious? After they destroyed every single Cube in the city?"

"Think about it Bernie. They failed to take me out, or Park and Rosen. We have Colonel Stapleton on our side, all of our equipment, and a team still available."

"Your volunteers are still with you?"

"Are you kidding? They're just kids, totally excited by what happened. Green says I can keep them, with his thanks."

Bernie laughed. "Most of my academic friends are saying it was just an elaborate internet hoax."

"We've got a long, long way to go Bernie. TAC and Byrnes are still out there, and the national media has ignored the most spectacular event since Pearl Harbor. But we still have a base of operations and a cultural agreement in Midland that a lot of things are being hidden from us. It's going to take very skilled media people and someone who understands the system to get our message to the national public. Are you ready?"

We clinked glasses and swallowed some really good single malt. "I'm ready," Bernie said.

My next move was to look up Danielle Menard.

— 38 —

After the Battle of Midland Stapleton talked to Byrnes over the headsets. He told me that Byrnes is determined to suppress the new technology.

"For all the usual reasons, claiming it will cause massive economic upheaval and will find its way into the hands of terrorists and unbalanced persons."

Stapleton looked at me and grinned. "He considers you a lunatic."

I had to laugh, but the colonel grew serious. "Byrnes is convinced we have weaponized the Pulsar and that further attacks on us could result in the destruction of his men and his fleet of exotic aircraft. He isn't willing to risk another attack – yet."

This has bought us some time at least, but the situation is not resolved. Stapleton is fatalistic about violating his oath to TAC. "If they get me they get me," he said.

There were dozens of videos posted on the net as people filmed the exotic aircraft, but nothing much came of it. There were too many wild claims that aliens or Martians were attacking the city. Eventually the national public dismissed the event as another UFO sighting from a lot of hysterical people. "Sixty Minutes" showed interviews with several people on Midland who were just attention-seekers. The program also showed the press conference that occurred that evening in Midland, with FBI and military officials present. When angry citizens demanded to know why ETs had attacked the city, a man dressed as an alien in a green costume came out and said that the city was being punished by his brothers from the planet Remulac, who were angry that Carleton University had lost its first football game. Everyone laughed. Even I had to admit that the guy in the alien suit was a good comedian, and had trivialized the entire episode. In this way Byrnes' attack on an American city was pretty much ignored nationally. There was almost no property damage – just clean, four foot holes in sixty homes – so it didn't look like anything much had happened. The only real destruction was at 1457 Pine, and that was described as a gas leak. A big expose on Midland Consolidated (the local gas company) was broadcast the next day on Channel 7 Action News. The station accused the company of negligence!

We never found out where those amazing craft came from. Bernie and Stapleton say that the Technology Acquisitions Group is just a cell in the Network. Stapleton says that Zbigniew Byrnes is a player somewhere in the bowels of a private corporate organization that has developed some really remarkable technology.[15] It's exciting to think that such technology exists. Those headsets, for example, make our crummy cellphones look like a junky telegraph wire.

Incredibly, Berglin Enterprises quickly recovered its economic footing after the event. We have become famous within the classified community. I received calls from several former colleagues at Lockheed, who all claimed to know about the electrogravitic craft.[16] Others just said, "I wondered when something like this would happen," as if the Battle of Midland had been inevitable. We got so many software orders from security conscious businesses we couldn't keep up. We received a lot of congratulations from people who called anonymously, thanking us for standing up to a system that is broken.

After the Battle of Midland so many people from the town wanted to join Berglin Enterprises and UPower that the university (the biggest employer in town) would have lost half their support staff if we had been able to hire all of them.

Home services contractors shook their heads as they repaired identical and clean four-foot circular holes in walls, foundations, and basement floors. The insurance adjusters began to believe us when photographs of the damage were submitted to their offices. For several weeks the glass companies in town couldn't keep up with the demand. Unfortunately everyone who had Cubes had to go back on the grid, but I have had a few hand-made for myself and my employees. We're in complete chaos at UPower right now and nothing much is getting done until we can sort through all of the applications and put people to work efficiently. I wish Al Jordan was still here; he was the best organizer I've ever seen.

Heather McCloy and Mike Parsons got married. After the Battle of Midland, however, a shocked Heather wasn't interested in going to Laos. I offered Heather and Mike jobs in my Human Resources team at UPower. We can't find jobs for all those who want to work there yet.

Trevor Clarke and his three buddies got out of town as fast as they could. Apparently the sight of flying saucers over Midland shredded their worldview to such an extent that they could no longer live here. Mike Parsons explained it in psychological gobbledygook that I couldn't understand. About one-third of the population of Midland left eventually, apparently replaced by others who were OK with a paradigm-shifting event.

Surprisingly, Rachel DuPlessis (Ferrell) hired on as our Marketing director. When she saw the "lights in the sky," as she called it, she had a sudden and complete reality adjustment. She and her husband, Mark Ferrell, became reacquainted and she realized how warped her world had become. Zach was happy about that.

I'm sad to say that Max Jr., my son, also left. I found out later that he had been selling information to someone who worked at TAC. He had also been working with Trevor Clarke, Bob Justice, and Judge Massimino. All four of them thought I was crazy. Max Jr. told me that what happened was my fault and that I had ruined his life.

Larry Potvin, Zach's old employer, and Mark Ferrell, also found a home at Berglin. They expanded their restoring business to include an automotive service outlet. We have over 200 employees now (and growing) and Larry is an automotive genius. He is still bitter about what happened and the actions of military personnel. Ralph Zimring explained to him that the action was not sanctioned by any legitimate military organization. After that he calmed down and got to work. Larry and Mark's company maintain our fleet and fix most of the cars of our employees. Larry's son Karl is a programmer at Berglin.

One of our most effective employees is Hassan Bashari, who was Larry's boss at PANA. Larry introduced me to him. Hassan has demonstrated a great understanding of people and cultures. He's now working in Berglin Enterprises' International Sales division.

Stan Moyer quit the force after the Battle of Midland, only four months after his appointment as police chief. I went over to his house for dinner one evening. "I'm getting too old for this, Berglin," he told me. Stan now runs our Security service from a nice, comfy desk. His wife Lou Ann loves me for it.

After the Battle of Midland, Austin Park brightened considerably. When he saw Byrnes' exotic craft it confirmed that his frontier science work was legitimate. He and John Rosen are now working happily on the Pulsar. Austin told me the other day that in a few more years they might be able to develop a superluminal propulsion system. "It depends on whether we can make sense out of Tesla's notes. His concept wasn't fully developed." I wonder whether this idea has already been developed in the special access programs.

At UPower we have been able to restart work on the Cube production line. It took several weeks to get everything set up again in the lab, and replace the damaged equipment. Zach Ferrell is now working for us as an engineer. He had the foresight to get Yusuke Shiozawa, Roka Hatsumi's hotshot design engineer, to turn over a copy of all his work before he left for Japan. It has been slow going because we're so disorganized. But once that is completed Zach expressed a desire to continue his job setting up Cubes for residential customers. It's a perfect job for the kid, who has an outgoing and friendly personality. He likes to work with people.

Zach's electrician has a blog that shows images of the befores and afters, with pics of vaporized cubes and some homeowner images of "cold fire" energy emissions surrounding the damaged areas. They look just like the pics I saw after 9/11, which I mentioned at the beginning of the story.

Amazingly, the crime rate in Midland has dropped to almost zero. People here bonded I guess (at least for the time being). The city gave every officer who participated in the Battle of Midland a hefty bonus, and told everyone to go out on patrol and talk to the people. The police love it because everyone is now much friendlier toward them after their heroic work during the crisis. We have the best police-community relations in the country. A reporter from the *New York Times* even came to interview Tina Brooks to see what this was all about. Hardly anyone is misbehaving. I wonder how long that will last, human nature being what it is. Maybe I can get Austin and John to spread some radiant energy around. Don't laugh! Once the new age community heard about the incident at the warehouse, they were all clamoring for Research to make "healing wands." I would not be averse to trying them out myself.

I wonder what happened to that beautiful woman who called herself Tiki, and that asshole Elmo Tackett. I have never seen them again. There was something about that Tiki woman...but I won't miss Tackett. I saw Tiki talking to him after he tried to kill me, just before the attack from the skies. Stan Moyer told me that he cleaned out his basement apartment at Tavistock and disappeared. Maybe he went with Trevor Clarke and his buddies to wreak havoc in some other town.

The word is slowly trickling out about what happened. The sightseeing industry has increased threefold, and the police are becoming more tourist guides than law enforcers. Maybe they will be believed. There's something about a uniformed officer that inspires trust. Those guys were all at ground zero during the attack and speak with conviction, even though the damage from the attack has been repaired and everything looks normal in Midland again. However, there are over 60 houses and structures (including Larry Potvin and Mark Ferrell's auto shop) where those energy beams sliced perfect, four foot circular holes in brick walls, driveways, and foundations. You can see the new repairs next to the older structures; some people have drawn circles where the holes used to be. Some of the residents are charging money to curious people who want to see what happened. Mark Ferrell is trying to find a lawyer that will sue TAC for damages. Their lathe was damaged beyond repair when one of those energy beams sliced through it.

Unfortunately the entire incident is now almost an urban legend to the mass public. Only the outliers actually believe anything unusual happened in Midland, and they have always been on the fringe of society. The public doesn't care about UFOs anyway and thinks people who believe in them are kooks. Zbigniew Byrnes and his cohorts might be psychopaths, but they are clever bastards. Byrnes et al. surgically destroyed every Cube in existence, scared the shit out of an entire city, and got away with it.

A month after the Battle of Midland Clive Barnsely and the *Courier* began to resume their old stance that UPower is a danger to the community (and he has some supporters). "If it wasn't for UPower, Max Berglin, the Battle of Midland would never have happened." I have to admit he is right about that. The *Courier* keeps publishing articles about the "danger of unsupervised technology." Tina Brooks at the *Courier's* City Desk tells me she quit the paper ("Clive Barnesly is an idiot," she said) and has started her own blog, which is being widely read. But all those who had Cubes are talking them up and telling everyone how great they are (were).

I went over to Danielle Menard's apartment after the Battle of Midland and Zach Ferrell was already there. It looked like they were getting back together. It was all I could do not to fire the kid right there. I ground my teeth and wished them well, and received a grateful smile from Danielle for not being a jerk. Danielle and Zach got married a month later, which depressed me. Fortunately, I had so much work to do that I was able to get over it. I was mad at Zach for several weeks though, although he and I were so busy he probably didn't even notice.

One other thing happened: Pierce Menard came back to town after Danielle went to Boston to see him. He is now working at Carleton and is apparently out of the classified research area. I have never seen a bigger change in a human being; he looks a lot happier. Zach and Danielle and Pierce bought houses next to each other close to the university. He looks great and Zach treats him like a god, and pesters him about his experiences in the classified programs. Pierce is teaching him physics. Pierce is a cementing element in their marriage; Danielle is overjoyed that her husband admires her father almost as much as she does.

Ralph and Monster also got married. The wedding was attended by over a thousand people, most of whom watched it on their mobiles outside the church. At the reception everyone got smashed (including me) and the police actually had some work to do. Several people challenged Monster to a tennis match, and a good time was had by all.

Now for the best part. After I lost Danielle to Zach I saw her, Zach, and Jessie DiPietro in Sweetwaters. Jessie and I got to talking and, after several weeks, I fell for her. Turns out she was just the caring woman an assertive man like me was looking for all along. And I was just right for Jessie: she is very intelligent, but not terribly decisive or motivated. We get along great. Danielle and I never would have meshed; she and I were too much alike, too aggressive, too opinionated. My longing for her was just an infatuation combined with an admiration for her talents. But Zach is just right for Danielle: an understanding, outgoing, and laid back guy that loves her deeply and can keep her happy. I anticipate a few fights along the way, but that's natural with any couple.

Of course not all endings are happy endings. Jessie's parents, Wayne and Myra, objected very strongly to my marriage to their daughter. They even tried to interrupt the wedding. "You're over forty now, you're too old for her," Myra told me. "You're just a leech." I told her I needed a younger woman because I have the energy of a twenty-five year-old, but she thought I was just trying to get over. I wasn't. It's true, and Jessie knows it. We should age well together. Wayne DiPietro won't talk to me after I hired Larry Potvin. He thinks Larry is a crook and maybe he was, but he's doing work he loves now. We don't see Jessie's parents, which makes Jessie very sad.

Things also didn't work out well for the Katelians and the Nalbandians. The proposed Ginzburg Development Project was voted down by the City Council as an extravagance, so their crews didn't get the work they were counting on. The whole thing fell apart after Trevor Clarke, Bob Justice, and Judge Massimino freaked out and left town. Besides, Midland was now (at least for the time being) squeaky clean. Vahan has his uses, but only in crisis situations. However, being a man of my word, I signed a Founders agreement with Katelian. The agreement is to cut them in on ten percent of all profits from UPower, if and when we finally get it going again. It was their idea after all. They had the vision to begin cutting-edge research when even I had given up.

I thought that would keep those predators off my back, but Vahan, Zadig, and Vartan Nalbandian have been on me like blackflies ever since to speed up production. Vahan says the families are going broke. If there is trouble in the future, though, which I'm sure there will be, the families will (hopefully) be an asset.

Jim Stapleton (who I did kick in the shins after receiving a profuse apology for that debriefing) is now running our in-house Intelligence unit. "At least for the time being. Don't be surprised if you find me one day with a bullet in my head. There's no such word as quit in TAC."

The two men in Byrnes' group who stayed to help us idolize Ralph Zimring and Monster. Stapleton says that TAC is still very dangerous and he is keeping a sharp lookout. I ask him every day where those exotic aircraft came from but he doesn't know. "Maybe Nellis AFB, who knows, I saw one out there once. I'm working on it. I'm out of the loop now and no one at TAC will talk to me anymore." My guess, from my old contacts at Lockheed, that they're manufactured at the Skunk Works and at Boeing's Phantom Works. Those guys are doing some amazing things.

The question is, where do we go from here?

Unfortunately everyone who had Cubes had to go back on the grid, but I quietly have had a few hand-made for myself and my employees. Midland Edison knows that now and they will report it to the Illinois Commerce Commission, the state's utility regulation authority. We won't be able to stay under the radar for very long if we get production going again.

Stapleton says that TAC is afraid of the Pulsar's potential and will probably leave us alone, but I'm not counting on that. Julian Green says that Byrnes is very wary of us. I know one thing: the sixty people who had their Cubes destroyed are demanding more of them, and will pay for them. I've explained the risks but they are adamant: they want us to start making them again. Once you become energy-independent, there's no going back. The resource crisis is still with us, as well as the pollution problem and the energy problem. Hundreds of millions of people still live in poverty because of the scarcity and clumsiness of energy from fossil fuels. The battle to release the new technologies is still ongoing. According to Stapleton there are a lot of guys within the Network who want to go public.

How will it end? I have no idea. It's up to you and me I guess. We have to demand answers and not just accept the things we hear on the news and on the net every day. As my Grandpa Harold used to say, "Keep your hat on tight and don't believe everything you hear."

That's good advice.

Appendices

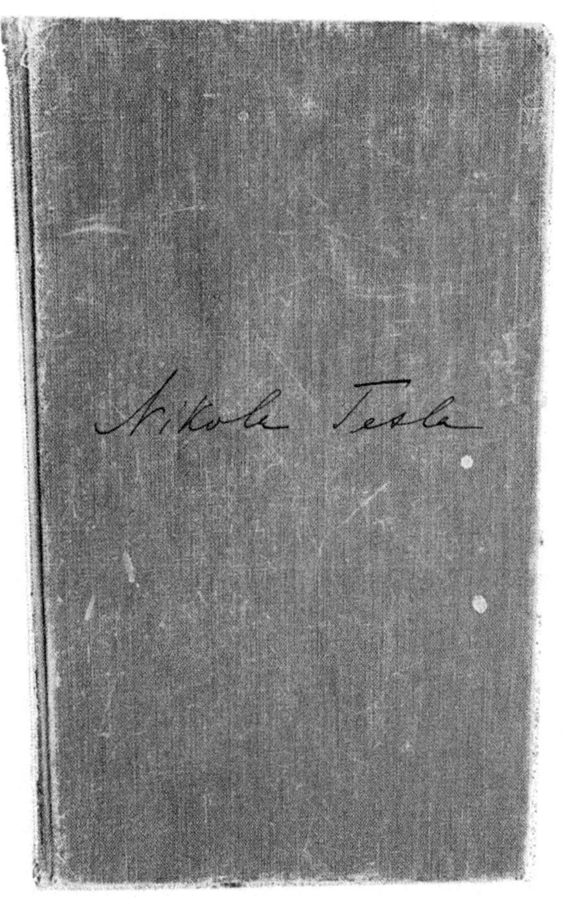

— Appendix A —

Author's Notes

(1) The story told here is a very toned-down version of what some say is really going on inside the special access programs, which apparently have exotic technology reverse-engineered from downed non-terrestrial spacecraft. In reality, perceived threats to national security are not tolerated. Max Berglin and his scientists would have been dealt with quickly, but then I wouldn't have a story! For a detailed briefing on the operation of the Deep State, see Dr. Steven Greer's briefing at https://www.youtube.com/watch?v=bPV-TNqoH2A Also see the movie "Unacknowledged."

(2) The Federation of American Scientists says that the U.S. Patent Office has sequestered more than 5,000 patents in the area of frontier science. See Schulz, G.W., Center for Investigative Reporting, April 16, 2013, "Government Secrecy Orders on patents have stifled more than 5,000 inventions," *Wired* magazine. https://www.wired.com/2013/04/gov-secrecy-orders-on-patents/

(3) In 1987, while chairing the Senate Select Subcommittee on Secret Military Assistance to Iran, Senator Daniel Inouye said, "There exists a shadowy government with its own Air Force, its own Navy, its own fundraising mechanism, and the ability to pursue its own ideas of the national interest, free from all checks and balances, and free from the law itself." The late senator was describing what I call in this novel the Network, and others call the Deep State. To hear a clip of what he said in committee, go to

https://www.youtube.com/watch?v=EbFphX5zb8w&feature=youtu.be

(4) The headsets used in this story use consciousness-assisted technology. Every point in space is connected to every other point via a universal field of

mind or consciousness. Apparently technology like this (and a lot of other mind-blowing stuff) has already been developed in the special access programs. President Eisenhower and President Kennedy told us in 1961 that the U.S. government had already lost control of these programs.

— Appendix B —

Nikola Tesla and Cosmic Energy

Nikola Tesla developed a "radiant energy" device to power loads (U.S. Patent No. 685,957, and 685,958. In an anecdotal story, he also developed a black box device that was hooked up to a 12 volt battery and an AC motor, which powered a converted Pierce Arrow automobile to speeds up to 90 mph (See *Secrets of Cold War Technology, Project HAARP and Beyond*, Gerry Vassilatos, pp. 86–93). In place of the engine Tesla had installed an AC motor of his own design, and in the dashboard installed what he called a "power receiver" that was about as big as a ham radio of the day, and which utilized "a mysterious radiation, which comes out of the aether." Tesla said that the energy itself "is available in limitless quantities" and could be used to power homes and factories.

Did this really happen? Who knows. Vassilatos was just a high school science teacher, but I became fascinated with the story and used it in the book.

The article below, about Tesla's radiant energy device, comes from the *Philadelphia Public Ledger*, November 2, 1933:

Tesla 'Harnesses' Cosmic Energy

Inventor announces discovery to displace fuel in driving machinery. Calls Sun main source. A principle by which power for driving machinery of the world may be developed from the cosmic energy which operates the universe, has been discovered by Nikola Tesla, noted physicist and inventor of scientific devices, he announced today. This principle, which taps a source of power described as "everywhere present in unlimited quantities" and which may be transmitted by wire or wireless from central plants to any part of the globe, will eliminate the need of coal, oil, gas or any other of the common fuels, he said. Dr. Tesla in a statement today at his hotel indicated the time was not far distant when the principle would be ready for practical commercial development. Asked whether the sudden introduction of his principle would upset the present economic system, Dr. Tesla replied, "It is badly upset already." He added that now as never before was the time ripe for the development of new resources. While in its present form, the theory calls for the development of energy in central plants requiring vast machinery. Dr. Tesla said he might be able to work out a plan for its use by individuals. The central source of cosmic energy for the earth is the Sun, Dr. Tesla said, but "night will not interrupt the flow of new power supply.

In 1901–1902, Tesla was also perfecting the wireless transmission of power at his Wardenclyffe facility on Long Island. Unfortunately, his funding was provided by J. P. Morgan. When Morgan discovered that Tesla was going to release wireless transmission of power technology to the world, he supposedly said, "Where's my meter?" Morgan cut off Tesla's funding and his facility was eventually destroyed. In 1943, Two days after Tesla's death, representatives of the Office of Alien Property went to his room at the New Yorker Hotel and seized all his possessions, including his precious black notebook, in which he wrote all of his notes and sketches for his inventions, along with all of his technical papers.

— Appendix C —

Would the President be Briefed on a UFO Special Access Program

By Bernie Haisch, PhD

(reprinted with permission from the author)

In 1976 presidential candidate Jimmy Carter promised the American people that he would open any government UFO files that might exist. Recall that while governor of Georgia, Carter had a UFO sighting and actually filed a report. After winning election to President, Carter met with CIA Director George H. W. Bush seeking a briefing on the topic. Bush turned him down, claiming that neither as President nor as Commander-in-Chief did he have a "need to know." Once in office Carter turned to NASA for information, directing presidential science advisor Frank Press to ask NASA administrator Robert Frosch to "form a small panel of inquiry" to investigate the UFO situation. This letter and other correspondence may be found in "UFOs and NASA" (*Journal of Scientific Exploration*, pp. 93–142, 1988). Nothing at all came of this as recounted by Richard C. Henry – then a young astrophysicist (now a prominent Johns Hopkins professor) working as a deputy to the director of what was the Astrophysics Division at NASA headquarters – on whose desk this "hot potato" request landed. For five months NASA went through some amusing twists and turns, recounted by Henry, before politely declining.

Discounting the NASA farce, and assuming that any possible UFO program would exist as a Special Access Program in the Department of Defense, on what legal basis would the President and Commander-in-Chief be denied access?

It is likely that the UFO topic is actually classified by one or more laws duly enacted by Congress in the late 1940s concerning national security – but without any overt reference to UFOs of course – and signed by President Truman. Only a handful of members of Congress, if any at all, would have known that more than Cold War issues were involved in this far-reaching national security legislation enacted at a time of near panic over a Soviet nuclear threat. There are at least two bins into which the UFO topic could have been placed such that a future President could not unilaterally release it (legally) or, in fact, maybe even know about it. One bin is the category of Restricted Data (RD) established by the Atomic Energy Act in 1946 and pertains to Special Nuclear Material (SNM); another bin would be what has since evolved into the Waived Special Access Program system set up under the authority of the National Security Council which traces back to the National Security Act signed by Truman in 1947 [interestingly only a couple of weeks after the Roswell episode].

[My note: The Roswell N.M incident occurred at the only nuclear bomber squadron in the world at that time, (the 509 CG), which conducted the atomic bombings of Hiroshima and Nagasaki, Japan, in August 1945. Redesignated the 509th Bombardment Group, Very Heavy in 1946, the unit was the host organization at Roswell Army Airfield, New Mexico in July 1947 during the Roswell UFO Incident.]

That means that even if an incoming President asked someone who knew about the existence of such a program, that individual would be required by law to not only not tell the President, but also to actively mislead him, if necessary. (Such a policy is actually spelled out in controversial documents that researchers Ryan and Robert Wood obtained and traced back to CIA Director Allen Dulles in the 1950s. The source of these documents is unclear.) If a president today tried the same thing without the appropriate clearances (which he could not give to himself) he would likewise be told (legitimately) that there was nothing disclosable. If this hypothesis is correct, then UFO information would be "Born Secret" by the Atomic Energy Act, and not releasable to anyone without at least an AEC "Q" clearance (and likely higher, R or above), plus a legitimate need to use it in his/her job. By law, all RD is "owned" by the AEC Commissioner at its inception. The AEC clearance standards are somewhat different than executive branch standards. In order to grant a Q or higher clearance, the Commissioner must find that the applicant is of "good moral character," among other things. Thus, if the Commissioner didn't like Richard Nixon's burglary at the Watergate Hotel, or Bill Clinton's dalliances, the Commissioner could withhold access to RD even on those grounds.

A new President who wants to know what the government knows about UFOs would have to be persistent, clever, and informed before beginning the quest, as Clinton's failed attempt via Associate Attorney General Webster Hubble attests. Simply issuing a presidential executive order declassifying the topic might yield the mistaken conclusion that there is no such material. The first step would be to determine under exactly what legal jurisdiction the matter is classified. This could best be accomplished by a small dedicated research team reporting directly and personally to the President with at least high enough clearances to be able to read all classified Presidential Decision Memoranda and the classified appendices to the Atomic Energy Act and the National Security Act.

—From ufoskeptic.org

Ufoskeptic.org describes itself as "an information site on the UFO phenomenon by and for professional scientists."

Notes

Chapter 1

1. Quote from the *New York American,* Nov 1, 1933

Chapter 2

2. Quoted from RareHistoricalPhotos.com at http://rarehistoricalphotos.com/nikola-tesla-1943/
3. Nonsensical? Please see "Would the President be Briefed on a UFO Special Access Program?", Dr. Bernard Haisch, ufoskeptic.org, reprinted in Appendix B.

Chapter 5

4. The lives of the aforementioned characters taken from an unpublished book by Ralph Shepard titled, *Could I Have? I Could Have, but I Didn't.*

Chapter 13

5. See "Tesla, Life and Legacy, Tower of Dreams," at PBS.org, https://www.pbs.org/tesla/ll/ll_todre.html

Chapter 15

6. Based on (my) embellished version of a story narrated by Dr. Steven Greer during one of his presentations.
7. "The Invention Secrecy Act of 1951 requires the government to impose 'secrecy orders' on certain patent applications that contain sensitive information, thereby restricting disclosure of the invention and withholding the grant of a patent. Remarkably, this requirement can be imposed even when the application is generated and entirely owned by a private individual or company without government sponsorship or support.

"There are several types of secrecy orders which range in severity from simple prohibitions on export (but allowing other disclosure for legitimate business purposes) up to classification, requiring secure storage of the application and prohibition of all disclosure.

"At the end of fiscal year 2016, there were 5,680 secrecy orders in effect." Source: "Invention secrecy," Federation of American Scientists, https://fas.org/sgp/othergov/invention/index.html

Chapter 25

8. Taken from an interview with mercenary John Geddes. See Dixit, Jay, 12 Jan 2009, *Psychology Today,* "Ask the mercenary, Commando-for-hire John Geddes on the life of a mercenary."

Chapter 27

9. See S. DOC. 105-2 - REPORT OF THE COMMISSION ON PROTECTING AND REDUCING GOVERNMENT SECRECY, US Government Publishing Office, at https://www.gpo.gov/fdsys/pkg/GPO-CDOC-105sdoc2/content-detail.html

10. Taken from "On Black Special Access Programs," Dr. Bernard Haisch, ufoskeptic.org. Used with permission.

11. See President Kennedy's speech at https://www.youtube.com/watch?v=zdMbmdF The speech title is "The President and the Press," given on April 27, 1961 at the Waldorf-Astoria hotel in New York City. Kennedy said, among other things, "The very word secrecy is repugnant in a free and open society; and we are as a people inherently and historically opposed to secret societies, to secret oaths and to secret proceedings. We decided long ago that the dangers of excessive and unwarranted concealment of pertinent facts far outweighed the dangers which are cited to justify it....

"We are opposed around the world by a monolithic and ruthless conspiracy that relies primarily on covert means for expanding its sphere of influence–on infiltration instead of invasion, on subversion instead of elections, on intimidation instead of free choice, on guerrillas by night instead of armies by day. It is a system which has conscripted vast human and material resources into the building of a tightly knit, highly efficient machine that combines military, diplomatic, intelligence, economic, scientific and political operations.

"Its preparations are concealed, not published. Its mistakes are buried, not headlined. Its dissenters are silenced, not praised. No expenditure is questioned, no rumor is printed, no secret is revealed..."

Chapter 32

12. See http://nrgnair.com/MPT/zdi_tech/tesla/common/radiant/TRE1.htm, "Tesla's Discovery of Radiant/Dark Energy." In 1889, Tesla began experimenting with capacitors charged to high voltages and discharged in very short time intervals, which he called a "magnetic discharger." When the duration of the pulses were changed, various "radiant energy" phenomena were observed. When the duration of the pulses were under 1 microsecond, "spontaneous illuminations capable of filling rooms with white light, were produced. Even shorter pulses produced cool room penetrating breezes with a accompanying uplift in mood and awareness."

Chapter 34

13. This comes from a story about William Harvey's discovery that the heart pumps blood, and that blood circulates throughout the body. The prevailing view, supported by Galen, the noted medical authority of the time, supposed that blood passed between the ventricles by means of invisible pores. This famous statement was supposed to have been said by a physician who supported Galen even though Harvey's findings were proven to be correct. It is sometimes used to show how shortsighted persons refuse to accept new ideas.

Chapter 37

14. A video of an actual flying triangle, called the TR-3B, is available here: http://www.military.com/video/aircraft/military-aircraft/tr-3b-aurora-anti-gravity-spacecrafts/2860314511001. For models and images of these man-made ETVs based on verified sightings, see the presentation given by Dr. Steven Greer of the Disclosure Project on November 2016 in Las Vegas, "The Cosmic False Flag."

Chapter 38

15. See Authors Notes, (3).
16. If you want a good laugh, look up the definition of "electrogravitics" on the home of orthodoxy, Wikipedia. Also check out other frontier science concepts such as "torsion field" and Dr. Rupert Sheldrake's proposal of "morphic resonance." Concepts that threaten the validity of fossil fuel technology are labeled "pseudo-science."

About the Author

Kenneth J. M. MacLean is a freelance writer, editor, typesetter, and home services contractor who lives with his wife Jennifer and their two cats in Ann Arbor, Michigan.

Websites: kjmaclean.com, macleanediting.com

Other Books by the Author

A Geometric Analysis of the Platonic Solids and other Semi-regular Polyhedra (geometry textbook)

The Vibrational Universe (nonfiction)

The Manchild (SF novel)

The End of the Universe (SF novel)

Beyond the Beginning (metaphysical novel)

Dialogues: Conversations with my Higher Self (metaphysics)

Miracles Can Happen (novel)

The Old Soul (novel)

The History of the Future (novel)

The Intervention (novel, Spring 2023)

Available on Amazon.com and at kjmaclean.com/Products/MainProductPage.php

www.ingramcontent.com/pod-product-compliance
Lightning Source LLC
Chambersburg PA
CBHW070541030726
47505CB00001B/120
9780988212541